THE FEUD ON DEAD LANE

A BARTELL CRIME THRILLER
BOOK 1

ROBERT W KIRBY

Copyright © Robert W Kirby 2022
This book is sold subject to the condition that it shall not, by way of trade or otherwise, be lent, resold, hired out, or otherwise circulated without the publisher's prior consent in any form of binding or cover other than that in which it is published and without a similar condition including this condition being imposed on the subsequent publisher.

Robert W Kirby has been asserted his right to be identified as the author of this work.

(eBook): ASIN: B0B7TQ5F7P
ISBN (Paperback): 9798840308073
ISBN (Hardback): 9798840308462

Copy Editor Helen Baggott

This is a work of fiction. Names, characters, businesses, places, events and incidents are either the products of the author's imagination or used in a fictitious manner. Any resemblance to actual persons, living or dead, or actual events is purely coincidental.

This book contains graphic violence, drug use and disturbing scenes.

"Cover design by Martellia"

1

He heard distant waves crashing nearby and the cold hit him hard. It struck with a sudden, stinging impact, making his entire body shiver, and he could say with complete certainty that he'd never experienced a cold so raw and severe. His mind spun as he strove to focus on his surroundings. He tried to recall where he was heading and why, but his groggy head hurt and his vision spiralled wildly. His legs felt so heavy too, and walking seemed almost impossible – like wading through gloppy cement in a pair of oversized clown shoes. Upon hearing the voices and laughter, a surge of relief came to him, because at least he wasn't alone out here. Then he thought someone called out his name. There must have been at least two people present, because both of his arms were grabbed in a steadfast hold, and he received some assistance to walk; although a wooden shuffle would be a more accurate description. He tried to speak to them, but his voice sounded alien-like, and this freaked him out enough to clamp his mouth shut. Whoever held his right arm stumbled, causing the second figure to release his left arm and let out a hissing, drunken laugh. He tried to laugh too, but a stabbing pain hit his head and his legs crumpled. The pain was like an internal crushing sensation – akin to his brain being slowly compressed by a giant hand. As he peered up, he noticed the figures were standing over him. He tried to focus, but their faces resembled nightmarish portraits of men with smudged features; like someone had used a massive eraser to wipe out their identity. They sounded like men, anyway. The figures hauled him back to his feet. Then he realised his legs were moving again. The figures dragged him, and the waves were getting louder. The wind whipped at his face and a heavy sickness swirled in his guts. He didn't want to be here. Wherever *here* was. He cried out as he attempted to pull his arms free from the figures, but they gripped him tighter in response to his protests. They squeezed so hard his biceps hurt as their fingers pinched against his skin. He called out for them to let go, though what came out of his mouth resembled a garbled moan. His legs, now like rubber, could not support his weight, and without help, he'd have gone straight back down. The figures were talking in whispers, but they may as well have been speaking in a foreign language because he couldn't decipher their conversation, though he thought they spoke his name again.

They laughed, but he somehow sensed pure anger emitting from them now.

Then they let go of him, and the wind became much stronger. It slapped against him in an intense, noisy barrage.

He panicked uncontrollably, as a falling sensation enveloped his entire body. He just had time to comprehend that he was plunging down towards the sea before everything went black.

2

Kent, 10 November 2002

Nino awoke with a start. He'd been dreaming about the creatures lurking in the shadows again and now he gazed around his gloomy surroundings, clutching his tatty ape soft toy. He hated it up here, and he'd convinced himself that the eerie loft room he shared with his brother was haunted. Nino was certain he'd seen shapes shift around in the shadows. In the dimly lit corners and recessives. He calmed himself and settled back down under the blankets, until he heard men shouting, which caused him to freeze and listen. Then horns blasted. He bolted upright.

Craig, naked save for a pair of baggy boxer shorts, shot up from his bed, raced to the roof window, yanked the blind aside and peered out.

The noises sounded like several car horns simultaneously going off. They hooted nonstop. The dogs were barking and howling in distress, though Nino couldn't fathom if the spaniels were outside or downstairs in the kitchen.

Nino slipped out of bed and put on his dressing gown, all the time holding his toy. 'Craig… what's happening? Is there a fire?'

Craig pushed his face against the glass of the window. 'No. The courtyard is full of cars. And men.'

Nino stood next to Craig and tiptoeing, peeked through the roof window. He could see blinding headlights and shadowy shapes moving about the vehicles. He gasped and pulled the blind shut. 'I need a pee, Craig. I'm scared.'

Craig just gave him a quick glance and grabbed his jeans from the floor, where a pile of dirty clothes lay strewn about. He didn't even seem fazed by the intruders outside.

The horns were hurting Nino's head now, so he wedged his palms against his ears. The door flung open. Barry stood in the doorway, tugging a white vest over his bulky frame.

Craig shut the blind and turned to Barry. 'Who's out there?'

Barry clapped his hands together. 'Kitchen. Now! Chop, chop, you two.'

Nino almost fell down the steep wooden stairs as he raced for the kitchen between his stocky brothers.

As the three of them darted into the kitchen, the horns stopped and Nino took in the scene before him. The entire Bartell clan was gathered here.

Maria, dressed in a worn pink bathrobe, sat with her elbows on the table. In front of her, a bottle of gin and a smoking cigarette perched on a tin ashtray. Maria flashed Nino a look of contempt, then picked up her smoke and took a deep pull. Maria looked terrible. She always had dark puffy circles around her sagging eyes and fuzzy hair, but in this moment she appeared more bedraggled than ever. He'd never once seen a dab of makeup on her fleshy face, and she never took much care of her shabby appearance.

Johnny, wearing an opened wax jacket over his naked torso, and a pair of dirty jogging bottoms, stood with his arms crossed and winked at Nino. Johnny would be seventeen soon, but he was already larger than most men Nino had come across. Nino glanced at Johnny and was in awe of him. He acted like a man, too. Unlike his dad and brothers, who were short and broad, Johnny was tall and already stood a good six feet two.

Whilst Johnny seemed calm, Barry was pacing around, kept smashing his fist into his palm and his face appeared fixed in an angry snarl. Barry was always brash, arrogant, and quick-tempered. Barry was two years older than Johnny, but somehow Johnny seemed like the eldest in Nino's eyes. Perhaps he just behaved in a more mature manner, he considered.

Nino's father, Jack, searched under the sink, frantic and flustered. He was fully clothed, and Nino noticed he still wore the same gear he'd had on during dinner yesterday evening. Black suit trousers and a white shirt – though now that shirt appeared crumpled and stained. He'd only noted his dad's attire because he'd never seen him wearing anything but jeans and a T-shirt, or the occasional black vest back in the summer months.

Jack stood up, and clutching a handful of shotgun cartridges to his chest, said, 'Johnny, you ready?'

'Yeah,' said Johnny.

Jack moved to the kitchen counter and dropped the cartridges down and they flew everywhere. Craig dashed to his knees, scooped them up, and handed them back to his dad. 'Who are those fellas, Dad?'

In that moment, Nino spotted his dad's shotgun leant against the fridge, and he felt himself wobble.

Jack grabbed the weapon, snapped open the barrel, causing Nino to flinch, and then slid two red cartridges inside.

For the first time since Nino had known his father, this bull of a man who Nino would wager could take on a crazed boar and win, appeared frightened. But of what? Who were those people outside? Nino jumped as the horns sounded again. He gripped his toy and the urge to pee became so strong he felt a small squirt of wee come out. Though he wouldn't ask to go to the toilet. He couldn't have uttered a word during that moment if his life depended on it. His dad must have sensed his terror, because he stepped over to him and patted his head. 'Go with Craig. Hide in the store shed. Don't leave until one of us comes out to get you. Understand, son?'

Before Nino could respond, Craig said, 'I'm coming out front! I'm not hiding in the barn like some cowardly chicken shit.'

Johnny strolled to the other side of the kitchen and removed two steel carving knives from a scratched and dented wooden knife-block. He handed one to Craig. 'Do what you've been told.'

Still, the unrelenting horns blasted. Nino wanted to scream, and when Johnny approached, offering him the handle of the second chunky knife, he almost did. Though somehow he resisted the urge to breakdown, and instead, held the blade awkwardly in his trembling hand. It seemed heavier than it looked, and he wondered what they expected him to do with it. Did they expect him to defend himself? Fight back against... he didn't even know what, or who.

Barry brandished the wood chopping axe they used to split firewood. Speaking to Johnny, he said, 'How many?'

'I counted thirteen,' said Johnny.

The horns' incessant blasts continued.

Jack grinned. 'My lucky number.' Then he walked into the hallway and turning to Craig, said, 'Take the dogs. Lock yourselves inside the shed. I'm counting on you to guard Nino and my dogs. You hear me? If any of those fellas try to get inside, you stab them in the nuts... and don't slash... I mean stab them. Hard as you can.'

Those words made Nino's legs tremble and tears welled up in his eyes, but he fought them back down.

Maria, swigging her drink, glared at Nino. If he wasn't mistaken, Nino could make out the traces of a sly smirk. No doubt seeing him this fearful pleased her no end. But why did she appear so unmoved by this ordeal? Wouldn't most normal people be in a blind panic?

Johnny and Barry readied themselves to leave with Jack. Nino caught the fear in their eyes now. Barry, breathing heavily, curled his lips, and the veins in his neck went taut.

Jack, gun pointing to the floor, placed his hand on the handle of the front door.

Maria slugged her gin, slammed down her glass and shouted, 'What the hell did you *do* last night, Jack Bartell?'

Jack didn't respond. He pushed open the door. As the chilly night air blew through the hallway and into the kitchen, the horns stopped and Nino caught a brief glimpse of the mob of shadowy people standing in the courtyard, drenched in headlights, motionless and menacing.

'Get going, Craig,' said Barry.

Craig, reluctant, did as he'd been ordered and ushered Nino in the other direction.

'Make sure you take care of your father's precious pooches,' said Maria. She poured another drink and chuckled hoarsely.

'Mum, don't stay in here. Hide with us,' said Craig.

Maria sipped her gin, then prodded a finger at the back door. 'Get out of here.'

Craig paced the barn like a caged beast, slashing the air with the knife whilst muttering and cursing under his breath. His long, thick hair kept falling in front of his eyes and he moodily flipped his head back to remove it from his face.

Nino crouched down behind some cobwebbed covered pallets with his dad's springer spaniels. The three alert dogs sat scanning their surroundings, ears high, nervous, with heads cocking to one side as if listening intently. Charles, the eldest spaniel, a grizzled gun dog with only one eye, sat closest to Nino. The dog's eye had been removed after an injury caused by a sharp thorn damaged the optic nerve, though this disability didn't seem to bother the dog. The other two younger dogs, Rita and Reg, let out soft whimpers. All three had similar liver and white coats, with white being the dominant colour, and cropped tails. But Rita's fur had a shaggier appearance, and her ears were fluffy and ringleted. The dogs loved Nino, but he considered the dogs seemed wary of Craig. Rita, especially, would cower away from the boy, and didn't seem keen to be petted by him. Even now, Rita watched Craig with untrusting eyes. Nino wondered if they sensed something bad in him. Nino didn't trust him. He detected a darkness in Craig. A nastiness that unnerved him. He loathed sharing a room with him.

Craig, only a silhouette now, stood at the door. 'This is bollocks. I should be out there. Not stuck in here babysitting a seven-year-old. I'm twelve, for fuck's sake.'

Nino knew he wasn't speaking to him. Craig was just rambling. He also wanted to point out he was eight, but thought better of it.

'I'm not doing this. I'm not! I won't hide up like this,' said Craig, as he pulled up the thick wedge of timber that acted as a giant door bar. It clanked as it hit the ground and Nino flinched at the sound.

'What are you doing, Craig?'

'Helping my family.'

'No. Don't leave me here. Not on my own.'

Craig, ignoring Nino's pleas, pushed open the door and left. When the heavy door slammed shut, Nino felt urine seeping into his pyjamas.

Nino cuddled his soft toy as he shivered in the gloom. Cobwebs were tangled in his hair, but he couldn't move to wipe them away. He'd heard distant raised voices for a moment. Men shouting and guttural yelling. He reckoned he'd sat there for ten minutes now. His entire body frozen stiff, Nino just focussed on the shed doors. His eyes hadn't moved from them the entire time. The dogs sensed movement at those doors and they whimpered. Charles growled, and Nino felt the dog's body stiffening – Nino's body tensed at the same moment. As the doors creaked open, he dropped his toy and raised the knife. He knew he wouldn't be able to defend himself; he barely had the strength to hold up the knife, let alone thrust the blade at an unknown attacker. Nino gripped it with both hands. But that didn't help. He held it out in front of him, shaking and sobbing. Charles stood up, his fur raised, and moved forward a few paces. Reg and Rita cried in unison, still sitting, but fidgety now.

Nino saw a figure standing in the doorway. Whoever it was stayed frozen like a silent, sinister statue.

Nino dropped the knife and cried out.

Then the figure stepped out of the shadows and began heading towards him.

3

Kent, 29 March 2018

Duncan, squash racket in hand, approached the waiting mustard coloured Nissan Micra, and the driver's door swung open with a grating squeak. This wasn't quite the vehicle Duncan had expected to see out here, though he shouldn't have been surprised, as his best friend liked to exaggerate and often deluded himself.

Karl smiled proudly. 'Well?'

'You told me you'd purchased a sporty little number, Karl?'

'Ooh, someone sounds a tiny bit envious.'

Duncan grinned. 'Yeah, I am... I mean, baby-shit yellow being my favourite colour and all, you must have known I'd be racked with jealousy.'

Karl adjusted a green Yankee air freshener hanging from the interior mirror. 'I see this more of a Dorset cream, or sunburst lemon.'

'It smells nice in there, at least. And the upside is no one with any dignity will steal it.'

Karl started the engine. 'I'm getting the impression you would prefer to walk to the club?'

'Leave off,' said Duncan, walking to the passenger side and clambering in. 'But do me a favour and don't go past anywhere that somebody might recognise me.'

'Why not hide in the back? Or better still, I'll shove you in the boot.'

'I wouldn't fit in that boot. Please don't drive like a twat.'

'Let the fun begin at ten miles per hour.'

'What do you think?' asked Karl.

Duncan shrugged. 'Can you afford it?'

'I won't lie. Things will be tight. But I have to leave my old man's place. His constant nagging drives me bonkers. It doesn't matter what I do, it's never good enough. I could tell him I'd just got a job as a top London investment banker, and he'd still find fault.'

Duncan nodded, but didn't comment. What was there to say? They both knew Karl's dad could be a difficult man. In all the years they'd been friends, Karl hadn't once spoken of his father in a positive light. When they'd been kids, Duncan had been fearful of Donald Rogers and so rarely went to Karl's house to play. Being a hard-nosed secondary school English teacher, he'd been intimidating, always addressed him in a harsh, booming voice and spoke frankly. In Donald's eyes, Karl was a big disappointment – a total underachieving doofus (his words) that spent his school years clowning around and wasting every opportunity to learn. OK, Duncan did kind of see where the guy was coming from. Karl had always been a liability, and whilst Duncan kept busy, cracked on with homework and studied unremittingly, Karl stayed glued to his PlayStation, and often turned up late for school resembling a bleary-eyed ghoul, because he'd been playing well into the early hours. He would tell Duncan that he'd set his sights on working in the gaming industry, therefore it was essential that to become an accomplished games designer, he needed to be an avid gamer, too. Though Duncan agreed with his friend, he'd also pointed out that a degree in computer programming, or computer science, would likely come in handy, and that knuckling down and getting good GCSE grades would be a great start towards such a career path. Like a lot of Karl's ideas, it didn't bear fruit. Karl's younger sister, Beverly, however, did fully apply herself, and went onto study physics and astronomy at Manchester University. Beverly had been the golden child from the day she'd been born, but this academic acquisition didn't exactly help Karl's situation.

'Plus, he's putting the house on the market. He's going to be working full time in Cambridge, so he's moving there later in the year. It makes sense to go my own way.'

'Don't get me wrong, Amy is a lovely girl…'

'I sense a big, boring *but* coming here, Dunk.'

'You've only been seeing her for eight months.'

'Ten… I really like her. A lot.'

'But does she feel the same, Karl?'

'I guess I'm about to find out.'

4

Duncan ordered up a pint of pear and raspberry cider and gulped down half of it. After the squash session with his cousin earlier, he was beat and the sweet drink slipped down way too easily. Duncan loved cider. Pear, apple, strawberry. He didn't care, but he couldn't stomach beer in any form. He struggled to see the appeal of going out and necking ten pints of the stuff. At a push, he'd sometimes drink one to be sociable. Some guys he knew, his cousin Scott for one, would neck Stella and Guinness like it was orange juice, but it just gave him a brutal migraine and a belly ache.

Although it was still early, the pub was getting busy, and Duncan felt a tad paranoid that he smelt unpleasant. The showers at the sports club weren't working great; the infuriating dribble that came from the shower-heads made it nigh on impossible to have a decent scrub-up, so he'd opted for a generous spray of underarm deodorant and tossed on a fresh T-shirt and joggers. Now though, as a couple of foxy girls strode by the bar area, he couldn't help but giving himself a quick, covert sniff. Not too ripe, he considered.

Duncan could see Karl and Amy sat at a corner table. The pair laughed as they spoke, and so he assumed that their sprightly demeanour meant that things had gone well, and that Karl's proposal had been met with the enthusiasm his friend had been banking on.

Now bored with waiting for his friend, Duncan walked to the fruit machine and started slotting in coins.

Out of the corner of his eye, Duncan glimpsed an iffy looking lad who sat slouched at the bar. One of those characters you just knew was trouble. The lad's unfriendly eyes intermittently flicked between the entrance and the football playing on the wall-mounted big screen.

Duncan noticed Karl heading for the toilets, and Amy strolled over to the bar. The iffy lad followed her with his eyes, as though he were undressing her in his mind.

Amy waved at Duncan from the bar. He flashed her a smile and continued to slot in coins.

Amy wore tight jeans and a red body-hugging cami top that had tiny white love hearts printed on it. The top had several black buttons at the front, but the top one must have popped undone, and left little to the imagination. The lad at the bar couldn't remove his gaze from her cleavage, which she must have noticed, because she shyly moved a hand to her chest and secured the top button. He then gave her a slimy smile, but Amy pretended not to notice. With high cheekbones, full lips, and long, brunette hair in a feathered style, Amy was stunning and always drew attention.

'Hey… hold up. Excuse me,' said the lad.

'Um, hi,' said Amy.

'You alright?' the lad asked with a leering expression.

Amy just gave him a confused smile, but didn't offer any reply.

'What are you drinking? How about a cheeky cocktail, hey? Go on, any drink you fancy?' said the lad.

'Sorry, no… I'm actually waiting for—'

The lad didn't let her finish. 'I'm Craig, by the way. What's your name?'

Duncan wasn't the most chivalrous of chaps, but felt he should drift over to support Amy. This guy wasn't really doing anything wrong. OK, technically he was attempting to pick up his best mate's girlfriend, but then anyone as smoking-hot as Amy Mullard must have had their fair share of advances to contend with, so he guessed she would be capable of dealing with this annoying pest. Only this guy gave Duncan the creeps. He was around five-foot five, with a stocky frame and must have been in his mid to late twenties. His grin oozed menace and Duncan knew this Craig looked like real trouble.

Craig sipped his beer. 'You don't need to be shy. Wow, you smell sexy as fuck.' Then he placed a hand on her shoulder and winked. His hand sported several chunky gold rings.

Amy shrugged the hand off. 'I'm leaving…'

Karl, now out of the toilets, headed straight for Amy.

'With my boyfriend,' continued Amy.

Karl joined Amy at the bar and placed a protective arm around her shoulder.

Duncan overheard some guys chatting in hushed tones further along the bar, and although he couldn't be certain, he could have sworn he heard them muttering about the guy at the bar. 'Yeah, mate, that is defo Craig Bartell,' one voice said.

Duncan froze.

Craig shook his head and sniggered. 'Looks like your boyfriend has strutted over to his little hottie to state his claim.' Then to Karl he said, 'You look like that Steve-O mush from the Jackass show. Dead ringer apart from the ginger hair.'

Karl smirked. 'He's a good-looking guy.'

Craig looked back to Amy. 'Nah, I'm not having this. Please, tell me El-gingero here, ain't really your fella? I won't sleep tonight knowing that this idiot is banging youse!'

Amy scrunched up her lips, her cheeks flushed, and she turned away from him, utterly shocked.

Karl spat out an over-the-top laugh. 'Oh, and you think she'd rather sleep with a bloke with a face like a dented potato and hair like Elvis dragged through a bush backwards?'

A couple of blokes drinking at a nearby table sniggered at that comment, though they were also quick to hide their faces behind large food menus.

Craig's eyes raged. 'You best watch your mouth, you stupid ginger wanker!'

'Ha, yeah, good one, mate. Hey, you know that acting like a massive dick won't actually make *yours* any bigger, right?'

'You have a smart mouth on you. You man enough to back up your big talk?' said Craig.

Karl laughed. 'Oh, man! Please just stop talking. You're like an annoying little duck. Quack, quack, quack.'

Duncan moved closer to his friend, who seemed oblivious to the danger he was unwittingly putting himself in. Duncan had never seen Craig Bartell, but he'd heard a rumour about him. And from what he'd learnt, Craig and his family were notoriously violent. Duncan knew he needed to get his best friend out of there and pronto, because he was one smart-arsed comment away from receiving the pummelling of his life. Karl never backed down from a disagreement.

'Hey, Karl. Let's grab that burger,' said Duncan. They'd planned to eat here, but staying put wouldn't be a wise move now.

Craig instantly rounded on Duncan, eyeing him with malice, though he needed to crane his neck to do that, because Duncan towered over him. Though despite the size difference, Duncan shrunk away from the lad and couldn't hold his fierce gaze for more than a few seconds.

'How about we finish our chat outside?' said Craig, focussing back on Karl, as if deciding Duncan didn't pose any real threat.

Karl winked at him and spoke in a buoyant tone as he said, 'Nah, you're good. I'm done flirting with you, mate. You're just not my type, I'm afraid. You're a bit too pikey for my liking. No offence.'

Amy tugged at Karl's arm. 'Come on, let's go! Now, Karl.'

'Yes, let's go,' added Duncan.

Craig turned back to Duncan, his glare penetrating, and for a brief second, he thought the guy was going to strike him.

'You hulking mug. You fancy a square go? I'll put a pint glass straight in your fat mouth,' said Craig in a low, nasty voice.

Duncan shook his head and swallowed nervously. 'No... I don't want any trouble.'

'Do one then, you dopey cunt,' sneered Craig.

'Oi, don't get bitchy with him because *you* got the major brush off,' said Karl.

Craig's features darkened and Duncan seemed sure things would turn violent.

Suddenly, a shrill, donkey-like laugh came from the bar's entrance, and Craig's focus shot to the noise. A skinny man with twig like arms waltzed in. He wore a baseball cap perched sideways on his head. A small entourage of students followed him. The man locked eyes with Craig. He stopped dead, gave a gormless grin and his nose twitched as though an elusive sneeze was rankling him.

Craig stomped towards the man, who took off his cap revealing a shaven, bony head shaped like a giant jelly bean.

'Hey Craigy-boy, that's like so weird, man, coz I was literally about to call you up, mush,' spluttered the guy. The group of students, sensing the animosity radiating from Craig, dispersed, leaving the man standing alone.

'My stupid phone won't hold a proper charge. It's been temperamental all day,' said the bald man. He even whacked it against the bar as if to emphasise the point. As if somehow that would help his predicament.

'Outside, Trev,' snapped Craig.

This Trev guy shuffled out the door like a naughty schoolboy trudging off to visit the headteacher's office.

Duncan guessed this Trev must have been in his late-thirties, yet had the mannerisms of an annoying sixteen-year-old chav.

'What a total twat,' muttered Karl.

Duncan nodded in agreement and suggested they left without delay. His heart was thudding like crazy.

'Can't we go back later? I had my heart set on a rocket-man burger,' said Karl, walking fast to keep up with Duncan and Amy.

'Didn't you just hear what Duncan said?' asked Amy.

'Oh, so what? The guy was a massive dickhead,' said Karl, glancing back as he walked. 'Surely if he was going to start any trouble, he'd have done it in there,' he continued, though with less surety now.

Duncan could see Craig and Trev debating across the street. Craig was jabbing an angry finger at the other man. At least he seemed uninterested in them now.

Amy checked her phone. 'Well, my sister is parked up here. Try to stay out of trouble, kids, won't you?'

'Wish your mum happy birthday from me,' said Karl, kissing Amy on the lips.

Amy said her goodbyes and headed off to a waiting Ford Fiesta parked on the other side of the road. She gave a quick wave before getting into the passenger side of the car. Karl waved and grinned boyishly as the car drove away.

'So, you didn't get an invitation to the birthday bash?' asked Duncan.

'Mmm, no I didn't. Just family. I'm sure I will next time.'

'Wait up, dickheads!' bellowed a loud voice.

Duncan recognised the voice before seeing the bulky figure come strolling across the road. He held a portion of chips that could have fed five people. Duncan noticed that his cousin, Scott, still wore the same blue Adidas tracksuit he'd been wearing earlier, with visible sweat patches blotting his arm pits. His light-brown, wavy hair looked a total dishevelled mess.

Scott crammed a handful of greasy chips into his gob. 'I was just popping down for a swift one, lads. You off already?'

'Sorry, Scott, we're grabbing a takeout instead,' said Duncan. The waft of stale perspiration coming from the big man almost made him gag.

'Fair enough, I'll bugger off home then. Probably for the best, cos the showers down the club are knackered and no doubt I smell like a rancid old nut sack.'

'You, Mr Blunk, are definitely correct there, pal,' said Karl, stepping backwards as he dramatically waved his hands to fend off the stench.

'That's the aroma of a hard workout, Karl... you should try it sometime,' said Scott, trying to put an arm around Karl, who darted out of his way, laughing.

'Sod off, Scott. You can keep well away from me. You stink like rotten cabbage,' said Karl.

'We need another player for the five-a-side footy next Wednesday, Karl... if squash is not your thing,' said Scott.

'Sport in general isn't my thing.'

Duncan clapped Karl across the back. 'The only time you'll see him running is when it's last orders at the pub.'

'Come on, Karl. Be a laugh,' said Scott.

Karl grinned. 'I'd rather have intercourse with a cheese grater.'

Scott rammed a wedge of chips into his mouth. 'So, I'll stick you down as a maybe?'

Karl laughed. 'If that makes you feel better.'

Scott flashed a cheeky, lopsided grin. 'In all seriousness, you might want to stay in shape, though, mate. A bird like Amy won't want to date a lard arse.'

'Leave off, I ain't a lard arse,' protested Karl, patting his stomach. 'I am lean and buff, bro.'

Scott offered his last chips around and got no takers. 'Just saying, Karl... she's well out of your league. You should beef up, dude,' continued Scott.

'Aw, thanks, Scott. You know how to cheer a guy up,' said Karl.

Scott stepped back several paces, scrunched up the chip wrapper, and locked eyes with Duncan. 'Ready?'

'Yep.'

Scott tossed the now ball shaped wrapper to Duncan, who effortlessly stepped forward, headed the rubbish, and landed it straight in a nearby bin.

Scott punched the air. 'He's only gone and done it first time!'

'Dunk and Blunk strike again!' hollered Duncan.

Karl let out an embarrassed sigh. 'Please don't call yourselves that. It makes you sound like a very dubious nineties boy band.'

'How'd you crack that delicious little nut anyway, Karl?' asked Scott.

'We work together... well, for the same firm.'

'What, she delivers bogs too?' asked Scott.

'No, she's a receptionist. And I don't just deliver bogs, as you so eloquently put it. I distribute stellar bathroom supplies,' said Karl.

'What, so like posh crappers? Do they sell those things that can squirt warm water straight up your bum hole? I've always fancied one of those. Can I get a discount?' asked Scott with a devious grin.

'Bidets. And no, you can't get a discount. Plus, I doubt they stock any bidets that could handle your huge, reeking arse anyway.'

'Amy's hot though. Loads of my mates have tried to get it on with that knockout. How did you manage it?' asked Scott, sounding genuinely interested.

'We were friends for a... sorry, what? Who's tried?' asked Karl, now gazing incredulously at Scott.

Scott made a face. 'Um, anyway, I best make a move. Catch you lads later. Let me know about the footy!'

Karl slurped on a large milkshake. 'That poor excuse for a burger was no consolation. It was like chewing on a wedge of old leather. Aw, crap, now that's given me major brain-freeze.'

'I'm not convinced my chicken surprise was actually chicken,' said Duncan.

The pair approached a carpark set at the rear of a darkened office block on the outskirts of the city. The parking area belonged to a solicitor's firm, and though the entrance had a barrier, it seemed to be permanently up.

'What was the surprise?' asked Karl, rummaging inside his jeans for his keys. 'Or maybe the surprise comes early tomorrow morning when you bolt out of bed and dash to the loo.'

Duncan laughed. 'Hurry. Open up, I'm getting chilly here.'

'I will, when I find my keys,' said Karl, now digging deep into his grey fleece jacket.

'One day, your car will get stuck in here, Karl.'

'My mate Bill's mum works here… she told him they never shut the barrier.' Karl placed the milkshake on the roof of the car, still searching. 'Amy wants a kitten.'

Duncan laughed. 'You didn't tell her you're allergic?'

'Um, no, I tho—' Before he finished his sentence, Karl crashed down under a flurry of wild punches. Duncan hadn't even seen the attacker approach. He rushed to the other side of the car. Karl, now rolled into a ball and half under his Nissan, was being kicked and stamped on. The hooded attacker bellowed obscenities as he delivered the merciless beating. Duncan watched in terror, but somehow couldn't drive his body forward to assist his friend, who now shrieked in panic and cried for help as the powerful blows continued to thud down.

Duncan forced himself to snap out of his frozen daze – and piled into Karl's assailant, grabbing him from behind, pulling and holding him with all the force he could muster.

This caused the man, at least a foot shorter than Duncan, to go insane with rage. The man yelled, cursed and bucked in Duncan's arms like a deranged kangaroo. He repeatedly slammed the back of his head into Duncan's face. Pain seared straight up Duncan's nose. He tasted warm blood in his mouth and, as tight as his grip was, he had no option but to release his bear-hug hold. The man attacked the moment he did so, and Duncan, forced backwards, shielded his face with his hands as the attacker laid into him. The relentless blows rained against him. One punch connected with his chin and sent a stabbing pain from his lower jaw all the way back to the nape of his neck. Duncan didn't have the chance to hit back; he didn't even know how to swing a proper punch, let alone take on someone so aggressive and hellbent on bashing him.

The next flurry of fists sent him down, and he instinctively shoved his forearms over his face.

He expected more blows… but they didn't come.

Karl yelled something.

The attacker bellowed insults.

Duncan became aware of a scuffle nearby.

Then he got to his knees. As he did so, Duncan heard an awful sound in his head – like two huge trucks colliding in a tunnel. Then all the noise ceased and his mind swam. Everything became hazy. Then darkness took over as he thudded against the ground.

Duncan lay there in stunned shock. How long had he been down? He felt his entire body shaking, and although he knew he'd taken some hefty wallops to the face, the pain didn't seem too intense at that moment.

'Duncan… Dunk… you OK?' whispered Karl. 'Come on, get up.'

Karl helped Duncan to his feet. He gazed around, searching for signs of the attacker, though he couldn't see him.

Karl looked disorientated. Then he walked to a nearby wall and peered over. The wall was only three feet high. Duncan was unable to see the drop on the other side. He assumed the attacker had gone over the wall and he envisioned the man climbing back over any second, enraged and ready to kill them both. But no sound could be heard.

Duncan viewed his friend, taken aback at how awful he looked. His right eye was swollen, his forehead carried a nasty gash, and under the orange glow of the nearby lamppost, he looked sickly white as he walked around in circles, taking in deep gulps of air.

Duncan took a few slow steps towards the wall. He couldn't help himself. He had to check. Something inside him made him step over to it and take a peek.

The drop behind the wall wasn't far, and down below sat a row of wooden picnic benches set on a small grassy area surrounded by skinny trees. It was no doubt used as a lunch area by employees of the nearby business. When he clapped eyes on the attacker from this viewpoint, he recognised him straight away. He seemed much younger, as he lay there, sprawled on his back, one leg bent at an ungainly angle. The image was horrific, yet cartoon-like. The lifeless eyes were open wide in a sort of over the top surprise. His mouth had set in a wide O-shape. But in those horrible few seconds, Duncan still identified him easily and the impulse to throw up hit him like a hefty thump to the belly. A frightening thought struck him – their lives would never be the same again. Craig's head had landed on a railway sleeper, one of many that acted as a border separating the grass and the seating area. A pool of dark blood had spread out behind Craig's head and flowed in thick rivulets down the side of the wood. Duncan couldn't bring himself to go down and investigate further, but suspected that if he did, he'd discover Craig's head had been impaled on a piece of metal sticking out of the sleeper. He shuddered and turned away.

Duncan then realised Karl stood aside him, gaping down in horror. Neither of them spoke for some time, but Karl broke the silence as he snatched out his phone. 'We need to call somebody.'

Duncan pulled the phone from him. 'Don't use your phone!'

Karl just gawped at him like he'd gone nuts.

'Are you OK to drive?' asked Duncan.

It took Karl a while to comprehend what Duncan was suggesting. He walked to the car and leant against it, his breathing uneven and rasping.

Duncan placed a hand on his shoulder. 'Find your keys.'

This time, Karl located those keys in an instant. He shoved a hand in his back pocket and tugged them out. They were both in that car as soon as the locks pinged. Karl fumbled to get the key in the ignition. It took several attempts to get the key to hit its target, and when the engine came to life, it seemed horrendously noisy and caused the pair to wince.

'Milkshake!' shouted Duncan, springing out of the car and racing to the driver's side to retrieve it. As he scooped it from the roof of the car, he became aware of a presence by the entrance to the carpark. Out on the road, engine humming, lights shining, was a BMW with its passenger door open. Duncan gazed at the car in dismay, as though it were a living beast about to charge straight at him. What he saw next caused him to jolt backwards so suddenly, the milkshake almost dropped from his grasp. A shadowy figure moved in the car. Someone in the driver's seat had been silently watching the altercation, though the shape had moved from his sight now. But it *had* been there. Or had he imagined it?

As they fled, with Karl driving like a dazed pensioner, Duncan knew he'd better wait until they were far away from here before he dropped the news about the witness he'd clocked.

5

Duncan didn't know where they were, and guessed Karl wasn't sure either. He'd driven them away from Canterbury and ended up travelling aimlessly through a maze of twisty lanes that were surrounded by thick woodland. They hadn't seen a building for miles now. After around twenty-five minutes, Karl manoeuvred the car onto a puddle-filled byway that was towered by alder trees, switched off the engine, and gazed out of the window.

They sat in silence for a long time, absorbed in their grim thoughts. Duncan kept mulling over what he knew about the Bartells. His cousin once spoke about a man called Paul Becker, who'd got into strife with Craig last year. Becker's problematic kid brother owed Craig a substantial amount for a drugs debt, so Becker tried, tactfully, to sort the matter out himself, and save his little brother a nasty beating. Becker's interference resulted in him receiving four cracked ribs and two broken legs. Once, Becker had been a terrific flanker for Canterbury Rugby Football Club, but he'd never play the sport again, because of complications with the breaks. This wasn't surprising, because, if the story were true, the Bartells had crushed Becker's legs under the wheel of a car. Though another of Scott's friends who'd been part of the discussion, said they'd attacked Becker with metal bars, and the other story had been a fabricated version that somehow circulated. Whatever did happen, Becker never pressed charges through fear of reprisals from the family. The once strong, jolly guy was left a broken man. And by all accounts, the poor bloke was a depressed alcoholic these days. Duncan remembered feeling so upset for the man when he'd heard the story in the pub.

'So... what do we do?' said Karl, his voice barely audible.

Duncan hurt all over now; especially the back of his neck and top of his shoulders, that flared with a stabbing pain every time he moved an inch. His nose, now some two sizes bigger than it had been earlier that evening, hurt like hell, and a strange pain throbbed behind his eyeballs.

'What happens when you accidentally kill someone?' asked Karl.

It's manslaughter, guessed Duncan, though he didn't say it. He didn't want to say the sentence out loud. As if by somehow saying those words, it would turn this messed up incident into a reality. It was still like a bizarre dream at this point. A God awful nightmare.

Karl touched his forehead and squirmed. 'We can claim self defence... right?'

We, mused Duncan, then said, 'You didn't have a choice, Karl. You did what needed to be done. End of story... It wasn't even a big drop, was it?'

Karl stayed silent... apart from his shallow breathing.

'Pure bad luck that he landed like that. But it's not like you meant to shove him to his death, it's just... it was rotten luck,' said Duncan.

Karl scowled at him for a moment, then said, 'Rotten luck? Duncan, rotten luck is when you stub your toe on the door. This is a bloody catastrophe!'

Of course, they shouldn't have fled like that. They should have phoned the police, contacted a decent lawyer, and dealt with the matter head on. But standing in that carpark, Duncan envisioned Paul Becker screaming in agony as a car tyre crushed his legs. He even imagined the sound, like dry branches snapping.

Now, feeling feverish and ready to puke, an idea sprang into his mind. 'Do you have your passport?'

Karl closed his eyes, balled his fists and kept bashing his head as he brooded over the situation. 'You reckon we should run, don't you?'

Karl appeared about set to have a meltdown. So, Duncan waited for

Karl to compose himself. Then he told him about what he'd seen in the BMW. And also told him the story about Paul Becker's quarrel with the Bartells.

Afterwards, Karl put his head in his hands and let out a strange moan. 'Aww tits. We're so shittin screwed!'

They pulled up outside Duncan's house in Boughton-under-Blean at eleven. Duncan's parents were asleep, and so he silently went to his room and packed his things. Before leaving the house, he cleaned his cuts and petted his labradoodle, Lenny, before sloping back out to Karl's car. The next stop was Karl's dad's place, where Karl slipped in via the back door to grab his belongings. He returned to the car twenty minutes later with a large rucksack slung over his shoulder, and wearing a khaki-coloured baseball cap, which he'd tugged right down over his head to disguise the gash. They walked two streets away and only had to wait five minutes before the taxi arrived to take them to Ashford. The driver seemed reluctant to engage in conversation, which suited them, as they huddled in the back and travelled in total silence. Booking the Eurostar had proved costly, but Duncan just handed over his Visa with zero complaints and thanked his lucky stars they could get on the early Friday train at such short notice. As the train left the UK, Duncan once again felt terrible pains behind his eyes and worried that something wasn't right, and that he needed medical attention, which he would have sought immediately had the circumstances been different.

When the pair reached Brussels' South Station, Duncan and Karl shuffled off the train, avoiding direct eye contact with everyone; neither had uttered a single word since the train sped from Kent.

Within five minutes, they were en route to Brussels Centraal, where, on arrival, Duncan purchased a pair of one-way tickets to Eindhoven. Karl had yet to offer any readies towards the travel fare, but Duncan considered they could sort all that out when they got their heads around everything. At the station, they waited in dejected silence as eager passengers whizzed about their business and rushed for the correct platforms. Duncan noticed they were waiting on the incorrect platform only five minutes before their train rolled in, so the pair joined a throng of scurrying commuters as they hurried to the right one.

The intercity, compared to the Eurostar, seemed to crawl along, but with just one change at Breda, they rolled into Eindhoven a little after lunchtime.

Like two wandering schoolboys, they followed directions on Duncan's phone to the Market Square. This was a place his brother often mentioned when they'd spoken about his time here.

Karl stopped and nodded towards a McDonald's. 'Hungry?'

Typical Karl, thought Duncan. They could have been exploring the lost islands of Fiji and he'd sniff out a Big Mac. Duncan decided his stomach ached because he was hungry, and so the pair went inside. Whilst they ate, Duncan sent a text message to his brother – *Hi bro, guess what? I'm in Eindhoven. Let me know when you're free.*

Within thirty seconds, a reply pinged through, saying – *WTF???*

He listened, chin rested on steepled fingers, as though Duncan and Karl were pitching a ridiculously lame idea in the Dragon's Den and he couldn't wait to notify them *he was out*. But overall, Duncan concluded, his brother had taken the disastrous news well, considering this was the same individual who would scream at him like a banshee when he dared to borrow his favourite Lynx shower gel or his new Billabong T-shirts.

'I'm sorry to drag you into this, Ryan. I... I didn't know who else to turn to,' said Duncan.

Ryan leant back on the chrome chair and scanned the cafe; even though there wasn't anybody within earshot of the quiet corner they'd chosen to huddle into. 'I want to make this crystal clear. Should you ever get implicated in this business, I never knew what transpired last night. Are we one hundred and fifty per cent clear on that, lads?'

Duncan and Karl nodded.

'You came here for a change of scenery and asked me to put you up for a few days. I thought it seemed odd and asked if everything was

OK. You both assured me that everything was all hunky dory. That's it. And don't video call anyone until those bruises fade.'

Duncan and Karl both nodded again, more firmly this time.

'Did either of you check for CCTV?' asked Ryan, directing the question at Duncan.

Duncan and Karl shared a nervous glance. They hadn't even considered this. Karl tugged off his cap and squeezed it with both hands and begun wringing it as though it were a wet towel.

Ryan sucked in some air. 'Moving on then. How certain are you that someone was in that car, Duncan?'

Duncan stared at his older brother, and in that moment, he'd never felt so envious of him, as he waited for his response like an astute solicitor. Ryan, thirty in a month, with his trimmed goatee, sharp haircut and small, shrewd eyes, was a whip-smart individual who had done well for himself. At just twenty-six, Ryan landed a fantastic job at a huge firm that operated in London, Hamburg and Eindhoven, the name of which Duncan couldn't even pronounce, as a customer services representative for the European Market. Well-spoken in both Dutch and sufficiently spoken in German to hold an adequate conversation, Ryan soon became an invaluable member of the company and got paid handsomely for his endeavours. When Ryan lived at home, they'd not been close, but ever since he'd left, he and Ryan became the best of mates, and Duncan would spend at least one weekend a month staying at his brother's flat in Hackney. They'd go to all the trendy city centre bars, watch comedy shows, attend football matches and frequent decent restaurants. When Ryan announced that he'd been promoted and would be transferred to the Netherlands branch, Duncan felt gutted, but Ryan assured him that travelling to his new residence would be super easy, and he should still visit as often as possible. Though despite nearly two years passing, Duncan hadn't made the effort to come... until this morning. A shroud of guilt descended over him as he sucked up that fact.

'I dunno... I mean, I'm fairly sure,' said Duncan.

Ryan dragged a hand through his blond hair. 'Look, on the upside, if you couldn't see them, perhaps they couldn't see you. Not clear enough to give a description.'

'What if they took Karl's registration?'

Karl groaned at this.

Ryan tapped his fingers on the table. 'Right, we need a plan. Firstly, you both need a phone blackout. So, send a brief text to anybody who might miss you and explain you've taken a few days away in Europe. A mad, spontaneous trip. Give no more detail than that.'

'What about our jobs? I'm due in tomorrow and Karl should've been at work hours ago,' said Duncan.

'Call in sick,' said Ryan, 'and don't use Facebook or anything online. Temporarily shut the accounts, or just don't use them. And don't start searching online. No news reports or googling. I'll monitor the situation on a secure laptop in the office. And I'll speak to Mum and tell her you've surprised me with a visit and that you kept shtum in case she blabbed to me. She'll buy that.'

Duncan wasn't convinced she would, but nodded anyway.

A young waiter approached with a tray of coffees and apple tarts. Ryan conversed with the guy in Dutch, exchanged what seemed like a bit of banter, and the waiter left their table, chuckling as he left them.

'What's he sniggering about?' asked Duncan.

Ryan picked up his coffee. 'He asked why your nose is such a mess. I said you went over the handlebars of your push bike.'

'Oh, lovely, and he found that funny, did he?'

'He said "don't drink and ride".'

And don't mouth off to thuggish maniacs, thought Duncan sombrely, as he glanced at Karl, who was busy cursing and twisting his baseball cap.

6

Kent, 30 March 2018

Elena sat outside on the tatty swing seat and popped a smoke between her lips. The courtyard was quiet and Jack's dirty Land Rover Defender was the only vehicle present. Elena scanned the house, eyes hunting for movement, but everything was still. She lit the smoke and took a deep drag as she gazed back at the scruffy unit they lived in. The static caravan looked more decrepit than ever today in the early spring sunshine. Strips of cracked PVC cladding hung lifelessly from the sides and the roof was covered in moss and patched with dark pitch, where they'd hastily filled in several holes that had caused some leaks last winter. The ancient unit had been rooted to the same spot for decades. The shanty looking lean-to that covered the entrance steps looked like it was about ready to keel over if someone dared cough near it. Yet somehow, the crappy wooden structure had survived all this time. Every time a strong wind hit, Elena expected to step outside to find the shelter had been blown into the paddock, but the stubborn structure always held fast. The inside was cosy enough; cramped, but cosy. Nino called it the *Hippy's Nest* because of the dream catchers, colourful drapes, psychedelic tapestries, and rainbow cushions decorating the place. Elena just wanted to add a touch of zing to the dreary old dwelling. When she'd moved in with him, it smelt like a hovel and resembled a homeless man's squat, before she added her vibrant and jazzy touch to the place. The scented candles were the first things on her list, and then she'd transformed the place into their own homely, sassy love den. Elena dreamed of owning a cosy cottage in the middle of nowhere – far from here, where she and Nino could raise their own family. Without the interference of the Bartells. OK, they already lived in the middle of nowhere, but she felt trapped and isolated here, like some sort of prisoner in her own home. With no proper means of transportation of her own, in a way, she was. She sometimes took long strolls into the surrounding fields and woods. It was nice to escape the place. But with the majority of her family in Uttoxeter and York, there wasn't anywhere for her to go, anyway. Even if she'd wanted to. As her father said, 'You've made your bed, Elena O'Carroll, now lie in it, lass. I hope that boy is worth leaving us for.'

Nino was. She loved him more than anything. He'd die for her, and vice versa. That wasn't just some sappy shite that they said and didn't mean. They both meant it. Their bond couldn't be broken. Not ever.

Elena focussed on the main house again, sure she'd spied movement in the loft window. Craig's room. She took another drag on the smoke and a chilly shudder ran through her. Things seemed different here today. Serenely quiet and strange.

Elena only left their little home and ventured into the dreaded main house for two reasons. The first was to enjoy a nice hot bubbly soak in the tub, and she'd pick the opportune moment to nip upstairs to the bathroom; usually when most of the family was absent. Or at least, when Maria, Craig and Barry were not lurking around. The second was for Sunday roast with the entire clan, which seemed to be unavoidable, despite her continuous complaints to Nino when she'd first agreed to move in with him two years ago. Although, she had to admit, Barry, despite being an utter toss-bag, could cook a fabulous roast with all the trimmings, and during mealtime, he'd be reasonably civil to her. Although Maria couldn't manage this even for one mealtime. She'd scowl and mutter and make snide remarks under her breath, tut whenever Elena dared to open her mouth and generally be a mardy-faced cow throughout. Jack would occasionally try to control his wife with the odd. 'Jesus, enough, Maria!' or he'd slam down his beer glass and throw her an icy stare. Elena often noted Maria retort with a tiny sly smile, like she'd been trying to goad him on purpose. Elena had been unnerved by the woman initially, but soon grew less afraid of the fat trout as time passed. She hated that woman so much, and wanted to pull out her waspish tongue, or slap that irritable grimace straight off her vile face. But she knew that wasn't possible, and so instead, she'd smile girlishly and be the little innocent victim. She'd learnt the best way to deal with her was to act like Maria ruled the roost and that she was too quiet and timid to react. But, now and then, she'd give Maria a secret look that said, 'Yes, I am a massive threat, Maria, you total bitch.' And she'd witness the fury light up in those dark, evil eyes as though at any moment she'd fly into a rage, but she never did, because deep down she knew it wouldn't be justified.

Elena would always moan like hell to Nino when they left. She'd swear and promise that it would be the last time, but Nino always talked her round, telling her to be the bigger person. Maria disliked Nino too and only had a fondness for Craig and Barry – the arseholes of the family. There used to be a third reason to enter, and that was to use their washing machine. This meant heading straight into the bitch's lair, and so after only two attempts at laundry duty, she delegated that job to Nino.

Elena hadn't seen Nino since yesterday afternoon. He'd texted her to say he'd be out all night, and she assumed he'd been dragged into one of Craig's schemes, or made to run errands for one of the brothers. She was, however, enjoying the peace. This was short-lived though, and she tutted as Barry's crappy Range Rover broke the silence as it pulled into the courtyard and parked near the unused steel water tank. Johnny was behind the wheel and Barry sat in the passenger side, head slumped in his hands. Elena decided it was a tad early, even for Barry, to be in such a wasted state that he was incapable of driving. Being blathered didn't normally stop the inconsiderate pig from getting behind the wheel, anyway. Maybe he'd been hitting the bevvy hard last night, she considered. Then she looked closer – Barry was sobbing, and now Johnny awkwardly rubbed at his arm. Barry gazed up at his brother, tears rolling down his cheeks as he spoke. Elena had no clue what words were being spoken, but it seemed clear that something terrible had transpired. The brothers were in bits. She flicked the cigarette away and lit a fresh smoke, viewing the scene with intense intrigue now. The vehicle's back doors opened and Nino got out, appearing mournful and dejected. Then Jack, his face hard and unreadable, as he opened the passenger door and crouched down to Barry, whispering to him and rubbing his son's shoulder that bobbed up and down as he sobbed.

Nino stood there, hands jammed in the pockets of his jeans. He wavered as though he didn't have a clue what to do next.

Elena sucked hard on the smoke, not too sure how she felt about seeing Barry in such a sorry state. Tough guy Barry, with his smart arse comments. The ever tenacious, argumentative and irritating, Barry, weeping like a child. *Mummy will make it all better soon*, she thought, trying not to crack a smile that she could feel fighting its way to the surface. Or, perhaps Maria had keeled over and croaked it, she considered optimistically. Though she doubted that. Even death would be scared of that sour-faced old bint and she'd no doubt outlive the lot of them.

Jack and Johnny helped Barry from the motor. Nino shuffled away from the vehicle, and headed towards her.

Behind Nino, Barry roared, fell to his knees, and cried. It looked so dramatic and over the top that Elena slipped out a tiny snigger. She considered that the only thing missing from the scene was some melancholy piano music playing in the background.

Then Nino was standing in front of her, and said, 'Craig died last night.'

Elena fixed her face, feigning the look of grave concern. 'Oh, no. Shall I make a nice brew?' she asked. It's the sort of thing her ma would have said, she mused.

7

Nino finished making the tea and zigzagged through the noisy congregation of burly men and their sour-faced partners. He headed to the lounge, where he found Maria slumped in an armchair. One of Jack's spaniels, Moose, sat at her feet, his head placed on her knee, and she stroked his ears. She was dressed in black, her eyes were red, and her mascara smudged; but Nino still thought she appeared better presented than usual.

'I made you a strong coffee. With a generous splash of whiskey,' he said in a soft and friendly tone. 'A good turnout at the funeral today.'

Maria stopped stroking Moose and gave him an icy glance, making no move to take the drink.

Nino placed it on a table. 'I'll pop it down here.'

'Big shoes to fill. Big shoes,' said Maria, eyeing him with a look of pure malice.

Nino didn't have any desire to fill Craig's shoes. Not now, not ever, but he didn't reply. He just smiled and turned to leave.

'I know!' she spat.

Nino turned back to her. 'Know what?'

'That you're not telling the truth. I *know*,' she said in a low, unfriendly tone.

Again, Nino didn't respond. He guessed there'd be no point. The best thing he could do now would be to leave the forlorn woman to grieve in peace. So, he gave her a sad smile and left. He decided he'd go and join Elena.

8

Saturday 5 May 2018

Nino watched the two lads at the bar with disguised contempt. Stefan Chillcott, tall and broad shouldered, puffed out his chest and raised those big shoulders every time he moved. He had skinny, twig-like legs that looked out of proportion to his well sculpted top half. His jet-black hair was slicked right back and his sharp facial features gave him the appearance of a self-absorbed male model. He scanned the room with an air of superiority as he sipped on his pint. Next to him, his new crony, who was another in a long line of sycophantic idiots. This one was called Nathaniel. He was a jumped-up student-type playing at being a drug dealer. The rich *my daddy didn't give me enough attention* type. A thankless super-brat that was only rebelling and being a bad boy, just to prove some nonsensical point. Probably just to prove that he can still make it without daddy's money. The fact that this lad had so many other options available, yet still chose this path for himself, rankled Nino immensely. Nathaniel was younger than Stefan, perhaps twenty-one. He had thick, dark spiky hair and Nino thought he looked a lot like a younger version of that famous actor, Riz Ahmed. He wore a woollen jacket over a turtleneck jumper, faded jeans and black leather Chelsea boots. Nino had heard the lad boast that his dad wanted him to go to university, but he'd scoffed at the idea. *Arsehole*, thought Nino.

Stefan laughed and rubbed his nose. No doubt he'd been hitting the party candy. It was hard not to chuckle at Stefan's getup. Tonight he wore a tight black Hugo Boss vest to show off his bulging biceps, and the thick gold chain that hung about his neck appeared so weighty, Nino suspected that even Mr T would refuse to don it. The back of the chain was even held together by a chunky carabiner style clip, like something a mountain climber would use to secure himself to a rock face. Earlier, when he'd glimpsed Stefan's phone screensaver, he'd bitten his lip to hide a snigger. The photo was of Stefan, posing in the mirror, with his muscles tensed. This summed the lad up. Nino visualised the idiot waking up each morning, caressing and kissing each bicep before jerking off to his own reflection in the mirror.

A short, tarty looking girl, wearing a pink bralette that barely covered her nipples and a tight, denim mini-skirt, tootled over to the pair, laughed at something Stefan said and headed to the toilets, causing a wave of stares and leers from half of the scumbags in there.

Stefan's light-blue eyes locked onto Nino and he gestured he join the pair at the bar. Instead of going over, Nino just raised his drink, forced a polite grin and turned away from the pair.

Stefan and Nathaniel had both tried to engage Nino in idle chatter earlier, but not one for bullshit small talk with wannabe drug dealers, Nino soon found an excuse to slip away from the pair and left them lording over the bar area. Nino opted to sit in a corner where he messaged Elena, telling her how much he missed her. He'd much rather be home with her instead of being stuck here with a bunch of boisterously drunk Neanderthals. But his brothers had insisted that he must show his face. The Chillcott family wanted to show their respect for Craig by having a knees-up, and the Bartells and their friends were being treated to a free bar all night.

Reilly and Mills Chillcott had both attended the funeral too. Apparently, they thought highly of Craig. Nino reckoned his brother would've made a good addition to this violent, messed up family. Not that this his family weren't those things of course, but the Chillcotts made his lot seem like a bunch of mischievous kittens in comparison.

Reilly, who'd previously been explaining something to a confused-looking Mills, joined the pair at the bar, playfully punching both the lads in the stomach. Then they laughed raucously at something his younger brother whispered in his ear.

Reilly, shorter and slighter than Stefan, always carried an amused expression that suggested he was privy to something funny that you were not. He, unlike his older brother Mills, who resembled something right out of a terrifying fairy tale, was a regular-looking guy. He had an unforgettable face. Just an average Joe. It could be hard to read Reilly too; most of the time he seemed calm, and he spoke softly; but apparently once that switch clicked, his temper was ferocious. Nino hadn't ever witnessed any anger from the man, but even Craig had never dared to cross Reilly and bent over backwards to stay in his good books. That was testament to his reputation. And that put Reilly on another level of psycho, because his late brother wasn't prone to being easily scared.

If Reilly was a real life psychopath, then Nino wondered what category Mills belonged. Reilly, ninety-five per cent of the time, came off as charming, friendly, and approachable, but Mills was very different. He came across as detached, sullen and unfriendly. And it was common knowledge that the gigantic man could barely keep a lid on his explosive temper. Nino got a bad vibe from Mills. He guessed that controlling his rage must be an arduous task, especially working in a rowdy pub full of noisy scrotes and mouthy idiots. Where Reilly was manipulative, street smart and business minded, Mills was... well, an aggressive oaf. Nino believed neither brother felt much in the way of empathy for others.

Out of the three brothers, Nino detested Stefan the most. The way he swaggered about acting the big hard man. How he constantly exploited his family's reputation for his own gain. How he liked to stir up trouble for others by slyly dropping gossip in Reilly's ear, who had such a fondness for his younger brother that he'd believe anything the lad told him. He'd do anything Stefan asked of him, and that put the fear of God into people. That made the slimy toe-rag so dangerous. Because one word from him and you had a colossal problem.

Nino liked Reilly the most. He'd always treated him with respect, made time to talk to him, and seemed genuinely interested in what he had to say. He was also utterly terrified of the man, so on the occasions they'd spoken, he always watched what he said.

Nino joined his brothers and must have looked bored or annoyed because Barry tutted and said, 'Stop walking about with a face like a slapped arse, boy. Make some effort to socialise for once. And stop texting *her*!'

Before Nino could respond, Reilly plonked down at the table, with a big grin plastered on his face.

'How's your old man doing, Reilly?' asked Johnny.

Reilly shrugged. 'He has good days and bad, you know? But his mind is going to shit. And things will only go downhill. It's hard, I tell you. Seeing him so… weak. So confused. He deteriorated so rapidly.'

Johnny sipped his beer. 'Sorry to hear that.'

'He's being well cared for at the centre. It just does your noodle in when you visit and he's not quite there. He says some really weird things and gets everything all muddled up,' said Reilly.

'What's wrong with him?' asked Nino.

'He suffers from what's called Lewy body dementia. He's at stage six. Which is a severe decline. We tried to care for him ourselves, but… we knew he needed professional help. He's always been such a strong figure in our lives.' Reilly continued smiling as he spoke, though this was now a pained smile and Nino felt bad for asking for details.

Reilly raised both palms in the air. 'Can't control these things though, hey? How's your old fella?'

'We hardly see him these days. Stays at his place on the coast with Mum,' said Johnny. 'And the spaniels.'

Barry swigged his pint. 'Yeah, they have a static caravan near Whitstable. A tidy one, not like that ramshackle shit hole Nino prefers to stay in!'

Nino ignored that comment.

'Fair play. That sounds nice. Wouldn't mind waking up on the seafront myself every day. My dad used to talk about Jack all the time. Sounds like he's mellowed right out now. I heard some crazy stuff,' said Reilly.

'He's still a nut job,' said Johnny.

'So, any news about what happened with Craig?' asked Reilly, lowering his voice.

Barry grunted and shook his head.

'The police reckon they can't even rule out accidental death, because he had booze and sniff in his system. What did they call it? *Misadventure*. But that's not true,' said Johnny.

Reilly shook his head. 'Don't rely on the police finding the culprit, lads. It's been over a month, so they clearly have nothing. Keep digging. Someone must know what happened. I've been keeping an ear to the ground.'

Barry nodded sternly. 'Good to know.'

'I didn't like to ask at the funeral, but what was the actual... you know, cause of death?' asked Reilly.

Barry took a sharp intake of breath and cringed. 'A metal spike. He... fell backwards onto it... the bloody thing drove straight into his brain... killed him instantly.'

'Blimey,' said Reilly, then he gazed over at Nino. 'Wasn't you with him that night, Nino? Any thoughts on what went down?'

Nino nodded. 'Yeah, I... I was driving his car that night. I'd dropped him off in Canterbury because he was looking for someone who owed him money.'

'Who owed him money?' asked Reilly.

'Trev Smith. He's a nobody,' said Barry. 'We know he wasn't involved.'

'Oh, yeah, that pill popping moron couldn't kill a leg-less fox!' said Reilly.

'He doesn't know anything,' said Barry.

Reilly, now only half listening, gazed at the bar. 'Hold up, lads. I need to chat with someone. Let me grab you all another round in whilst I'm up.' Reilly mooched over to the bar and started conversing with two dodgy looking guys huddled there. Nino didn't know the pair, but earlier his brothers referred to them as Silas and Grey Baker. They both wore tanned, faded leather jackets that hung down almost to their knees. They were both shaggy haired and flinty eyed and didn't seem to socialise with anyone else in the bar, save Reilly. Silas was much shorter than Grey, and the pair looked rather odd standing next to each other. Apparently, the brothers were inseparable – you never saw one without the other. Nino noticed Johnny and Barry throwing the pair a dirty look. Not for the first time that night.

Nino finished his wee and was about to slip back to the bar area when Stefan swaggered in. He tried to slip out without having to talk to him, but Stefan had other plans.

'Hey, Nino mate, I know you're probably feeling so lost without Craig… the geezer was a big part of your life. The fella was a legend, right? None of us will forget him.'

The alcohol flowing from Stefan's breath made Nino's eyes water. He just nodded despondently, wishing this cretin would leave him be.

'You should work for me. I'll see you right,' said Stefan, sounding so serious it was hard for Nino not to laugh in his face. Who did he think he was? Besides, he'd spent most of his life being Craig's dogsbody, so he didn't intend to become somebody else's lackey anytime soon. He imagined Elena's face when he relayed the news of this offer. She'd be in hysterics.

Nino didn't enjoy communicating with people. In truth, he disliked most people. Especially the individuals in the world he inhabited. Elena kept telling him he may not feel that way about people outside of this world. She'd say it was because he'd never associated with normal, average people. Even at school, he'd never been allowed to mix with the other kids outside of school hours, and most of the pupils were too afraid of him anyway, because of Craig's reputation. Nino enjoyed school, though. He'd been happy to knuckle down, bury his head in the books and keep himself to himself. He'd thrived at English and Mathematics.

'Did Craig tell you about the Association?' asked Stefan.

'What's that?' asked Nino, pretending to sound intrigued.

'It's a group of like-minded people. Young people, with big plans. Understand?'

Nino nodded, thinking he'd like to tell this chain wearing dickhead to shove his shitty Association right up his skinny arse.

. . .

The scruffy band, who had played some lame, cacophonous nineties Indie covers all night, continued to drone on with their cover of Blur's 'Beetlebum', and neither Barry nor Johnny had looked enthralled to be there. Nino guessed they'd both received more than enough condolence speeches for one lifetime and were as keen as he was to leave. He'd overheard plenty of Barry's muttering complaints, with the latest being, 'I'm gonna murder that whiney-arse singer with his own guitar if he starts one more bloody song!'

A scuzzy bloke with a short ponytail made his way to their corner, rested his hands on the table and grinned like a maniac. The guy was steaming drunk.

'Bazzzaa knows me. He knows me! Don't you, Bazza?' said the man in a loud, Liverpudlian accent.

'I don't know him,' grumbled Barry.

The man put his arm around Nino and grinned. 'And who's this handsome fella, hey? You could be an Italian. Bet the old fanny loves you, hey. Am I right, hey? Am I?'

Nino pulled free of the man, who smelt of stale ale and earthy tobacco.

'Look at that big, manly nose. That's a Roman's honker that, bruv. You're little Nino Bartell, right?' asked the man.

Nino nodded, eyeing him dubiously.

The man put his arm around Nino. 'Little Emperor Nino! I'm made up to meet you, lad.'

Barry and Johnny scowled at the man.

'So, what's Nino short for?' asked the man.

'It's short for nosy idiots fuck off,' said Barry.

The man scratched his chin as if considering this. 'No, that doesn't work. Nosy idiots naff off... you could use that, Bazza.'

'Don't call me Bazza,' said Barry.

Reilly came to the table. 'Eee, you being a pest over here, Sean?' he said in a mock Liverpudlian accent.

Sean pretended to be offended, then bounded over to Reilly and playfully tickled him on the stomach. 'Oooooh, Reilly, you prick teasing hunk of spunk,' he said in a silly voice.

Reilly took all this in good spirits, slipped out a fat roll of notes from his jeans, and handed Sean a tenner. 'Here, go grab one for the road. Go on, off you trot, you bloody loon.'

Sean pointed at Barry. 'You watch this one, Reilly, he's being a right meff, him.' He then winked at Nino, gave two thumbs up to Barry and Johnny, then staggered to the bar area where he pushed his way through the crowd of misfits, unstoppable in his attempt to reach his goal.

'Who the hell is that utter muppet?' asked Barry. 'What's a meff? Is he taking the piss?'

'Supply me with a bevvy!' came Sean's loud voice.

Reilly laughed. 'Sean Teller. Or Sean Tell-us-a-story as we like to call him. He's a regular. He's alright.'

Nino could see Sean ordering up the local Wolf-Bane beer that the locals called Cunted – an eight per cent ruby ale that the regulars here loved and probably attributed to ninety per cent of the violence that kicked off.

'Scouse clown,' said Barry.

Reilly laughed. 'He's harmless, Barry.'

'Bloke stinks,' grumbled Barry.

'He's quite the character once you get to know him. Until he's had too many jars… Then he just annoys all the punters until they buy him a drink to get rid of him. Mills calls him the Sponge,' said Reilly.

Barry muttered something under his breath.

'He reckons he ran with a biker mob that used to do over crack houses in Liverpool,' said Reilly.

'Course he did,' said Barry.

Reilly ignored Barry and continued. 'He said after they ripped off some yardies, the gang sent out a kill-squad that scoured the city hunting down the thieves. They nabbed Teller outside a boozer in Toxteth, took him down in some cellar and threatened to dismember him with a chainsaw. They held him for two days, but he blagged his way out, convincing the gang it was a case of mistaken identity. He said that he worked for a charity that specialised in helping out victims suffering symptoms of PTSD.'

'And they let him walk unscathed?' asked Johnny.

Reilly grinned, showing immaculate white teeth. 'Nah, the biggest guy, a massive black dude with long dreads and rows of gold teeth goes, "PTSD. I'll be giving you PTS fucking D, boy!" The guy then cranks up the chainsaw, but he's so off his nut on crack, he drops the thing and slices off half of his own foot!'

'What, and you believed him?' asked Barry, face scrunched up as though he could smell something nasty.

Reilly grinned boyishly. 'No, leave off, Barry. Bloke's full of horseshit. But he tells some entertaining stories. And Sean knows everything about motorbikes, I'll give him that.'

Fresh pint in hand, Sean weaved his way back to the table, sipping the drink as he came. He then bumped into Stefan, who aggressively shoved him away and started mouthing off at him. Sean just laughed and pulled a funny face and Nathaniel had to restrain Stefan from charging at him.

Nino, pleased to be leaving at long last, shook hands with Reilly.

'Chin up, mate. You take it easy, yeah,' said Reilly, turning to shake hands with Barry and Johnny.

Reilly made to leave, but stopped, turned, and smiled at Barry. 'My dad said some weird stuff the other week. Started talking about that big deal that went sideways… the German one. You ever hear about that?'

'Is that right?' said Barry suspiciously.

Reilly nodded. 'Started saying, "That Jack Bartell knows… he knows who took all those bloody pills." Then he got quite angry and Veronica ended up calling the nurse.'

Barry drunk the last mouthful from his pint, swilled it around in his mouth and made a face like he'd tasted something sour. 'Really?'

Reilly gave a toothy grin. 'But the other day he thought I was his uncle Sid for the entire visit, so we take everything with a pinch of salt lately.'

Barry flashed a sarcastic smile. 'Do give him our best, won't you?'

A commotion erupted outside. Several glasses smashed. Then belligerent shouts from several men filled the air. Through the window, Nino spotted a mob of people arguing outside. More glass smashed, curses were screamed and a man with a gravelly voice bellowed, 'Yeah, I'll DO you right now!'

Reilly raised his eyebrows and flashed a mirthful smile. 'Mmm, sounds like the kids are playing too rough again.'

More punters piled outside, eager to get in on the action as the screams and shouting intensified to the point where Nino felt unsafe.

A young lad wearing a bomber jacket raced into the bar area. He spotted Reilly and gestured he should go outside. 'Teller's starting shit. You best come out, Reilly.'

Reilly nodded and followed him outside, with Silas and Grey skulking off to join them.

'Wanna check it out, Barry?' asked Johnny.

'No, we ain't getting involved in that carnage. Com'n, get me outta this circus.' He grabbed his faded black leather jacket from the back of the chair and tugged it on. 'Who does that wanker think he is? What was that all about, Jon? Is he implying Dad ripped off Marcus? Prick! That business was back in the mid-nineties, for Christ's sake. And Dad would never have done that.'

Johnny slipped on his Aviator sheepskin jacket and adjusted the fur collar. 'Come on, Barry, he's just on the wind up. Don't start.'

'Aw, fuck him!' spat Barry.

Nino couldn't wait to leave this shit hole.

9

Letter Dated 1 December 2017
Page 1

"I understand saying sorry is not enough. How could it possibly be? But I need you to know that I am. I need you to know that if I could change the past, I would. And I need to tell you the truth. So, I'm going to tell you everything right from the beginning. Some things you'll learn will upset you. They will hurt you very much, but I still must give you all the facts. In order to validate I genuinely am who I claim to be, I've enclosed two photos. I have marked the dates and places on the back. My heart bleeds when I look at these. These were all I've ever had (I have copies, though these are the originals). On the coming pages I've outlined what happened. This won't be an easy read, so be prepared for what you are about to learn. I suggest you sit down as you get ready to digest my words, as they will almost certainly turn your world upside down…"

10

Kent, 21 June 2018

Ravi adjusted his tie as he approached the run-down shop. He quickly glanced back to his Jaguar XE, uneasy about leaving his beloved car in this iffy area. He focussed back on the shop and read the faded metal sign hanging from the door stating that this was *Nick's Tackle and Bait shop*. He wondered if he'd punched the incorrect postcode into his satnav. As Ravi entered, a bell rang above his head and two men, one slouched behind a wooden counter, another with his elbows resting on it, eyed him with open hostility. They'd been chatting away as he'd entered, but stopped upon seeing him and they seemed peeved by his interruption. The man behind the till, a burly chap with a hooked nose and bushy beard, said, 'Other door. Go around the back.'

Ravi, thinking how incredibly presumptuous it was to assume he wasn't a customer, just because he wore a suit and tie, sternly replied, 'Thank you.'

Ravi had been an avid angler when he'd been an adolescent, though he hadn't cast a line for over four decades. Not since he'd left the West Indies. Ravi left and scanned the secluded back street. The neglected building was tucked away on the outskirts of Chatham, and he guessed a suited businessman was an uncommon sight in this sketchy part of town.

Ravi headed through the backdoor and took the steep steps up two flights until he spotted a slim bronze plaque on a door that confirmed he'd arrived at *The L S Agency*. He tapped on the shabby door.

'Come in,' called a voice.

Ravi entered. He'd been expecting to be greeted by a man in his forties or fifties, so as the young, fresh-faced lad with sandy coloured hair bounded over to him, offering his hand, he'd been a tad dumbfounded.

'Mr Sookdeo?' the lad asked.

Ravi would have been surprised if Schneider, if indeed this was Schneider, was much older than twenty-eight. He wondered what sort of young person would seek to work in such a business, because Schneider dealt in the grief game; where adultery, missing persons, unwanted court papers and hours spent observing individuals were all part of the daily grind. Ravi's solicitor had been the one who recommended that he contact Schneider. She advised him that all their branches used him as a process server and he never failed to get the job completed. No matter how difficult or slippery the defendant was, Schneider always located them and served them with no issues. He also carried the reputation of an agent who worked doggedly to track down missing debtors and held an astounding success rate when it came to tracing gone away tenants and elusive swindlers.

Ravi accepted the handshake. 'Are you Mr Schneider?'

'I am. Take a seat, Mr Sookdeo. Please, call me Lewis.'

Ravi considered the youngster appeared, and sounded, very unmasculine, as he sat at the desk and surveyed the room. The building appeared old and tatty, but the spruce office furniture, wooden blinds and tall houseplants made all the difference and helped ameliorate the compact space.

'I have no milk in, so I can only offer you a black coffee.'

'I'm fine. Thanks.'

Schneider tapped his fingers on the desk. 'Right, so I have your first report here.'

'You've found something?' said Ravi, unable to hide the surprise from his voice. It had only been four days since he'd spoken to him over the phone and exchanged a few emails.

Schneider rummaged in his desk and pulled out a brown envelope. 'It's my initial findings. I wanted to skim through a couple of points with you before I proceed further.'

Ravi accepted the envelope. 'Funding the investigation isn't a problem.'

'That is good to know. I have clients that expect miracles on a shoe-string budget… but that's not the issue here.'

Ravi, the intrigue too much to take, slipped out a plastic covered report from within the large envelope as Schneider divulged his findings.

As Ravi absorbed Schneider's words, his world began to darken by the second. No, more than that, his world started collapsing around him. Schneider, now aware of Ravi's anxiety stricken features, watched him furtively.

'I understand it is difficult to hear this, Ravi.'

Ravi straightened himself in the chair and spoke in a steady voice as he said, 'No, no, no. Incorrect. My son wouldn't be involved in such a filthy business. He did not need to be. Callum must have, at the very least, fabricated part of the story he told you.'

Schneider gave him a level stare and held it. 'I just report my findings. I don't come to my own conclusions, and I certainly don't speculate.'

'But I have spoken to Callum Anderson myself. Several times, in fact, and not once did he mention any of this to me. I have known that boy since he was six years old. I'm friends with his parents. They've been guests at my house.'

'That's *why* he didn't tell you the truth, Ravi. He said he didn't know how to tell you. But he spoke freely to me. Callum made it clear he'd been relieved to get this all off his chest, what with Nathaniel being missing for over a month. He'd been desperate to divulge the information to the police officer that spoke to him, but he'd been worried he'd implicate Nathaniel.'

Ravi struggled to control his breathing and had to take three deep nostrils of air to compose himself. He never displayed his emotions, not even in front of his wife, so he'd be damned if he would start getting all tearful in front of a complete stranger, especially a lad young enough to be his son.

'Are you OK, Ravi? Shall I get you that coffee?'

Ignoring the questions, Ravi said, 'These… substances he'd been… supposedly selling… the cocaine,' Ravi whispered this last word, as though even speaking it out loud would be considered illegal. 'Did he confirm who supplied him?'

'Callum doesn't know, and is reluctant to ask around. But, he said that Nathaniel's new friend, this guy called Stefan, could be involved somehow. After this guy dropped onto the scene, your son started acting differently. Callum thought this Stefan lad seemed like trouble, but Callum doesn't mix in the sort of circles where he'd be able to ask about him. He said his friends are all geeks and outcasts, and Nathaniel was once like them too. But not anymore.'

Ravi bit his lower lip hard. Nathaniel knew his stance on drugs, and therefore would know what a massive kick in the teeth this would be. Why would his son *do* that to him? Hadn't he brought him up well enough to respect his own family and to abide by the law? Did the boy have such disregard for his own family that he'd be so callous and selfish? The shame this could bring to his name… and God forbid his business, should news of it ever leak out that his son was no more than a common narcotics pusher. Some of his top clients would run for the hills if they caught a whiff of this scandal. These notions made his mind spin and his temples throb. He ran a hand over his balding head, feeling the perspiration on it.

'I spoke to another college student who confessed to buying a gram of powder from your son,' said Schneider. 'And he'd become known as the guy to go to if you needed any… illegal substances.'

'Right. So, you need to find this Stefan character,' said Ravi. It wasn't a question. He emphasised his point by jabbing a finger at the young man. 'You find him, you hear me? Pronto.'

Schneider nodded, though Ravi saw the young man's eyes narrow in annoyance. Ravi needed to keep a lid on his haughty behaviour. He wasn't in his office now, dictating to his own staff. He rubbed at his creased forehead.

'Any additional news on the van you mentioned?' asked Schneider.

'The police suggested it could have been a couple of burglars staking out potential targets,' said Ravi.

'Sounds plausible.'

Ravi huffed. 'The day after Nathaniel went missing? No, I can't believe that. Especially after what you've just informed me. Now I'm even more convinced those people were searching for him.'

'You think he's on the run from somebody?'

'They confirmed the van had false plates. They were doing something devious.'

Ravi recalled what he'd seen that late afternoon. As he'd approached the van, the engine roared to life, and it sped away. He'd caught sight of a strange decal on the rear window; a gorilla wearing a fedora hat and brandishing an assault rifle, with the words *Ape Shit* circling the image. He'd spent hours scouring the internet to find the same one, but couldn't find anything that came close to the crude sticker he'd remembered. He'd also received some weird phone calls on the landline from different callers asking to speak to his son. Nathaniel never received calls on that line, which seemed suspicious in itself, but when Ravi asked for the caller's name, they cut the call. On the last day Ravi had seen his son, he'd organised a grand birthday dinner for his wife and Ravi called his son late that Friday evening, leaving an irate voice message and expressed how disappointed he was that he'd not made an appearance and that Nathaniel had ruined his mother's special day. The next day, there'd been no reply, and they grew more and more concerned with every call they made, all of which went straight to voicemail. Ravi had spent the last weeks worrying like crazy, but now, knowing that his son had been acting like a common criminal, he felt an agonising dread he'd never before experienced. 'Find my son, Mr Schneider. I don't care what it costs. Just bloody *find* him.'

11

Eindhoven, June 2018

Duncan sat in silence, and his mind drifted. Around this time, on a Sunday afternoon he'd be settling down to one of his mum's legendary roast dinners. Not the kind that would fit on your average size plate, instead they used deep plates, the size of a lorry's steering wheel. After consuming that, which was quite a task, he'd mooch off to the lounge and watch a lame film with his dad, and one or both of them would snooze for an hour. They would wake to find Lenny snuggled between them, sleeping off his dinner of the leftover scraps and farting during his slumber. The Dutch didn't do a traditional roast that he knew and loved, and though this wasn't by far the top of the list of things he missed, it depressed him. He also missed a good cider, because for some bizarre reason Duncan could not fathom, finding good cider here was harder to locate than rocking horse shit. One of the Irish bars sold Strongbow... but fruit cider – nope. Fruit beer – yep, but that was about your lot. Duncan hated fruit beer more than he did normal beer. He'd rather drink stagnant pond water. He'd also come to an early conclusion that the Dutch were amazing at cooking steaks, and he'd consumed some delicious slabs of beef at some of the local eateries. And their burgers were epic. Every restaurant in the city could make a scrumptiously good burger. But he wasn't so sure about the rest of the general fare available. Duncan was a notoriously fussy eater though and he'd be the first to admit that. He wasn't very adventurous when it came to trying new cuisine, either. Karl on the other hand loved all the food here.

He gazed around the busy square, and the surrounding tables packed with chatting customers. The bars, restaurants and cafes here were always bustling and even the rain didn't stop the alfresco dining in the city centre. The Dutch certainly didn't get put off by rubbish weather, which was lucky as it rained here a lot. Today was pleasant though and the sun half showed itself from behind broken clouds and had sneaked its way under their giant red parasol and onto Duncan's side of the table, warming his hands as he fiddled with the bent menu. It seemed as though the entire population of Eindhoven appeared content and cheery today.

The laughter from the others gathered at the table jolted him from his thoughts.

Opposite Duncan sat Karl's new best friend, Joost Claasen, a blond, bearded man originally from Haarlem who seemed to be forever dressed in the same worn jeans and blue and white chequered shirt. Karl befriended Joost at one of the local cafes, after nibbling some olives placed on the bar that he'd assumed to be complimentary. They hadn't, but Joost found the incident hilarious and the pair started chatting and hit it off. Karl now spent more time at Joost's place than he did at Ryan's, which Duncan didn't mind, considering the pair shared the small spare bedroom. But of late, it seemed all of Karl's conversations revolved around the wonderful Joost – *Joost did this. Joost said that. Joost recommends I smoke this...* He'd had bloody *Joost* up to his frigging eyeballs. Now, the amazing Joost had even bagged Karl some part-time work at the commercial cleaning company he worked at, where he'd help his new best buddy buffer office floors and shine office block windows for euros in hand.

Joost offered his cigarette pack to the man next to him, who declined the offer. This was Noah Eikenboom, a tall black guy who sounded American when he spoke English. Duncan thought a lot of Dutch people spoke with American accents. He'd even made himself come across as a right twit a while back, when he'd asked a waitress whereabouts in the US she was from, to be told she actually lived in Tilburg, only thirty minutes away. Joost had told them that Noah loved the States, was obsessed with American TV and yearned to work in the US as a film producer. His dream was to live in Laguna Beach, California. He was quite a friendly character and Duncan liked him.

Joost offered the packet to the third Dutchman at the table. Faas Van Ankeren accepted, and Joost flicked the flame on his lighter and lit the smoke for him. Faas, a spindly guy with a youthful face but the heavily receding hair of a forty-five-year-old man and a laugh like a seal choking on a fish, smiled his gratitude. Duncan couldn't take to Faas. He found the guy way too outspoken for his liking. To the point of being downright insulting. He'd already told Duncan that he sounded like a camp presenter from some children's TV show he could not recall the name of. He also said that Duncan often carried an expression that resembled a disturbed sheep caught in a car's headlights.

Karl seemed to be having the time of his life, and he'd adapted to his new Dutch lifestyle within a few weeks. He'd been despondent and upset for the first week as they both waited in Ryan's flat, pacing, unable to focus on anything else except what news Ryan might learn. And when Ryan's key turned in the lock, they'd scurry to the door like frantic dogs, eager to hear any updates surrounding Craig's demise. But each day brought no worrying news. He'd even scanned Google street-view and seemed confident that no CCTV covered the area. The media coverage hadn't even been that major. And most importantly, *they* hadn't been implicated. Or at least they hadn't been mentioned in any news reports or social media outlets in connection to the incident. That didn't mean that people *weren't* looking for them, of course, but the police didn't show up at their parents' houses asking questions, which they took as a good sign.

After some ten days, Karl, convinced they were in the clear, told Duncan they should think about heading back home, but Duncan point blank refused and said they should wait a while longer. Ryan agreed too.

Now, over two months into their stay, they were stuck in limbo. It was now Duncan who craved to go back home, and Karl who no longer had any desire to leave.

Joost prodded Karl's shoulder. 'You should have seen this guy, Duncan. What an absolute superstar.'

Duncan smiled thinly as he cast a glance at his oldest friend, who, these days, seemed like a complete stranger to him. He even resembled a stranger with his unshaven face, unkept, wild ginger hair and lopsided smile. Duncan knew his friend wanted to morph into another person. He wanted to become someone else and leave Karl Rogers, the man who killed a drug dealer, behind. And he'd succeeded in that. No doubt the name change would come soon and he'd reinvent himself as Lars Smit or Finn De Jong.

'Dunk was at the karaoke too,' said Karl.

'Hiding in the back, no doubt. So we didn't make him sing. Huh, I bet he sings like a horny fox screwing,' said Faas, which he followed up with his seal-like laugh. Then he grinned, reminding Duncan of a devious, hungry shark.

Duncan had never witnessed Karl get up and sing at a karaoke, and so he'd watched in total astonishment when he'd sung – no, belted – Alice Cooper's 'Poison', whilst standing on a table crammed with bottles and glasses. The stoked Dutch crowd cheered, hollered, and whooped along. Afterwards, they clapped him on the back, and high-fived him. Karl then pranced around the establishment like a rockstar. They loved him here.

'What have you done to your neck?' asked Joost, gesturing at Duncan's eczema flareup that seemed to worsen daily.

Duncan hid the rash by resting his neck on the palm of his hand. 'Just an allergy thing.'

He'd not had an angry break out like this since he was sixteen. His mum always used a special steroid cream that would rapidly deal with the itchy, irritating rash, but he could only get the stuff on prescription. Clara, Ryan's girlfriend, had given him some cream that she thought might ease the itching, but it didn't seem to help. If anything, the stinky cream just aggravated it. The patches on his upper arms were even more scaly and sore, but at least they were hidden.

'Perhaps you are allergic to the Netherlands,' said Joost.

'It is a stress rash. You should chill more,' said Faas, matter-of-factly. 'Maybe you should also shed a few pounds, hey? I think that would help you. Your skin is quite unsightly. You look like you have leprosy.'

'No more Hagelslag on buttered toast for Duncan!' said Joost, giving Duncan a quick wink.

'We lived on that stuff during our first days here,' said Karl, who seemed oblivious to Duncan's ever growing annoyance.

Noah and Faas started conversing in Dutch and for a moment it sounded like they were bickering, but then Faas burst out laughing and slapped Noah across the back.

Noah caught Duncan's eye. 'Ignore Faas… just call him a zakkenwasser.'

Faas shoulder barged Noah. 'You're the only zakkenwasser here.'

Joost prodded Karl in the stomach. 'The amount of Vla that this one consumes, I am surprised he hasn't fattened up.'

'Aw, Dunk, the vanilla one is amazing. You gotta try it,' said Karl.

Faas tutted and wagged his finger. 'Don't put ideas into his head. And hide the chocolate sprinkles, Karl, I see Duncan likes them a bit too much.'

Noah let out a deep laugh. 'Says you, Faas! You eat more chocolate than Augustus Gloop.'

Faas tutted. 'Hey, that's not nice. That's Duncan's German cousin you're talking about!'

Joost rubbed Karl's hair. 'Wasn't he a redhead?'

'Depends which version you watch. In the Depp version, he's got red hair,' said Noah. 'I liked the original.'

Duncan, bored with being ridiculed by Faas, decided not to stay and eat with the group. He made his excuses and left the table.

'What is it with you? You are being a right moody bitch today. Why are you being so tetchy around our mates?'

'They are not *my* mates, Karl.'

'Of course they are.'

'Faas is a total twat!'

'Leave off, Dunk. He's just titting about. Don't be so sensitive.'

'He never ribs you. Why does he dislike me so much?'

'Dunk… come on, he's joking.'

'He's not funny. So, just go back and eat your battered horse's balls.'

'It's Bitterballen.'

'I don't care what it is. I don't want that crap.' With that, Duncan marched off across the busy Market Square and onto Nieustraat. His brother's apartment was only a ten-minute walk from the centre and he would do it in less if he went quickly.

Karl jogged ahead of Duncan, almost colliding with other pedestrians, and stopped him with a hand to his chest. 'Just say it. Tell me why you are doing this?'

'Because I just can't see how you can be this happy... your optimism... it isn't right.'

The pair shuffled out of the throng of people and stood in the doorway of a casino. Next door was a waffle and ice cream parlour where three kids gleefully consumed giant bowls of multicoloured ice cream scoops, whilst the bored father tapped away on his mobile. Those kids seemed so content with life as they greedily lapped up their treats. They didn't have a single care in the world. How Duncan envied them.

'What's wrong with being optimistic? I look on the bright side.'

'You killed someone. That should change you.'

Karl eyed him for a few moments and said, 'It has.'

'You could have fooled me.'

'I won't let it dictate the rest of my life, Duncan. Neither should you. We didn't run over a tiny child whilst speeding, or smash a helpless granny over the noggin during a burglary.'

There's that we again, thought Duncan.

'Why did you run your mouth off in the first place? You never know when to button it.'

'Because... unlike you, I speak up for myself. I don't shy away just because I don't want to get into a disagreement with some idiot. Joost likes my frankness.'

'That's because the Dutch are all plainspoken.'

'Yeah, I like that, Dunk. And I like it here.'

'It wasn't so long ago you were obsessed with the idea of setting up a love shack with Amy. Now you pretend like she didn't exist.'

'We had to make a clean break. Besides, like your cousin said, I'm out of her league, anyway.'

'Right, because everyone listens to that plonker.'

'I realised I wasn't ready for that. I was confused and rushing into things without thinking. This whole affair has opened my eyes. Given me a glimpse of broader possibilities. Life is for the taking, Dunk. We can do anything… go anywhere. Look at Clara. A travel blogger. Talk about a dream job.'

'I'm sure it's not all it's cracked up to be.'

'Come on, Dunk. Let's go on adventures. Go off the grid. Explore the unknown and write about it. Grow massive bushy beards and buy trekking poles. Maybe all this is fate and we're on the right path.'

'Ease up, Columbus. What's all this *we* business? I don't intend to spend my life being eaten alive by fleas in crappy hostels. I have my own business plan.'

'So setup the landscaping stuff here.'

'Karl, I can't speak Dutch.'

'You can learn. You'll pick it up, no problem.'

'I've tried, and it's not been working out so well.'

'Um, I'm with you on that. So far I only know, *the farmer got on the bus, beautiful and run.*'

'What use is the first one?'

'None whatsoever.'

They stared at each other for several moments, then burst into laughter.

'The Dutch all speak English, Dunk. You know that. They like it. It just pisses them off if you try to speak their lingo.'

'Go back to your Battered-balls, Karl. I'll catch up with you later.'

'Duncan… I don't enjoy seeing you so unhappy.'

'I'm fine. My skin is driving me bonkers. I'll try the pharmacy again.'

'I'm working with Joost in the morning, so I'll crash at his. Perhaps I'll see you tomorrow?'

'Yeah, sure.'

Karl went to leave, but stopped and flashed a warm smile. 'It will all be OK, mate. Trust me.'

'Sure,' said Duncan, though he didn't believe for a moment that it would be.

Three days after his disagreement with Karl, Duncan received a phone call from his dad that changed everything. He'd been working on his new website on Ryan's spare laptop when the call buzzed in. Duncan knew before his dad uttered a single word that it would be bad news. He could sense it. And when he'd said, 'Your mum's in hospital, Duncan,' the emotions that overwhelmed him in that moment were impossible to describe. He sat down and listened to his dad, the resilient and robust Tom Parvin, whom Duncan had idolised all his life, sob like an infant as he told him what had occurred that morning. After speaking with his dad and assuring him he'd be heading home that night, Duncan raced to the toilet, flung up the seat and threw up for a good five minutes straight.

Ryan raced into the lounge, and even though there were clear traces of panic written all over his face, he spoke unflappably to Duncan as he said, 'It's probably got nothing to do with what happened. We shouldn't get all worked up.'

'I have a terrible feeling about this, Ryan,' said Duncan, pacing the room and hugging himself tightly. He'd circled the sofa umpteen times.

'Are you going to visit her?' asked Clara. She was sprawled on the sofa with her MacBook on her thighs. She was wearing light blue pyjamas with a large cartoon French bulldog on the chest and a towel wound around her head.

Ryan nodded. 'This afternoon. Can I take your Polo?'

'Sure. I'll go pack,' said Clara, shutting down the MacBook's flap and jumping up from the sofa.

'You're coming too, Clara?' asked Duncan.

She flashed him a confident smile. 'Of course. I'll be your bodyguard.'

Clara was slight, with ash-brown hair which she usually had tied up in a high ponytail, and soft brown eyes that reminded Duncan of warm caramel. Her mother was Dutch and her father was Japanese.

'What about Karl?' asked Clara, sliding her laptop into a padded travel case.

Duncan wouldn't say he fancied Clara, because that would just be weird, but he admired her, and unlike the rest of the city's occupants, she thought Karl was quite annoying and respected Duncan. Clara hadn't been present in the apartment when they'd first arrived in the city, as she'd been working away, and after she'd returned home, Duncan had been livid to learn that Ryan had told her everything that had happened in Canterbury. Though he quickly established that he could trust Clara unequivocally and understood how his brother had fallen for her. She was funny, bright, and savvy. She ran a successful European travel blog, and she loved what she did.

'Yes, what about Karl? Will he go back?' asked Ryan, now with a hint of indignation in his voice.

'No,' came Karl's voice from the kitchen. He popped his head around the door. 'I mean, I hope your mum is OK and everything, but I'll pass on heading back.' Then, seeing Ryan's face darken, he added, 'I'll stay over at Joost's place.'

'Don't you want to see your family?' asked Clara.

Karl flashed a thin smile. 'Um, nope. Coffee anyone?'

'You know what this could mean, Karl?' asked Duncan.

'Dunk, mate, don't get all paranoid about this. It was just a car accident,' said Karl.

'A car slammed into her and drove away. You know this could be connected,' said Duncan.

Karl let out a long sigh and gave him a look like he was being an overly dramatic child. 'I doubt that, Dunk. Relax.'

There's that super optimism again. Duncan gritted his teeth, his anger boiling. 'This could be a message. Or a ploy to drive us out into the open.'

'You are over thinking this. But if you're that worried, maybe don't go back,' said Karl soberly.

'So I just leave my parents in the firing line? I don't think so. I'm not prepared to sit back and just hope for the best. God knows what will happen next. You may not give a crap about your dad, Karl, but I care about my parents,' snapped Duncan. The veins in his head were pulsating, and he knew another headache was winging its way. He'd been getting them daily.

Ryan and Clara shared a concerned look, and Ryan moved over to Duncan and put an arm around him. 'I don't think we should get too carried away. Chances are Karl is right, but... I suggest we need to err on the side of caution here. Until we know if the incidents are connected, then—'

'Then what?' asked Karl, stepping out of the kitchen with his arms crossed. 'We hand ourselves in? Say what happened?'

Ryan ran his fingers through his hair and drew in his lips. 'I didn't say that, Karl.'

'But you're saying that we might have to consider it,' said Karl.

'If our parents are in danger, I'll tell the police everything,' said Duncan. He eyed Karl with contempt, almost wanting him to disagree. He wanted to tear into him. He'd never outright blamed Karl for the events that unfolded that night. Not to his face, anyway. But now Karl was pushing his luck and Duncan was getting narked by his devil-may-care attitude.

'Fine,' said Karl. 'I agree. Tell them everything. But I'm still not returning. And for the record, just remember that I wanted to call the police straight after. I never suggested we run.'

Duncan went to speak, but stopped himself, as Karl's words sunk in.

Karl returned to the kitchen. 'I'll stick that coffee on.'

Duncan snorted and muttered. 'Yeah, that's right, leave everyone else to mop up your crap.' But nobody heard him.

12

Elena strolled to the front gate and checked for the post. Nothing. Four days with no bloody post. This was ridiculous. She had online orders to fulfil and didn't have all the materials required to finish the majority of the pieces her clients were waiting on. Elena made her way back home, fast walking across the courtyard and heading past the main house, and doing her very best to avoid gazing through the kitchen window, just in case she locked eyes with Maria. She hadn't clapped eyes on the woman since the funeral. It had been three months since Craig's passing and the Bartell residence was quiet these days. Not a nice, serene and pleasant quiet, a more sinister, eerie quiet that chilled her to the bone. The calm before the storm, she considered. Normally there would be fortnightly gatherings in the barn, or The Den as they called it. Nino's brothers built and converted the place into a bar and hangout several years back. These gatherings would always coincide with Jack and Maria being away at their second home in Whitstable; or holiday home, as Jack liked to refer to it. On average, about thirty-odd boisterous arseholes would descend upon the place. Usually men, but occasionally she'd hear the odd holler from some young trout-mouth up there. Most of them were Craig's cronies. A real rogues gallery of prison hardened psychos, aggressive chavs with dead-eyed stares, and bad boy coke-heads. Plus a few brown-nose flunkies, desperate to seek approval from the brothers as they lapped up their bullshit and treated them like famous movie stars, the sad lemons they were. Nino and Elena would barricade themselves inside their place and would struggle to get any sleep during those long nights. The noise levels would gradually increase as the night wore on. And as excessive amounts of drink and drugs were consumed, things would get crazy. There'd be the odd fight, of course, but generally it would be Craig kicking off with some piss-head that had mouthed off or dared to stare at him the wrong way. She'd once witnessed him frogmarching some young lad off down towards the lane, punching him in the back of his head as he protested his innocence during his banishing. After escorting the lad from the property, Craig swaggered to where the lad's car was parked, and set about it with fists, bricks, and kicks. Then all his cronies flowed out from The Den and whooped, jeered and egged him on, with others hurling bottles at the car.

Two days later, the sheepish lad dared to return for his motor, with his dad and uncle in tow. The trio didn't say a word as they got in the battered car, heads bowed, and as they tried to leave, they received a barrage of nasty abuse from Craig. The dad drove the car. The poor guy had to drive with his head hanging out of the window, due to all the cracks in the windscreen.

She considered that most quarrels and feuds resulted from drink fuelled disagreements. So-called criminals coming to blows and risking everything over banal comments and over the top banter. Taking the piss and slagging off others in the game behind their backs. All such petty nonsense, Elena always thought. If they concentrated on being proper crooks, instead of messing about and taking lumps out of each other, they might actually make some real money.

On the warmer nights, the gang would spill out into the paddock and bang out drum and bass at an ear-splitting volume. Not counting them, it wasn't like there were any neighbours to complain about the racket, and they probably wouldn't have given a shit if there had been. Sometimes they'd get their windows banged on and some muppet would shout to them and demand they get their arses out to join the fun. But they never did. Because it never sounded fun. It sounded terrifying, and the group was a hideous bunch of unruly trouble-makers that neither of them wished to socialise with. Sometimes they'd have massive fires out in the paddock and on occasions, they'd have drunken firing practice with shotguns, which would lead to a very uneasy night for Nino and herself.

Elena spotted Barry scurrying across the courtyard, hands loaded with fresh eggs, and unavoidably, their paths crossed. She gave him a thin smile, making it clear by her disgruntled expression that she had no desire to partake in small talk with him.

'Hey Mouse, you want some eggs?' asked Barry. He spoke friendly enough, even though those dark, deep-set eyes glowered at her, belying his upbeat tone.

Elena shook her head. 'No, you're alright, ta.'

'Where's lover boy then, Mouse?' he asked.

Elena hated it when Barry called her Mouse. 'Gone for bike parts. He was jabbering on about pistons and cylinders. It's all alien to me.'

'Tell him I'm cooking up my specialty omelettes. If he gets back soon.'

No invite for her as per normal. She sighed. 'OK.'

Barry continued to stare at her, making her feel uneasy. Barry was an intimidating character, with a round, rugged face that looked like it had been chiselled from stone. He often wore a deadpan expression and his smile, if you could even call it that, would only be reserved for those few special people in his life. If asked, most people would have put Barry's age at around forty-eight, because it seemed impossible to believe he'd not reached thirty-six. He rarely had many words for her and those few he did offer were usually offensive. Elena had always thought he was weird, but since Craig's passing, he acted even stranger.

'I best get back to it,' said Elena.

Barry grunted. 'Still making your little gypsy beads and bangles?'

'I have some orders.'

Barry nodded and gave her a look that suggested he didn't believe a word of that, but she couldn't care less what this fat pig thought. OK, so her online jewellery shop didn't make a massive profit, but she had repeat customers that loved her handmade pieces and she'd also started an eBay shop hoping to generate more sales. She'd be lucky to make over one hundred pounds profit per month, but she saved every penny she could – putting it in the *get the hell out of here* fund. Besides, she made those pieces because she loved crafting. She'd go insane with boredom without something to focus on. It had started as a hobby, until Nino suggested she could easily sell her stuff, and that he knew there'd be a niche market out there for the things she designed. One day, once they left this place, she'd have her own shop somewhere far from here and would make a proper, big business out of it. Nino had promised her that.

'Tell Nino I need a chat,' he said curtly.

'See you, Barry.'

Elena went back home and sat down in her cramped work corner where an assortment of beads, shells and coloured stones awaited her on the pull-down shelf. She gazed at the door. After a moment's deliberation, she decided to nip back and click the lock into place.

13

The metallic blue VW Polo drove off the Eurotunnel shuttle, rattling over the unloading ramp and hitting UK soil, making Duncan's stomach lurch. As darkness crept in, the car left the departure area and slid onto the M20. Duncan felt uncertain about everything. Clara must have sensed dread pouring from him, because she turned in her seat and flashed him a reassuring grin. It seemed like there was no turning back now and suddenly he envied Karl being miles away and safe.

Ryan approached with a tray of drinks. He passed Clara a big glass of red wine and handed Duncan a large glass of fruit cider. 'There you go, bro. I'll just use the toilet and we'll grab some menus.'

As Ryan headed off, Duncan gulped the cider and his eyes surreptitiously scanned the quiet hotel bar area, as though at any moment shadowy assassins would spring from under the surrounding empty tables and hack him to pulp. They'd arrived too late to visit his mum in hospital, so Ryan had checked them into a Premier Inn a few miles from where she'd been admitted, and agreed with his dad to rush over as soon as visiting hours allowed the next day. His dad argued they should all come straight home and stay there, but Ryan insisted his dad already had plenty on his plate without dealing with extra guests. Duncan wasn't keen on being referred to as a guest and envisioned returning home to find his bedroom turned into a sewing room or a reading den. But he knew what his brother meant by it.

Clara sipped her red wine and gave him a warm smile. 'You OK, Duncan? You went white as a sheet when we came off the train.'

Duncan nodded, though in reality he was far from OK.

'I think all this is a shame. Everything that's happened to you. It isn't fair. I would have liked to have met the old Duncan, before all this crazy mess. The guy your brother always told me about.'

'I'm not sure where *he's* gone. Though I wish he'd bloody come back, because this Duncan is driving me bonkers.'

'He will come back. In time.'

Duncan doubted that, but nodded politely.

Clara moved closer to Duncan. 'I shouldn't tell you this, because my pa swore me to secrecy. He'd be pretty annoyed if he found out I'd told anybody.'

Duncan swirled the ice in his cider. 'Tell me what?' He'd remembered Clara had mentioned that her father used to be a high-flying businessman in the Tokyo's Shimbashi district, and that he'd met her mother on a business trip to Rotterdam. They'd fallen in love and, after a long distance relationship, they bought a house in Dordrecht, where they brought up Clara and her brother Nicolaas.

'My pa got into trouble back home. He fled his home country as he was wanted for questioning by Japan's National Police Agency.'

'Blimey, what did he do?'

'He'd been embroiled in some unscrupulous plot. Something to do with a shady syndicate linked to a criminal organisation.'

'You mean, like the… Yakuza?' said Duncan, speaking in a conspiratorial tone and gazing around at the other tables, just to double check they hadn't filled up within the last five minutes. They hadn't. Duncan's limited perception of the Yakuza syndicates derived from his fondness for Marvel and Manga comics, in which they were depicted as brutal foes who followed strict codes of honour. He owned hundreds of comics, some of them from the eighties and nineties and most likely now collectors' editions worth a few quid. He considered it would be useful to have his own Yakuza hit squad right now; hardened criminals ready to protect him – ready to die for him, should the Bartell family seek revenge. He sipped his drink as he visualised two slim, suited Japanese hoodlums flanking his every move, Samurai swords sheathed on their backs, as they flashed blazing, malevolent stares at anyone that dared to approach, or even glance in Duncan's direction.

Clara shrugged. 'He never elaborated. He just said they were dangerous men. And he promised me it wasn't his doing. The person who pulled him into that world was once his best friend. A person he'd trusted since his childhood. A friend who stabbed him in the back and placed him in an impossible position with some very dangerous individuals. That's why I use my ma's maiden name, De Klerk.'

Duncan gulped the cider. It tasted like the best fruit cider in the world. Then he wondered why Clara had decided to unload all this onto him, though guessed it was her way of showing him they could trust each other with cardinal secrets.

'He told me you can only ever truly trust your family. Nobody else,' continued Clara.

'Don't you trust Ryan?' asked Duncan.

'Of course. We will be married next year. That makes us family.'

Duncan got the impression that this was Clara's way of saying he shouldn't trust Karl anymore. That he should cut his ties to his oldest friend. Perhaps he already had.

'I think you should talk to someone, Duncan. A specialist.'

Duncan laughed. 'I can't tell a shrink about everything that happened.'

'No, but perhaps you can get help with your anxiety.'

Duncan forced a grin. 'I need to crack on with my own life and stop focussing on… him. I'll be fine.'

'If it all gets too much, you know where we are. You will always be welcome.'

'Thanks,' said Duncan and smiled at her, believing every word.

As they entered the hospital ward, Duncan became dizzy and incredibly hot. He could hear his own deep, wheezing breathing.

Duncan, Clara and Ryan headed to the door of Sandra Parvin's room, loaded with chocolates, grapes and flowers.

'Are you Mr Parvin?' said a female voice that sounded full of authority.

Duncan's legs turned to jelly, and he almost dropped the grapes.

'Mr Parvin?' came the voice again.

When Duncan turned to see the two uniformed officers heading their way, he jolted.

Ryan, sensing his brother's desperate plight, shoulder barged him and through gritted teeth said, 'Keep it together, Dunk.'

The uniformed female officer, accompanied by a younger male officer, strutted towards them, smiled, and then continued further along the waiting room to where Tom Parvin jumped up from where he'd been seated. He spotted his sons and gave them a relieved grin as he approached the officers. Then to Duncan and Ryan he said, 'So good to see you boys. I've got to chat with these police officers, and I'll be with you in a tick. Pop in and see your mum. She's dozed off, but wake her because she's not stopped asking for you both. Hello, Clara, catch up in a jiffy, love.'

'Hey, Tom,' said Clara.

Tom hurried off with the officers and they headed over to a quiet corner, where he shook hands with them. Duncan considered his dad looked so vulnerable and tired, and it was painful to see him this way.

'Just relax, Duncan,' said Ryan. 'Take some deep breaths.'

Duncan, trembling all over, took some deep lungfuls of air. 'I'm OK,' he said.

They arranged the flowers and chocolates as Sandra began to stir. Her hair was a mess, her arm in a sling, and the entire right side of her face was covered in an angry mass of purple and yellow bruises, though despite all this, she looked joyful and flashed a jubilant smile as she forced herself into a sitting position. The movement seemed to rack her body with pain, but she continued smiling through it. 'My boys! Oh, Clara, you came too. So nice to finally meet you in person. Sorry, I look like a scarecrow that's been mauled by a grisly lion.'

Clara kissed her on the cheek. 'So glad you're alright. I can't believe how perky you are. You must be a real tough lady, Sandra!'

'Aw, bless you for coming. You're even more stunning in person. It's no wonder Ryan is besotted with you!'

Ryan took his mum's hand. 'We came over as soon as we found out, Mum. We would have visited last night, but we didn't hit the UK until late.'

Duncan stood in the corner, holding the dead flowers he'd swapped over with the fresh ones. He could barely look at his mum's injuries. If he'd caused this to happen, he'd never be able to live with himself.

They made small talk until Tom came into the room. Then they all turned to him, eager for an update on his discussion with the police and what information he'd gleamed.

'What did they say, Dad?' asked Ryan.

Tom puffed out his cheeks. 'Well, they caught the silly son of a bitch.'

Duncan gazed at his dad. The vulnerability had lifted now and Tom Parvin appeared so uncharacteristically angry that Duncan stepped away from him. Tom was friendly with everyone, and didn't find fault in people. He always made the effort to be polite in any situation. Duncan had never seen him even come close to losing his cool.

'If I get my sodding hands on the bastard responsible,' grumbled Tom, before noticing all eyes were fixed on him. Then he lost the incensed expression and smiled apologetically. 'Ark at me, sounding off like some thuggish moron. Sorry, ladies.' He walked over to Sandra and held her unbruised hand in both of his. 'Anyway, all your mother was concerned about was seeing you two. She's not stopped pestering me to get you both here. Thanks for coming, boys.'

Duncan, desperate to learn the news the police had divulged, fidgeted, but failed to find his tongue.

Sandra let out a raspy cough and winced. 'So, this is what I have to do in order to get my laddies back home together again, hey? Well, it was worth it.'

'Um, Dad, what did the police officers say?' asked Ryan.

'Bloody drunk driver! Some idiot that lost his job and went on a mad bender. After hitting your mother's car and speeding off, the bloke jumped a red light and ploughed into the side of a Tesco delivery van. They caught that on camera, so he's banged to rights.'

Duncan caught Ryan's eye. The pair shared a reassuring look.

'Pass me some water please, love.'

Duncan poured the water from a jug into a cup and handed it to his mum.

She took a tiny sip. 'Sooo, come on, Duncan, what's going on?'

'What?'

'You thought my crash was something to do with why you've been hiding away at your brother's place.'

Duncan was so dumbfounded by his mum's words that when he spoke, he just came out with an incoherent babble.

'I'm not stupid, son. What happened? Why did you run off like that? What were you lads running from?'

'No. We weren't running!' said Duncan, cringing at the outburst that had made him sound like a querulous toddler. He smiled sprightly, but could see she wasn't buying it.

'Don't you be lying to your mother, Duncan Parvin. I wasn't born yesterday.'

'Mum—'

'Why was your Face-page what-sit turned off? And that Insta-thingy you go on? Huh?'

Duncan tried to think of how she could know he'd switched off his social media accounts, and if reading his thoughts, she added, 'I had your auntie Caroline have a nose on there. She's into all that online stuff. She told me you and Karl had both gone offline. Accounts inaccessible. Why would that be?'

Duncan hated lying to his mum, but how could he tell her the truth? Why did he switch off the account? That just made him look even more suspicious.

'OK, I'll tell you what happened,' said Duncan, racking his brain for some excuse that she might buy. 'Karl wants to be a travel blogger,' he blurted.

'A what now?'

'Karl, he wants to travel around Europe and write about his experiences. For a job, like Clara does. I said he was full of bull, as per normal, and bet him a hundred quid that he wouldn't do anything about it. And he called my bluff, and we ended up in Eindhoven and a few other places, setting up his new business.'

His mum pulled a confused expression. 'And what about his *actual* job? What about your job and your business plans?'

Duncan shrugged. 'What can I say? He surprised me, Mum. Looks like Karl really wants this. I helped him get set up, and he wanted me to stay…'

'I see, have you decided to pursue this?'

'No, Mum. That travelling lark isn't for me. Karl's going to stick with it. He seems to be enjoying it. For now. But he'll get bored after a few more months.' Duncan shocked himself at how easily the lies had flowed out like that. He guessed it helped that there had been a shred of truth to the fib. But he couldn't think of an alternative. 'Plus, I wanted to visit Ryan and meet his girlfriend.'

'Aw, she's sweet, isn't she? What a lovely couple they make,' she gushed.

Duncan nodded, wondering how he'd have got through this entire ordeal without his brother. He prayed his mum wouldn't mention the social media blackout again, because he didn't have an answer for that.

'And don't you be so hard on Karl! He's a trier. So good for him having a go at something like this. Bless him. It will do Karl the world of good to get out from under that domineering father of his. Grouchy old sod. You support him, Duncan.'

Duncan nodded again, though with some reluctance this time. It drove him insane that she was once again giving golden boy Karl all the praise. She thought that boy crapped gold. It drove him bonkers at times. And technically, he'd just said he'd been out there helping him with the sodding blog. What more did she want him to do? OK, that part wasn't true, but that wasn't the point.

'Your skin has flared up, I see. I'll get you an appointment with the doctor.'

Duncan, about to protest and say he was more than capable of doing that himself, instead nodded.

'And I hope you boys weren't smoking all those funny-fags out there.'

'No, Mum.'

'You don't want to be getting all hooked up on that whacky-hash. That will mess with your marbles, son. You don't need that.'

Duncan decided, almost instantly, that the high life wasn't going to be for him, and despite having Karl and Joost nagging him that he needed to experiment with different strains in order to find the perfect fit, he wasn't invested enough in the stuff to bother. It made him feel feverish and gave him a heavy, weird sensation in his chest area and sometimes a blocked nose. Not to mention the paranoia. Duncan wasn't sure if being high made you move slower or your mind just made it seem that way; but even simple tasks like locking the door, brushing your teeth or finding the toilet for a pee in the dark could become a demanding undertaking. Plus, it made him think too much. Way too much. His hazy mind would go into overdrive and Craig Bartell would be forefront in his thoughts.

The first thing that hit Duncan was the smell of fusty dog and fabric washing conditioner. He surmised that the house always smelt this way, but guessed when he lived here his nose had become accustomed to the homely scent. What was he saying? He still lived here.

Lenny bounded in from the kitchen whimpering, his tail whipping frantically as he bounced around Duncan like a hyper puppy. He petted the old dog and felt guilty that he'd not given Lenny all that much thought during his time away. Lenny often slept in his room, and relied on him for walks, treats and copious amounts of ear rubs. Lenny was his dog, after all, and judging by the mega fuss he was now receiving from the pooch, he'd missed Duncan.

Duncan headed to his room, gazing up at the loft hatch as he went. He wondered if he should pop up and check all was well with his model collection. He didn't know why he kept all the stuff up there, because it wasn't like he used it anymore. But he couldn't get rid of it. Duncan would spend all of his spare time up there as a kid, meticulously painting his Space Marines and building the gaming world. Duncan scratch-built everything. He'd crafted detailed bunkers, complete with realistic finishing touches like bullet holes and rusty water patches. He'd used sheets of chunky polystyrene to create complete modular sections of terrain, like rugged mountain passes and wastelands dotted with battle debris and craters. Duncan had even carefully cut plywood and used resin glue to construct polluted river sections that, with some trial and error, looked crazy good; professionally made even. There were entire woodland and jungle sections with handmade boulders and barricades for the miniatures to use for tactical cover. Despite all his efforts, finishing the epic gaming campaigns with Karl was often impossible, because Karl was always getting grounded. Duncan would knock for his friend, eager to revisit the action, and Karl would peer around the door with a sheepish look on his face, and lie, saying he was unable to come to Duncan's house because he had tons of chores to do. Then his dad's booming voice would shout out, 'Don't you make plans, Karl! You know damn well you're grounded all week.' Karl would then look away, embarrassed, and they'd both ignore the blatant fib he'd told. This would be a regular occurrence and sometimes entire summer holidays would be wasted. Duncan would be so annoyed every time he gazed at the board; seeing his squads of Blood Angels stuck in a never-ending standoff against Karl's Chaos Marines, as they all waited for Karl to be released so they could continue their grand battle. Duncan never got grounded and wondered what on earth Karl kept doing that always warranted such a harsh punishment. Often he tried to replace Karl with some nerds he'd met from the Canterbury Games Workshop. Callum Anderson and his cronies, the Howard brothers. But they were such serious players who debated every minor detail of the game, they ended up sucking the fun right out of it and the entire experience became such a drag. They'd be consulting the rule book every five minutes and would bicker and discuss every single element of the game and gripe over measurements, incorrect dice rolls, and other petty stuff. Plus, they didn't seem to own a can of deodorant between them, and the unventilated loft was often ripe with geek BO and on occasions, he'd feign going down to the toilet just to escape the funky stench up there. With Karl as an opponent, the gaming was always enjoyable. They would stick to the rules, though less fastidiously, and his best friend's zest to play added the extra oomph. The other gamers strove to win and would play so strategically it would bore him silly. Whereas Karl would seek carnage and destruction, choosing risk over the safety of keeping holed up in an advantage spot. Sometimes his hazardous play would pay off, sometimes it would be a total disaster and he'd wipe out complete squads of his own team in a vain attempt to take down an enemy bunker, or take a wild stab at assassinating a rival commander. On occasions it would pay off big time and make the win even more exciting. Whatever happened though, it was always dramatic and riveting to have Karl as an opponent and they'd lose whole days enthralled in the little adventures, whilst stuffing their faces with Pringles and popcorn. He'd do anything to return to those days again. Anything.

His mum had stacked up a thick wad of unopened letters in the dining room, and Duncan found his P45 amongst them. Before the day – well, *that day*, Duncan worked for a moody landscape gardener called Mitch Gilligan, who owned Lawns, Patios and More. Gilligan never seemed to struggle to find good paying customers, despite his miserable nature, and Duncan and the small team of youngsters were always kept busy. Gilligan was overweight, walked with a limp and never got his own hands mucky. But he paid a fair wage and let them get on with the job with minimal involvement. Duncan's plan had been to work for Gilligan for another year, and then go self-employed. He was already in the process of launching his own business. He couldn't think of anything worse than a long-time job that involved lining the pockets of a lazy old goat like Gilligan, and knew working for himself was paramount. Then all his hard work would have greater rewards. Duncan wanted to offer grand, outside creative spaces, contemporary garden designs, bespoke summerhouses, and luxury garden bars. The website looked fantastic and the next step was to find a reliable van, buy decent equipment, and prepare a marketing plan that couldn't fail. He'd saved a few grand to invest in the business and had already started working on the amazing ideas he intended to pitch to prospective clients. Although he'd dipped into his savings for the Eurostar tickets; plus, there was no way on earth he'd wanted to take handouts, so he'd insisted that he buy groceries every week in Eindhoven, even though both Ryan and Clara assured him it wasn't necessary.

Duncan sighed and binned most of the letters without even opening them.

14

Kent, 5 September 2018

Ravi stepped out of the en suite shower and hearing his phone ringing, tugged on his bathrobe and bolted into the bedroom to snatch his phone from the bedside table. It was Schneider.

'Hello,' answered Ravi, his heart pounding. 'Any news?'

Schneider's investigation had been stale for months, and although he'd been in touch with the young investigator every couple of weeks, no productive information had come to light. The police hadn't reported on any further money withdrawals, and the last trace of his son was on the third of June, where Nathaniel's card was used at an ATM in Broadstairs, where he'd removed two hundred pounds from his account. The officer asked Ravi to identify Nathaniel from a still taken from the footage, so at least he could confirm that it was Nathaniel who'd used the card, which gave him some reassurance at least.

'Hi Ravi. Yeah, I've just taken a call from Callum Anderson and he's identified Nathaniel's elusive dealer friend.'

Ravi sat down on the bed. 'Go on.'

'So, whilst sitting in a dentist waiting room, Anderson got bored and flicked through an old newspaper that was stashed at the bottom of the magazine pile. Where he spots an article about this lad who died back in May. And he's adamant it's him.'

Oh, dear God, thought Ravi.

'How soon can you get here?' asked Schneider.

An hour later, Ravi sat at Schneider's desk whilst the young man spoke on the phone. Several times, he smiled apologetically at Ravi as he spoke and said, 'Right, yeah, um... I will phone you back in an hour to further discuss this. There is another client waiting in my office... that's no problem. Thanks.' Schneider ended the call and raised his eyebrows. 'Another timewaster no doubt. I get plenty. Sorry to keep you hanging on.'

Ravi shrugged. 'It's fine.'

'I try to avoid the adultery cases, as it sometimes brings in the crackpots. But I take the odd job on.'

Ravi shrugged again, uninterested. 'Right.'

'Does the name Stefan Chillcott mean anything to you, Ravi?'

'No. Why?'

Schneider placed his finger on a piece of paper and slid it across the desk. Ravi picked it up and inspected the contents. It was a printed news story. The title read man found dead near Firelight Cove, Hastings.

Ravi read the article; according to the story, an elderly dog walker had discovered a body washed up on a quiet section of the beach on the morning of Saturday the twelfth of May. Ravi stopped reading and eyed Schneider. 'That's the day after my son went missing.'

Schneider clenched his jaw and nodded.

Ravi continued to read the article. It named the deceased as Stefan Chillcott, a twenty-five-year-old man from the Faversham area. Postmortem revealed large traces of MDMA, Ketamine and a drug called Spice in the man's system. And a large amount of alcohol. The police investigation was ongoing, and they were appealing for witnesses. The reporter had displayed a photo of Stefan, in which the lad appeared indignant and menacing as he stared at the camera. It looked very much like an offender's mug shot. Ravi's eyes were glued to the grim photo. On face value, this lad came across as a total degenerate. A wrong'un, or, as his father would say, a bad egg.

'Spice?' asked Ravi.

'Horrible stuff. It renders the user into a zombie-like state. It's a synthetic marijuana type drug. Spice was a legal high once, but became illegal back in 2014… I had a client whose son became addicted to the stuff and went missing in Brighton.'

Ravi wanted to ask if Schneider found the missing boy, but could discern by the way he'd spoken about the case that he hadn't, so didn't bother to question him further. Perhaps he didn't even want to know the outcome.

Schneider cleared his throat. 'I… we will need to tread carefully now, Ravi. This changes things.'

Ravi's eyes were still fixed on the photo as he muttered, 'Why?'

'The Chillcott family are… let's say… unsavoury characters. If I dig around, things could get a tad… tricky.'

Ravi didn't respond, but his chest tightened.

'Stefan's father, Marcus Chillcott, was rumoured to have been a big drug dealer back in the nineties. A serious and respected figure in the criminal underworld. These are not people who'd appreciate having someone prying into their business.'

'You're giving up the case,' stated Ravi tonelessly.

'No. I didn't say that. But I suggest you take this information to the officer dealing with your son's case. Let them take an in-depth look. This is a worrying find.'

Ravi cast his mind back to the things he'd located in Nathaniel's room. It took him several hours of dogged searching to unearth the items. After he'd first learnt about his son's involvement with drug dealers, he'd rushed straight home and tore his room apart. He considered telling Schneider about the findings, but knew that would only add to the obvious concerns the young man now had about working on this case.

'The Chillcotts purchased a pub six years ago. A place called The Swan Inn. A country establishment on the outskirts of Canterbury that the villagers have dubbed as a "villain's paradise". On one online piece, a local man quoted, "You may swan in, but you'll run straight out. You should avoid that sinister place if you value your safety. The entire village does".'

'So, what now? Surveillance at the pub? Perhaps you could speak to some regulars?' asked Ravi.

Schneider ran a hand through his messy hair, sighed, and puffed out his cheeks. 'With all due respect, Ravi, I think you've been watching too many TV crime shows. There is no way I could safely observe the comings and goings of this property for long periods of time. It's a rural spot. And even if I could find a way, to what end? We don't know how deep Nathaniel's ties are to these people. We should consider the dangers. I have a family, Ravi.'

Ravi placed his hands on the desk, tapping his fingers, frustration growing.

Schneider moved more newspaper clippings across to him.

Ravi snatched up a printout and waved it about. 'Yippie, more bloody newspaper articles. Is this what I'm paying you for? For you to pull up some old news stories. I could've done this myself. I'm paying you to investigate.'

'If you're not happy with my progress, we can call it quits now. Just say the word.'

Ravi wanted to tell this pup to grow some balls and show some initiative, but instead grunted and tried hard to calm himself. In an effort to keep his cool, he plonked one of the articles onto the desk, moved his harsh gaze from Schneider and focussed on the printout. The piece, a Kent Online report, was a missing person story. The subject, Tristan Vickers, a sandy haired twenty-three-year-old who vanished in February 2006. And according to the journalist's findings, she claimed to have found witnesses that verified Vickers had fallen out with Reilly Chillcott, co-owner of The Swan Inn, who had convictions for unlawful wounding, burglary and actual bodily harm. Her sources revealed that several days prior to his disappearance, Reilly had been putting the *word* about various pubs and clubs, that he was going after Vickers, though he denied these rumours when questioned by the police. The report confirmed that The Swan Inn had itself been the centre of several other stories relating to the previous owner, Herbert Penn, and about how Penn begrudgingly sold up, and that many of the locals were adamant that the sale was suspicious. One unnamed resident stated that some sort of unscrupulous deal was afoot and that the well-liked pub owner wouldn't have agreed to let his cherished bar go so easily, and especially not to the likes of the Chillcotts, who had an iffy criminal background. A different source stated that every resident in the village intended to boycott the pub, confirming that the Chillcotts were nothing more than a bunch of thugs and thieves. Another resident called them murderers and believed they had ties to organised crime and were in deep with hardened travellers.

'Reilly is one of Stefan's older brothers,' said Schneider, his face now turning a light shade of red as he crossed his arms.

Ravi knew he'd annoyed the PI, but couldn't care less now. 'Just give me *every* single piece of information you have about this family.'

Ravi pulled his Jaguar onto the huge gravel driveway and stared at the oast house conversion he once called home. The gorgeous grade two property boasted seven bedrooms, two lounges, a family room and a huge dining room in the roundel, which overlooked a picturesque natural pond. But with his wife and daughter staying away at his London apartment, and news of his son's likely involvement with common criminals, it now seemed like the most uninviting place on earth. He felt like a stranger in his own home. He'd been rattling around in the vast property of late, and he was feeling lonely and oppressed. Even his long-term gardener and handyman, Hashim, had threatened to quit, after Ravi had been impertinent with him one too many times. That had cost him a small pay increase.

Ravi walked into the kitchen and the automatic overhead lights beamed on, displaying a freshly buffed white tiled floor that gleamed, and spotless kitchen counters, confirming that at least his cleaners hadn't abandoned him, despite the fact he'd forgotten to pay them for over two weeks. Suddenly comprehending that he'd not drunk anything today, he hurried to the fridge and grabbed a cold bottle of Evian. He drank deeply and finished the bottle in one hit. As he shut the door, a family photo grabbed his attention. Nathaniel was just eight in the shot. His daughter was eleven. They both looked so happy, with vivacious expressions as they prepared for their first exciting day in Disneyland Paris. His wife, Chandra, had a relaxed smile on her face, and even Ravi himself was managing a tight-lipped grin, despite knowing the day ahead would be filled with negotiating crowds, listening to moaning children, and coping with aching feet. He always considered that everyone viewed their photos through rose-tinted glasses; only remembering them as *the good days* as you block out the memory of the awful weather, siblings bitching in the car, or the extortionate price for a few lousy ice creams. Though during times like Ravi was currently experiencing, he considered those days were everything. They were special – they were of crucial importance. And when your life starts to fall apart like his was, that's when it hits you. That's when the sadness becomes overwhelming. Because those days were long gone. They would never come back. Not only that… the son he knew had gone, and Ravi seemed convinced he'd never find that boy again. *Even if he located his whereabouts*, he mused bleakly. The boy in that photo no longer existed.

Ravi made some manuka honey and ginger tea, finished off with a large wedge of lemon. Then took the drink into his office and fired up the PC. As soon as he hit the internet browser, the missing persons charity page flashed up. He'd being viewing the page late last night, and once again found himself scrolling through the myriad of listings. All the boxes contained a close-up photo of the person, age at the time of disappearance, date they went missing and from what area. He stopped at the listing for a Terry Gold, a twenty-nine-year-old missing from Tonbridge in Kent. In the photo, a cap wearing Terry gave a slight, smug grin, but a deep sadness clouded his eyes. The next poster was a woman called Mia Pham, a twenty-year-old Vietnamese girl. Mia had her chin rested on her hand as she gazed longingly out to sea, in a pose that was most likely meant for a social media post, and not a desperate call for help. The next, Henry Collins. At the time he went missing, he was seventy-six. He'd been missing from Ashford for well over a decade now. In his grainy photo, Henry seemed relaxed and happy, and Ravi tried to think how a pensioner like Henry could just drop off the grid and couldn't help wondering if the poor old bugger was lying in an isolated ditch somewhere, or if he'd fallen into a deep river and been dragged to the bottom and lost to the world. An undignified way to finish your time on this Earth, he considered. There were many more faces flashing past as he scrolled. So many stories. So many families that were left broken. Left wondering. So many lost souls. He stopped when he saw the poster for Nathaniel Sookdeo. He stared at it for ages. Seeing his son listed here was surreal. It all seemed so... impossible. And all he could think was, *why?* Just *why, why, why?* Ravi put his hand over his mouth to stop himself from screaming. He felt like he was going crazy. He read the charity's message.

Nathaniel, we are here for you whenever you are ready; we can listen, talk you through what help you need, pass a message for you and help you be safe.

Ravi prayed his son would see the message and send word that he *was safe.* Or he'd reach out to him and beg for his help. Ravi would give it, of course he would.

Ravi pressed the button on the handset to power up the Sonos music system. Ennio Morricone's 'Chi Mai' rose through the speakers he'd had embedded into the ceiling. This haunting piece of music always stirred emotions in him he never understood. But today, as he sat sipping his tea, thinking about his life, he sobbed his heart out. He'd never cried so much before, not even when he'd lost his parents.

After the music ended and all the tears were gone, he placed down his cup, slumped back into his bulky leather chair and gripped the arms so tightly his fingers dug into the expensive material. He wasn't used to this... losing control... having *no* control over the situation. In that moment, he decided he'd do what he always did. He'd take full control of the matter himself. And he didn't care about the dangerous path ahead. He'd find out what had happened to his son, and couldn't care less about his own safety. It was his duty as a father. He knew what he needed to do.

15

Ravi had never used an Air B&B before, and he'd only selected this one because there were no other places to stay within ten miles of the Chillcotts' rural pub. He guessed there wasn't much in the area to warrant a big tourist interest. The few reviews didn't inspire confidence in the place. One listed under the name Pat Paws simply said 'Meh', and another under the name Gareth Kermit stated, 'Count Dracula's crypt during dinner time would be more inviting than the Donavans' property'. But Ravi wasn't here for a pleasant stay, so it mattered not.

The owner, Maggie Donovan, a wizened faced lady, showed him to his room. She tried to be chirpy and friendly, but Ravi knew this was an act. Underneath her merry exterior, he could see a weary and dispirited lady. He saw it in her eyes.

'Towels are in the bathroom. Breakfast, should you want it, is served between seven and nine. Cereals, toast and coffee. No cooked breakfast, I'm afraid.'

'Thanks. Um, Maggie, I spotted a pub on the outskirts of the village. Is that worth a look? For dinner?'

'No!' she snapped. 'Stay away from there. There are some takeout menus downstairs. Those are the only businesses that will be prepared to deliver this far afield.'

Ravi grinned. 'Is the pub food that bad?'

Maggie's features darkened. 'It's a terrible pub. Full of loutish builders, unruly travellers and drug addicts. There is a lot of trouble there. Especially during the weekends.'

'Oh, what a shame.'

'It was once owned by a lovely local gent. And it was a friendly place. The heart of the village where everyone was welcome. Then they took over... *that* family.'

Ravi tested the bed. Solid as a rock. He'd need a few stiff drinks if he stood a chance in hell of falling asleep on this.

'Trouble often spills out into the village. They are dire people. Loud, lowbred and violent.'

'You don't expect that. Not in such a peaceful area.'

'Poor Mr Barrowfield had a bunch of them brawling in his back garden. They squashed all of his cabbages and tomato plants.'

'That's just not on.'

'After the fracas, he found a battered drinker in his flower bed. Those animals had beat him so badly he ended up stuck in a wheelchair.'

'Oh, no. Really?'

'And hear this... the chap still drinks there. Can you believe that? I have seen him rolling into the pub. No one was even charged. The God-awful place is lawless. The authorities won't help and the local police can't, or won't take action...' Maggie suddenly stopped talking, and looked annoyed with herself for spouting ugly gossip to a customer, realising how bad for business that was. 'Tea?' she blurted.

'No thanks. I'll perhaps head out for a walk and stretch my legs.'

It was a five-minute stroll through the quaint and serene village to The Swan. The pub was positioned on the edge of the village, at a point where two skinny lanes leading to the built-up area met. It was early and still light, though black clouds were forming in the sky and rain looked likely, which is why Ravi had opted to wear his parka jacket. On the approach, things appeared calm. He could hear a bit of boisterous talking and laughing, but assumed that was normal for a drinking den. Not one for being accustomed to pub life, Ravi didn't know what to expect, anyway. He strolled past a few work vans and a scaffolding lorry parked inconsiderately in the rear carpark. He stopped to have a sly peek to make sure none of the vehicles matched the Renault with the weird sticker. They didn't. Ravi adjusted his parka jacket and walked into the pub. He'd been apprehensive on the way here, but, as he walked in, casual and confident, the fear lifted and he strode up to the bar to order a brandy and ice. He received a few quick glances from other drinkers, but nobody paid him much heed. The barmaid, a brown-haired lady with deep crow's feet, even offered him a civil smile as she took his money. He considered this might be the older sibling, Veronica, that Schneider had mentioned in one of his reports, but couldn't locate a photo of.

As Ravi paid for his drink, he caught sight of large tattooed hands collecting glasses from the bar. They belonged to a huge, hulking bald fellow, with chiefly black tattoos covering the back of his neck and back of his head. The big guy spoke to the barmaid, with an almost pained expression slapped on his face that didn't seem to shift. Ravi considered the man appeared to have the countenance of a mean-faced ogre straining for an enormous poo. Ravi knew who this man was. Schneider had provided details of Mills Chillcott, the eldest brother from the Chillcott clan.

Mills gave Ravi a quick once over, but then picked up a paper, disinterested. Ravi couldn't imagine any sane person being stupid enough to cross such a fearsome looking individual. He didn't want to meet the thug down a dark alleyway anytime soon.

Ravi sipped his drink and scanned the room. A few rowdy workmen supping pints. A couple of young lads, likely underage, that were more interested in their phones than each other's company. And two louts working the fruit machine.

Ravi sat in a quiet corner for an hour and nursed two drinks. The bar area now heaved with punters and many of them were shifty looking individuals, but he'd been completely ignored thus far. Ravi got a sense that as the night drew on, and more punters streamed in, the bar took on a more inauspicious feeling. He guessed this to be paranoia – hoped it was paranoia. Then, as one sinister looking youth started studying him, he shifted nervously in his seat, thinking that he'd perhaps outstayed his welcome. Then he spotted a man slumped in a wheelchair and knew he'd need to stay a while longer. He headed over to the bar for a refill, careful not to bump shoulders, make direct eye contact, or interact in any way with any of the bruisers at the bar.

With a fresh drink in hand, he slumped back to his seat and waited.

The pub exterior looked in a shabby state. There were tiles missing, walls with peeling paint, and one window had been boarded up with what looked like a combination of cardboard, bubble wrap, and gaffer tape. The building invoked a depressing feeling, but the sight of the dilapidated children's play area was enough to make you want to walk in front of a bus. Ravi could only imagine the type of parent who'd be happy to sit there and swig cheap lager whilst letting their child loose on, what could only be described as, a death trap slide, complete with shards of glimmering glass at the bottom, and a wonky climbing frame that looked like it had been erected by a bunch of drunk chimpanzees. Utter pond life, Ravi considered grimly, that's who.

Ravi approached the man in the wheelchair. He'd parked up next to a rickety picnic style table and was rolling a cigarette. The man spotted Ravi drifting around the garden and glared at him with blatant animosity.

Ravi flashed him a soft smile. 'Evening.'

The man scowled, leant over to the bench and snatched his pint, as though protecting it.

'I wondered if I could ask you something?' Ravi asked.

The man's eyes narrowed, but he didn't speak, instead he hawked and spat a nasty wad of lumpy phlegm onto the ground.

Ravi stepped closer and was hit by the sudden stench of the individual. He smelt rancid. Stale booze, cheap tobacco and the body odour of a man that hadn't changed his attire for days, possibly weeks. He was skinny, unshaven, and his lank, greasy hair hung to his shoulders. Under normal circumstances, Ravi would have deftly crossed the road to avoid even breathing the same air as such an unsanitary wrench; but these were not normal circumstances.

The man licked his front teeth, sneering.

'I haven't been here before,' said Ravi, with nothing else coming to mind.

As the man scratched his bony cheek, Ravi considered when this unhealthy looking soul had last consumed anything remotely nourishing. Apart from the odd brandy, Ravi monitored his diet with such precision it drove his wife insane. She found eating out with him embarrassing, as he would often nit-pick over every item on the menu. But you only had one body, so why would you want to pollute it with any old poison? Some people disgusted him. They were worse than pigs as they gorged themselves on fatty foods, guzzled gallons of sugar-filled fizzy drinks and smoked themselves in to oblivion. Nobody seemed to care about keeping healthy anymore. Especially the younger generation. Not that this guy was young. He must have been close to forty.

Ravi smiled. 'I'm looking for somebody. Perhaps you can help me.'

The man studied him for a few moments. 'Why? What's this got to do with me?' The man appeared uninterested as he tried to light his cigarette with a lighter that refused to provide a spark.

'I'm trying to find out if my son ever came here. My son is called Nathaniel.'

The man tapped the lighter against the side of his wheelchair. 'If you are filth, mate, that lot in there will rip you to pieces.'

'Do I look like a policeman to you?'

The man gave up with the lighter and threw it into the play area. 'I dunno, maybe. You don't belong here, that's for certain. So, if I were you…'

'Please, just a couple of questions.'

'How about I call them out here and tell them you're snooping about asking me stuff?'

'Why would you? Aren't they the very people that did *this* to you?' asked Ravi, pointing to the wheelchair.

The man glowered. His eyes flicked to the door, then back to Ravi, but he didn't answer him.

'I would hazard a guess that you hate those people with every fibre of your body. I'd say that you only come and drink here to show them they didn't break you. That shows real courage. You have a gutsiness most people do not possess. I admire that,' lied Ravi. He thought the man was a total fool for coming back here after such an incident. What sort of idiot drinks and socialises with the very people that turned him into a paraplegic? It was utter insanity.

'Aww, I feel so much better knowing that *you*, a complete stranger, admires me. I really do. I'm glowing with fucking pride here, mate. Now either piss off… or buy me a pint.'

'What would you like?'

'I'll have a pint of Cunted… but just ask for Wolf-Bane.'

'Sure.'

The man sniffed, and a smile crept on his lips. 'I wouldn't go talking to anyone else in there.'

'Do you know my son?' asked Ravi.

The man opened his mouth to speak, but stopped as two broad, scruffy men left the pub, chatting boisterously to one another.

'I'll talk to you,' said the man, his voice now lowered. 'But it will cost you. My information won't be free. And we don't talk here.'

'Where?'

'Give me your number, I'll call you.'

Ravi discreetly checked the two men as he reached into his jacket pocket. The men were drunk and almost every word they blurted was a swear word. Although the pair didn't seem interested in what they were up to. They spoke so aggressively, as though they were about to fight, but they were laughing too, so Ravi guessed it was just their way of communicating. *Strange people.*

Ravi handed the man his business card. 'Here. Call me anytime. I'll make it worth your while. Trust me.'

The man studied the card. 'Ravi Sooloo.'

'Sookdeo,' corrected Ravi.

The man scratched his stubble as he scrutinised the details on the card. It seemed to Ravi as though the man was working out how much money he could gain from this situation.

'Financial advisor, hey. Nice. So loaded, then?'

Ravi didn't reply to the question, and instead went back into the bar to order the beer the man had requested. When he returned, the man had a lit cigarette between his lips and the other two aggressive men were no longer present.

The man snatched up his pint and gulped it back in three slobbery pulls. He then let out a big belch. 'Cheers. I'll see you around.' With that, he rolled his wheelchair to the back entrance of the pub and rolled up a makeshift wooden ramp. Once outside the door, he turned back to Ravi. 'They built this *just* for me. Sweet, aren't they? I'm Arnie Baxter, by the way.' He bashed the door open and rolled himself inside.

Ravi shoved his hands in his pockets and left the pub.

The thought of his son frequenting such a dire place made his head hurt. None of this made any sense.

16

Kent, 15 September 2018

Elena opened the second bottle of red wine and poured them both a generous helping.

'I'm already tipsy,' said Nino, smiling heartily, but accepting the refill.

The wine had gone straight to Elena's head, and she was in a mischievous mood. 'Let's do something fun, Nino.'

'Such as?'

'Let's go on a cheeky ride. It's Saturday night. I don't want to stay cooped up inside.'

'You think that's sensible? I have been drinking.'

'Screw sensible.'

Thirty minutes later, Elena held on to Nino's waist as the bike hurtled through Craven's Cross Forest. Neither wore helmets, and she felt exhilarated and free as the cool night rushed by. Foxes and rabbits darted from the glare of the bike's harsh beam as it raced along the bumpy byways and weaved along narrow paths. She knew Nino could navigate these woods blindfolded and had absolutely no concern for their safety. Nino had made a secret network of tracks and routes all around the property. The tracks passed along the side of Dead Lane and linked up through all the surrounding fields and woodlands.

They sped down an incline, through a shallow stream, and into a tunnel of aged, twisted trees. He sped up and the engine roared as the bike raced through the tunnel. Elena yelled in elation and held tighter.

Now this was more like it.

The tunnel seemed endless. The forest zipped by in a flashing blur.

'Faster!' she screeched.

They sat against a log and shared the wine that Elena had packed in her rucksack. No glasses this time. They made do with swigging straight from the bottle. They sat in silence as they viewed a family of badgers crossing the pathway they'd used to ride up to the clearing. One badger eyed them curiously, before joining the others as they scurried into the thicket. Once the badgers were out of sight, Elena set about making a fire.

The pair talked, joked and got drunk as they watched the dancing flames and enjoyed the clear night sky. When Elena saw a shooting star streak above them, she gasped. 'We should make a wish.'

'What do you wish for?' asked Nino, a euphoric grin plastered on his face.

She gave him a playful shove. 'You already know what I wish for.'

Nino laughed. 'I'm still working on that.'

'Not fast enough, mister! Not fast enough.'

17

'Duncan... this kitchen... you've been here all day.'

Duncan scanned the unwashed plates, mugs and discarded Pot Noodle pots. How on earth did he make so much mess in one day? His mum looked peeved.

'Have you not been out again, Duncan?' she asked.

'I have been working... on the new business.'

'I see,' she said, sounding unconvinced. In fact, she may as well said, "*Oh, piss off, Duncan, you lying slob!*"

'Your auntie Caroline can still get you that job at the pharmacy. You'd work as a delivery driver for the dispensary. The pay isn't great, but it will get you out of the house, love.'

'I'm starting my own thing, Mum. It's just taking time to set it up. The website is looking so good. I'll show you later.'

'Mmmm.'

'And I'm thinking about leasing a van, rather than buying some unreliable crap-heap.' He doubted he'd even be able to afford the insurance on a van, but it sounded good.

'Scott's been talking to your dad. He says you've been ignoring him for months. That you won't go to the five-a-side games anymore. And you won't even meet him for a pint.'

'What's he like? Plonker. I'm meeting him in a few days to play squash.'

Sandra let out a long, sad sigh. 'I'm worried about you, Duncan. You need to see the doctor. Maybe get referred to the dermatologist. Your baddies haven't flared up like this since you were twelve.'

'I will,' said Duncan, scratching at the dry patch on his neck. His mum never used the nasty 'E' word.

'You're turning into a bit of a recluse. And you never sleep. Why don't you sleep anymore, love?'

Duncan considered his response. What could he say... Well, because if I do nod off, I wake up in a cold sweat every time I hear even the tiniest noise... Because when Lenny barks, my blood turns to antifreeze... Because I'm convinced they are going to come for me and drag me from my slumber.

'I do nap in the day. You know me, I'm a night owl, Mum. Now let me make you a brew and I'll wash up this lot.'

The noisy, beaten-up blue Berlingo van came to a stop at the top of the slipway track. Hashim got out and trudged down towards Reilly.

Reilly tapped his watch. 'Come on, Hash, ten minutes late.'

'Do not call me that,' snapped Hashim. 'My name is Hashim. What do you want from me?'

Reilly popped a piece of gum in his mouth and chewed vigorously. He quite liked Hashim, especially his directness and ballsiness. Most people were shit scared of him, but this guy didn't give a monkey's ball sack and that was refreshing. When Reilly had referred to him as a Turk, the man blew his top and informed Reilly he needed to stop talking nonsense. 'I am Lebanese,' he'd spat.

Reilly looked out to the River Medway, leant back against his car and crossed his arms. 'Any updates? It's been some time.'

'No updates. No sign of the boy. Or the wife,' said Hashim testily.

'You think they are getting divorced?' asked Reilly.

Hashim sneered. 'What am I, their bloody marriage counsellor? I mow the lawn and sweep up leaves. How should I know?'

Reilly laughed at this. 'You said you suspected his missus had gone to stay at his gaff in the city.'

'And I suspect she's still there. I have no idea for certain. He doesn't talk to me other than to bark orders and complain about my work. I'm like the shit on his expensive shoe. Hindu asswipe.'

'You got a house key?'

Hashim shook his head. 'No key needed. It's a code.'

'Do you possess that code?'

Hashim narrowed his eyes. 'Why?'

'Just asking?'

Hashim reached inside his dirty coat and pulled out his phone. He showed Reilly a photo. 'That's him.'

Reilly studied the photo of the balding, grave man who must have been in his late fifties. He decided this guy resembled his dad's Pakistani physician, Doctor Usman.

'He's Trinidadian. So is his wife. She told me that. She used to talk to me sometimes,' said Hashim.

Mills stepped out of the car and trudged over to the pair. Hashim eyed Mills as though he were sizing him up. Zero fear. Yes, Reilly liked this bloke. Most people bricked it when faced with the looming, frosty beast that was his older brother. Not Hashim though.

'Mills, this is Nathaniel's old man,' said Reilly, nodding at Hashim's phone.

Mills studied the photo on the screen. 'He's been in the pub. Over a fortnight ago, I'd say. But I have seen him. I never forget a face.'

Reilly handed Hashim a wedge of cash. He'd added mostly tenners in the bundle to bulk it out and make it appear like a fair amount, though there was only three hundred.

Hashim pocketed the money and offered a disdainful glare by way of a thanks. 'I'll be in touch if I find anything useful.'

Reilly smiled. 'Can't wait.'

Hashim turned and trudged back to his van, mumbling and muttering to himself as he went.

Mills crossed his arms and watched him go. 'What a moody cunt.'

'I like him,' said Reilly, thinking his brother was the bloody biggest hypocrite going.

18

Somewhere in the Netherlands – September

Karl opened his eyes and wondered why he'd been sleeping on the floor and using his dirty trainers as makeshift pillows. He blearily scanned the room. Asleep in the chair was a Chinese man with dark, spiky hair and a jutting forehead. He'd never seen the guy before in his life. Another figure, a curvy female, lay sprawled on the bed. Her mini skirt had ridden up, showing a lemon-coloured thong that did little to hide her fridge-white, sagging bum cheeks. A patch of what looked like vomit, was smeared on the pillows by her face. For a second Karl thought she was dead, but then she snorted, kicked out a leg, scratched her bum, and started snoring and grunting.

'Aw tits,' wheezed Karl. He did not know what had happened here. Or where here was. There were signs they'd been smoking. A lot. On the low coffee table there were clumps of weed, Rizlas, and ashtrays overflowing with roaches and fag butts. There were bottles of booze and discarded cans of beer everywhere. The place smelt of stale vomit, rank sweat, and dank ganja. Plus something else, the kind of putrid smell that follows a dustbin lorry.

A stabbing pain hit his guts, and he knew if he didn't find the loo immediately, he'd crap his pants. He located the bathroom and slipped inside. He found the sink overflowing with bright yellow sick, mixed with water, a toilet crammed with crushed beer cans, and Joost, asleep in the bath, naked save his tight, red pants. He had a shower curtain wrapped around his legs and a toilet brush and an assortment of flowers lay in the tub with him.

'Joost! Joost, wake up!'

No reply.

Karl shook the Dutchman's shoulder. 'Joost… Joost, where the hell are we? Who are those people in there? And who blocked up the sink? I am not putting my hand into radioactive spew.'

Joost let out a gurgled, 'Mmmmm. Ahhhh. Whaaau. Huhhhh.'

'Get out of here. I need to go. Now!' yelled Karl.

'Uhhh.'

With a cramping pain that made him double over in agony, Karl knew he was incapable of holding out any longer. He pulled out the piss covered cans from the toilet, tossed them onto the floor and slammed down onto the filthy seat, just as an epic explosion of runny crap hit the pan. The poo, grim and fast flowing, seemed endless.

Joost, though still half asleep, grumbled, 'Man, tell me you are not doing a fucking big shit in here!'

'Sorry, dude, I couldn't wait,' groaned Karl, unable to stop.

Joost sniffed the air, heaved and vomited a brownish liquid from his mouth and nose. It splashed over the tatty linoleum flooring. The colour of the slushy puke made Karl think of his funny little car back home, abandoned on the driveway. He wondered if his dad had scrapped it. Probably. He'd sold the house now and would be moving away in a couple of months.

Karl noticed a yellow rubber duck in the sink, floating on the puke. At a closer inspection, he could see the duck had an Elvis style haircut.

Is this what the travel blogging life would be like? Then another awful thought hit him. 'Joost! The travel wallet. Where is the travel wallet?'

'I dunno… I think you had it. You… you put it in the rucksack,' said Joost, hunting around and looking for something to wipe his face on. He made do with a wet towel from the floor that Karl guessed was soaked in urine.

Karl sprung up from the toilet and raced into the main room. He flung stuff around the room in a desperate search for the rucksack.

A begrimed sock flew across the room and landed on the sleeping man's face, which did not wake him.

A spinning shoe knocked over an arched, green table light that looked like it belonged in a seventies motel. Actually, the entire place looked reminiscent of a seventies motel.

Karl located the rucksack by the bed and tipped out its contents – clothing, a dented can of deodorant, a packet of squashed Stroopwafels, one broken flipflop, and the long black leather travel wallet, all tumbled out.

Karl exhaled a long breath and held the wallet to his chest. 'Thank God.'

Joost walked in, scratching his groin and yawning. 'You didn't wipe. That is disgusting. I must have coffee. Right now. I need coffee.'

Karl held up the wallet. 'It's here.'

Joost begun rifling through the ashtray. 'See, in the rucksack. Like I said.'

Karl popped open the wallet's lid and rummaged inside.

'How are we doing on funds? I'd like proper food today,' said Joost, tying his hair back into a ponytail, a blackened cigarette, or joint, now clasped between his lips. 'Have you seen my lighter?'

Karl checked inside again.

'I hope I haven't lost my favourite lighter. I love that lighter,' grumbled Joost. 'Can you help me find my lighter please, Karl?'

'The euros are all gone. The travel fund has… gone,' said Karl.

19

Fifteen days had passed since Ravi's chat with Arnie, so he'd now assumed that the vile man had just been pulling his leg about his proposal to help him with his search. So when Ravi took the call from an unrecognised number, he'd been shocked when the caller identified himself as Arnie Baxter and that he wanted to speak with Ravi.

'Can we meet?' asked Ravi.

'Yeah, we can. How would you like to treat me to breakfast?'

'Where?' asked Ravi.

Ravi took in the surroundings with disdain. The stench of polluted sea air, rotten seaweed and stale grease hit him. Ravi disliked seaside towns. Or at least, he disliked the typical British seaside town; especially in the South. He pulled his overcoat over his suit jacket and scanned the spiritless, dirty road where flocks of seagulls squabbled over the first pickings from yesterday's discarded chip wrappings and Styrofoam burger packets.

The dreary cafe, Arnie's chosen spot to meet, was located between a small arcade, and a property undergoing a renovation. The neglected building had been boarded up years ago by the look of the place, and mediocre graffiti covered the weather-worn boards that screened it. A cracked drainpipe had leaked green, stagnant water down one board, and Ravi stepped over the pooling, rancid liquid, careful not to get any splashes on his pristine brogues.

Ravi started scanning the area for any signs of suspicious activity. For any signs that he was being watched. Two young men inside the arcade caught his eye. They both had an air of *dodgy waster* about them, but they only seemed interested in filling the noisy machines with their coins. One smacked away at the buttons and the machine bleeped, chimed and eventually rewarded the idiot with an annoying melody and further toots and bleeps. Ravi couldn't help wondering why these lowlifes weren't at college or at work.

After deciding that there were no eyes on him, he ventured inside the cafe.

The smell of unpleasant food hit him and despite skipping breakfast, the desire to eat now fled his stomach.

Two burly builders sat in the corner, one tucking into a sandwich, the other sipping from a can of Red Bull as he flicked through *The Daily Mail*.

Arnie sat in the far corner, eyes fixed on his phone. Ravi felt certain Arnie had already clocked him enter, but was putting on a little charade and pretending not to notice him standing there.

The cook, who Ravi spied through the serving hatch, looked like a cross between an ageing Rasta and Captain Birdseye. He was jiving away to some groovy reggae sounds as he tossed sausages in a huge frying pan. A young girl, who was cleaning tables, smiled politely at Ravi and also bobbed her head to the background tunes. She had messy hair, dyed a hideous purple colour, and thick, round spectacles. Why were these people so happy? How anyone could be this cheery serving up eggs to sour-faced builders seemed beyond comprehension to Ravi. They were surely high on drugs. That seemed to be the only rational explanation for their upbeat mood.

Ravi walked to Arnie's table and coughed. 'Arnie?'

Arnie moved his eyes from his phone to Ravi, then back to the phone. He was engrossed in some sort of battle game.

Ravi pulled up a seat opposite him, brushed off some crumbs, and somewhat begrudgingly, he sat down. Then he scanned the room, the entrance, and lastly fixed his gaze on Arnie, who continued to play the game on his phone. The song changed to another funky reggae number, which the cook started singing along to.

Arnie finished his game and acknowledged Ravi. 'Nice to be down here, hey? I love the seaside.'

Ravi just snorted at this.

'So, you have a few questions for me?' asked Arnie, tossing his phone on the table.

'Yes, I—'

Arnie cut him straight off. 'Hold up! Let's just take a step back. We need to talk about money first. And I'm not talking about what financial advice you can give me.' He laughed at that.

Ravi detested this man. If he could give him some advice, it would be to go and buy a toothbrush and clean his damn teeth once in a while. He'd have to bite his lip and stay in control. He needed this reprobate's help, so would need to keep that notion forefront of his mind before opening his mouth.

'How much di—'

'Five hundred,' said Arnie, cutting him off again.

Ravi took a deep breath. Now five hundred would not break the bank. Five grand would not break the bank. But what exactly was this loser offering him for that money? Did he even have anything to offer? For all Ravi knew, this was some ruse to line his own pockets and, in reality, the man had no intention of assisting him. But he'd hit a brick wall, so trusting this deadbeat really was his only option right now. Schneider had all but given up. The police hadn't been able to help, and he was going insane with worry. And he'd walked the streets of Broadstairs and neighbouring seaside towns, flashing Nathaniel's photo for days at a time, to no avail. Ravi knew he needed a fresh approach. Not that anything was remotely fresh about this smelly weirdo.

Ravi cleared his throat. 'If you have adequate information, then yes, I will agree to five hundred.'

A frown creased Arnie's forehead, and he appeared to look displeased; as though he was now wondering if he'd just sold himself short. He had, because Ravi would have paid considerably more for any lead that boosted his chances of finding his son.

'Where is it?' asked Arnie.

'Where is what?'

'My dough.'

'In my car. Whether it is yours is still up for debate.'

'Where is your car?'

Ravi, about to tell Arnie to hold his horses, was interrupted by the waitress appearing at their table. 'Hey, what can I get you?' she said, a bright smile on her face.

'Gut-buster breakfast. Strong tea. Extra toast. Butter, not marge. Cumberland sausage sandwich, with lots of onions. And he's paying. Oh, and a large orange juice with a small splash of water,' said Arnie.

The waitress scribbled down the order and turned to Ravi.

'Just coffee for me. Thanks.'

Arnie rapped his knuckle on the table. 'Whoa, come on, Rivi, don't make me eat alone. That's not very sociable.'

The waitress waited, pen poised above the pad, as she looked from Ravi to Arnie with a strange smile fixed on her face.

'Fine. Eggs on toast. Wholemeal, or seeded loaf preferably, please.'

'Fried, poached, scrambled?' the waitress asked.

'Scrambled will be fine. Hard, not slushy,' said Ravi. He was very particular about how his eggs were cooked. He didn't intend to eat a single mouthful of food in this grubby den anyway, so wondered why he was being finicky about his order. Force of habit, he considered. He would dread to think how sullied their cooking utensils were back there in that dirty, poor excuse for a kitchen.

The waitress scampered off.

'So, let's talk about Nathan,' said Arnie.

'Nathaniel! My son's name is Nathaniel. And my name is Ravi. Not Rivi!' hissed Ravi.

'Cool your jets, pal.'

Ravi, feeling hot, stood up, removed his overcoat and lay it across the back of his chair.

'Sometimes people called him that,' said Arnie.

'What can you tell me about my son?'

'I have never spoken to him. We're not mates or anything. But I have seen him hanging about in the boozer with Stefan.'

'And this Stefan… he was good friends with Nathaniel?'

Arnie grinned. 'I assume by saying *was*, means you know what happened to the lad?'

Ravi nodded sombrely. 'Yes.'

'Yeah, they *were* good mates. I think your son enjoyed hanging around with a Chillcott. It made him feel special. I mean, no disrespect, but in their world, Nathaniel is a nobody. But he swanned about with Stefan like he was gangster number one.'

'Did Stefan deal drugs in the pub?' whispered Ravi.

Arnie shrugged. 'Probably. I mean, he wasn't a big player himself. He liked to think he was in the big leagues, but his older brothers are the major players.'

'Reilly and Mills?'

Arnie laughed. 'Look at you, Mr Super Sleuth. Been doing some digging, hey?'

'Who else did Stefan and Nathaniel associate with?'

'There was a little gang of them, from what I heard. They were setting up some sort of crew. But in the lead up to his death, it was only Nathaniel who frequented the bar with Stefan. The pair were tight.' Arnie leaned in closer to Ravi. 'Nathaniel was supposedly the last person to see Stefan alive. They'd been out together at a pub in Canterbury.'

'What?' exclaimed Ravi.

'Yeah, they left together... and the next day, they found Stefan washed up on a remote stretch of that Sussex coast... and your son disappeared. I heard the Chillcotts put the word out that anyone with news of Nathaniel's whereabouts should go straight to them.'

Ravi scanned the room again. An overweight man wearing a flat cap and thick scarf waddled in through the door, waved at the waitress and took up the seat nearest the door.

'Arnie, do they... oh, my word... do the Chillcotts think my son is involved in what happened?'

'All I heard is they want to talk to him. I dunno what they think. But, looking at the situation from their point of view, Nathaniel doing a vanishing act isn't helping his case. If he wasn't involved, then they assume he knows something about what went down that night.'

Ravi's temperature seemed to rise by the minute as an overwhelming sensation of dread flooded over him. He went to speak but felt disoriented and short of breath. His son had got himself into some serious trouble here. More serious that Ravi could ever have imagined.

'So, you've not had any contact with him yourself? No indication where he might have gone?' asked Arnie indifferently.

Ravi wondered if he should be here. He'd already considered Arnie could be in cahoots with the Chillcotts, as insane as that seemed, given what had transpired. But surely that wasn't impossible. Or was it? He decided to veer the conversation.

'What happened to you, Arnie? How did you… you know?'

'End up in this old cripple-copter,' said Arnie, slapping the side of the wheelchair. 'You know how it is? Too many shandies. You talk shit to the wrong person. Forget your place.'

'So, who was actually responsible?' asked Ravi.

Arnie sniggered. 'Why? What difference does it make to your life? You gonna help me take down the culprit? Help me pay them back and get revenge?'

'Why didn't you go to the police?'

'Why?' asked Arnie. 'Because I—'

Their drinks arrived and Arnie stopped talking, toyed with his greasy hair, and waited for the waitress to leave. They were about to restart the discussion when the waitress returned with their food. They'd cooked that far too fast for Ravi's liking.

The pair sat in silence as Arnie drenched his oversized plate of food with watery ketchup, bright yellow mustard, and an unhealthy dusting of salt.

'The name Sookdeo, that's pretty unusual. What's that, South African?' asked Arnie.

'Yes,' lied Ravi. He had no intention of giving this scumbag any more information than was necessary. Ravi's heritage was none of this man's business. His family were all proud Trinidadians who'd moved to London in the late seventies, and before they emigrated, Ravi had spent much of his youth in the West Indies, which were fond memories he cherished. He still had relatives in San Fernando where his parents were from, but it had been many, many years since he'd visited. He considered that taking Nathaniel there for an extended trip was long overdue. That could be something worth considering, once… *if*… he located him. Because getting him far away from all this mess would be imperative.

'Do the Chillcotts own a Renault van?' asked Ravi, picking up a fork and wiping it with a napkin.

Arnie held up his sausage sandwich, took a ravenous bite, causing a surge of onions to spill out and land on the plate. 'No, not as far as I know. Why?'

Ravi shifted the unusual coloured eggs around his plate. 'I'm looking for one that's been staking out my house.' He took a gamble and tried the eggs. They were fluffy and tasted delicious.

Arnie chewed uncouthly and raised his eyebrows as if intrigued.

'There is a distinctive sticker on the rear window. A gorilla with a gun. Have you ever seen it at the pub?'

'Ah, yes, wait… yeah, that van,' said Arnie, spitting food as he spoke. 'I know whose van that is.'

'You do?'

'Barry Bartell.'

'Who is that?'

'Well, not the sort of man you'd want to be watching your house. Though not quite in the same league as the Chillcotts, the Bartells are not a family you'd want to have on your back, Ravi.'

Ravi put down the fork and pushed the plate away.

Arnie, now done with the sandwich, started tucking into the gut-buster, making Ravi feel nauseous.

'Both families are crooked as a barrel of angry snakes. And they do have something else in common. Both families lost a son this year,' said Arnie.

'What?'

'Craig Bartell. Another lad that died under suspicious circumstances. Found dead in a carpark in Canterbury,' said Arnie, licking sauce from his lips. 'Back in March, I believe.'

Ravi, dumbfounded, made no reply.

'The Chillcotts and Bartells have a lot of history. Stefan's and Craig's dads used to run together back in the nineties. Drugs and robberies. I have heard rumours of some major deal going tits up. I don't know the ins and outs. But from what I do know, Jack Bartell picked up a massive shipment of Es from Germany and loaded them onto a boat on the Belgium coast.'

'Es?' asked Ravi.

'Ecstasy… disco biscuits… mollies… Get with it, Ravi. Anyway, the boat delivered them to Ramsgate, where Marcus Chillcott loaded them into a van… but en route to their lock up in Essex, they got ambushed and the whole shipment was pinched.'

Ravi just gazed at Arnie, wondering how he could respond to such information.

'They turned the criminal underworld upside down, hunting for the culprits. But to this day, no one knows who poached those drugs. Some say they even suspected each other in the end. It ruined their partnership anyhow. Placed a weird rift between the families ever since.'

Ravi shifted in his seat. Nathaniel had stepped into a murky world that would swallow up the average, law-abiding person. What the hell was he going to do?

Ravi's stomach was in knots as he turned his Jag into Dead Lane. He'd checked the road out on street view, but that only covered a brief part of the track and the aerial map hadn't been very useful. It did, however, clarify that Hunter's Cottage lay at the very end of the lane, and that the property sat in a remote area surrounded by nothing but dense woodland and vast fields. The nearest building was a place called Greytree Farm, and that was a ten-minute drive across a completely rural area.

The lane was an unmaintained flinty track, and as the Jag bounced up and down on the potholes, Ravi's heart pounded in his chest. He couldn't remember the last time he'd been so apprehensive about anything. The drive was painfully slow, and the more ground the car covered, the more shredded his nerves became. It had looked a fair distance on the map, but actually undertaking the drive seemed to be taking an eternity. The car hit a dip, hidden under leaves, and he cursed as the Jag groaned and shuddered, causing him to ease off the already meagre pressure he'd been applying. A quick getaway in this motor wouldn't be an option. This was four-wheel-drive territory.

The lane became tighter and even more rugged, so he searched for somewhere to stop and venture the final part of the journey on foot.

Ravi parked up the car in a lay-by next to a weed covered iron gate and switched off the ignition. His nerves were shot to pieces, and he struggled to bring himself to get out of the car. He took a deep breath and forced himself out of the vehicle and walked to the boot to change his footwear. After changing his shoes for hiking boots, his overcoat for a waterproof Burberry jacket, he slipped on a beanie and took the dog lead and collar from the Pets at Home bag. Ravi tugged off the labels and stuffed the items in his pocket. He'd purchased them earlier, just in case anyone questioned his presence here. He then grabbed his mini telescopic binoculars, locked the car, and headed down the lane.

It was so silent here. Not a peaceful silence, either. More of a nerve-racking silence that jangled your nerves and put you on edge. The lane got even worse. Broken and rutted. Ravi would have cursed himself if he'd pushed his precious car further along here. Though he had to admit, he felt far more exposed and skittish now he was walking; claustrophobic too. The trees and thicket were getting more compact and there'd be few places to hide should an unknown vehicle approach.

Ravi stopped as he noticed several signs pinned to a wide oak tree. The first was a metal notice, red with big white writing, stated – *Private Property Keep Out*. Underneath that, a large sheet that had been laminated. This had a red *STOP* symbol, with the following words – *This is NOT a footpath*.

Ravi kept walking, faster now, though he suddenly had the urge to urinate. On he walked, and still the signs continued – *No cycling. No motorcycles. No dogs. No hikers. Strictly NO public right of way.*

Ravi fingered the dog lead in his pocket, now thinking that his plan hadn't been so clever after all. He stopped and gazed behind. Nothing. He looked forward – nothing but more twisting lane ahead. What sort of people lived out here? How did they ever get anything delivered? You really could apply *arse end of nowhere* to this place.

. . .

Ravi turned the corner and walked under two enormous chestnut trees, where he found a barn-gate marking the entrance to Hunter's Cottage. The house plaque had a picture of two white and tanned spaniels on it. On the other side of the gate sat a stone statue of a creepy goblin creature that appeared to be bursting up through the ground. It seemed to stare right at him. It had a squashed face, sinister eyes, and a huge, flat nose. It reminded Ravi of Mills Chillcott. From the gate, the track wound along another forty metres or so, where it opened up to a large courtyard. By the gated entrance was a wooden cabin with high, thin windows, and the crude building looked as though they'd constructed it themselves. Out the front of the building lay various bits of junk, pallets and oil drums, plus a skip, which looked rooted to the spot with vines and weeds creeping up its sides. Poking up from inside the skip were rotten doors, a stained mattress, and pieces of twisted metal that perhaps once belonged to a storage unit.

Ravi took out a small set of binoculars from his jacket, unfolded them, and used them to scan the main house. This was an old, rustic red bricked building. There were some outbuildings too, several metal sheds, and a shabby mobile home with a swing seat out the front of it. The premises, Ravi surmised, were once part of a working farm, but it didn't appear to be being used for that purpose any longer. Everything looked unkept, rundown and altogether inhospitable. Though in contrast, the woodland regions and hilly fields beyond looked charming.

Ravi then scanned the vehicles – a dark blue Ford Ranger truck, an old-style white Range Rover, and a mud covered Land Rover Defender with a big roof rack system, chunky chrome front bars, and huge, round spotlights. There was also a vehicle under some blue tarpaulin. The final vehicle he laid his eyes on made his heart flutter. A greyish-blue beaten-up van. He couldn't see the sticker because the front was facing him, but Ravi knew this was the Renault Traffic that he'd seen surveying his house. Arnie's information had been correct, and he now considered that the money he'd given the man was well spent. He reached into his jacket to retrieve his phone, wondering if he'd be able to sneak into the courtyard unseen for a snoop about and snap some photos. He dismissed this reckless idea and left the phone. He slid the binoculars back into his pocket. No sooner had he put them away, a deep voice cut through the silence. 'Are you lost?'

Ravi's heartbeat momentarily stopped. He kept his face neutral – his best poker face that he could easily deploy when required for work meetings or important business conferences. He spun to face the intimidating voice and said, 'A thousand apologies. I am aware this is private land.' Ravi fumbled for the leash and collar, awkwardly pulled them free and dangled them.

A stocky man in a long, padded wax jacket eyed him with a curious smirk.

'My damn dog pulled free of his collar and darted off,' said Ravi.

Ravi's eyes fixed on the shotgun in the man's hands. Though, thankfully, he had the thing pointing low, and the barrel lay open. But the fact he was armed made Ravi's legs turn numb with fear.

Ravi shook his head and tutted. 'Bloody dog.'

The man nodded. His face was unreadable. 'What breed?' There were two spaniels flanking the man, watching Ravi with interest. One had a dead pheasant clamped in its jaws, the other was panting urgently. Ravi's mind went blank, and he struggled to recall any breed of dog. He almost said spaniel, but decided that would have been rather suspicious. 'One of those bearded dogs. Looks a bit like a grumpy old man,' said Ravi. He could have kicked himself for not thinking this far ahead, but then he'd not expected to be questioned about his pretend pet's details. Ravi knew next to nothing about dogs, though he recalled a time many years back, when his daughter had showed him a photo of a puppy her friend had received for a birthday gift. She'd pleaded with him to have one, too. She'd cooed, 'Aw, but look at his sweet little face, Daddy! He's just like an adorable teddy bear. I'd love him so much.' Ravi said no, of course, without even giving the idea a moment's deliberation. She'd not attempted to debate the decision.

'A schnauzer?' asked the man.

'Yes, that's the one. It's my wife's dog. She's gone away and I've been lumbered with him.'

'Right. What type?'

'Type?'

'Miniature... giant?'

'Uh, a small one.'

The man gestured the collar in Ravi's hand. 'No wonder he escaped, then.'

Ravi held up the big collar and could have slapped himself. He was clearly useless at all this clandestine stuff. 'Aw, yeah. I say small. But he's big for a... miniature. Or so the vet said.'

The man grinned. It was a grin that said, *Do you think I'm a total bloody idiot?*

'Anyway, I'll get out of your hair. Again, my apologies for trespassing. But nice speaking with you.'

'I'm Jack,' said the man holding out his right hand.

'Um, Isaac,' said Ravi, accepting the handshake that lingered far longer than he thought necessary. The large hand was coarse and strong. Jack must have been mid-sixties and stood with a slight stoop. Ravi noted a large, jagged scar running down his left cheek, and tried not to focus on it. Jack hadn't come across as menacing, or even unfriendly. Just impassive. Ravi also sensed a sadness clinging to him. This made him think about the boy, Craig, that Arnie had mentioned in the cafe. He wondered if this was the dead boy's father. It made him feel a deep sorrow for this stranger. He then wondered if there was a connection between Stefan Chillcott, Craig Bartell, and Nathaniel. He contemplated telling Jack who he really was to see if he had any answers. But decided not to risk it.

'Would you like my dogs to pick up the scent from the collar?' asked Jack.

Ravi peered down at the dogs, then set his eyes back on Jack. 'No, I'm sure he'll be waiting back at the car now.'

'If you're sure.'

'They can do that?' asked Ravi, genuinely interested.

'Nah, I very much doubt it. Anyway, I hope you find him.'

Ravi grinned and nodded. 'Good to meet you.'

Jack shoved open the gate and headed through. 'Moose. Cracker,' he bellowed. The dogs charged in behind him.

Ravi, about to leave, noticed another man, well-built and younger, standing in the courtyard with his gaze fixed on him. What he saw next sent a shiver straight through him. He realised the man's left hand wasn't visible as it was tucked up the sleeve of his jacket. And poking out of that sleeve, he glimpsed several inches of what looked like the blade of a wide, sharp, carving knife.

This place was dangerous. Ravi had already sensed that. Now he knew it. He turned and strolled away, and after going a short distance he quickly glanced back. Both Jack and the other man were leaning over the closed gate, openly staring at him. Then a pheasant bolted out of the undergrowth by Ravi's feet and nearly gave him heart failure.

Ravi fast walked back down the lane, looking over his shoulder every so often, so sure he'd see a vehicle racing down the track towards him. About halfway down, his rattled nerves could no longer take it and he broke into a jog.

When he reached the car, he did a painstakingly slow ten-point turn to change direction, then he left Dead Lane much faster than he came in. The car bounced, clonked and protested, but this time Ravi forgot about damaging his suspension, because all he cared about was getting himself clear of this place as rapidly as possible.

Ravi hadn't heard from Schneider in a good while, but guessed his several missed calls from the young PI were most likely related to his outstanding invoices that he'd neglected, on purpose, to pay. Of course, he intended to clear his debt, but felt that Schneider's lacklustre service should at least be subject to a lengthy delay, which would lead to him worrying that Ravi wouldn't pay. He guessed this would result in one of two things happening. Either he'd give up and refuse to work on the case, or he'd stop being a keyboard detective and grow some balls and investigate his son's disappearance properly.

Ravi picked up his phone and slumped into his office chair. 'Afternoon, Mr Schneider.'

'Hey, Ravi. Listen, I tracked down Lacresha Carr... the partner of Tristan Vickers. The missing guy who—'

'I remember,' said Ravi, cutting him off with a curt tone.

'I called her. She was very reluctant to speak to me. Understandably, she's pretty cut up. Tristan is the father of her three girls and she strongly believes that her partner is dead. There has been no trace of him.'

'Did she mention the Chillcotts?' asked Ravi.

'She didn't want to say much about them, only what we know, that he'd had some grief with Reilly over a debt. But the day he went missing, Tristan told her where he was heading.'

'Where?' asked Ravi.

'To a meeting at his friend's place. Some guy called Johnny Bartell. She gave me the address. It's right in the middle of nowhere. Hunter's Cottage, Dead Lane. Near Faversham.'

Ravi smiled to himself, thinking that maybe he should be the detective, being as though he was way ahead of this pup. Though at least Schneider was now digging in the same spot. He'd consider settling up his latest invoice soon.

Ravi sat up straight. 'So, are you going to talk to this Bartell character?'

'I'll do some research on the Bartells and get back to you soon. I won't head out there.'

Of course you won't, considered Ravi and said, 'Keep me posted.'

'Yes, sure. Ah, yes, also, on another note, we have some outstanding—'

Ravi cut him off. 'I must go. I have an online meeting. Speak soon.' He ended the call. A bit of money motivation often helped to get the job done. Anyway, who did he think he was? *You watch too many TV shows...* The jumped up little twerp. Then he peered up at his office wall. The cork board pinned up there resembled something out of a TV police procedural drama, with maps, photos and newspaper clippings stuck all over it. Perhaps the lad did have a point.

20

After eight hours of intense labour, an epidural and plenty of cursing, Amy gave birth by c-section at two-thirty-three am, on Monday the twenty-ninth of October at Canterbury hospital. The ordeal had been horrendous and terrifying. But now, holding her newborn daughter, Francesca, weighing just over seven pounds, all of that trauma evaporated. Her partner, Oscar, barely left her side during the entire delivery, and although he wasn't the baby's biological father, he beamed in wondrous bliss when he held the baby. When she'd first spotted the child's tiny mop of light gingery hair, she'd have been lying if a small wave of concern hadn't washed over her. But that soon lifted when she'd seen her partner's expression as he held her baby for the first time… held *their* baby. Throughout the pregnancy, Oscar had been there for her, and he'd promised that he would always treat Francesca like his own flesh and blood. And she'd believed him. He was a good man, after all. Although, because of the age gap, her parents were dead against their relationship. Her sister kept moaning at her too, saying she'd moved on way too fast and Oscar wasn't right for her. Plus, Oscar's mother seemed to think Amy was a total user, though most of the time she'd be amicable to her face and pretend to like her. Amy knew otherwise. She sensed the bitterness. She'd win her over. In time. And if she didn't, then that was her loss.

None of that mattered now. Not in this moment. They were a family and as she contemplated their future, Amy felt a serene hopefulness and knew that everything would work out. She was exactly where she was supposed to be.

Oscar kissed her on the cheek and whispered, 'She is so amazing. You were amazing, Amy Mullard. I love you so much.'

21

Page 2

"I'd always dreamed of being a professional cabaret and burlesque dancer. Ever since I was a young girl. I thought about it every waking moment. I'd been told I had pure talent, and I was destined to perform. A true artist, they'd tell me. I yearned for the big stage and the immense crowds of appreciative spectators. And when I spent time with Valletta's Bedazzle Troupe, we were a sell-out act that entranced and excited every single audience. That feeling of intense elation as the crowds watched in awe was amazing. Exhilarating. Life changing. Indescribable. That's the life I thought I wanted… until you came into my world and everything changed. I knew things would never be the same again. I didn't mind that. I soon learnt this: all that mattered was you… Sometimes I see you in my dreams – still a tiny baby in my arms and I don't want to wake up, because when I do, I know I'll sob my heart out and think of everything I've missed out on. All those key moments in your life. All those special times. I've contemplated suicide. If I'm honest, I've more than contemplated. I almost attempted it more than once. But what's always held me back is knowing that one day you'll find your way back to me… Sometimes I pray to God that you will. I plead with Him. I sometimes try to form a picture in my head of what you look like now. I see your little smile when I close my eyes. You were such a gorgeous baby. Big, ice-blue eyes, and tiny dimples in your cheeks. We often went for picnics on the beach, and from the moment you could walk, you loved the sea. You were drawn to it. I would call you my little mer-boy. I wasn't able to offer you much, but I loved you with all my heart. But I struggled. Financially and mentally. It was hard for me to cope on my own. I let things slide. That's when *he* returned and when he learnt of your existence for the first time. He'd only come looking for sex. That's what he always came for. I meant nothing to him. He'd used me in the past… made me feel wanted when it suited him and tossed me aside like a used beer can once he'd had his way. When he saw you, he sussed it straight away. He stared at you and you at him. He got angry. Furiously mad. He told me I was a wicked bitch for keeping you a secret from him. You won't remember anything because you were only a toddler, but he smacked me in the face with a wine glass – right in front of you. I still have a deep scar on my forehead from that attack. He shouted that he'd kill me with his bare hands. Beat me to death, were his exact words. He said he was taking you away, because I was an unfit mother and that I made you live in a filthy flat and didn't feed you right. If those are the things he told you, which I guess they are, then please, please, please believe me when I say it was all lies. I didn't have much, but I did my best and we had a wonderful little life together. You were so happy. I begged him not to take you. I cried like I've never cried before. I even tried physically fighting, but I had no chance against that brutish monster. He told me two things before he left. The first was that you had his blood in your veins and, therefore, you belonged with him. The second was that should I ever search for you, he'd kill me. And he'd do it slowly and savour every moment. I didn't even get to say goodbye properly. He let me hug you briefly before making me pack up a small bag with a handful of clothes and your passport. And you were taken from me. And my life crumbled around me."

22

Kent, 22 November 2018

'Has he been chasing some Dutch-muff? Admit it. That jammy shit. That's why he stayed out there. He's met someone. I dunno how that little jerk does it.'

Duncan sipped his strawberry cider and shrugged. 'No. I dunno, Scott.'

Duncan didn't know why he'd agreed to meet his cousin. Well, actually he did, because his mum's incessant moaning about him becoming a hermit had driven him to crack and agree to go out and play squash. He'd met up with Scott at a new gym complex he'd now joined. This one at least had working showers, a decent changing room and a modern bar area, so was a far cry from the pants sports club they used to frequent. The game itself had destroyed him. He'd not been particularly fit before. Or ever. But Duncan could at least play squash and footy without feeling like he was about to keel over and flake out in a panting, withering mess. The months spent hiding away at home and doing nothing but online gaming, eating crisps and binging on naff TV had taken its toll. Since March, he'd put on two stones and his skin flare-ups were the worse they'd ever been.

Now every time he ventured out of the house, he'd get hot and cold sweats, heart palpitations and fuzzy migraines. Even now, sitting in this gym bar, surrounded by healthy, cheerful people, and wearing freshly changed clothes, his underwear and T-shirt were soaked in sweat. It wasn't even warm in here, the temperature was pleasant, but even still his boxers were sticking against his backside and thighs because they were so heavy with perspiration. He wanted to remove his hoody, but that would only make the wet T-shirt visible, and therefore make it worse. He got in this state as soon as he ventured anywhere. Even the local shop. Also, any sound would make him jumpy. A stern shout. A slamming door. Cars skidding. Sirens. And it seemed as though he had hypersensitive hearing these days; especially during the long nights, which would drive him insane with panic. A glass smashed in his street a few weeks back during the early hours, which caused Duncan to shake for twenty minutes. It was like his blood had been replaced by iced water and nothing could stop the horrible shivers assaulting his entire body. Not even three blankets and a dressing gown over his pyjamas. Then he'd woken up before six, saturated with slimy sweat, and ended up waking his parents after knocking the back-scrub off its hanger and causing it to clonk against the shower door. They'd not been impressed.

Duncan noticed Scott eyeing him with mock suspicion.

'What?' asked Duncan.

'Come on, Dunko-man. It's quite obvious what went down. Just come clean.'

Duncan felt the shakes coming on again. He had to play it cool, keep appearing unconcerned, even though he could now detect the sweat beads gathering on his forehead and slipping down his nose. He moved to pick up the glass for a quick sip, but his hand trembled, so he shoved it into his pocket.

Scott flashed him a smug grin. 'Karl got wind of the sprog and did a runner. That's why he bottled it on the flat and zoomed off overseas. That's why you came home and Karl stayed hiding out over there. Come on, I'm right, aren't I?'

Duncan just blinked, stunned by Scott's revelation.

'Fine. I get it. Secret squirrel. My round,' said Scott, making for the bar. Duncan grabbed his arm and stopped him. 'Are you serious, Scott?'

'What... you didn't know?'

'No!'

'So, does that mean—'

'He's not been in touch with her. He... lost his phone out there. Left it on a bus.' Accidentally on purpose, thought Duncan.

'Ooh my shit. Aww, whoa. That's awkward. I assumed you both knew about the sprog. Shit-ola.'

'Are you sure? Amy has a baby?'

Scott grinned. 'Yeah, my mate James Starr... well, his bird, Melissa, knows her. And when Amy posted photos on Facebook, Melissa showed James. Little baby girl with tiny ginger curls. Born a few weeks back. Uh, now, what did he say her name was?'

'Jesuuuus, this is insane. So, you're telling me you think Karl has a kid? Karl? Karl, who is currently twatting about in the Netherlands pretending to be some sort of cultured, bearded travel blogger... and all this time Amy—'

'What? Karl's a travel blogger? Interesting. I always wondered how those bloggers got paid. Advertising, right?'

'No, Scott, he's not a travel blogger. No more than I'm a bloody astronaut. And that's not the point here. He has a baby that he's got no idea about.'

'I remember when you were adamant you wanted to fly to the moon. You remember that? You had that cool suit with the helmet and everything. But you wouldn't let anyone else play with it.'

'Scott! I have to tell him.'

Scott waved his hands. 'Nah, Melissa told James that she's settled down with this Maplethorpe guy. Top bathroom supplier and king of the shitters.'

'Oscar Maplethorpe? As in... her boss? Karl's old boss!'

'Yeah, Melissa reckons they've dated before. They stayed friends or something. She must have got back with him on the rebound.'

Duncan shook his head, unable to process all this.

'I heard he's a total plum, but he can provide for them, so she's better off. Let Karl do his thing. Why ruin it? It's a win for everyone.'

'Until he finds out, Scott. He'd never speak to me again.'

'You think he's the first bloke out there who has no clue they have a nipper? Maybe I have... maybe... well, not you, Dunk, but it happens.

Look, don't get me wrong, I think Karl's a decent bloke, but he'd be no use to her. We both know he's not father material. He's a daydreamer. And he's self-centred. I was amazed she'd been interested in the first place. It would never have lasted once she figured him out.'

Duncan wiped the sheen of sweat from his forehead. 'It's not down to us to decide. It's down to him.'

'Dunk-ola… mate, are you sure this isn't about you?'

'Meaning?'

'You miss him. I get it. He's always been around. He's been a big part of your life. But people change and move on. You thought he'd be about forever, but… stuff happens. Life changes. We disconnect from people.'

'It's just… he'll be furious if he found out we'd kept this from him. I would be mortified.'

Scott shrugged. 'But you are not like him. Look, Dunk, I'd personally stay out of this. You'll only complicate matters. And it's not like life won't go on without him.'

'Right.'

'You'll get over him. It's like losing your first love,' said Scott.

'Just shut the hell up!' spat Duncan vehemently.

'Whoa, hold up, Dunk.'

'My life *will* go on without him, because I want it that way. I'm choosing that path.'

'Why are you getting so angry? I was winding you up. It's OK to miss him. He is your best mate.'

'My life doesn't revolve around that stupid prat.'

'Stop shouting and chill. You're going bright red. Let me grab another drink.'

'Stick it.' Duncan made to leave and caught the expression, a mixture of outrage and total confusion, on Scott's face as he stropped out, already feeling like a total idiot for losing his cool so easily.

Duncan just about heard Scott say, 'Stop acting like a big bloody baby, Duncan.' Then the cool air hit him and he marched away from the complex, shivering with each step. The soaked underwear was cold and uncomfortable on his skin.

. . .

Karl studied the Elvis duck again. He'd been carrying the thing in his bag and kept telling himself he'd bin it, but somehow couldn't bring himself to toss it away. Some of his mid-September travelling adventure stayed missing from his mind. Those days he'd spent in Amsterdam. A few things had come back to him in hazy, fragmented flashbacks; most notable of his recalled memories were that of the Amsterdam Duck Store. He recalled virtually nothing else of his time in the dam. He remembered spotting the duck on the shelf loaded with an assortment of other ducks. It had been wedged between a native American Indian and a hipster duck. After showing Joost the Elvis duck, he'd been in complete hysterics and pictured himself telling the Dutchman about how he needed to purchase 'Craig' and keep it on his person as a reminder of what happened. So did he blab to Joost about the events back home? He couldn't remember. If so, then Joost had said nothing to confirm this. Also, should he be concerned that part of his brain, albeit a highly intoxicated brain, found hilarity in this situation? Like it was all some kind of joke to him. This thought disturbed him. *A lot*. He gazed at the duck again and wondered what Duncan would say. He guessed his friend would find no humour in the situation and give him a stern telling off.

23

Kent, 24 November 2018

Things were changing at the house in recent days. The months of mourning were past, and the place was no longer peaceful. Jack and Maria seemed to have pretty much moved out of the house and spent most of their time in Whitstable, although the pair still made the occasional appearance to check up on everything and stayed for the odd day. Barry had met some middle-aged skank from Dorset on a dodgy dating app, and spent most weekends away on romantic trips to Bridport. No one had yet seen a photo of the mysterious woman, so everyone had concluded she was a total old dog. Or at least, she and Nino had assumed that.

Johnny had spent most of his time out in The Den, drinking alone and listening to music. Some days he didn't even leave, and Elena could hear the Chilli Peppers and Foo Fighters blaring out and see Johnny slouched at the bar area that he and Craig built from repurposed building pallets last year. Other days she'd spotted Johnny out in the back paddock working the battered punch-bag that hung from the small dead tree. One day last week, he'd been hitting that bag for nearly three hours with very few breaks.

Today, Warren Green and Fraser Moore were here. Which meant

trouble. They'd turned up with Barry a few hours ago and they were having a boys meeting in The Den.

Warren, who Elena had nicknamed Spooks, though never to his face, was tall, with dark, lank hair and pallid skin. He had big, bug eyes and a slit-like mouth. His tiny, almost non-existent nose, at a quick glance, appeared like two tiny black holes where his nostrils should be. Elena couldn't believe what a knockout his girlfriend was when she'd once seen her here. How any lass could date somebody with such a disturbing mug seemed impossible to comprehend. They say love is blind and all that, and in Warren's case, she'd say his bird must be as blind as a senile wombat.

Fraser Moore, she sort of knew through her brother Brennan, who once worked with him on the marquees, back when they'd been in their late teens. He'd also helped the O'Carrolls in the past with the odd job. Most people mistook Fraser for a fresh-faced lad in his early twenties, despite him being close to thirty-five. The Scotsman was a major heavy metal fan. He wore a Black Sabbath T-shirt that looked about three decades old, worn black jeans, with a baggy black hoody tied about his waist. Fraser was a bit of a fruitcake who carried a fascination for all things sharp and dangerous. He'd done time for possession of a dangerous weapon and almost got a serious sentence for GBH with intent, but got acquitted on a technicality. Brennan once told her that years back, Fraser tried to remove one of his rivals in Glasgow by tossing a hand-grenade through his opponent's lounge window, which nearly killed several people in the explosion. It turned out he'd been furnished with the incorrect address and targeted the wrong house. She didn't doubt the story. Fraser was crazy. Now he was here. It meant serious trouble was brewing.

Johnny tossed Nino a set of car keys. 'Go with them.'
'Where?' asked Nino.
'There are overdue collections that need picking up,' said Johnny.
'Why do they need me to go?'
Johnny glanced to the other side of the courtyard, where Warren and Fraser chatted to Barry. Nino got the feeling that Johnny wasn't keen on the pair, by the way he kept eyeing them disapprovingly.

'You know all Craig's old customers, what they look like, and where all the addresses are. Plus, Warren's on a driving ban,' said Johnny. 'Unless you'd prefer to do the collections solo?'

Nino didn't. But the thought of doing the rounds with a couple of psychotic weirdos didn't excite him either. He assumed business must be bad if they'd called in these nasty weasels to help straighten things out, but guessed this was Barry's doing. Most sane people would be quick to clear their debt, with those two nutters turning up demanding payment.

Things had collapsed since his brother's death. Craig was pivotal to the family's illegitimate business, and without him, things were a mess. Barry and Johnny's contribution to the operation had been key, but minimal. They'd use their source to procure a regular and substantial amount of cocaine, amongst other stuff, and then Craig would step on the drugs, distribute to his network of dealers and contend with sales, arrears and the vetting of any potential punters. Craig was always very thorough and diligent when it came to selling to new buyers, and if they didn't come via a trusted recommendation, he'd not go near them. He'd run his side of the business well, and his reputation meant very few buyers would dare have him over. His network of people included students who sold to fellow pupils, wide-boy criminals who dished out gear on their own patches, and even single mums that sold to other parents on the school run. Other buyers that purchased for their personal use would WhatsApp Craig and have their goods delivered to a place of their choosing as easy as ordering a Chinese takeaway. But all that had changed now. Buyers had gone elsewhere for their gear, dealers owed money and his older brothers had done nothing for many months to take control of the sinking business.

Fraser and Warren approached and gazed at Nino, as if sizing him up.

Then Barry marched over and flashed Nino a snake-like grin. 'Don't crash my motor, Nino!'

Then Nino remembered Maria's words. *Big shoes to fill...* He wanted to scream. Then he saw Fraser slipping on his hoody and spotted the glint of a blade under the belt of his jeans.

· · ·

So far, the money collections had been easy. They'd not located every customer but the ones they'd found, paid with little hesitation. Nino gazed out of the window at The Meads estate. The local paper referred to this area, near Margate, as *The Wild West* and with good reason. The place carried a bad reputation. There were frequent robberies, arson attacks and even the odd stabbing. After dark, the streets were like racetracks, with hot-headed loons speeding about in their jazzed up shit heaps or stolen motorbikes, with little regard to anyone else using the roads or pathways. Parts of the estate were practically lawless.

Nino drove past two abandoned sofas occupied by stony faced youths who scowled at them. Nino let out a heavy sigh. *Screw living here*, he thought. He felt bad for the law-abiding residents. It must be hell for them to live in such a disruptive area. It was a teenage delinquent's dream come true. Come to think of it, Craig had liked it here and had spent several weekends staying in the area and hanging out with the likes of Davey Keane, whom his companions were about to call upon. His brother had been the one who'd introduced the impressionable Keane into the enthralling world of cocaine dealing.

Nino pulled the motor into a small carpark strewn with litter and approached the building the locals had dubbed as *The Fortress*. An imposing high-rise block of flats surrounded by a tall black metal fence. Nino eyed the looming structure and felt a lump in his throat. He'd be staying with the car, that was for certain.

'What floor?' asked Warren.

'Sixty-one. Second from the top,' confirmed Fraser, peering out of the window to get a better look.

'And if he isn't home?' asked Warren.

Fraser shrugged. 'We come back doon here and wait, I guess. Nino can identify the lad. Right, Nino?'

Nino nodded.

Warren opened the door. 'We best take the stairs. I'm not using the lift in there.'

'Aye, too right,' said Fraser.

They all got out of the vehicle. Warren gazed up at the tall, dreary building. 'I used to holiday near here as a kid. Don't remember ever coming to this part, though.'

'I cannae see why not. It's a lovely picnic spot,' said Fraser drily, gesturing to a small grass area littered with an assortment of beer cans, nappies and even a discarded trainer.

Nino felt on edge. But he wouldn't have said he was scared. Most of the so-called hard nuts on the estate would be no match for this pair of headcases. The gangs around here, though intimidating, were made up of wide-boys, chavs, and wayward kids trying to make a name for themselves. They were desperate to be deemed as tough criminals and strutted around thinking they were tough, though if faced with real danger, they'd most likely crap themselves in an instant. *Or so he hoped.*

Nino was forced into this grim world because of his family, but what was their excuse? Money? Admiration? Escapism? Why not set a goal on a legitimate enterprise that wasn't surrounded by all the dangers and risks that this unscrupulous business held? Why not aspire to be a top athlete or seek a noble profession like a paramedic or fire fighter? God knows they needed plenty of firemen around here, judging by the several blackened car carcasses they'd passed on the way into the estate's centre. Nino couldn't comprehend why so many of these youngsters sought a life of crime and idolised the likes of his brothers. Although, if rumours were to be believed, the Bartell name had begun to diminish. Their dangerous reputation was dwindling, brought on by the demise of Craig. The one who many said was the Bartell who should be feared the most. The unpredictable one who had climbed his way up the criminal ladder because of his penchant for extreme violence and appetite for dangerous confrontations. Those who concluded Craig had been the brother to fear were foolish and misinformed. His older brothers' barks were quieter than that of his late brother's; but their bites were fiercer and far more dreadful. And their memories were long. They never forgot, and they rarely forgave. But unlike Craig, they picked their battles carefully, striking when they knew it was an apt time to do so. Not to say they didn't make foolish and rash decisions, especially whilst under influence. Both could be quick to snap and act senseless whilst intoxicated. He should know, he'd witnessed it first hand.

'Here we go, the wee cockroaches are emerging from their shite holes,' said Fraser, gesturing at three skinny youths who were watching them warily from the opposite side of the road. The youths whipped out phones and started texting. The tallest of the trio, a black youth with a harelip and an afro that resembled a mushroom, pressed his mobile to his ear.

Two mopeds came into view. They drew up in front of a neglected bus shelter. The riders wore no helmets and watched the trio with undisguised hostility. The lad with the afro finished up on the phone and jogged up the street to the moped riders. They spoke animatedly as they jabbed fingers their way.

Fraser stepped into the road and took several quick paces towards the mopeds. The afro lad started swaggering towards him, but lost his confidence and bravado as Fraser lifted his hoody to give him and the other spectators a good view of the large machete handle protruding from his jeans. He removed a few inches of the gleaming blade from its sheath and eyed the cocky youths, daring them to approach with a baleful sneer.

The kid with the afro jumped onto the back of the nearest moped and the rider tore away, the tiny bike engine screeching jarringly as it zipped into the distance. The other rider moved past Fraser, revving the bike and smirking at him as though he knew a secret only he was privy to. Fraser flashed him a predatory grin, walked to him with purpose, and he too raced away.

Whilst Fraser had been attempting to intimidate the local young thugs, Warren had been pressing every button available on the intercom system, but had yet to get any response, which was infuriating him.

Fraser, walking over and hiding his weapon once more, came back to where Nino stood guard in the carpark. Nino's eyes flickered around the surrounding streets and buildings for any more signs of trouble. He had a bad feeling it was all about to kick off.

Warren stabbed at the buttons in frustration. 'Keane isn't answering. Nobody is answering!'

'Try the tradesmen's button?' shouted Fraser.

Warren appeared to be sizing up the door to see if he could boot it down. Nino didn't think that would be likely.

'There isn't one,' said Warren, hammering his fist against the solid door. 'Someone open up!' He booted it hard.

Nino, about to suggest they try checking for a rear door, flinched as a loud thud sounded off next to him. Fraser, with a more perplexed than concerned expression, gazed at the hand-sized dent that now sat centre of the Land Rover's rear passenger door. Nino scanned the building for the culprit responsible. Then the driver's side window exploded and Nino instinctively ducked down.

Warren raced over, his mouth dropping open in horror at the damage caused to Barry's motor.

Fraser yelled, 'Ooh, fuuuuck me! Doss bastards!'

There were bellows and insults coming from the street now. Lots more youths had joined the group, and the now sizeable posse was getting pumped and rowdy. Some teenage girls had joined the gang, and they shouted various unladylike comments. But the angle at which the Range Rover was parked meant there was no way the projectiles had come from the street. Nino was sure they'd come from the tower block. Then Nino spotted a figure up in a window several stories up. He was holding something… no, he was aiming something – a catapult. 'Heads up!' bellowed Nino.

But it was too late. A gut wrenching WHAMP followed and Warren went down in a crumpled heap.

The gang hurled bottles and bricks from the street.

They smashed and thudded all around them.

The ever-growing crowd roared and screamed.

Warren cried out as he clasped both hands over his face.

Fraser tugged Warren up from the ground and shouted, 'Radge bastards! Go, Nino.'

In the horrendous moments that followed the assault on Warren, Nino's mind drifted. He tried hard not to focus on the bloody scene in the rear of the vehicle. He tried to focus on something else – anything else. His mind cast him back to another traumatic day. As he raced the Range Rover from the tower block, darting down a narrow street to get away from the uproar of the rowdy youths hurling more bottles and bricks, he started remembering that day those strangers came that grim night.

The Range Rover whacked off the wing-mirrors of several parked cars, then almost collided with a moped in his efforts to flee; the biker just about mounted a pavement to avoid the impact.

24

Kent, 10 November 2002

Charles crouched, let out a low, hissing growl and slunk back from the intruder. Rita and Reg whimpered. Nino gripped the knife's handle as he held the blade out as far as his reach would allow.

The figure stepped closer, and relief washed over Nino once he established Craig had returned. His relief was short-lived when he acknowledged his brother's enraged expression. 'You've pissed yourself,' growled Craig.

Nino dropped the knife and inspected his pyjamas. Through the terror, he'd not even noticed the urine seeping into the material, and now he was fully aware how soaked his bottoms were.

The dogs, sensing the anger emanating from Craig, didn't let their guard down, and followed Craig with wary eyes.

'What's happening?' asked Nino. 'Who are those men? What do they want?'

Craig stepped closer to Nino and his wild eyes seemed to blaze with fury. 'You're needed inside. Kitchen. Go. Now!' he ordered.

Nino, about to protest, thought better about objecting, and did as he was told. He trotted out into the chilly night and, feeling ashamed and conscious of the dampness spread over his crotch area, scurried across the courtyard.

As Nino reached the back door to the kitchen, he hesitated as he held the handle. He entered, heard a commotion inside, and instantly regretted stepping into it.

Nino knew this day would be etched in his mind forever. He gawped in pure grim fascination, disgust, and utter wonder.

Jack sat in a chair, trembling all over. He gripped a bottle of whiskey in both hands. There was so much blood. His shirt was drenched in it. The floor, fridge and kitchen counter were also smeared with the stuff. Jack, spotting Nino frozen in the doorway, turned to him. The horrific facial injuries became all too visible then, and Nino gasped. He'd never witnessed anything so gruesome, and his blood turned to ice. He could now see the reason for the carnage. The right side of Jack's face was swollen, the eye closed and the surrounding area bulging out the size of a big apple. But the left side looked grotesque and disgusting. A part of Jack's cheek hung limply from his face. The gouge was so deep, Nino could see traces of shiny bone under the pulpy mess of flesh, as well as teeth and gums.

Jack mumbled, 'Nino… no.'

Maria, needle and thread at the ready, shot her gaze to Nino. 'Out. Get him out.'

Johnny and Barry, now also spotting him, charged over and shooed him backwards. Nino obeyed with little hesitation and started edging away from the horrors. But not before glimpsing Craig's face. His summoning was now clear, because his expression told all – Craig had wanted Nino to witness the aftermath of the night's events, because a gloating grin had spread across his face as he watched Nino back away and crash clumsily into cupboards as he tried to exit.

25

Kent, 25 November 2018

Barry sat down with his breakfast, lifted his backside and let out a trumpet sounding fart. Johnny noted Barry had his usual today: half a box of Frosties served in a cake mixing bowl and filled to the brim with full fat milk. The slurping and irritating chewing followed as his brother devoured his food with as much grace as a starving camel.

'I wouldn't mind a decent omelette. I'll make us one with the two cheeses, Jon. You get the eggs in yet?'

Johnny sipped his tea. 'Nope.'

'Any news on the collections?' asked Barry with a hopeful gaze as he drove his big spoon in for another helping of the soggy flakes.

Johnny was glad he'd already eaten, as watching his brother slurp his food whilst slouched at the table in a white vest and tight boxer shorts was enough to put a scrawny mongrel dog off their grub. For someone with OCD like Barry seemed to have, he ate like a right messy sod.

'You haven't spoken to Nino?' asked Johnny.

Barry scratched the ridge of his nose and belched. 'No, why? Problem?'

Johnny finished his tea and went up to the kitchen counter for a refill. 'Nino was at the hospital all night. Warren got hurt. A ball-bearing fired from a catapult. The bloody thing was the size of a walnut.'

'What? Where?'

'In Margate. Davey Keane's tower block.'

'Fucking hell… I mean, where did it hit him?'

Johnny took his tea back over to the table and sat down. 'In the gob. So hard, his entire lower jaw was hanging off his mug. Fraser had to hold it in place while Nino drove them to A and E. The back of your motor resembles a murder scene.'

Barry tossed down his spoon. 'Great. And Nino didn't bother to clean up the mess?'

'Nope,' said Johnny, thinking that he'd neglect to tell his brother about the many melon sized dents in his motor. He'd let him establish that for himself.

26

Kent, 26 November 2018

Amy tucked Francesca up under a cotton blanket imprinted with teddy bears and love hearts. It had been a present from her lovely nanna Lizzie. Amy couldn't resist touching the sleeping baby's tiny button nose. She couldn't believe how well she'd taken to motherhood, and despite her sister and some of her more outgoing friends, blathering on about how she was way too young to be settling down, she felt more content now than ever before.

Amy went to push the pram down the driveway when she noticed a big chap wearing a baseball cap, jeans, and a navy peacoat heading down the driveway. At first, she assumed the guy had a delivery for her, but as he peered up and caught her eye, she stopped dead and glared at the visitor in disbelief.

They spoke for a few moments about how the baby was doing. About how living here was so convenient, because her parents lived a few streets away and that's where she was heading. Then he spoke about his trip to his brother's place and how Karl wanted to start a new career blogging, or some crapping nonsense. Amy kept a lid on her anger for a short while as the awkward small talk flowed, but the big stupid lump that stood before her would not get off too easily.

'So, let me get this right. Karl tells me he's renting a flat and wants me to move in with him, and the very next day, he packs up and joins you on a trip overseas. A trip you never even mentioned to me. Just like that? Not only that, all I receive is a quick text telling me he'd made a mistake and needed time away because he wanted different things.'

'Amy, you don't know Karl like I do. He can be a complicated guy. Things were moving too fast. He panicked.'

'Karl is many things, but complicated is not one of them, Duncan.'

'He's an idiot. He treated you badly. I'm not defending his behaviour. That's not what I'm doing here. But... if he'd have known about this little one, he would have acted differently. I promise you that.'

'Yet, it's you here, and not him,' she said tartly.

'He doesn't know.'

'Well, if he hadn't of vanished before I had the chance to tell him, or if he'd bothered to answer my calls, then he would know!'

Amy cast her mind back to the day Karl had surprised her about the flat. She'd been itching to tell him about the baby at that moment. It seemed like the exact right time. But she'd only been five weeks into the pregnancy. She still had lots to think about and decided it would have been too early to discuss everything. Her auntie miscarried twice whilst she was in her mid-twenties, and that had been at the forefront of her mind.

'Amy, please. You will tell him, won't you?'

Amy gazed at Duncan for a few moments before she said, 'I know... I know why you both left!'

Amy saw Duncan's face twitch as he tried to appear unfazed, but failed miserably.

'Come again?' he said.

'Karl always used that carpark. So he didn't have to pay.'

'You've lost me,' said Duncan, a confused frown creasing his forehead. 'Carpark? What carpark?'

'Anderson and Buckley solicitors.'

Duncan made a face like a surprised fish sucking air, then smiled as if baffled. 'Solicitors?'

'Duncan, I saw the guy in the paper. Craig Bartell. The loudmouth from the pub. They were appealing for witnesses. The lad died under very suspicious circumstances.'

She'd seen Duncan's eyes widened at the mention of that name. His nostrils flared, and he chuckled nervously. It was so obvious he was bullshitting her.

'Who?' asked Duncan.

'Please give me some credit.'

Oscar sat in his office and watched his phone. As far as Amy was aware, the camera he'd installed was picture only, and you received no audio through it. But a direct live stream could run via the app on his phone. You could hear everything. His first thought was that Karl Rogers' mate had turned up to pave the way for his friend to reconnect with Amy. His blood was boiling at this idea. That was unthinkable. That smart arse Karl worming his way back into Amy's life felt like a knife in his guts. He wouldn't be able to bear it if Karl wanted to be a part of Francesca's life. It would tear him to pieces.

But now the conversation had taken a very unexpected and intriguing turn. Oscar raced to his office PC and fired up the live camera feed on the bigger screen.

'I don't have a clue what you're on about, Amy,' said Duncan.

'I can see it on your face. There's no hiding it,' said Amy.

'What do you think we did, Amy?'

Amy lowered her voice. 'I'm guessing that Craig Bartell came across you in that carpark and probably attacked you. And things got out of hand. That is my theory.'

Oscar turned up the volume, listening intently.

'And I think you, or Karl, killed him… by accident,' she continued.

'What? That's insane,' spluttered this Duncan fella.

'I think that you both panicked, fled to your brother's and waited to see if you'd been implicated.' Amy was whispering now, but Oscar could just about hear her.

Duncan flapped his arms. 'Come on, this is crazy talk, Amy.'

'What hurts the most is that you both decided you couldn't trust me enough to tell me the truth. Karl said I was his world. Then he just shut me out. Any idea how that felt? He broke my heart, Duncan.'

Oscar, hearing Amy say this, winced as though someone had slapped him.

Amy, as though suddenly remembering where she was, glanced back at the house and eyed the camera. Then she spun back to Duncan. 'I'm late,' she said, then headed down the driveway and out onto the path – out of earshot.

Oscar turned off the camera feed and googled the name Craig Bartell on his phone.

'What about Karl?' asked Duncan.

'My number hasn't changed. If he wants to see his daughter, it's down to him to contact me. But tell him not to expect a warm welcome, because personally I'd rather never clap eyes on the selfish idiot ever again,' said Amy.

'He lost his phone. I can give you his new number.'

Amy stifled a yawn. 'Let me get my head around this. I'll call you in a few days. We will discuss *all* of this. And I want the truth! OK?'

Duncan swallowed hard and nodded meekly. 'You can reach me on my old number. It's back on.'

Amy gave him a hard nod, gripped the pram, and sauntered off up the street.

She got far from the house and Duncan, before stopping and letting the tears flow.

Duncan scurried away from Amy fast. When he got to a busy section of road, he trembled. Queues of cars urgently duelled for poll position, whilst hordes of rowdy school children congregated, and what seemed like Canterbury's entire work community were mixed in a busy, nerve-shredding Monday morning melting pot.

A group of tall schoolboys were using a lump of polystyrene as a football.

Another schoolboy held a pretend cigarette to his lips whilst puffing out cold air. His shorter friend chuckled like this gesture had been extremely creative and hilarious.

A bald, cherry-faced van driver beeped his horn and waved his fist at a cyclist, who'd dared to zip across the zebra crossing after the lights had changed.

A suited man in an Audi leered openly at a group of schoolgirls in tight skirts and black tights.

A chunky lady in an SUV screamed like a deranged beast at three rowdy toddlers who were leaping about in the back.

Duncan became hot and sweaty. He turned and fast-walked back the way he came, knowing it would take twice as long to divert from this course. It would be worth it. He recounted Amy's words and baulked. The thought of someone else knowing their secret filled him with utter dread.

Oscar was perched at his desk for a while before he plucked up the courage to make the telephone call. He'd been thinking about Amy's conversation all day and decided he needed to take drastic action. He didn't have any other choice.

The other offices sat deserted now and the warehouse staff had left for the day, so he was alone in the huge building. It was a little dramatic, but earlier he'd purchased a burner phone to make his intended calls and he'd set it all up earlier, putting Rafiq's number into the contacts.

The phone was answered after two rings.

'Hey, Raf, how you doing?' said Oscar in the breeziest tone he could muster.

'I'm sorry. Who is this?'

'Oscar.'

'Who?'

'Oscar Maplethorpe. Your old boss, Raf.'

'Right, yeah. Course. Didn't recognise this number. What's up?'

'Look, I need you to hook me up.'

'Thorpy, mate, all that was years ago. I can't get that stuff anymore. Sorry.'

'No, no, no. You misunderstand me. I need to make contact with somebody. I'm thinking you can help with that.'

'Um, who?' said Rafiq, sounding puzzled.

'I need to speak with one of Craig Bartell's relatives. Ring any bells?'

'I don't know them. So, not really sure I can help. Sorry, bro.'

'Raf, come on, pal. You must know somebody who knows them. A friend of a friend. I'd appreciate it.'

'I don't mix with those types of people anymore,' said Rafiq, his voice sounding pathetic and whiney.

'Just ask some of your old buddies. You must be able to pull in a favour. It's very important. I need a direct line for one of them. Ideally, one of his brothers. It would mean a lot, Raf.'

'Fine. I'll ask about. But I'm not promising anything. And be careful. This is a different world, Thorpy. I won't even ask for your reason. Because that's none of my business.'

Oscar put his feet up on the desk and stared at the photo on his desk. Amy and Francesca – his entire world now. 'You're a star, Raf. Quick as you can, yeah.'

Duncan had sat in silence for a long time as he contemplated his talk with Amy that morning. It was now late. He'd done nothing all day except compile several messages for Karl, but deleted every one before pressing send. How could he tell him all this via a quick text? He considered phoning him, but decided against that, too. He'd just have to wait. Wait for Amy to contact him. How stupid had they been to not even consider Amy wouldn't connect the dots? It hadn't even crossed their minds. The only thing stopping him from going insane with panic was the fact that, in all this time, she'd not acted on her hunch. Why would she decide to drop them in it now? If she'd intended to tell on them, wouldn't she have done that in the very beginning? But should he come clean and tell her everything? He considered that this idea would be reckless... yet it also seemed the only option available, because she knew everything and holding back might be an even more dangerous move.

Duncan lay down on his bed and closed his eyes, wishing he could just sleep for a while to escape the incessant, spinning thoughts constantly crushing his mind and driving him nuts. He wondered if Karl was spending all his time worrying too, though guessed he wasn't. This thought annoyed the hell out of him, and he knew Karl would probably be swinging his pants and having a wonderful time.

27

Kent, 27 November 2018

Ravi watched the YouTube video for the third time before he'd been confident enough to set up the correct browser on his old laptop that enabled him to access the Dark-web. All very easy. He found a website called Euro Guns, Ammo & More. The store that claimed to sell all the firepower you'd ever need and apparently had thousands of fabulous reviews from happy, presumably now gun toting, buyers. He'd intended to buy a gun and scrolled through the listings, but opted for an EPS high powered stun gun capable of delivering a whopping 500,000 volts and used by security agencies and military personnel. It cost ninety euros, and he paid in bitcoins, using his Coinbase account where he had a decent amount of Crypto Currency already stored up. They promised shipping within ten working days, but he changed the shipping to the global priority option that guaranteed delivery within two working days. Ravi was sceptical about ever receiving his item, but he was desperate enough to risk losing the money in this case. He scanned the guns again, and though very tempted, he couldn't quite bring himself to add one to his basket. He viewed the Walther P22 pistol, thinking that the Walther was Bond's weapon of choice and would be his choice, too. This option was based solely on the fact 007 favoured it, so considered it must be a dependable piece. Because, in reality, Ravi didn't know the first thing about guns. He also viewed a Glock-19 semi-automatic and a Beretta M9, but checked out with only the stun gun in his basket. He didn't think he could take the worry of having a firearm delivered to the house by bloody UPS or somebody. That just didn't seem right. Plus, he'd be too scared to fire the damn thing in case it was faulty, backfired and blew half of his arm off. The stun gun would have to do. It would make him feel a tad safer, anyway.

28

Nino turned up the electric heater to full power and sighed. It would be December in a few days. The temperature seemed to drop daily. Unlike Elena, who thrived in the winter, Nino hated the freezing cold weather. She'd happily sit outside drinking wine in front of a roaring fire-pit during the coldest of nights. Nino, on the other hand, would rather hibernate until late March. Nino glanced over to Elena, asleep on a beanbag with a Lisa Jewell novel on her chest. He sat down on the beanbag next to her and watched her as she slept. He couldn't imagine life without her. She'd been the one thing that had always lit up his dark existence.

He recalled the day Elena came into his life. And it had been thanks to Craig. The one good thing he'd ever done for Nino, although that certainly hadn't been on purpose.

Nino leaned over and kissed her softly on the cheek as he visualised the first time he saw her perfect smile.

29

Kent, 1 July 2007

'Where are we going?' asked Nino.

'Keep up. This way,' replied Craig, skidding on his backside as he made his way down towards a slow running stream.

'I don't want to get lost,' said Nino as he scanned the unfamiliar surroundings. Craig had led them both north of their house, out of the woodland they referred to as Craven's Cross Forest, across several fields in which they had to fight through towering crops, and then into a densely wooded area sectioned off with a shoddily erected mesh fence. Here, several signs hung. One, painted in a red scrawl, that stated – *shooting in progress* and another was marked – *stay out!*

'We've come too far out, Craig,' moaned Nino.

Craig's response was an annoyed tut, followed by an angry wave of his hand, beckoning him to follow his path towards the stream. Before Nino could protest further, Craig scrambled onto a fallen tree trunk and traversed the water. Nino, sweating profusely from the beaming summer sun, became tempted to skip the climb and wade through the appealing looking water. His feet were on fire, and the idea of slipping out of his trainers and socks and cooling off in the flowing stream became a hard to resist temptation. Then he considered Craig might not wait for him and he'd be lost out here. Nino wasn't certain he knew the way back now, and it wouldn't be the first time his brother had ditched him in the wilderness. With this thought forefront of his mind, he followed Craig's path down and clambered across the makeshift bridge to find him. He found Craig balanced upon a log, waving him on.

They continued into the woods. This place was unlit and cool. Although it seemed a tad bleak and creepy, he was glad to be out of the blasting heat. The insects were buzzing around like crazy here, and he batted the annoying bugs away as the pair plodded along in silence.

They soon found their way onto a snaking track and the area opened up to a vast space where most of the trees had been downed, and those few left standing were far taller and spindlier than most of the trees they'd seen. There were huge logs piled high and wood dust everywhere. There was a heavy scent of wood-chippings and burning bracken.

Craig followed a set of deep tyre tracks that wound down towards a rise of twisting smoke.

'I've got something digging in my foot,' said Nino, tugging off his dusty trainer and emptying the wood shavings and stones that had found their way into the shoe. 'Wait up! Craig!' called Nino.

But his brother, ignoring his yells, strutted off out of view.

Nino, slipping on the trainer and almost falling over in the process, jogged after Craig, grumbling as he went.

When Nino located Craig in a clearing at the bottom of the hill, he wished to God he'd turned back and tried to find his own way home. His brother stood amongst a large crowd of unfamiliar kids, and every set of eyes turned to him, cold and hostile. The group appeared to have been busy constructing a hut that they'd erected with pallets, logs and Perspex sheeting as improvised windows. The roof, made from jagged corrugated metal, balanced precariously on top of the structure. But now work had been interrupted, and the unsmiling, intimidating youths eyed the new arrivals. One lad, a bulky boy, bare chested with a shaven head, held a saw over a half-cut lump of timber. He curled his lip into a snarl, his red face shiny with sweat. Another lad, gangly with greasy, shoulder-length hair and goofy front teeth, held a mallet. He seemed more interested in the new arrivals than annoyed, as he cocked his head to one side and eyed Nino with a curious smirk.

'You two shouldn't be here!' A girl stepped forward. She was short, round, with thick legs, and arms that almost appeared way too short for the rest of her rotund body. 'You shouldn't be here!' the girl repeated, this time with a tone that held a clear edge of warning.

Craig smiled. 'Come on, Sally. Don't be like that. Our dads go way back.'

'You're trespassing,' Sally hissed. Then, as if just noticing Nino, shoved Craig aside and waddled over to him. 'Who is this?' she asked tersely. She spoke in a harsh Northern accent, but Nino didn't have a clue where it was from.

Craig smiled again. 'My brother. Nino.'

Sally looked Nino up and down, scowling. 'Well, that's a weird name if ever I've heard one. He doesn't look like a Bartell to me. He looks foreign. Greek or Italian.'

'Yeah, he's illegitimate. My old man fucked some Maltese tart. She croaked it, so we got lumbered with the smelly little half-breed. Just one of those things,' said Craig matter-of-factly.

Some of the group chuckled at this. The lad with the saw let out a hoarse, grating laugh.

Nino's throat felt dry. He desperately needed a drink of water. Sally inched closer to him. Nino could smell cheese and onion crisps on the sour-faced girl. She stood a foot shorter than he did. She gazed up at him. 'So, you got a girlfriend, Ninooo?' she asked, with her nose crinkled.

'No!' blurted Nino, and straight away regretted his answer as he spotted Sally's eyes widening. So he quickly said, 'I mean, yeah. I do.'

Craig coughed, 'Bullshit,' under his breath and Sally's eyes hardened again. The girl seemed to have no neck, and her facial features appeared to be squeezed into the centre of her pumpkin sized head, leaving a massive forehead, which was worsened by her dark brown hair being tied back in a scraggly ponytail. Her cheeks were blotchy and bloated, as though she had a gob full of food stored in them, like some giant hamster. Sally pulled a face like Nino had just taken a crap on her shoes. 'You Bartell boys best do one! This is O'Carroll territory.'

She licked her front teeth, which were stained, and one front tooth was chipped.

The lad with the saw stood up tall and said, 'You Bartell boys are nothing but a bunch of inbred, plastic gangsters.'

'Uh-oh,' said Craig, putting his hands on his hips and dramatically puffing out his cheeks. 'Nino won't take that type of shit, Brennan. He said to me on the way in, "those O'Carrolls are a bunch of pig rapists, and I won't put up with their nonsense. I'll slap the granny right out of them".'

Brennan glowered at Craig. 'What?'

Craig shrugged and let out a nonchalant sigh. 'His words, not mine. Not sure you want to start any beef with him. He's a scrapper, Bren. He'll tear you a new one, mate. I'd wager a score on that all day long.'

Nino could only watch, flummoxed, as the bulking Brennan slammed the saw into the timber with such force, the entire blade disappeared deep into the wood. He tensed, upper arm muscles bulging. 'Is that right?' he said.

Nino swallowed, his voice lost in his dry, rasping throat. He noticed Craig was loving this. He didn't appear fazed or scared in the slightest. Craig was revelling in their plight. Or maybe *his* plight.

Brennan swaggered towards Nino, big shoulders swaying. Sally stepped aside, swishing her hair from side to side and smirking.

Brennan prodded Nino hard in the chest. 'Are there any rules for this straightener?'

Before Nino could respond and try to talk his way out of the bout, Craig said, 'Nino fights like a dirty little rat, Bren. If you want rules, pal, then you've picked the wrong opponent. He'll gouge your flipping eyeballs right out.'

'Rip his ears off, Bren,' squealed Sally.

Before Nino had a clue how to react, the rest of the group circled and began hooting and baying for blood to be spilt. Mere seconds before the first hefty punch connected with his nose, Nino spotted a face in the crowd that commanded his attention. A face that, amongst the angry, yelling youths, appeared out of place; friendly even. A black-haired girl that fixed him with a look that, if it he wasn't mistaken, said – *You can beat him. I want you to beat him.*

As he rolled with the first punch, Nino decided he'd fight back with everything he had.

Nino tried to sit up, winced in agony from pain that seemed to attack every inch of his body. It turned out that everything he had was, in fact, not that much at all. 'Where is Craig?'

The black-haired girl smiled thinly. 'Oh, he's still here. At this moment, he's getting sloshed with my brother and cousins over in one of the woodsheds.' She had a Northern accent too, though hers was much softer than Sally's aggravating tone.

'He's drinking with them?' asked Nino, flabbergasted.

The girl dabbed his nose with a tissue. 'Yeah, they sound like they're all having a fabulous time.'

Nino shuddered in pain. 'What happened?'

'My brother knocked you unconscious.'

Nino touched his lip and pulled away when he felt the huge swollen and mashed mess where his lower lip should have been. 'He is *your* brother? I think I need to go to the hospital.'

The girl flashed him a sympathetic smile. 'We're miles away from anywhere. I need to check your wrist. It looks swollen. Don't think it's broken, though.'

Nino tried to move and groaned in agony. 'I'm not so sure about that.' A sharp pain seared up his wrist and he moaned.

The girl scanned the area. There seemed to be a faraway look about her. A hidden sadness, Nino considered. She was slim, dressed in ripped khaki shorts and a dark grey baggy T-shirt. Her black hair, long and springy, covered half of her face. Her skin was dark, not as dark as his, but she carried the well tanned tone of someone who spent many hours of their day outside. Nino gazed at her, absorbed in the moment, despite the awful pain he was in. Then he started remembering the moments before the brawl kicked off. 'I never said the O'Carrolls were a bunch of pig... you know... I don't know why Craig said those horrible things.'

The girl shook her head. 'Because he's a nasty, spiteful boy. I don't envy you for having him as a brother. And that's saying something, because my lot are a bunch of no good turds.'

Nino managed a grin at this, but even that hurt his stomach and ribs. 'What's your name?'

'Elena. Elena O'Carroll,' she said. 'Com'n let's find the others. I sent a couple of the group to find some medical stuff.'

'No. I can't face them. I want to go. Awww, my arm hurts like hell.'

'Brennan told me to bring you over once you woke up. The fight is over. There'll be no grudge. Actually, he was pretty impressed. Brennan is a total wild animal, and you downed him.'

Nino vaguely recalled the fight spilling over into the woods behind the hut. They wrestled and fell onto the dusty ground. When they found their feet, he somehow managed to shove Brennan down into a ditch and the boy rolled aimlessly amongst a thicket laden with coarse brambles and giant stingers. He'd roared and screamed in pain as he charged back up the ditch, bare torso scratched and oozing bright blood. Nino sort of remembered the terror in that moment, though it had been short lived once the furious lad had reached the top and pummelled the hell out of him.

'Here he comes, *Hong Kong Phooey*,' said Craig, perched on a stack of pallets with Brennan and the boy with the long hair, who was swigging from an unlabelled bottle of brown liquid. This boy eyed Nino with a big, gleeful grin.

Brennan stood, torso blooded and slashed. He approached Nino and said, 'You elbowed me in the solar plexus. Barbaric, mush. Took the wind out me, ya little spud.' He chuckled childishly and slung a beefy arm around Nino's shoulder, causing him to recoil.

Nino hadn't been aiming, and if he was honest, didn't have a damn clue what, or where, the solar plexus was. So he shrugged and said, 'Yeah, my signature move.'

The long-haired boy winked at Nino. 'I'm Vince. You alright, mate?'

Brennan snatched the bottle from Vince and passed it to Nino. 'You deserve a drink, boy. Anyone willing to have a square go with me is alright in my books.'

Willing, thought Nino. Not exactly the word he'd have used.

Nino caught Craig's sly expression. He could tell his brother hadn't banked on Brennan's amiable mood towards him. He caught sight of

Brennan's large hands, the knuckles missing patches of skin and incrusted with blood. This made the pain in Nino's face flare up.

'Let me see that,' said Craig, inspecting Nino's swollen arm. 'Looks sore, that,' he said, then squeezed tightly.

'Awww, nooo!' screeched Nino, now feeling sick with pain.

Brennan grabbed Craig's arm and yanked him away.

Craig scowled at Brennan and let go.

'I don't think your brother likes you very much, Nino,' said Brennan, looking at Craig with baleful eyes.

Nino and Craig eyeballed each other.

The feeling is mutual, thought Nino.

Elena approached, carrying a small red medical kit. 'Someone swiped this from inside one of the diggers.'

'Aw, little Nino's got a guardian angel,' said Craig, flashing Elena a nasty smile. 'How sweet.'

30

Kent, 30 November 2018

Johnny walked out of the kitchen and headed across the courtyard in the bitter morning duskiness. He enjoyed being up this early, and the cold didn't bother him. He sipped the hot coffee from his travel mug and scanned the fields, taking in the pleasant autumn morning. A low mist hovered in the paddock and Hetty trotted over to the fence to greet him. He rubbed her snout as she let out a snort, her breath visible in the chilly morning air.

Johnny made his way to the old store shed and fought with the stiff lock to gain entry. He opened up and headed into the cluttered storeroom in the back. First, Johnny grabbed his old quad bike crash helmet, removing the cobwebs stretched across the visor. Then he collected Berty-Bash, Jack's well-used police battering ram.

Happy he had everything he needed, Johnny took the items to his Ford Ranger. He was wearing black jeans and his thick padded leather jacket. He considered going back in the house for his gloves, but decided not to bother in case he woke anyone up. Johnny wanted to get this job done solo and knew Barry would insist on coming. As much as he loved his brother, he could be a massive pain in the arse. With Barry, nothing ever got done without a ridiculous amount of drugs and drink and he didn't want this quick trip to end up being another booze fuelled cockup. The last one had caused enough issues. It was too early for that. He'd not even had any breakfast. Not that the time would make a difference to Barry. Any time of the day was good for a session as far as that bloke was concerned, though Johnny suspected Barry just couldn't function under pressure without intoxicating himself. But he understood that.

Johnny put the helmet on the passenger seat and slid Berty-Bash into the front footwell. He'd heard plenty of stories about that police ram, and if he lost it, Jack would go ballistic.

Many years back, Jack, Marcus Chillcott and Greg O'Carroll worked with a crew of real sinister fuckers who went around Kent, London and Essex undertaking dawn raids on dealers. They'd go dressed in black military wear, with ski masks and resembling a squad of action ready riot police, and they'd batter down the victim's door, screaming, 'Police!' as they charged in with battens and pepper spray. The gang would steal drugs, cash, and anything else they desired from the unfortunate criminal. They rarely met much in the way of resistance and they'd even spoken to concerned and nosy neighbours during the raid, telling them to stay in their houses and that everything was under control. They'd even receive the odd shout from a nosey neighbour saying, 'About time those scumbags were caught!'

Nobody ever buzzed the police. And why would they? They'd turn up in black Beamers with tinted windows and would often put one of those blue magnetic lights on the roofs for added authenticity. They were so brazen it was insane. Key to their success was speed. More often than not, they'd locate the goodies in minutes, but if the occasional hard-man tried to play games, Marcus would employ his time-tested method, involving the victim's fear shrivelled family jewels and a sharp razor blade. They were always in and out within ten minutes. On one occasion, Jack told Johnny they'd burst in on one luckless muppet who'd been trussed up like a giant turkey and was in the process of receiving a brutal early morning spanking from the missus; and yet this guy still had the audacity to lip off and call them dirty pig cunts, amongst other obscenities. They all had a cracking good laugh about that one for weeks. The gang's fearsome reputation grew and not only did half the villains in the South want this lot caught, the police had even setup a serious task force to stop them. They became a legend in criminal circles and we're often referred to simply as *The Men in Black*. Jack never divulged where their information came from, but Johnny suspected they were receiving tip-offs from buyers, other dealers and maybe even bent police officers. Nothing stolen in the area ever got sold off in the South. Instead, they dealt with a Manchurian that took the lot and distributed it to various dealers in Liverpool, Birmingham, and Newcastle. The scam worked well, and the cash made went towards a big future deal. A deal that did not end so well and destroyed the long partnership between Jack and Marcus.

Johnny started the Ranger and sped off. He wanted to get this shit dealt with pronto.

The estate was eerily quiet and the tall tower block seemed depressing in the morning gloom, though Johnny considered there most likely wasn't a time when this place ever would appear charming and inviting. He'd come early, knowing most of the youngsters that were part of Davey's little crew would be tucked up at home with their warm, fluffy pjs and snuggle bears. They'd unlikely be roaming the streets during this hour.

He'd parked away from the block and already slipped on the helmet and taken hold of Berty-Bash as he headed to the square leading to the tower's entrance. He'd taken no chances where the lookout was concerned, as he very much liked his jaw fixed firmly where it was and not hanging down towards his tits. When a shot walloped against the top of the helmet, he felt the impact and heard the plastic crack. The projectile would have knocked him clean out and most likely fractured his bloody skull had he not been wearing it. He gazed up to the window and glimpsed a kid aiming the catapult straight at him before the next shot smashed into the visor, cracked it and messed up his field of vision. This little piss-stain had a quality aim on him, he'd give him that. He also had to admit that despite the precautions he'd taken, he hadn't *actually* expected the look-out to be active at this hour. Fair play to him. This lad was committed to his job. There was some distance to cover before the entrance, and though tempted to run, Johnny continued to walk on in a relaxed manner, trying to ignore the pain in his shoulder from the ball-bearing that bounced off it with a dull thwack. The little turd had changed tactics and was now aiming for unprotected body parts. The thick leather did little to soak up that blow, or the one that followed and struck him on his chest, taking the wind right out of him. But he didn't even flinch. He just kept a steady pace, made it to the door and prepared the ram. Two hefty whacks that sounded deafening in the quiet morning gloom, and the door split open.

Johnny headed up the stairs, taking two steps at a time.

He didn't need force for the next door. A half-naked Davey had already opened it and stood guard with a chrome baseball bat poised and ready to swing at him.

Johnny lifted the broken visor.

'Bloody hell. What's happening, Johnny?' asked Davey, eyes wide with fear.

Johnny leant the ram against the wall and walked into the flat, pushing past the younger man. Davey didn't try to stop him.

'You should have called. I'd have told Mum to make you breakfast,' said Davey.

Johnny could smell burnt toast and fatty bacon. The aroma was not in the least bit inviting. Johnny made his way into the lounge where a kid wearing red pyjamas with a cartoon lion print on them sat tapping away on an iPad. He was probably only four. The lad gave him a sideways scowl, but didn't take his focus from the screen. He wore a pair of chunky ear defenders that looked way too big for him.

Johnny took in the flat and considered it wasn't half bad. A big flatscreen, a decent plump sofa and a nice bit of oak flooring.

'Look, Johnny, I know you think I've been avoiding you… But I've been trying to get my shit together. We had some serious problems with another crew down here from London trying to flood the place with their gear. It's been a nightmare.'

Johnny, ignoring him, picked up a family photo and studied it before gently placing it back down.

'I know I messed up. Please, don't start anything here. My mum… she's not well. And my brother has autism. I didn't think my debt vanished just because… you know, because of Craig. I didn't.'

A woman appeared in the doorway and screeched, 'Do you want beans or not? Davey! Davey!'

The woman's hair was so messy and frizzy it looked like she'd recently stuck a screwdriver into a plug socket and electrocuted herself.

'There is only brown sauce,' she yelled. 'I said red, not brown. Why'd you get brown? Why? Why when I said I hate brown? Davey? Did you hear me?'

'I'll get the red sauce, Mum. Go sit down,' said Davey, physically squirming.

'Oooo no, you've cracked your helmet,' she said to Johnny with genuine concern in her voice.

Johnny smiled. 'Yeah, but it could have been worse, Mrs Keane. Could have been my head.'

'Mum, you need to take your pills,' then Davey looked at his brother and mimicked eating, though he only got a rapid shake of the head in return.

'Johnny, please not here,' said Davey meekly. 'Please, mate.'

Johnny fixed his eyes on the unnerved man.

'I can tell you where Nathaniel is,' exclaimed Davey, looking utterly ashamed of himself the moment the words left his mouth.

'Where?' asked Johnny.

Davey sighed. 'Holed up in an empty flat on the top floor. I put him up there.'

'OK. Get dressed and we'll go and wake him up,' said Johnny.

Davey's shoulders slumped, and he tutted.

'Oh, and Davey... if there are any of your buddies waiting downstairs for me, I won't be pleased. Now, let's go.'

Davey appeared as though he was going to refuse, but after a moment's deliberation he nodded and said, 'There won't be.' Then he scurried off.

The boy gazed at Johnny with big mistrustful eyes, then his eyes once again flicked back to his screen.

31

'What are you doing up so early?' asked Nino.

Elena took a puff of her cigarette and gave him a lazy smile. 'Couldn't sleep.'

Elena was wearing a tight, black V-neck top and frayed jeans shorts. Nino noticed her pert nipples fighting against the material, confirming that she had no bra on. Elena rarely wore underwear. If they lived on their own somewhere, she'd spend most of her time indoors starkers. Not that he'd see any problem with that.

'Me neither. Geeez, girl, you not freezing out here?' asked Nino, wrapping his fleece-lined coat about his naked torso.

Elena shook her head. 'I'm part Viking.'

Nino laughed. 'Yeah, well, that would explain a few things, Elena.'

Elena flicked her smoke away and flashed him a suggestive look. 'You want this ice maiden to warm you up?'

'Wouldn't say no to that.'

'Make me a brew first. Warm my hands up. They are a little nippy.'

Nino winked at her. 'I've already put the kettle on.'

'I wasn't the only early riser. Johnny-boy was heading off before six-thirty.'

'Elena, why the hell were you up at six-thirty?'

'You were dreaming again and were fidgeting and kicking me.'

Nino thought about the dream last night. He couldn't remember it clearly, but he recalled seeing a long stretch of calm, turquoise sea. The rest had now faded into oblivion. He'd have like to have remembered it, because he'd somehow recalled the dream making him feel quite optimistic.

'Nino. Have you decided when we'll do it?'

'Soon.'

'You can't keep saying soon. We need to decide... we need to prepare. I don't have your patience.'

'We will. We need to wait for the opportune time. Now can we go inside? I can't feel my toes.'

Elena nodded to the gate. 'He's back.'

Johnny's Ranger drove into the courtyard and stopped outside the main house. Johnny and two men got out.

'Who are they?' asked Elena.

Nino surveyed the visitors. The shorter of the two lads strolled alongside Johnny. He wore a red padded gilet over a white long sleeve T-shirt, blue jeans and bright white Nike trainers with no socks. His dirty blond hair, styled in a side parting, looked freshly waxed into place. Nino knew Davey Keane, but not well. He also knew the taller lad in the light blue Adidas tracksuit too. Though they'd only met a few times. Nathaniel Sookdeo caught his eye, held it for a few moments, then shoved his hands in his tight tracksuit bottoms and scurried after Johnny and Davey. Nathaniel certainly looked different from when Nino had last seen him. He looked almost tough with his shiny bald head and thick goatee beard.

'I need to pop over to the house for a moment,' said Nino. He kissed Elena on the lips, dashed inside to throw on the nearest clothes he could find, then sprinted over to the main house.

Nino hurried across the courtyard. Barry stood in the doorway and beckoned him to come inside. Nino, surprised he'd got an official invitation to the meeting, rushed into the kitchen.

Inside, the atmosphere wasn't as tense as he'd been expecting. Nathaniel and Davey were seated at the table, which Barry began setting for breakfast, and Johnny stood cracking eggs onto the aga, where strips of bacon were already frying.

Davey seemed relaxed and had already helped himself to a slice of bread and jam.

Nathaniel looked more apprehensive, and when he'd caught Nino's eye, he'd averted his gaze elsewhere.

'Davey, you best have washed your hands, you manky wanker,' said Barry.

Davey nodded. 'Course, mate.'

'Nino, make everyone a brew,' said Barry.

'Coffee for me, mate,' said Davey.

Nino shuffled over to the kettle, peeved that, as usual, he'd been called in to be the sodding skivvy.

Davey devoured the bread and licked the jam from his fingers. 'Craig foresaw the problems coming in from the city. He was right on the ball.'

Barry picked up a bread knife and hacked away at a chunky crusty loaf with the elegance of a handcuffed cow. 'Why would this North London firm be interested in our shitty little coastal towns?'

'County Lines, Barry. It's happening everywhere. You must be aware of these networks,' said Davey.

'Well, course I am,' said Barry with a puzzled and somewhat irate expression.

Nino smiled to himself, thinking how out of touch Barry was with the entire game. Craig had already known about this threat a long time ago.

Davey, sensing he'd not quite answered Barry's question, elaborated. 'In London, competition is high. You've got a ton of crews fighting over the same postcodes. But, ultimately there isn't enough custom for everyone to make a maximum profit. So, the gangs have diversified. Spread the operations further afield into areas that have less dangerous opposition.'

Barry sniffed. 'Right.'

'They establish a supply line out of the city by taking over trade in smaller towns. Then they push out local dealers and supply the area with cheaper, better gear. On our estate, a new number got passed around, with free samples dished out. That's how it started. These crews are on the lookout for areas being supplied by inadequate gear.'

'Our gear is decent,' said Barry in a defensive tone.

'Their stuff is much better. Plus, they supply everything from crack cocaine to some of the best MDMA out there. Before a few months ago, crack wasn't even a thing on the estate. Now there are junkies skulking about that will knife their beloved old granny for a hit of this stuff. This lot no longer desire my crappy coke.'

Nino plonked the teabags into the cup and couldn't help but wonder how many times the powder the likes of Craig and Davey pushed had been cut, and how much actual cocaine the end buyer received. Less than ten per cent actual coke, he guessed. They'd been too greedy, peddled their drugs to a market that didn't have other options, and now karma had arrived to bite them on the butt. New players wanted a slice of the action, and they'd take it with force if need be.

Barry grinned wolfishly. 'Well, Davey lad, now it's time to step up and grow a pair.'

Davey suddenly looked nervous as he ran a hand through his hair. 'These are serious dudes, Barry. We're talking large-scale drug trafficking, contract killing, and arms dealing. This is a major network of very bad people and they have set up shop in our estate.'

Barry scratched his stubble and shrugged. 'Not our issue, pal. Nip up to London and have it out with them.'

'No disrespect, Barry, but we are nothing to them. It's a bit like comparing... I dunno, a small crack in the wall after slamming the door a bit too hard... to say, a full-scale ground-splitting Richter ten earthquake. We're not the earthquake, by the way.'

Nino could see Barry's face changing. His lips were scrunched and his face turned a light shade of red.

Davey continued. 'We don't know who they are, anyway. The runners don't know either. They are just kids. This lot prey on the young and the vulnerable and exploit them. No one knows who the major players are. They hide in the shadows and run everything from the city. Probably from some fortified crack-den. That's how these networks work. The stash house they took over belonged to a pair of complete muppets that got reliant on the gear. They didn't have a clue what was happening. They had to hold and sell the stuff that got delivered… or there'd be consequences.'

'You're talking about the disabled couple whose house you doused in petrol,' said Johnny.

Davey glanced at Johnny. He appeared shocked that Johnny knew this. 'We made sure they were out first.'

Barry sniggered. 'Aw, thoughtful of you.'

'They knew the score. This couple knew these Tottenham lads were not to be messed with. The runner told them how dangerous the crew was and that if any of them screwed up the operation, there'd be no second chances,' said Davey.

'These London boys won't be thrilled with you then, Davey,' said Barry.

'We had to do something. Some of my dealers were threatened at knife point and robbed of all their stuff. A couple of others have fled the area owing me a ton of cash. They've already cuckooed another place in town, so it was bloody pointless!'

Barry yawned and checked his watch.

'It's a disaster. My business has crumbled around me this year. But I will make this right. I promise you. I'll square up with everyone I owe. You guys included,' said Davey urgently.

The waft of smoked bacon smelt good and Barry sniffed the air. 'Yeah, well, you best make it quick. Sounds like you're running out of time.'

Johnny flipped the bacon that looked well-done. He turned to the table. 'Craig mentioned a County Lines organisation had taken Southend by storm. Took over the entire area and wiped out the competition with ease. He did mention we should look at getting on board with the operation instead of fighting against it.'

'I don't remember that,' snapped Barry.

'Anyway, grub's up,' said Johnny, scraping off well-done bacon and not so well-done eggs. He started serving up.

Barry viewed the food with a disappointed sneer. 'Burnt bacon, as usual, I see, Jon. This is why I normally do all the cooking, lads.'

Nino, though he'd prefer not to be a part of it himself, carried a real fascination for the drugs trade and the characters that inhabited its murky world. The way the business worked interested him. He'd once overheard Barry and Craig discussing how their cocaine supplier received his goods, and one method was by using hollowed out fruit, such as pineapples, stuffed with narcotics which was shipped to Tilbury via Rotterdam and Antwerp. Although Nino only took a very minor role in the business, he'd overheard plenty. He'd often heard Craig talking about how Barry's source, a shady Lithuanian gypsy, was unreliable, overpriced and untrustworthy and they'd soon need to find an alternative seller. The supplier, based near Erith, purchased his gear from a gang who ran their operation near the Dartford crossing. Craig often complained that the supplier was cutting the drug significantly before it reached Barry, because the purity was inadequate. Craig said they should hunt elsewhere for a better deal and should consider using Reilly's brother-in-law to broker a deal with the Albanian clan he had ties to. But Barry had scoffed at that idea, saying they'd all end up at the bottom of the Thames if they got involved with Albanians. Nino also suspected that some people at this table had big ideas about pushing themselves further up the chain of command, because Barry and Johnny were too lazy and unambitious to push for such a change. Their reputation could only get them so far, and times were changing. But Barry was way to pig-headed to listen, and it was always his way – full stop. Nino remembered Stefan's boasting about the association he was setting up and he gazed at Davey and Nathaniel in turn, wondering if they'd been involved in setting up this new organisation. This seemed more plausible since Davey had helped hide Nathaniel.

Nino put the radio on and distributed the tea and coffee to the group.

Barry took a sip and pulled a sour face at his drink. 'You use two bags? This tastes weak.'

Nino hadn't, but nodded anyway.

Davey stuck some egg and bacon in between two slabs of bread and took a huge bite. 'Nice, I love my bacon all crispy like this.'

Nathaniel nibbled his food like he was being poisoned.

'Wow, this bread, mate. It's the absolute dog's beanbags,' said Davey.

'I make that myself,' said Barry.

Davey studied the bread. 'The fuck you do.'

'You calling me a liar?' said Barry.

Davey tore open the bread and fingered the dough inside. 'You seriously bake this?'

Barry, clearly not sure if Davey was jesting with him or not, nodded.

'It's good. It's insane. No joke. You should blow-out the blow business and go legit, bro. Barry's Bad-Boy Baguettes. Hard on the outside, soft and fluffy on the inside.'

'Are you taking the piss?' growled Barry.

'No, no, mate… deadly serious. Best bread I've had. You must have French ancestry or something.'

Nino saw that despite himself, Barry couldn't fight back the urge to present a tiny, proud grin, and he noticed even Johnny seemed to bite his lip to curb a smile.

Nino joined the group, and they all ate the breakfast. Davey munched away, chatted and joked like this was just any old ordinary mealtime. Where in contrast, Nathaniel ate little and appeared as though he could be eating the last meal before attending his own execution.

After they'd all finished, Nino was sent to make more drinks for everyone.

Davey held up his cigarette packet. 'Can I?'

Barry gave Davey a look like he'd just whipped out his erect penis and slapped him straight in the face with it. 'No! You bloody can't!'

The song 'Sunglasses at Night' started playing in the background. Nino liked this track, and although he'd heard it several times before, he didn't know who the singer was.

Davey put the smokes away. Then Barry got up, the movement so sudden, Nathaniel flinched. Barry stomped over to the far side of the kitchen and Nino couldn't help conjure up an image of his uncompromising brother doing a daft dance and clicking his fingers to the tune as he went. The picture was so strong in Nino's mind, he needed to choke down a silly chuckle. Barry yanked open a drawer, pulled out a large monkey wrench and tested its weight. As Barry marched back to the table, swinging it at his side, Nathaniel and Davey shared a terrified glance and Davey sat bolt upright in his chair.

Nino watched open mouthed as Barry stood over the table, because for a moment he'd convinced himself that Barry was going to swing for one of them.

Nathaniel's jaw dropped and his eyes bulged.

Davey opened his mouth as if to protest, but said nothing.

Johnny sipped his tea, calm and unmoved.

The music continued.

Nino considered looking away, but then Barry tossed the wrench onto the table and it landed with a loud thud, making Nathaniel jump.

Barry, eyes fixed on Davey, said, 'You take that, and you use it on the mug that did Warren. You return the favour and you film it. I want to see it go down. Understand me?'

'Barry, mate... come on, he's just a kid. Not even thirteen. I told him to see off anyone that looked like trouble. I pay him in weed. He thought your lot was from London. All the estate did,' pleaded Davey.

'Well, if you'd have bothered to return our fucking calls, then you'd have known I was sending someone to collect our money!' bellowed Barry, now going blue in the face. 'So DO it!'

Davey nodded, palms up in front of his face as though surrendering.

'And you owe us. Understand? Not just the cash, but if we need your help, you come running,' said Barry.

'Cool, cool. No questions, sir. I'm there.'

Barry tutted. 'Don't call me sir. We're not at school.'

'Sorry... I'm sorry. I want to make this up to you,' croaked Davey.

Nino couldn't believe the rapid change in Davey's character. All the swagger and coolness had been replaced with an embarrassing feebleness. Davey knew how to play the game. And knew that stroking Barry's ego was obligatory.

Nathaniel spoke for the first time during the sit down. 'I have an idea. A way of getting your money back. Plus a way for me to get some start up cash together. So I can move far away.' He'd not looked up as he spoke, instead he kept his eyes locked on his plate.

Davey shook his head. 'Nah, mate. We talked about this. It's messed up. I said I didn't want to get involved in that shit.'

Nathaniel moved his eyes from the plate and focussed on Davey. 'If we keep it sensible, we can do this. Everyone wins.'

'How?' asked Barry.

Nathaniel looked at Barry. 'You ransom me.'

They spoke about Nathaniel's idea for a short while and decided on a plan of action. Nino, not part of the discussion in any way, found all of it very intriguing, and was surprised his brothers hadn't made him leave.

Barry stood up and gestured to Davey that they should be going. Davey got up. Nathaniel was about to follow, when Johnny put two big hands on his shoulders and stopped him. Nathaniel gazed at Davey, eyes wide and fearful, but Davey was already being led out by Barry, who also carried the wrench.

Johnny sat down opposite Nathaniel and stared at him, impassive and unreadable.

Nino spotted Davey's lighter on the table, scooped it up, and dashed after them.

Nino raced outside, waving the lighter. 'Davey, you forgot this.'

Davey took the lighter, lit up his smoke and sucked the life out of it. 'Nice one, Nino.'

Nino stepped back and lingered by the door, expecting Barry to tell him to scarper, but he didn't.

Barry held out the wrench. Davey accepted it, apprehensive and timid. Nino considered it looked heavy in Davey's grasp, and the thought of what needed to be done clearly sickened him to no end. He took a long drag on the cigarette and glowered.

Barry fixed him with a stony stare. 'And… what did *he* tell you?'

'About what?' said Davey, though Nino could see in Davey's eyes he was fully aware of what Barry meant.

'What did he tell you?' repeated Barry with more menace this time.

'He doesn't know what happened, Barry. I believe him too.'

'So why'd he run off? What did he tell you went down?'

Davey flicked the rest of the cigarette away. 'He just panicked. You know what *they* are like… he shat himself, Barry. Go easy on him. He's alright.'

162

Barry's eyes went down on the cigarette. 'Ark at you. You were quick to give him up.'

Davey retrieved the butt and stuffed it in his pocket. 'My family come first... For God's sake, don't tell the Chillcotts that I hid him in that flat.'

Barry shrugged and concentrated on sending a text whilst he cheerily said, 'As long as we get everything we want... then I have no need to mention it.'

Nino walked back into the kitchen. There, a nerve shredding silence lingered as Johnny and Nathaniel sat at the table sipping tea.

Johnny's phone beeped. He read the message and peered up at Nathaniel. 'So, you didn't tell Davey?'

Nathaniel shook his head. 'I swear on my family, I didn't tell a soul about that night. And I won't. Never.'

'It's lucky you didn't. Otherwise, today would have gone... much differently.'

'Look, Johnny... I know I'm stuck in the middle of this... I understand that I need to get far away from here. I will do that.'

Nino's eyes flicked from his brother to Nathaniel. They'd not even taken any heed of him returning.

Johnny nodded and, after a moment's contemplation, said, 'Why?'

'Because I knew if I blabbed... one way or another, I'd have ended up in the shit. That's what I believe.'

Johnny nodded, satisfied with that. 'You can stay in The Den.'

'But I can't leave?'

'No.'

'What about when... if we sort the money... then I can, right?'

Johnny grinned, though his eyes stayed void of emotion. 'Let's see what happens.'

Oscar stood at the far side of the bar and watched as Rafiq put down his phone, scratched at his thin, receding hair, and rolled his eyes.

Rafiq's companion, another Asian guy wearing a baseball cap, said, 'Not answering that, Raf?'

Rafiq snorted. 'It's bloody Maple-dork again. I sold the guy a gram of party powder a few times, and he thinks I'm some-sort of criminally connected go-to-guy.'

'Your old boss? He wants… drugs?' said the other man, whispering the last word, though Oscar just about caught it.

'Nah. He wants my help to make contact with somebody. And he will not stop pestering me. I've asked that skag-bag Trev Smith to pass on his number to… this *other* person, but he ignored me and Thorpy won't let up!'

The other man pulled a face. 'That sleazy skin-head Trev? The nobody who knows everybody… Why would you even get yourself involved in this, Raf?'

Rafiq sipped his beer. 'Thorpy is a pushy, overbearing bully. He treats people like dog-shit and grins cheerfully whilst doing so. He was a pig of a boss. And I know he won't leave me be until he gets what he wants. The guy is a total narcissistic arse.'

Oscar stiffened at Rafiq's words. He'd heard spiteful stuff like that said of him before and he would again. The joys of being the boss.

'I might change my number,' said Rafiq, more to himself than his companion.

Oscar picked up his drink and walked over to Rafiq's table, enjoying the look of shocked embarrassment on his face as he squirmed in his seat.

Oscar grinned. 'Rafiq, what a complete surprise running into you. I was about to phone you… again!'

32

Page 3

"I fell into a deep depression. I went to hell and back. I wanted to die, and I drank all the time. I lost my way. It wasn't until many years later that I met somebody. An American called Bernard Teach. We fell in love and we married after just six months of dating. Bernard worked in Lambeth and he rented a lovely apartment. Then I had a baby girl… your little half-sister, Lia. She was like you as a baby. Adorable. She had your eyes too… but sadly, she was taken away from me too. And once again, I was left heartbroken. Sudden infant death syndrome, they called it. She spent only five months on this earth… only five. How could life be so cruel? After this, Bernard struggled to cope with my rapid slide into a deep depression and as the cracks in our relationship soon became gaping holes, we ended our marriage. During my time in England, I'd met a new friend called Evelyn Cassey, who lived in Bromley. We got to know each other during my time working at a Mexican restaurant and we became the best of friends. Evelyn helped me so much over the years. I'd be dead without her help. That I do not doubt. I owe her so much and one day I hope I can repay her kindness somehow. Evelyn suggested I track you down. She wanted to help me.

She wanted to ease my pain. And so she did. It took nearly two years of searching, but Evelyn found where you were. And that's when things got really messed up."

33

Kent, 1 December 2018

Duncan could hear his mum singing 'Silent Night' as he plodded down the stairs. The decorations were already up and the festive season was well underway. As far as his mum was concerned, the season to be jolly started on the first of December in the Parvin household and you'd better run with it or else. Even Lenny would be wearing the obligatory reindeer ears soon. As he entered the kitchen, she was busy whisking a cake mix by hand and the singing now replaced by a low humming of the song 'Rocking Around a Christmas Tree'. She'd be especially merry this year because Ryan and Clara were over for Christmas Day and Boxing Day. So having the entire family altogether for the first time in two years would make her almost pop with excited glee by Christmas Eve. Duncan liked Christmas, however he found it all a little over hyped and sometimes being forced to socialise and act cheerful with elderly, germ-riddled relatives he'd not seen all year a tad taxing. Also, there'd be such a huge build up and months of stressing and preparing over what was basically a huge roast, a few presents and several days of over indulging. He couldn't wait to spend time with Ryan and Clara, though. He'd had no one to talk to, and of late, he'd felt like he was on the edge… like he was alone and swimming in his own madness. Craig's face never seemed to leave his mind.

Duncan spotted the painkillers on the side and he picked up the pot. 'Are you still taking these?'

'Ooh, didn't see you there. I'm making carrot cake,' she said with a cheerful smile.

Duncan shook the pill pot. 'Is your hip still playing you up?'

'Now and then. They said I'd suffer with the odd pain periodically.'

'That driver is a total prick!'

Sandra whacked the whisk against the bowl. 'I was just in the wrong place at the wrong time. It happens, love. No sense in fretting over it. There is nothing that can be done to change what happened.'

Duncan's sudden flashback of Craig attacking him in that darkened carpark made him flinch as though he'd been punched in the stomach. He must have pulled a strange expression, because his mum eyed him with concern.

Duncan grinned. 'So, be fantastic having Clara staying for her first Christmas with the Parvins! I hope she knows what she's letting herself in for.'

'I cannot wait,' gushed Sandra.

Johnny headed over to The Den with a Tupperware container filled with a cheese omelette and toast. As he approached, his eyes instinctively flicked to the ground. To *that* spot. Ever since Craig's death, Johnny had been thinking about his friend Tristan Vickers often; most days, in fact. Johnny kept finding himself fixing on the spot – the spot where it had happened – when things had changed. When *he* had changed. The turning point in his life, or so he'd always considered. Twelve years ago. That seemed impossible to wrap his head around. He stood there now, eyes transfixed on the ground.

On the day responsible for this eternal torture, he'd organised a meeting in The Den to resolve a dispute between Reilly Chillcott and their mutual friend, Tristan Vickers, who at the time, owed Reilly twelve hundred quid. Reilly let Vickers off paying his debt, because he'd been well liked by the Chillcotts. Reilly told Vickers that he'd wiped the debt, but he still owed him a big favour instead of the cash.

No one liked owing favours to the Chillcotts, and Vickers was no exception.

So, rather than being content with the outcome, Vickers supposedly bragged to anyone who would listen that Reilly didn't have the bottle to come after him for the money. According to all the gossips, he'd even been overheard spouting off that Reilly was full of shit and nothing but a jumped up little cunt and a scrawny mummy's boy. Which were not wise words considering Reilly's mum had passed away not long before the incident. After this, Reilly put the word out that he wanted to find Vickers, and a game of cat and mouse ensued. Reilly knew Johnny and Vickers were good friends, so he approached him about sorting out the issue.

When Johnny called Vickers about setting up a meet, his friend had been against the idea, which was more than understandable, but Johnny promised his friend that he'd be safe, and that he'd get his say, and even offered him his protection against the Chillcotts.

On the arranged day – a day Johnny knew the rest of the Bartell clan were not present – Reilly arrived in a dirty, beaten-up Jeep. He'd been dressed in a dark red tracksuit and sports cap and swigged from a can of Stella as he approached the pair. He also wore a pair of heavy work boots that didn't match his attire. Three young men emerged from the back. Reilly introduced the three stony-faced men as Kreshnik, Silas, and Grey. Johnny knew the three young men by name and reputation only.

Kreshnik was a tall and brooding Albanian, who was now the husband of Reilly's older sister, Veronica. The two younger men were travellers and weren't fellas to get on the wrong side of. Their notorious families were feared in the Southeast. The only positive he could see was that at least that sinister lunatic Mills hadn't joined the group.

Johnny, acting as mediator, led the men into The Den, where Vickers sat at an oak dining table – the old one from the kitchen that everyone had etched their name on over the years. Vickers drunk a beer, which Johnny had told him to take from the fridge earlier, then he urged the other guys to help themselves, too. Vickers looked ashen faced when he spotted the backup with Reilly, though he tried not to show it as he sat straight, chest puffed out, and eyed them all defiantly. Vickers wasn't soft; he could take care of himself, but he knew he couldn't compete against Reilly. This would be a feud he needed to end, or he'd be forever peering over his shoulder.

Tristan Vickers, being a proud man, explained that he felt mugged off by Reilly. He confirmed he'd spent several days working his tits off to get the readies together to clear his debt; he'd even sold his beloved mountain bike. But after all that, Reilly just turned his nose up at the cash, belittling him in front of his other mates that were present during the exchange.

Reilly nodded thoughtfully, listened to everything Vickers said, and replied by saying, 'Yeah, I get where you're coming from, mate. I understand why that pissed you off.' He continued to sip his beer and even cracked the odd joke. The other men drunk beers and the atmosphere seemed quite chilled, considering the volatile situation. Vickers also assured Reilly that he'd not been slagging him off behind his back, adding that he'd heard the rumours floating about and they were all false. He assumed it must have been someone being a massive arsehole and attempting to stir up trouble. Reilly said he'd look into it, and when he'd established who the loud-mouthed prick was, then they'd both pay the idiot a visit and break his arms. 'One each, right?' Reilly joked.

After the beers were drained and a few more anecdotes shared, the group drifted outside, and Johnny breathed a silent sigh of relief. He'd expected arguments, threats and even a scrap to break out. Johnny had witnessed Vickers fight. The man boxed for many years. If drugs and booze hadn't taken over his life, he could have been a pro. Johnny considered that perhaps Reilly knew Vickers wouldn't be a pushover, so decided that pursuing the trivial dispute wasn't worth the hassle in the long run. Vickers produced five hundred quid from the glovebox of his metallic blue Skoda Fabia, and insisted that Reilly accept the cash, and promised to pay him the rest of the debt in a few days. He'd apologised for no longer having the full amount, but he'd needed to pay the garage for an emergency fix on his car. Reilly took the cash and thanked him, saying that he could pay him whenever.

As Vickers walked Reilly back to his Jeep, they chatted between themselves and were smiling and laughing. It seemed like the matter had ended. But Johnny had been very wrong.

Kreshnik hovered by the driver's side of the Jeep and Reilly opened the passenger door.

Grey and Silas were walking alongside Johnny, making small talk about how much space he had available, and that he should consider setting up some music events out here.

He should have seen it coming – he'd let his guard down big time.

'Take it easy. Glad we sorted all this, mate,' said Vickers, holding out his hand.

Reilly accepted the hand and then flashed a wicked smile. 'So, I'm a jumped-up little cunt, am I?' Reilly pulled Vickers to him and landed a head-butt that would have wiped out a sumo wrestler. It sent Vickers straight to the deck. Without a single moment's hesitation, Reilly jumped high into the air and brought his boot down on to Vickers's head with such force, Johnny heard the man's skull crack. The sound had been diabolical. If the first stamp didn't kill Vickers, the follow up stamps finished the job. The other men stood and watched with a silent aloofness that chilled Johnny to the very bone.

The travellers were no doubt by Johnny's side, so they'd have been able to deal with him if he'd attempted to stop the execution.

Reilly stamped on Vickers over and over. It seemed to go on forever. Johnny could only watch in utter horror as his old friend's head got stomped into a gory, mushy pulp. Johnny assumed the entire thing had been premeditated – hence the big burly boots Reilly opted to wear that day. He was certain he'd even seen one of Triston's eyes pop from its socket.

After the horrendous ordeal, Silas and Grey dragged the remainder of Vickers to the Fabia and heaved the blooded body into the boot, whilst Reilly went to the rear of the Jeep and removed his clothes and boots. He bagged them, and handed them to Grey, who tossed them into the back with Vickers's remains. It was all so casual, as though Reilly were finishing up a work shift and removing his dirty factory overalls.

Then, with no one muttering a word, the travellers got into the Jeep and Kreshnik got into the Fabia, started the engine and drove away.

Dressed now in fresh jeans and a grey, baggy sports jumper, Reilly said, 'Cheers, Johnny. I owe you one for helping me sort this out.' With that, he climbed into the Jeep and the vehicle sped off in a blast of dust.

Johnny then walked to the spot his friend met his awful end and stared at the grim mess left behind. The thought of cleaning the gore made him dry heave.

That day changed Johnny. It strengthened him. It made him wary of everyone. He'd been a naïve twenty-one-year-old. Stupid and clueless. But he told himself that wouldn't happen again. Not ever.

Johnny didn't sleep for weeks after the murder of Vickers and received awful dreams for months after. He'd dished out violence on plenty of occasions. He'd gone at blokes with bottles and fists, but usually under the influence of booze and drugs which dulled the memories. Johnny remembered everything that happened the day Vickers died with crystal clear clarity. Every tiny detail. Sometimes it appeared he was replaying a scene from a terrible movie he'd watched as a child. Each sickening and memorable moment forever etched into the recesses of his mind, which would forever torment him. At that point in his life, Johnny had yet to see anyone die. And he'd not yet killed anyone himself. He'd often lay in bed during the early hours, reliving the moment; hearing that grim sound as Vickers's head got mercilessly caved in. Gone. Just like that. Over what was really just a bunch of bullshit. Would they have killed *him* too, if he'd attempted to intervene? He wondered that many a time.

When Vickers's partner, Lacresha Carr, showed up on the doorstep, Johnny freaked out. It turned out he'd told her all about the meeting, and the distraught and tearful woman was worried sick that something bad had happened to her fella.

'He didn't show up, Lacresha. I've not heard from him,' Johnny had lied. He could see in her eyes she didn't believe him. He later found out she'd been pregnant with his third child, and hadn't yet told Tristan she was expecting again.

Barry went ballistic when Johnny had relayed the news of their mate's grisly demise. He went blue in the face as he threatened to retaliate, and that he'd stab Reilly in the head, burn him alive and do various other methods of murder. Barry had been away in Spain whilst the meeting took place, and he told Johnny that he'd never in a million years have let Reilly do their mate like that. If *he'd* been present, things would have been different. Johnny explained that it all happened so fast. That Vickers hit the deck and got set upon so quickly there had been sod all he could have done to prevent his death. But Barry blanked him for many days. He still occasionally mentioned it.

Finally, drunk out of his skull one night several weeks later, Johnny plucked up the courage to take revenge. But this time, Barry bottled it, and dragged Johnny from his car, and wrestled with him until he calmed down enough to listen. 'One day, bro… one day we'll do that horrible little shit. But now's not the time, Jon.'

Johnny eventually agreed.

The Fabia and Vickers's remains were, to this day, never found. He'd later discovered that Reilly's brother-in-law had inherited a macabre reputation for making people disappear.

Johnny snapped out of his grave thoughts and continued his walk to The Den to give Nathaniel his food.

Karl woke from a fidgety, dreamless sleep. He rubbed his eyes and focussed on the disgruntled, blurry face gazing down at him. For a moment he didn't recognise his surroundings, but the events of the previous evening flashed by and he remembered stumbling into Ryan's place, making it as far as the sofa and passing out. He closed his eyes as a wave of weird sickness flooded him.

Ryan shook him awake. 'I'll make you a coffee, then I want you out of here.'

Five minutes later Karl sat sipping coffee and Ryan, looking rankled, sat, fixed him with an admonishing stare, crossed his legs and interlocked his fingers. *Here comes the lecture*, thought Karl.

'This isn't some doss house, Karl. I'd like you to return my key.'

Karl nodded, fished out the key, and placed it on the table.

Ryan sighed. 'Perhaps it's time you made your way home. You look terrible. No offence, but you look like you've been living rough.'

Karl scratched his unkept beard and grinned. 'I've been going for the rustic look.'

'Where have you been staying?'

'Here and there. Joost is between flats at the moment. Noah lets us crash at his now and then. I was kinda hoping to chat to Clara about getting the blog off the ground. I need some advice on how I can get ads with Skyscanners and the like.'

Karl caught Ryan's quick roll of his eyes and tight smile.

'I'm still serious about making this work, Ryan. I just had a rocky start.' As in, he spunked the travel fund on a two-day bender. The plan had been to spend a couple of days exploring each town and city between Eindhoven and Amsterdam, budget their money, buckle down and pour everything into the blog. Once in Amsterdam, they were meant to be working with Joost's friend for a few weeks to get more funds together, so they could continue their travels and add new posts to the blog as they moved between areas. The problem was, Karl found travelling alone dull and lonely, and Joost, although a fun and animated companion, was a total liability and the man seemed entirely motivated by booze and drugs.

'Clara's in Prague. She's visiting Christmas markets for one of her blogs,' said Ryan.

'Cool. Nice... Um, you heard from Dunk?'

'I haven't spoken to him in a while, but I've chatted to my mum... she's worried about him. He's not been himself.'

Karl missed Duncan, though at times he'd be a real party pooper and wasn't always the most outgoing of souls. Maybe that's why their friendship worked so well. Duncan kept the balance in his life and stopped him from going off the rails. Joost, on the other hand, brought out the hidden devil in him. Perhaps Karl needed Duncan in his life, and vice versa.

'It will take my brother a long time to get over what happened. You understand that, right?' said Ryan.

Karl nodded, he did. All too well.

'You've always been there to watch out for him... I don't think he's coping too well without you. Mum said he rarely leaves the house. Scott keeps trying to coach him out, but you know what a useless doughnut he is?'

'Yeah, total tit,' said Karl.

. . .

Reilly spat his gum into the river as the noisy van came to a stop. Hashim dragged himself out and trudged down the slipway, limping as he came.

'Good to see you, Hashim,' said Reilly.

'I brought you a gift.'

'You know where the boy is?' asked Reilly.

'No. I don't. Here,' said Hashim, handing over a crumpled business card.

Reilly studied the card. 'How'd you acquire this, Hashim?'

'If my client is stupid enough to leave his wallet on the side whilst in the shower... then that's a shame, no? I think that might be very useful to you, yes?'

Reilly rubbed his tongue against the front of his top teeth. 'Good. This is good. You shouldn't have taken this, though.'

'I didn't have my phone on me because I'd only gone inside to use the toilet. And my memory isn't what it used to be.'

Reilly fished inside the pocket of his joggers and pulled out some notes. 'I wasn't expecting to meet. There'll be more readies next time.'

Hashim eyed the meagre amount, licked his lips as though tasting something nasty, then nodded and left without another word.

Reilly got into his Fiesta and rummaged around in the glovebox for an old burner phone he could use to call the number on the card.

34

Johnny got out of his Ranger. Barry came strutting over to him, phone in hand.

'You gotta take a gander at this, Jon,' said Barry.

Johnny took the phone and viewed the spiralling footage. He could then make out a bunch of kids scuffling and a young lad started screaming for help. Then the group swarmed him and slammed him to the ground. Johnny grasped what he was watching, and so handed the phone back.

Barry tutted. 'No stomach for it this morning?'

'I don't wanna see that shit, Barry. It's grim.'

Barry viewed the screen, smiling. 'You'll miss the best bit.'

Shouts could be heard, and someone yelled out, 'Hold him! Hold his arms.'

'Pin him. Pin him down,' shouted another irate voice.

The boy being attacked screeched and pleaded for them to get off him. He sounded so young, and Johnny found it harrowing to listen to. He caught his brother's absorbed expression as he viewed the footage, for what was no doubt the umpteenth time. Barry was a sick bastard at times.

'Here it comes,' said Barry.

'No, nooo, no!' came the awful screams. Then a sickening crack was heard, followed by more stomach turning screams and ululations from the aggressors as they viewed their morbid handy work.

Barry crinkled his nose and sniggered. 'Whooooa fuck. That's messed up.'

'Was that necessary?'

'Necessary? Warren is still drinking through a straw, the poor bastard! The surgeon said he's likely to have a speech impediment for the rest of his life.'

'I'm not talking about the payback. I meant the video. It's sick. That's all.'

'So, don't watch it, princess. It wasn't for you, anyway. I'll take it to show Warren. Might cheer the ugly bugger up for five minutes.'

'Yeah, sure, he'll be doing naked cartwheels around the ward after seeing that bleak shit, Barry'

'Anyway, talking about films, we have our own little masterpiece to get on with.'

Elena walked across the paddock with a bundle of hay and headed to the old open fronted metal shed which Hetty used as her stable. As she pretended to distribute the hay, she watched as Barry and Johnny mooched off into The Den. Things were getting interesting around here of late. She'd asked Nino what Johnny and Barry intended to do with Nathaniel after they'd carried out their plan, but he'd shrugged and said he didn't have a clue what their end game was. It would not matter to them in the long run, but she hoped they'd let the lad go.

Hetty ambled over and nibbled on the hay. Elena looked after Hetty but never rode her. She'd been an avid horse-rider once. Until the day she witnessed the mare at her uncle's stables throw one of Sally's friends from the saddle. The shaken girl returned to her feet and dusted herself off, and the mare kicked out and cracked the girl in the chin and she'd screamed in agony. To make things worse, Sally bombarded the poor girl with insults, blaming her for being an inept rider. The kick resulted in her leg being kept together with metal pins and gave her a permanent limp. If Elena remembered correctly, the poor girl hadn't even wanted to ride and Sally pressured her into mounting the giant horse in the first place.

After that, Elena became nervous around the beasts. She'd often feed and pet them, but with caution, although she no longer had any desire to ride. She trusted Hetty, though, but was never tempted to mount her.

At the time of the grim incident, all Elena could think was why couldn't it have been Sally that got her chubby leg pulverised? Even now, thinking about Sally's bloated, spiteful face riled her to no end. She'd never forgive her for what happened that Christmas Eve when she'd stayed over at her aunt and uncle's place. Her uncle Greg was renting a big house in Shropshire at the time. She'd been fifteen, and she'd pleaded with her parents not to leave her there. Her uncle was a drunken bully, her aunt Fran a feeble pushover, and she detested her cousins. Sally was a mean bitch of a girl. And Vince, a creepy weirdo who often made inappropriate comments to her and sometimes got way too close for comfort.

Left alone in the house, Vince got crazy drunk and came to the spare room where she'd been sleeping. Elena would never forget that rank smell on his breath as he tried to kiss her. She'd never forget a single moment of the entire event. It made her skin crawl and bile rise in her stomach, and sometimes she hated herself for not being strong enough to fight him off. What always stuck in her mind was the door opening and a sudden relief flooding her senses that someone had rushed to her aid. Then she saw Sally's face, watching the scene with a nasty, gleeful sneer, before shutting the door on them. Though he'd not raped her, Vince did more than enough to leave her feeling dirty and ashamed beyond belief.

Elena didn't utter a word about that incident until a few years later at her eighteenth birthday party, which her dad had organised at a remote community centre in Yorkshire. Whilst she stood at the bar waiting for her drink, Vince had shuffled up to her and offered to buy her a glass of champagne. She'd declined, and he'd secretly run his hand along the top of her leg. Her body went cold with fear and she felt racked with shame. Her birthday ruined, she found herself out in the children's play area, where she hid in a wooden house and sobbed her heart out.

Then Brennan located her and pressed her for the reason she'd fled her party. And the secret about the sexual assault flowed out. Brennan surprised her that night. He'd held her tight and sobbed as he promised to keep her safe and gave his word he'd never tell a soul about what she'd told him. If things got too much, he would be there in a flash.

After they spent a while talking, he'd told her to keep her chin up, go back inside and not to let anybody ruin this special day. He stayed close to her all night, and Vince stayed well away. She'd thought she'd regret telling her brother, because she expected him to go charging into the hall and pummel the hell out of the pig and make a dramatic scene. She could foresee family fallouts, fighting and feuding. But he didn't. Brennan respected the fact she'd confided in him and she loved him for that.

Late the following December, Brennan took Vince out for a Christmas drink at some rural pub on the far outskirts of Leeds. Vince got himself into a right rowdy state. After leaving the pub, Brennan walked with a stumbling Vince to a walkway bridge that crossed a busy dual carriageway, where he hoisted his cousin up, tossed him over the railings and dropped him down onto the road below. The fall caused catastrophic, life-changing injuries, but by some miracle, three vehicles, including an articulated lorry, swerved to avoid Vince's crumpled body and the traffic was stopped, which undoubtedly saved him from certain death. Most people considered Brennan to be backwards. But Elena knew otherwise. He'd picked that pub because he knew a guy that he'd once worked with who'd retired to the area. This guy just happened to be out walking his dog that evening. He gave a full statement to the police, confirming that he'd seen the idiotic man, drunk out of his mind and messing about on the side of the bridge. He said, 'The maniac was only trying to balance on the side whilst shouting nonsense at the traffic passing under him!' The man confirmed he'd watched in horror as the drunkard slipped and plunged over the side. Punters in the pub also recalled seeing the drunk man not long before the incident. They'd confirmed he'd been in a right mess and some of the locals had complained about his loud, unruly behaviour. And Brennan said he'd been arranging a taxi and didn't notice his cousin wandering off across the bridge.

Vince survived, but never walked again without the aid of a

walking stick, and he'd been affected mentally. He was never the same again. He now spoke with a strange, slow stammer.

Elena often wondered if Vince remembered what Brennan had done. If he did, then he'd never told a soul.

A few months after Vince's alleged fall, Sally was rushed into hospital after taking an almost fatal amount of heroin. She'd have died if her boyfriend at the time, Mick, hadn't left work early that day and come back in time to call the emergency services. A close call. The weirdest thing of all was that Sally didn't touch drugs. Not ever.

Hetty nudged Elena, bringing her back into the present. Elena pressed her face against the horse's snout. 'I will miss you, girl,' she whispered. 'I really will.'

35

'When are you coming into the office full time, Ravi?'

'Next week. Definitely next week.'

Ravi heard his wife sigh.

'You said that last week, Ravi. There are things that need your attention. Clients that want to talk to you in person. Two appearances a fortnight isn't enough.'

'I understand.'

A long silence.

'I have had to forge your signature more than once. This is getting beyond ridiculous.'

'I need a bit more time, Chandra.'

'Ravi, please don't let this consume you. Just... don't.'

'I have to know if he is safe.'

'He made his choices. He's an adult. And he's changed... you're chasing after a boy that no longer exists. You need to understand that.'

'So we just stop? Give up. Even though he could be in danger. Or—'

'We gave that boy every opportunity. He spat in our faces. And *I* have given up. It's only you that hasn't. Even Narissa saw the change in him. She'd become frightened of him. Narissa told me she was too scared to be in the house alone with him. Were you aware of that, Ravi?'

Ravi said nothing. He was aware of that.

'Why not focus on your daughter? The one who doesn't use drugs. The one who desperately misses her father and her home. Who needs the security of both parents living together... instead of apart like they are on the verge of a damn divorce.'

Ravi still didn't respond. In his mind, Narissa was safe, happy and despite his wife's attempts to once again guilt trip him, he knew his daughter would rather be in London. She'd begged him plenty of times for the keys to his apartment because she loved staying in the city. He missed his wife, though he'd never admit that to her. They'd been sweethearts since they were sixteen. They'd been forced to spend time apart when he'd left Trinidad with his parents, and they'd both pined for one another. And Chandra eventually sought him out in London.

'You can come home, Chandra.'

'Not until you promise to stop. Not until you promise to stop obsessing over that boy. Until then, I refuse to come home. We both refuse, Ravi. We can't take this anymore. Face it, you've lost this battle. You have no control over this. It's time to stop searching. You know I'm right.'

Ravi opened his mouth to speak, but she'd already cut the call.

Ravi walked to the bathroom and splashed cold water over his face, then went back to his office. He scanned his ever-growing investigation board where more newspaper clippings, headshots of the relevant parties were positioned around two Ordnance Survey maps. One of the area around The Swan Inn and another of the fields and woodlands encompassing the Bartells' property. He'd scouted this area twice more since his last visit, though he'd not ventured so close on those occasions. Getting to the house without using Dead Lane was tricky, but as he'd discovered, not impossible. By parking on another twisty lane set a few miles from the house, and by using bridleways and byways through an eerie woodland called Craven's Cross, he could reach a large field on the outskirts of the property. He'd marked the route on the map with a red marker. He'd considered finding a spot where he could get up close enough to view the house with his binoculars and observe the comings and goings for a few days. It wouldn't be easy and it would be dangerous, but he felt confident he could pull it off. If only Schneider had the fortitude to undertake the venture, because he'd have paid him a tidy sum to carry out the surveillance. He felt certain this family was involved in Nathaniel's disappearance. He'd even browsed the Dark-web again, considering hiring some-sort of mercenary or soldier, but couldn't be sure the sites were bona fide.

Ravi considered calling Chandra back. He hated their calls ending like that. It seemed to be the norm these days, if they even talked, because some weeks their only communication would be a few laconic text messages. He kept wondering if he should tell her about the things he'd found in Nathaniel's room all those months back. Would she still be so cold and unforgiving towards their only son then? If she knew about the van watching the house and Nathaniel's ties to two criminally connected families, both with recently deceased sons. Would she show any signs of despair then? Had she grown to hate him so much she didn't care if he was alive or dead? Such an awful thought.

Ravi's phone vibrated, and he snatched it up from the desk. He had a text message from a number he didn't recognise. He clicked on the message and there was a video file attached. Ravi played the clip and viewed in horror when the shaky image came into focus, revealing a figure tied to a chair with what looked like a dirty pillowcase over their head. The film was shot in a wooden shed or cabin, cluttered with tools and piles of wood. A stocky man came into the shot, dressed in dark blue mechanic's overalls, latex gloves and a ski mask. The man tugged the pillowcase from the figure and they gasped and scanned the room with wide, panicked eyes. Ravi saw immediately it was Nathaniel, despite the bald head and goatee beard. The man moved off camera. He returned moments later, brandishing a machete. Then, using considerable force, he grabbed Nathaniel's forehead and yanked his head backwards.

'What are you doing? Let me go!' screamed Nathaniel.

Ravi watched, hand over his mouth, as the man held the blade to his son's neck.

'I'll say it… I'll say it,' Nathaniel screeched.

The man removed the machete. After a short pause, he let go of Nathaniel.

Nathaniel gazed at the camera in terror. 'Dad, I need you to save me. Please help me!'

The man stood to the side of Nathaniel, weapon hanging by his waist.

Nathaniel sobbed. 'If they don't get forty grand… by tomorrow… they'll kill me. If you contact the police…' Nathaniel started whimpering, flicked his eyes at the man and gazed back at the camera. 'Dad, they're gonna kill me if they don't get what they want. That's not just a threat. They will do it. They will hack me to bits. They said they will text you instructions.'

The camera shook, the footage blurred, then the screen faded black.

Ravi, his hand shaking, placed the phone back onto the desk and stood silently trembling. It was a long time before he could force himself to move from the spot.

36

Reilly entered the small office and took in the surroundings. He'd been expecting a middle-aged guy, but Schneider couldn't have been older than twenty-eight and this surprised him.

Reilly shook Schneider's hand. The man's limp grip didn't impress him. 'I hope you don't mind, but I've brought along some family members too.'

'Um, OK. I've only got two chairs, though,' said Schneider, bunching up the paperwork strewn across his desk.

He'd given Reilly an odd look, as though he'd seen him before, but just couldn't quite place him.

As Reilly took a seat, Mills and Kreshnik entered and Schneider appeared to go rigid as he viewed the pair. Both men wore clear latex gloves and Schneider noticed this.

'This is Mills, my brother.'

Mills scowled at Schneider.

'And Kreshnik, my brother-in-law.'

Kreshnik gave the PI an uninterested look as he plonked himself down.

Schneider's mouth opened and closed a few times before he said, 'Um, hi.' He focussed back on Reilly. 'What, um… how can I help?'

Kreshnik took something from his pocket. A syringe loaded with cloudy liquid. Schneider saw the item and gasped.

Kreshnik placed the syringe on the desk next to Schneider's phone. The colour drained from Schneider's face. 'Ah, what...'

'You don't want to know,' said Reilly.

Mills stepped over to the filing cabinet and started yanking open the drawers, the noise of each making Schneider flinch.

Mills flung files about the room until he located one that caught his attention and he flicked through it.

Reilly stared at Schneider and offered him a thin, but reassuring, smile. He didn't want the lad to break down yet.

Mills handed the folder to Reilly.

Schneider's eyes moved back to the syringe. Or perhaps the phone. Did he think he could quickly grab it and somehow call for help? Reilly would like to see him try.

'You want to try some?' asked Kreshnik, touching his index finger against the syringe.

Schneider shook his head, his face growing paler by the second. It now seemed the colour of milk, and his eyes were huge and glazed.

Kreshnik moved the gloved hand to the phone and slid it away from Schneider. Then he studied the screen before pocketing it.

Reilly flicked through the report, which contained newspaper clippings, typed reports and Post-it notes with scribbled writing all over them. 'You've been a busy boy, Mr Schneider.'

'That case is closed. I'm no longer working for that client,' said Schneider, speaking machine-gun fast.

'So, you've found the boy?' asked Reilly.

Schneider shook his head. 'The client didn't pay his bills on time. We had a breakdown in communication. I assure you that I have no interest in this.'

Reilly puffed out his cheeks. 'It's a funny old business this. Snooping into other people's affairs. It's sad really, wouldn't you agree?'

Schneider said nothing.

'I mean, how would you like it if someone started sticking their beak into your personal business? Or dug up all your dirty little secrets?' said Reilly.

Schneider gulped. 'Please, you can take the file. I'll help you guys as much as I can.'

'What did you find?' asked Reilly.

'The police said the boy drew money out of his account a while back. No other trace has been found.'

'Where?' asked Reilly.

'Broad... stairs.'

Reilly opened the file and flicked through it again. But when he spotted the newspaper clipping about Tristan Vickers, his heart skipped a beat. He tore out the plastic file and slipped out the notes from within. This noisy fella had been digging... digging way too deep. He read... *Lacresha Carr confirmed Vickers drove his car to see Johnny Bartell for a meeting. But did he actually go?*

Reilly read the part. *She believes him to be dead.* And a flutter of panic hit him.

Reilly glared at the investigator. 'What's this Tristan Vickers guy got to do with this case?'

Schneider's jaw dropped open, pure panic flashed in his eyes and he made a pathetic sound, like a scared kitten meowing.

'And what connects Sookdeo and Vickers?' asked Reilly.

'Umm... I...'

Me, thought Reilly.

'His name just popped up,' said the investigator meekly.

Mills glared at him. His eyes narrow and bitter. 'We don't like people spying on us, you muggy little cunt.' Mills stabbed a fat finger at the screen. 'Is it on here?'

Schneider didn't even look at Mills. His eyes flicked to the syringe and then put a shaky hand on his mouse and opened up the file.

Mills glared at the screen. 'This everything? No backup?'

'That is the backup. It's on the cloud. If you delete that, it's all gone,' said Schneider.

'So... delete it!' said Mills.

Schneider clicked the mouse a few times and deleted the file. Mills never needed to ask twice.

'It's just a missing person's case. That's all. I swear on my daughters. It's just a case... a missing person—'

Mills grabbed Schneider by the throat, squeezed hard and shook him. The guy struggled, but this was equivalent to a guinea pig trying to fend off a silverback gorilla.

Kreshnik took the opportunity to snatch Schneider's forearm, rip back his shirt sleeve, and scoop up the syringe.

'Oh, God no. No, no, don't do that!' squealed Schneider.

'What about Stefan? You find anything about him? Are these deaths connected?' asked Reilly.

'No... I didn't find anything about that,' cried Schneider.

Kreshnik flicked off the syringe's rubber protector with his thumb, squeezed out a small amount of liquid and hunted the arm for a prominent vein. Schneider made a sound like a dog violently retching and hyperventilated. Kreshnik plunged the syringe into the vein, emptied the liquid, and smiled. 'There we go. That wasn't so bad, was it?'

Mills held the man tight as he went rigid and somehow his face became even whiter than before.

Schneider gasped and sputtered, 'What... what did... you give... me?'

Reilly stood up, thinking his brother-in-law wouldn't make a very good nurse, the sadistic sod. 'We don't want to return here. Understand?'

Schneider started sobbing. 'Am I going... to die?'

'I hope so, you skinny cunt,' said Mills, shoving the wretch onto the floor.

Reilly shrugged. They'd not come to kill him, just scare him.

'What was it?' asked Reilly.

'Horse piss,' said Kreshnik.

'What will that do?' asked Reilly.

Kreshnik shrugged. 'Probably nothing. I don't know.'

'Could cause blood poisoning,' said Mills.

The trio got into Reilly's grey Fiesta.

'Sepsis,' confirmed Mills.

Reilly handed Mills the file and fired up the engine. 'And how would you know that injecting piss can lead to Sepsis, Mills?'

'An article in the paper. Some junkie injected their own piss. They did it for a thirty quid bet or something. Killed them.'

Reilly sniggered. 'Eh, that's wrong… so wrong.'

Mills sniggered. 'Oh, and what we just did was so right?'

They'd meant to be putting the frighteners on the investigator. The injection was only meant to be for show, but there didn't seem much point bringing that up now. Though if he'd known that Vickers's disappearance was being investigated, he may have approached the situation differently. Maybe he still would.

'Hey, that's a piss-poor way to die, no?' said Kreshnik.

Mills rolled his eyes and opened up the report, muttering something inaudible.

Kreshnik howled with laughter. 'Ahhhh, ha ha. That's a good one, yes?'

Reilly laughed, though more at the Albanian than with him. As much as he admired the guy, only Kreshnik found Kreshnik's jokes funny. Reilly thought of Kreshnik as his own brother. He owed a lot to this man and without his guidance, he'd have been banged up years ago. Reilly earned a lot of money. And he could have the tasty cars, flash clobber and decent house, but all these things brought unwanted attention. He'd learnt this from his brother-in-law. The way Kreshnik and his kin worked made so much sense to Reilly, and from the moment his sister hooked up with the guy, he foresaw that by getting on board with the man instead of fighting against him would be the best plan. Mills didn't like the idea at first, but Reilly talked him around. Kreshnik's Albanian crime family lived like penniless pikies in run-down council flats and battered caravans. But back in their home city of Elbasan, however, the men owned big, flashy homes, expensive sports cars and openly showcased their wealth. In the UK, they lived modest lifestyles, drove crappy cars and stayed well under the police radar as they ran drug dealing operations, smash and grab jobs and prostitution rackets. It was known that Kreshnik had another wife back home in Albania, and he'd visit her several times a year. Reilly suspected his sister knew this, but she'd never mentioned it and he had zero intention of sticking his nose into their affairs. If Veronica knew, she didn't seem bothered about the arrangement. Kreshnik started his criminal life as a low-level burglar and although he still wasn't a top player in the clan, he was still a well-respected member that made them a lot of money. The majority of his crime proceeds would make its way back to Albania, and his sister probably saw little of the money. Reilly couldn't help admire these people, though. Their work principles and desire to do whatever is deemed necessary to get what they wanted. The old British crews would never reign strong again. They'd had their day. The old gangs, like his dad and Jack Bartell used to run, were finished. They'd be no match for the Eastern Europeans, whose dedication, ruthlessness and numbers could not be beaten. Reilly knew that. And as the old saying goes, *if you can't beat 'em…* Plus, the Albanians were super smart and business savvy. They'd dominated the UK's cocaine industry by setting up direct trade routes with Columbian cartels. They'd pushed down prices, increased purity and taken over the criminal underworld, especially in London and the Southeast. You just had to respect their work ethic.

When Reilly came close to losing his cool, Kreshnik would tell him – *You must keep your rage inside. Do not let it boil to the surface. Your revenge will taste so much sweeter if you wait for the perfect moment. I know this.* He knew what he meant, because flying off the handle and acting in a blind rage would only lead to one thing. Prison. Unfortunately, Mills didn't *do* much thinking. He often considered his older brother would have made a fierce warlord. He should have lived in a time when battles were fought with a massive broadsword. Mills would have loved spending his days beheading rival warriors and dragging knights from their charges and battering them senseless with a hefty mace. It might have even put a smile on his ugly-arse face.

'What am I doing here?' asked Arnie.

Arnie was sitting in the back. He'd opted for that spot because he wanted to stay out of sight, and would be able to duck down behind the seats if need be. Ravi suddenly wondered what exactly Arnie could do and realised he'd only asked him along so he wasn't alone. The thought of making the exchange on this uninviting estate felt like a daunting task. Upon seeing the footage, his initial reaction had been to pull up Schneider's number, but he stopped himself from making the call. The young investigator would have only encouraged him to contact the police, like he'd done throughout the enquiry process. He wouldn't have had the stomach for this, anyway. Ravi had settled the invoices and suspected the guy felt relieved to be stepping away from the case due to the many dangerous factors surrounding his son's disappearance. He needed someone with more mettle, and wheelchair or no, Arnie still ticked that box.

'Keep an eye out. Any trouble, call my number or hold down the horn to attract attention,' said Ravi.

'Whatever you say,' said Arnie.

'Are you sure that car wasn't following us?' asked Ravi, checking all his mirrors.

'Nobody followed us. There's nobody out there,' said Arnie.

Ravi made to get out. Arnie pulled him back. 'Wait, Ravi, what if you get set upon? Shall I call the cozers?'

'No… just… keep watch. If things get really bad, then call for help.'

'Wait, hold up… you got a weapon? You should take something out there. You got a knife, Ravi?'

Ravi revealed the stun gun attached to his belt.

'Is that… a taser gun?'

'I purchased it on the Dark-net. It came today by UPS, would you believe?'

'Whooa, look at you, going all Heisenberg! I like it.'

'Heisen-who?'

'Never mind. Hey, did you get me one? You know, in case somebody tries to swag the motor. They'll do that here, even with my crippled arse sat inside. I've always wanted to taser someone in the gonads… zaaaaapp! Have a taste of that, you stupid ass! Best place to aim for.'

'No. I only have this one. And I'm taking it.'

'OK, fine, but I hope you'll pay for my ransom when I get taken,' said Arnie.

'Arnie, this is Margate, not Mexico City. Just watch for suspicious cars and film anything that looks iffy.'

'I want danger pay for helping you with this.'

Ravi grabbed the money satchel, got out, and slammed the door. He had to admit, despite Arnie being an aggravating idiot, he felt glad to have him here.

Ravi scanned the deserted street and checked his watch. He was five minutes early. Though it was only just coming up to six pm, it was pitch dark and weirdly quiet. There weren't any people around. It was silent enough to hear a pin drop. He continued to the end of the street and found himself standing at a graffiti-covered wall where a skinny, unlit alley ran through the middle. He gazed back down the street, where he could just make out his Jag. Still no signs of life. No cars came, no movement from the terraced house windows, and no dogs barked. He placed his hand on the stun gun. He wanted to reassure himself he still had it.

The text pinged up dead on six as they'd said it would. The instructions were simple – go through the alley and wait. The downstairs light to the nearest house came on. He caught sight of an elderly man in a brown cardigan before a tatty curtain shut off his view of the man.

Ravi took one more glimpse at his car and walked into the alley. The walls were high, it smelt of urine, and it was so dark he was unable to even make out his shoes when he glanced downward. It seemed long too, and like Dead Lane, an overwhelming urge to sprint to the end where a faint luminous orange light awaited him became unbearable. His shoulder dragged up against something and he froze. Then, remembering the small torch he'd shoved in his raincoat. He grabbed it, but stopped, composed himself and walked on with purpose without using the torch. He forced himself on through the darkness, ignored the sensation that the surrounding space was shrinking and the tall, damp walls were closing in around him. When he emerged from the alley, the sense of relief was palpable. Though very short lived when he assessed the surroundings. He'd stepped out into an enclosed area made up of neglected garages, most of which were open and piled up with rubbish, or had broken doors that hung, twisted and bent. Under a street lamp, flickering with a dim orange glow, was a Transit van, dumped in the corner, with every tyre flattened. One side had been blackened by fire damage. He examined the van and checked the front. The seats were covered in glass and a wooden panel divided the cab from the back. He went to the rear, where he found a heavy-duty padlock securing the doors and a sign that said – *no tools left in this van overnight.*

When Ravi turned around, he jolted back in shock. He was no longer alone in here. Just a few metres away, five figures sat motionless and silent on BMX bikes. They all wore identical latex face masks.

Clown masks. They were hideous, evil looking things with the lips appearing as though they'd been ripped back, showing torn, blood-red gums and a mouth full of razor-sharp teeth. They all watched him, silent and grim. Though his heart was racing faster than it had ever done in his life, Ravi stood tall, adjusted his jacket and approached the terrifying group with his chin up. He fixed his face into a stoical expression – or at least as stoical as he could manage under the harrowing circumstances. He tried to look past the intimidating masks and see them as a bunch of kids. That's all they were – just kids. Then he caught the glimmer of a long knife in the hands of one rider, and a severe dread hit him that almost made his legs buckle in fear. For a moment, he considered he might die here. Hacked to pieces by a bunch of lawless teenagers and left slashed and bloodied, encompassed by a bunch of junk-filled, scruffy garages. He'd be headline news. *London businessman found butchered in the backstreet of a seaside council estate.*

Then the bikes moved. They circled him, and once surrounded, they stopped and resumed staring at him. The knife wielder pointed the blade at the satchel. Ravi could study the weapon closely now. It had a lime-green handle and the blade must have been two inches thick and fifteen inches in length. Now there was no gap he could even dart through if the situation didn't go well. They'd penned him in. The urge to snatch out the stun gun, wipe out the nearest rider and bolt for the alley was strong. But if he wasn't fast enough, then he'd be done for. He dare not risk it.

Then the figure waved the knife again, more urgently this time.

Ravi took the satchel off his shoulder and tossed it to the ground. The figure to the left of the knife carrier snatched it up, peeked inside, slung it over his shoulder and pedalled off like a madman.

The other riders didn't move.

Ravi wanted to say something – anything – but his throat had become too dry to swallow, let alone speak.

They stood silent for around a minute before a bunch of keys landed by his feet. He peered down at them, and as he did, the bikers all rode off and vanished into the darkness beyond the garage block.

Ravi tried every key and still hadn't unlocked the padlock. Then it occurred to him what they'd done. They'd stalled him in order to make their rapid escape, and he cursed himself for being so idiotic. He tried the keys again. His shaking hands made it difficult to slot each key in place, but this time one clicked home and the padlock ring snapped free. He yanked open the door, grabbed his torch, and aimed the beam inside the vehicle. Ravi scanned slowly, seeing bundles of grey furniture blankets, an old tyre, boxes of tools and right up the front... what looked like an arm poking out of more tatty blankets. Ravi froze and whispered, 'Nathaniel... Nathaniel.' He climbed into the back and shuffled in. Under the glare of the torch light, he distinguished the shape of a person under the blankets.

With trepidation, he moved to the shape, placed a hand on the threadbare blanket and pulled it back. He heard his own gasp and fell backwards at what he saw – or what he thought he'd seen. He composed himself and got back to his feet. A patter of rain started hitting the roof of the van, and within seconds it descended into a full blown thudding downpour that sounded like tiny rocks landing and dancing on the van's roof. Ravi shone the torch over the figure, so sure it was Nathaniel's body lying there. He spotted the grey hood of a sports jumper. Ravi pulled at the figure and the lightweight body shape rolled over to face him. A clown mask, much the same as the bike riders had worn, glared back at him. Only then did Ravi comprehend that this was not a person. It was a shop manikin dressed in jeans and a hoody. Ravi slumped down and fought back the urge to bellow out a raging curse. The rain started smashing down and the noise sounded deafening to him in that nightmarish moment.

The rage passed, now replaced with the urge to sob. His chest heaved, and he closed his eyes. How had he been so naïve? He felt his phone vibrate and removed it from his coat. He'd expected a message from Arnie, checking up on the situation. But it was from *them*.

Ravi, soaked and despondent, got into his car. He couldn't see Arnie for a moment sat in the darkness behind the seats. Then he heard him cough.

Ravi wiped the rain from his eyes.

'Do we need to go to another location?' asked Arnie. 'Where did you go? What happened?'

A good minute passed before Ravi could find his tongue. 'They said they're going to release him.'

'So… where is he now?'

Ravi shrugged. 'They said he doesn't want to see me and he's going away.'

'Does that seem likely to you?'

Ravi slapped the steering wheel. 'How can I believe a word they say? How can I be sure he's not dead already?'

'Who picked up the cash? Did you get a look at anyone?'

Ravi shook his head. 'Kids. Kids wearing masks.'

They sat in silence, listening to the heavy downpour of the rain.

'Ravi, let's get out of here. Come on, let me buy you a beer and you can dry yourself out.'

'I'm speaking to the police… I'm going to tell them everything that's happened! I have no choice,' said Ravi.

Ravi's phone sprang to life. He looked at the screen. It was his wife.

'Go around the back,' said Johnny.

Barry did as requested and drove his Renault Traffic into the services and headed to the unlit lorry park tucked away at the back. He backed in between two Romanian Luton vans that had blankets covering their windscreens.

The rain battered down, and when Davey and his companion pulled up on a noisy moped, the pair were soaked to the bone and miserable. Davey slipped off the back of the bike and approached the driver's side of the van. He held a dripping wet backpack.

Barry rolled down the window.

'That heat in there feels nice and inviting,' said Davey, shivering.

Barry gazed out at him. His expression was not in the least bit inviting. He snatched up the bag, grunted and tossed it to Johnny, and without a word, closed the window, started the engine, and drove away.

Barry, always the charmer, thought Johnny, as he stuck his hand in the bag, located the satchel, and inspected the cash. They'd need to get back quickly and count it. He considered it unlikely that Davey would have had them over… but it couldn't be completely ruled out.

. . .

Ravi and Arnie sat in silence as they drank their drinks. Ravi sipped a black coffee with a shot of brandy and Arnie supped on an Amstel beer.

Arnie broke the silence. 'Did you tell your wife about the money?'

Ravi sipped his drink, grunted, and shook his head.

'Shit. My other half would kill me if I lost all that cash.'

Ravi raised his eyebrows, but didn't say anything.

'Yes... I know, it's hard to believe. I was a catch once. I wasn't always... like this. Separated now, though. But she helps me out. Feels sorry for me, I guess.'

Ravi closed his eyes and rubbed his forehead as though in pain. 'What's her name?'

'Gail... she's tough as old boots... and bolshie. Oh, yes, she can be quite intimidating when she wants to be.'

'So can my wife at times!'

They sat in silence for a while.

'So, what about my payment?' asked Arnie.

Ravi glared at Arnie, eyed him with contempt for a few moments, then looked into the steaming coffee.

'I'll make a deal with you, Ravi. If... *if* I can come up with the information that leads to you finding Nathaniel, then you pay me. And I'll let you decide how much. Sound fair?'

Ravi rubbed under his eyes and the ridge of his nose. He was exhausted. No, more than exhausted... he felt unplugged and drained of energy.

'For what it's worth, I'm sorry, Ravi. Your lad... he's one lucky sod to have an old man like you. Whatever happens, at least remember that you did everything you could, and more.'

'That was my wife who called. Nathaniel spoke to her... not long after I delivered the money.'

'So, where the hell is he now?'

Ravi let out a long sigh. 'He said he is safe, but he's going away, so he can lie low.'

'But where will he go?'

'He didn't tell her. And it sounds like she didn't push him for information.'

'What, and he didn't think to contact you? Don't you at least deserve a thanks?' asked Arnie, angry now.

Ravi threw up his hands. 'Evidently not.'

'Your son… he doesn't deserve you, Ravi. I mean that!'

Ravi's phone rang. He checked the screen – Schneider. He answered with a gruff, 'Hello!'

'I'm closing your case. Do not contact me again. Understand?' said Schneider.

Ravi could hear terror in the PI's voice and knew something bad had transpired. 'What's happened? Are you OK? You sound shaken.'

'I'll live!' snapped Schneider. 'You are no longer my client. Delete my number. No, delete all our correspondence. Everything.'

Ravi went to reply, but Schneider cut the call.

37

'Where did you put it?' asked Johnny.

'My usual spot,' said Barry, taking a seat, a roguish grin on his face.

Nino washed up some cups, listening, but doing his best to appear uninterested.

Barry slurped his tea. 'I'll make the arrangements for the next few days. We'll soon be back in full swing.'

Johnny nodded in agreement.

Nino, so engrossed in their conversation, nicked his index finger on a knife in the foamy water and recoiled. He guessed what would be next. These two had big ideas for him. Barry's subtle hints of late had aroused his suspicions, and it was obvious where this was leading, because he knew what Barry meant by more responsibilities and a step up the ladder. He'd now be expected to fill Craig's position.

Barry cleared his throat. 'And the other thing we discussed, Jon?'

Johnny let out a long sigh. 'I'm against it. He kept his end of the bargain.'

Barry let out an exasperated sigh. 'He's a liability.'

'He has kept his mouth shut. I say we let him take his slice and leave.'

'And what if he comes back? You want him out there knowing what he knows? Really, Jon?'

Nino dabbed some kitchen roll on his cut and watched out of the corner of his eye as his brothers eyed each other contemptuously. A phone ringing broke the standoff. Barry looked at the screen and grunted.

'Who is it?' asked Johnny.

Barry cut the call off. 'That dopey penis Trev Smith. He's been calling me for ages. Left messages about some twat who wants to talk to me.'

'About?'

'I dunno. I've been ignoring the moron. It's Trev, it won't be important.'

'You should check,' said Johnny.

'I'm not dealing with Trev, or anyone associated with him. Craig did nothing but moan about the useless toss-pot.'

'Barry, he was the last person to see Craig alive. Perhaps he's remembered something.'

Barry let out a long, deep belch. 'I very much doubt it.'

'Just speak to him,' said Johnny.

'If he calls again, then I might pick up. If I'm not busy.'

Then the phone rang and Barry shook his head and snorted.

'Put him on loud speaker,' said Johnny.

Barry placed the phone on the table and put the call on speaker.

'Barry! My man. How you keeping?' said the caller.

'Trev, why you have you been calling me? What's the drama?' said Barry in a curt tone.

'My mate, Raf, has been in touch. Some guy, his old boss or something, says he's trying to get hold of you, bro.'

Barry sighed. 'Who, Trev?'

'Who?' repeated Trev.

'Yes, who is this guy?' said Barry.

'Ahh, yeah... what's he say his name was... my memory... let me check my messages,' said Trev.

There was rustling and a woman's voice crowing, 'What youse doing, you silly prick?'

'Where's my other blower, Kerry? The other phone?' screeched Trev.

Nino saw Barry eye Johnny with a, *I told you so* expression, as the pair listened to this Trev bicker with his girlfriend. After a minute of quibbling, Trev came back. 'Sorry, my man. Yeah, here it is. Orson Naple... stork... no hold up, I need my glasses.'

Some more rustling followed, and then the bickering ensued. Barry gritted his teeth in frustration and Johnny looked like he was fighting down the urge to chuckle.

'Shut it! Just do one, you soap-dodging skank!... Not you, Barry, sorry. It's Oscar Maplethorpe. Ring any bells?' asked Trev.

'No, Trev,' said Barry.

Nino thought the only thing ringing today will be Trev's scrawny neck, courtesy of Barry's hands, if this conversation dragged on much longer.

'Yeah, Raf said the guy mentioned Craig. He has some info or something.'

Barry's face darkened.

'Raf said it was important,' said Trev.

'Trev, why didn't you just text me all this?' growled Barry.

'Yeah, man... like, I thought about doing that, but I was thinking this is some important intelligence or something and maybe I should, like... you know, speak to you. And relay it all proper, like.'

'Stop waffling bollocks and send me this Maplethorpe's details,' snapped Barry.

'So, like now?' asked Trev.

Barry gritted his teeth. 'No, next week.'

'Hey?'

'Yes, now, Trev!' Barry cut the call and turned to Johnny. 'What the hell is this about, Jon?'

Johnny shrugged.

A good five minutes passed by and still no message materialised. Barry, fuming, picked up the phone with intent to call Trev back, when a text pinged up with Maplethorpe's number.

Nino did not like the sound of this.

Oscar's secret phone vibrated in his jeans and he left Amy snuggled on the sofa with Francesca whilst he nipped upstairs, locked himself in his small study, and answered the call.

'Is this Oscar Maplethorpe?' asked a gruff voice.

'It is indeed. Who's calling, please?'

'Barry... Barry Bartell. I hear you've been trying to get hold of me.'

Oscar's voice got caught in his throat. It took him a few seconds to respond. 'Hello, Barry. I really appreciate you taking the time to call me back.'

'What's this about?' asked Barry, his tone sharp and unnerving.

'Um, well... I have... I've come across some... information. I feel I should—'

'Where are you?'

'Excuse me?'

'Where are you right now?'

'Um, I am at my home,' said Oscar, a cold shudder shot through him.

'Where is that?' asked Barry.

'Um... the outskirts of Canterbury.'

'I'll text you a meeting place. Be there in thirty minutes.'

Oscar, about to confirm that he wouldn't be able to nip away at such short notice, realised the call had ended.

Oscar's pulse raced as he grabbed his woollen jacket, driving gloves, and poked his head around the lounge door. 'Hey, Amy, I have to pop out for an hour.'

'What? Where are you going?'

'Bloody alarm went off at one of the stores. I need to check it out. Find us a decent film to watch and I'll grab us a Mexican and a bottle of red.'

'OK, be quick.'

Nino hugged Elena and slid on his crash helmet. She smiled sweetly at him and Nino found himself reliving the night they'd first kissed, just a few days after his eighteenth birthday. He'd not seen Elena for a good five years as she'd been travelling with her family. So when Nino had learnt that the O'Carroll clan were back in the area and staying in one of the neighbouring towns erecting marquees, he'd rode his bike to the event in view of tracking her down. It didn't take him long to find her. He could still clearly picture her wearing that vintage biker's jacket, with tight leggings and hiking boots. Elena's long, wild hair was blowing in the wind as she caught a glimpse of him through a crowd of people. She'd flashed him a big grin. They'd talked nonstop and spent the entire weekend together. He'd fallen in love with her, he knew that. Elena admitted that she'd been ecstatic to learn her family was heading back to this area. She'd somehow known their paths would cross again. It was one of the best weekends of his entire life.

'You sure you want to go alone?' Elena asked, snapping him out of his daydream.

'Yes. This time I need to go alone. That seems right.'

'Are you nervous?' she asked.

'Yes. But excited too.'

'Go on. Move it. I need to get organised. I have lots to sort out.'

Nino got onto his Kawasaki, flicked the ignition and kicked-started her up. He revved the accelerator and roared the throaty engine to life. He was buzzing with anticipation, because soon everything would change and life as he'd always known it would never be the same.

Oscar followed his satnav through the suburb of Rough Common and into Blean Wood. It was a chilly night, and he'd whacked the heaters on full as he drove his Mercedes E-class into the enclosed parking area used for visiting the nature reserve. Although he was nervous about this meet, he kept telling himself that he had valuable information to divulge and there'd be no reason for this Barry to harm him. As he parked his car and scanned the dark, empty carpark surrounded by eerie looming trees, he started to wobble. This was an insane move. What had he been thinking? How could he possibly know for certain he'd be safe? Why would this Barry want to meet right out here? He decided the best, and safer, course of action would be to drive away, lose the burner phone and forget he'd ever had this idiotic idea. No, he couldn't do that… the guy had his full name and, as a listed company director, he'd easily be located. No, a better plan would be to text Barry and advise him, in a polite but firm manner, that he would not be prepared to meet in such a rural and isolated spot. He would therefore wait for him at a pub. There was a suitable place in Harbledown, less than a ten-minute drive from here. This option was taken off the table as a chunky Ford Ranger drove into the entrance and stopped. He made out two large shapes in the vehicle.

'Stay calm, Oscar,' he muttered to himself. 'Don't freak out, matey boy.'

The passenger got out of the Ranger. A short figure with a heavy build.

Oscar cut the engine, opened the door, and got out. As soon as he left the toasty car, the chill air hit him like an icy wallop in the face.

The man approached, taking big, confident strides. 'Oscar?'

'You must be Barry. Thanks so much for meeting with me. I know this is all rather unorthodox and clandestine,' said Oscar, speaking in his best business-like tone.

Barry approached so brashly, for a moment it appeared as though he was preparing to thump him one. 'What the fuck is all this about? Who the hell are you, Oscar?'

Oscar, so stunned by Barry's forcefulness, spat out a load of nonsensical noise.

The second guy jumped out of the Ranger. This chap was taller than Barry, with broad shoulders and a squarer jawline, though Oscar saw a slight resemblance and guessed this was a Bartell family member. Although despite his size, Barry appeared far more ruthless, menacing, and intimidating than this other man.

'You better start talking,' said Barry.

Oscar couldn't stop himself blathering on non-stop. His mouth just wouldn't stop moving. The taller man listened with his arms folded.

Barry chewed his lower lip, his hard eyes locked on him.

'So after hearing all this, I investigated the name Craig Bartell and, well… here we all are.'

Barry nodded and exhaled. 'Oscar, I'm going to need you to hand over your wallet. Now, please.'

Oscar swallowed. 'What? Why?'

'Wallet!' snapped Barry.

Oscar complied, located his wallet, and handed it to Barry, who opened it and sifted through its contents. He pulled out his driver's licence and handed it to the other man, who took a photo of the ID using his phone.

Barry slipped out a business card and studied it. 'You're in the bathroom business?'

Oscar nodded. 'My father's firm.'

Barry flicked the card. 'I'll keep this for future reference.'

'Of course,' said Oscar.

The bigger guy handed the licence back to Barry, who slotted it back in the wallet.

'I am so very sorry about your younger brother. So tragic,' said Oscar.

'What do you get out of this?' asked Barry.

'I decided you should be informed. It seemed like the right thing to do,' said Oscar.

Barry tapped the wallet against the palm of his hand. 'Not the police? You decided the best course of action was to come straight to us with this?'

'Well, I—'

'Think before you answer,' said Barry, eyes blazing.

'Because... because Amy and Francesca are my entire world. I'll do anything to protect them! If *he* comes back, he'll worm his way into their world and I'll be pushed aside... I love them so much.'

'Alright, Maplethorpe, ease off. I'm getting all choked up here,' said Barry.

'Sorry, it's just... Karl Rogers is an incompetent idiot. I don't want that man in my family's life.'

Barry gave him a threatening stare. 'What, you reckon we'll fuck-up this Karl just because you've concocted some bullshit about him doing our brother in? I reckon you're taking us for a ride, pal. And let me warn you now, if you've fed us a load of garbage, I'll personally run over your head. And I'll use your Mercedes to do it. Do you understand me?'

'Please, Barry, I assure you that everything I have told you is the absolute truth. I would never, ever lie about such consequential matters. You must believe me,' said Oscar, now using his best conciliatory tone.

Barry turned to the taller man. 'What do you reckon, Johnny?'

Oscar could see real traces of concern on Barry's face now as he continued to chew on his lower lip.

The taller man, Johnny, stepped closer to Oscar. 'This Duncan, what's his surname?'

Oscar gazed up at Johnny, unable to read this guy's expression at all. 'I don't know, but he's the key to finding out the truth. He saw everything.'

'You said he denied everything when confronted. What if your girlfriend got it wrong?' asked Johnny.

'No. This guy had guilt written all over his face. He was there, I have no doubt,' said Oscar, considering that if he had this all wrong, then he'd be signing his own death warrant. 'The day after the... incident, Karl and his buddy upped sticks and raced off to the Netherlands. Plus, Amy confirmed Karl always parked at that solicitor's carpark. He quit his job and dropped off the grid, whilst also in the process of leasing a flat. Until then, he'd been a reliable employee.'

'But that's not proof,' said Barry.

'Barry, it all adds up. It's not right that Karl gets off scot-free. It's completely unfair that he can get away with...' Oscar wanted to say murder, but decided against it, and instead said, 'With an atrocious crime such as this.'

Barry and Johnny shared a look. A look that said, *what do you reckon?*

'Barry, I have the camera file. I can send you a close-up shot of this Duncan guy—'

Barry cut him off. 'You get his address. Tonight. Understand?'

'I'll try, but I don't...'

Barry handed back the wallet. 'Tonight.'

'Um, yes. Of course, I'll get the address to you by tonight,' said Oscar.

'And you better pray you've got your facts straight,' said Barry.

Oscar slid back into the Mercedes and rested his head in his hands. The protruding veins in his temples throbbed as he took deep breaths and wondered how on earth he could obtain this Duncan's address, and more importantly, what would those men do to him if he failed to provide said address? He'd already tried to find the lad via social media, but drew a blank there and he couldn't ask Amy. That would be far to suspect. He needed to formulate a plan, and fast. He started the engine and sped out of the carpark.

Johnny pulled over the Ranger and Barry got out, shouted something and started pacing like a caged animal.

Johnny cut the engine and got out. 'Let's get all the facts first. We don't know who this Oscar bloke is. Could be a wind-up.'

Barry, face screwed up, shook his head over and over. 'Nah, nah, this is messed up. He might be a poncy prick, but he seems genuine.'

'Maybe he believes it. That doesn't make it a reality.'

Barry sucked in air through his teeth. 'Find Nino! And call Warren, get him down to ours to monitor things. Keep an eye on Nathaniel.'

'The poor bloke's only just got out of surgery. His jaw is all wired up.'

'So what? I only want him to keep watch, not nosh the bloke off. I'll call Fraser. I want this bloody mystery solved tonight, Jon. We'll give this Maple-wanker two hours to come up with the goods. Then we'll go to his gaff.'

Nino sauntered down the street with the biggest smile on his face. He felt amazing. He almost skipped to his bike, because now they could start the preparations for what he and Elena had planned. The next couple of days would be tricky… no, tricky was an understatement, they'd be extremely dangerous. But the rewards would outweigh the risks. His joyous mood was ruined when he took out his phone, seeing the many missed calls and text messages from his two brothers. He read the texts, which were all were demands for him to call them ASAP and to return home without delay. There were voice messages too, no doubt also from his brothers. He scanned the busy street, certain that eyes were on him. Had they spied on him all evening? Seen where he'd been. Seen *who* he'd been with. Cars and buses whipped by and the pedestrians trundled past like phone obsessed robots. He scanned his surroundings and didn't spot anyone lurking around or studying him. There was no way in hell anyone could have followed him to South London on the bike, not at the speeds he'd kept up. Unless they'd been an adept rider themselves.

Nino listened to Barry's voicemail, and he gasped when he said they'd found some more information about Craig's death and needed to speak to him urgently. Everything was in danger of collapsing and he needed to get a handle on the situation. Had he started something that he couldn't finish?

38

Nino sat on a wall and fingered his phone as he contemplated his next move. He needed to find out what his brothers knew and fast.

Nino thought back to when he'd set the wheels in motion and felt a surge of panic rush over him. It all sort of... just happened... it had been that night in The Swan, when Stefan started talking nonsense about Nino joining his stupid association, when the idea came to him. The following day, during breakfast, he'd taken the first steps towards hatching his plan.

Nino recalled that he'd been staring into his cereal bowl, eyes fixed on the swirling milk and doing his best to appear as downcast as possible. He'd almost forced a few tears, but decided not to overdo it.

Barry started huffing and sighing. 'Come on, out with it.'

'I... I don't know... I—'

'Stop stuttering and spit it out already.'

'I heard some stuff last night. Some messed up stuff, Barry.'

Johnny had joined them at the table. He'd sipped his tea, fixing Nino with a blank stare.

'Well? Don't keep us in suspense all morning,' Barry had asked.

Nino had shuffled uncomfortably in the seat. 'I was in the toilet. I overheard Stefan talking to some guy by the sinks. He was well hammered and didn't notice I was in a cubicle. He started talking about Craig. He was laughing... he thought it was hilarious that we were out there in the boozer, totally oblivious.'

'I want to know what he said, word... for fucking... word. Do you hear me?' Barry had growled.

'He said, "those thick twats out there don't have a clue, mate. Not a Scooby, the useless fat-headed pricks." The other lad asked what he was talking about, and Stefan sniggered and goes, "I done that loud-mouth wanker myself".'

Barry's jaw had tightened, his lips scrunched up and his ears glowed bright red.

'Then Stefan goes, "Too big for his boots. That Craigy-boy reckoned the association was his idea, and he was going to run things. Shame it was so easy. He didn't suffer, which was pretty disappointing. Craig didn't put up a fight either. The boy was nothing but a massive bully and a lippy prick, and when it came down to a real dust up, the pansy crapped his pants!" Then he laughed and said, "Obviously this goes no further. Like I even need to say".'

Barry and Johnny had both glared at him like they were about to explode with pure rage. After around ten seconds, when the words sunk in, Barry snapped. He'd bolted up, roared in fury and upended the table, sending mugs and bowls flying about the kitchen. 'Why are you only telling us now?' Barry had lunged at Nino and slammed him to the floor. 'You prick!' Spittle ran from Barry's mouth as he'd screamed in Nino's face. He'd put his meaty hands around his neck and squeezed. 'I'll do that Stefan! I'll rip his face off, the little fu—'

The next thing Nino remembered was Johnny pulling Barry off and his brothers wrestling. Whilst the pair grappled, Nino took the opportunity to drag himself up and dodge out of the way of the brutal fracas.

'This is why! This is why Nino didn't tell us last night!' Johnny had yelled, slamming Barry against a kitchen cupboard and sending an assortment of pots and pans tumbling. 'Calm down, Barry,' he'd shouted, wedging his forearm under his chin. 'You need to ease up. Nino did the right thing. If we'd have kicked off in there, it wouldn't have ended well for us. Use your brain for once, Barry!'

After a few moments of wriggling, growling and hissing, Barry stopped struggling and Johnny released his grip.

Barry, breathing fast and his face turning a peculiar bluish red colour, did eventually relax. Though Nino thought he'd resembled an angry cartoon character and he'd half expected steam to blow out of his ears, or his head to explode into a million pieces. He'd tried not to smirk at the images.

When Barry spoke, his breathing had been rough, and he'd lowered his croaky voice. 'OK. We do... this... do it right... I don't care who he... is. We wait for the right... moment... and do that, fucker.'

'We need to be careful. But we'll do this,' Johnny had said.

Barry took a huge gulp of air. 'That's what you said when I wanted to settle the score for Vickers, Jon. Remember?'

Johnny's eyes had narrowed, and Nino tensed as he'd anticipated more violence, but Johnny retorted with a sigh and he nudged an upturned bowl. 'You need to clean up this mess, Barry. And mend that table leg.' Then he'd walked out.

Now, Nino jumped down off the wall and considered calling one of his brothers back, but thought better of that idea. If they'd found out he'd lied about Stefan, they were going to kill him.

39

1 December 2018 [20.30]

After they'd eaten their burritos and spicy rice, Oscar watched as Amy took a final sip from her glass of red, puckered her lips appreciatively and scrolled on her phone. The TV was on, playing Saturday night trash that neither watched and acted as background sound only. She wore her tartan print pyjamas with her hair swept over one shoulder, and sat crossed legged, snuggled amongst the fluffy scatter cushions.

Man, she looked so frigging hot. Sometimes when he viewed his girlfriend, he wondered if he were dreaming, because that's how privileged and lucky he considered he was. Not to mention the big age gap. He'd also not had many partners and those few he'd been with were all rather pig ugly compared to Amy. It didn't all boil down to her stunning looks, of course. He loved Amy, and the idea of losing her was altogether unbearable. If keeping her meant bending the rules and playing dirty, then bring it on. Karl would soon learn the great lengths he'd go to in order to keep the things most precious in his life.

'That wine is delicious,' said Amy, pouring the dregs from the bottle into her glass.

'I should hope so at twenty-five quid a bottle. Here, finish my glass,' said Oscar, pouring his untouched drink into hers. 'I've got one of my migraines.' He rubbed two fingers to each temple to emphasise the pain. He assumed she'd not taken the bait, so he opened his mouth to request she get his pills, but she put down her wine and mobile phone.

'I'll check on Fran and grab your pills. Are they in the upstairs bathroom cupboard?'

'Aw, thanks, Amy. Yep, should be. Or in my bedside drawer,' he lied. He'd moved them, knowing she'd likely try to hunt them down and give him more time to execute his cunning plan. The plan which had struck him like a lightning bolt as he stood in the Mexican restaurant awaiting his order. He followed her movements out of the corner of his eye, but kept his focus on her phone. He wouldn't have long, so needed to move super quick. The plan relied on her not locking the phone's screen, or it not locking itself, because he didn't know her pin code. He dived to retrieve the phone, and almost chuckled in delight when he saw the screen was, in fact, unlocked. With shaking hands, he scrolled the contents, found the only Duncan in her list and texted him. *We need to talk. It's urgent. Please meet me at the chippy on North Street at 9.30pm.* He went to press send but as an afterthought added one x. Amy always added one, no matter who the message was for, which he considered weird and unnecessary. But there you go. And send. He chewed on the inside of his cheek as he eyed the screen and waited. A good minute passed... nothing. He flicked his eyes to the door, then back to the phone's screen. Still nothing. *Bugger reply already,* he thought. He moved to the door, phone cradled in his palm, and listened. No sign of her heading back downstairs yet. Come on, come on, you bloody dopey fool... text back... text bloody back.

He could hear Amy calling him, no doubt frustrated at not finding the tablets. He focussed on the screen again, willing a message to appear. Reply, goddamn you. Answer the text. The three dots appeared, and he froze... come on, Duncan, type back. The dots vanished, and he almost yelled – *Nooo, you idiot*, as he heard Amy coming downstairs, grumbling about not locating his pills. Then, the message appeared. *I'll be there x.*

Oscar rapidly replied, *Great see you x.* He deleted the conversation with his thumb, and tossed the phone onto the table. Amy walked in the moment he flung himself back on the sofa, heart thudding.

'Oscar, I can't find them. I looked everywhere.'

'Eh, do you know, I might have left them in the study. I'll grab them. Fancy some popcorn? We'll stick that movie on.'

'You OK? You look flustered.'

'Fine, yeah fine. Once I've had a couple of pills, I'll be good as gold.' He left the room, charged upstairs, locked himself in his study and texted Barry about the meet, together with a photo of Duncan he'd already stored on the phone. Oscar received an instant *OK* in response to this. He took a deep breath and shut down the burner phone. He'd toss the thing in the River Stour tomorrow. A sheen of perspiration had developed on his forehead and he wiped it away with the back of his hand. Oscar felt a pang of guilt for the big guy he'd thrown under the bus, so to speak, but they had left him with no option. He hadn't technically obtained Duncan's address as they'd requested, but he'd furnished them with something far better. He'd delivered the boy to them on a plate. This made the guilt amplify, and he hoped they'd not hurt the lad too much. Christ, what if they murdered him? That was a sobering thought. Would he be implicated? Would he be an accessory to this? He'd not thought that far ahead. No, they wouldn't kill him. They'd rough the boy up and once Karl got wind that the Bartells knew of his involvement, then he'd be forced to stay away. Forced to stay out of the area and away from his girls. His family. He'd done the right thing and shouldn't torment himself on the outcome of his actions any longer. He needed a stiff drink.

Duncan pulled on his peacoat with intentions of slipping outside unnoticed, but as soon as he turned the handle, his mum appeared in the doorway.

'Just nipping out for an hour,' he said, buttoning up the big, round buttons on his coat.

'Duncan, it's almost nine,' she said, gazing at him like she'd caught him with his mitts in the cookie jar.

'I'm a big boy. I can go out past eight.'

'It's freezing tonight. You don't want to be going out in that nasty old weather, love. Come and watch the box with me and your dad. He got you some of that funny fruity cider stuff you like. Mango and passion-whatsit.'

'Oh.'

'We could always play that racing game. That one me and your father are useless at.'

This was so typical of his mum, thought Duncan. She'd nagged him non-stop about him being a recluse, and as soon as he ventured out, she went all bonkers on him.

'You meeting your cousin?' she asked, fumbling around on top of the shoe cupboard and tugging out his gloves.

'Yeah, maybe later. I'm seeing another friend first.'

She handed him the gloves with a concerned smile and for a second it looked as though she wanted to say something, but stopped herself.

'I'll see you later, Mum,' he said, and ventured out into the frosty night.

Not that she'd been counting, but Amy had noted Oscar was whacking back the vodka and Coke tonight. She didn't have a problem with this in itself. She enjoyed a good tipple herself, but it struck her as odd. First off, he rarely touched booze and when he did, red wine would always be his drink of choice. And second, he'd told her he'd taken his painkillers for his migraine and always vowed not to touch booze whilst on the medication; after the last time, when he'd got so sick and dizzy, he'd contemplated ringing an ambulance. Which meant either he'd lied about taking the pills, or something was bothering him enough to warrant him not giving a damn. On top of this, he kept watching her out of the corner of his eye, and when her phone beeped a notification, it seemed as though his eyes robotically moved to the device, even though his face stayed emotionless as he pretended to be fixed on the movie. And she seemed certain he was pretending.

On the next notification, she snatched up the phone, read the news feed report and feigned a shock at what she saw.

As expected, she spotted Oscar fix her with a nervous stare.

'Mmm, ugh,' she muttered.

'Something wrong?' he asked.

Amy kept up the charade and switched her shocked expression to that of outrage.

'Who is it? What's wrong? Amy? Amy? Who's that from?'

'What the hell is it with you? You've been acting weird all night, Oscar.'

Oscar picked up his drink, his face pinched and grumpy.

'What, you think I'm up to something dodgy? You don't trust me?' she asked.

Oscar poured himself more vodka and necked it neat. 'Do you still have feelings for him?'

'Who?'

'*Him!*' he spat. 'If he came back, what would happen?'

'I'm with you and he is my past. What is going on with you?'

'It's just... I couldn't take it... the idea of losing you both... it drives me insane with worry.'

It was odd seeing her boyfriend like this. His self-assured and cool-headed persona being swapped with that of an insecure and mopey teenager did not add up. Something had happened to make him worry about their relationship. Then the thought came to her – perhaps Karl had returned, and he'd somehow got wind of this. Amy needed to speak with Duncan. She considered messaging him now, but decided instead to wait until tomorrow. Amy was certain he'd have spilled the beans to Karl by now, and it wouldn't be long before he showed himself. She should have contacted Duncan and discussed everything with him like she'd agreed to. Now things were bound to get messy.

The taxi dropped Duncan on North Street ten minutes early and he stood outside the *For Cod's Sake* fish and chip shop, which was nestled between a hair salon and locksmith. The surrounding buildings lay in darkness and the warm, inviting glow from within that chippy almost dragged him inside for some respite from the chilly night. Ice had already formed over the parked cars and glistened under the orange hue of the street lamps. Duncan slipped out the gloves, now glad his mum forced him to take them, and popped them on. Ten minutes would seem like a long time in the freezing cold. He watched two teenage girls, gripping sizeable portions of chips, exit the chippy and bound off down the road, knocking shoulders and giggling as they walked. The aroma of food hit him and he peered inside again, seeing a young Chinese man slouched at the counter, eyes glued to his phone. He'd maybe suggest to Amy they grab some food and eat at the table inside. He wondered why she'd picked this spot to meet, though guessed she could get here on foot within ten minutes.

Duncan drew a smiley face on the window of a parked Seat using one finger. To warm up, he paced the shopfronts and wrapped his arms around himself. A bitter wind started picking up, and he decided to head inside the chippy and text Amy to let her know his location. As he took out his phone, considering if he could text in the thick gloves, a sticker on the back of a parked van caught his attention. He walked over for a closer inspection. It was a large decal of a grinning gorilla firing a rifle, with the words *Ape Shit* wrapped around the image. This van's windows weren't iced up and when the engine roared to life, it startled the life out of him.

'Hey, could you do me a wee favour there, pal?' The voice sounded Scottish, and Duncan turned to see a short man in a thick beanie, struggling with a large box as he headed towards him.

'The door, pal. Can you whip it open?' asked the Scotsman.

'Um, yeah of course,' said Duncan, fumbling with the catch, his chunky gloves hindering the action.

'Nice one. You're a star, big man.'

Duncan yanked open the stiff door.

What happened in the moments that followed flashed by so fast it made his head spin. As the door flung open, dark shapes moved from within the vehicle. Duncan spun to get away and saw the Scotsman drop the box and lunge toward him. Then he was hauled roughly backwards and landed with a bone-shaking thud. He rolled onto his front and tried to crawl away, and realised he was going further inside the van and fear gripped him like a fierce stab in the heart. He screamed and heard the van doors slam. Now he couldn't move and became aware that someone was kneeling between his shoulder blades. In the chaos, he'd dropped his phone.

'Help! Help! Somebody help me!' Duncan screamed, his hoarse voice filled with terror.

A hand pushed his head hard against the floor. His face pushed against some rough carpet that smelt of mildew. He screamed, writhed like crazy and kicked out his legs, but the figures were too powerful and he couldn't break loose. The front door creaked open, and the van rocked, confirming someone had got into the front. The door slammed shut. Duncan's scream caught in his throat when he felt cold metal press on the side of his neck. Not hard, but enough to make him aware that at least one of his attackers carried a knife.

'You need to stay silent! Understand?' The man's voice was both calm and authoritarian.

Duncan froze. As the van drove away, he heard what sounded like tape rending.

As his wrists were bound and the enormity of the situation dawned on him, he felt himself losing control of his bladder.

The grim thought that Amy had betrayed him made him want to sob. But he didn't. He bit his lip, closed his eyes, and suffered the terrifying ordeal in utter silence. How could she have sold him out like this?

40

Nino heard police radios crackling and froze. As a Bartell, it was natural to be wary of the police. It had been instilled in him throughout his life – the police were the enemy, end of story. He slipped off his crash helmet and turned, as casually as possible, to face the police car. Traffic police. Two uniformed officers surveying him from within the patrol car. He cursed himself for stopping at the motorway services for a fill up. The passenger, a young female, spoke on her radio and kept flicking a glance in his direction. The door hung open, and it looked like the officer was about to jump out of the car in order to question him. Nino kept it cool, crouched down and pretended to fiddle with his bike's foot-peg. He'd be in trouble if they questioned him. Yes, he owned a bike licence, but he didn't have the correct insurance, V55, or certificate of newness to ride his trials bike on public roads. But he'd definitely come to the officers' attention. He didn't need this now.

Duncan heard some muttered voices and tried to work out how long he'd been travelling for. Thirty minutes? An hour? Maybe longer. Time seemed impossible to follow. His muddled mind raced with jumbled, petrifying thoughts about what his fate would be. He bounced and rocked about as the van jumped from side to side, confirming that they'd left the main roads and were heading off the beaten track. This thought caused him to go rigid with fear. Where the hell would he end up? And would he ever go home again? Somehow he knew his fate… these men would kill him. They'd hurt him, make him speak the truth, then he'd die in a grisly fashion, alone and scared. The van shuddered, and he thumped his head on the floor. He only wished the impact could have knocked him unconscious.

The police radio crackled again. The officer spoke on the radio and within moments the patrol car was tearing off, blue lights flashing. Nino exhaled the breath he'd been holding in. He'd noticed a Premier Inn on the far side of the services, so he'd grab a room and call it a night. Once there, he'd phone Elena and go through the next course of action. Going back to the house didn't seem a wise move. He'd already concocted a new variation to the plan that they already had in play. But he'd run out of time tonight. Tomorrow would be another day.

Elena heard the commotion outside in the courtyard and stepped outside to investigate.

Someone screamed and pleaded for help and Barry shouted, 'Shut up! Keep it shut.'

Then Elena caught sight of Barry and Johnny wrestling with a big lad, who was in a total fit of panic. He cried like a baby and pleaded with them to let him go. They forced him away from the van. It was awful to listen to the lad's distressing shrieks, and it made Elena's stomach tie up in knots. The big lad yelled and tried to wriggle free of the pair, and ended up with a ripped jacket as he collapsed to his knees. As the brothers yanked him up, Elena glimpsed the terror on the poor lad's face and she bit down on her clenched fist.

Elena slipped back inside and watched from the window. Fraser slammed the van's rear doors and said something to Barry and Johnny, who were busy dragging the lad across the courtyard. Fraser then gave them the thumbs up and set about changing the van's licence plates.

That van had received more registration numbers than she'd had hot dinners.

Elena hid behind the curtain as Barry and Johnny marched the lad past the window and then the trio disappeared into Hetty's paddock. Her mobile sprang to life and made her jump.

'Shit! Where are you, Nino?' she asked, peering back outside into the gloom.

'Motorway services. I'm in a hotel room. Have you spoken to them? What's going on?'

'They've got some lad here. Big fella in his mid-twenties.'

'Right, listen, we need to go ahead with everything tomorrow, Elena. Do you know what to do?'

'What about your brothers?' asked Elena.

'I'll get them away from the house as soon as I can. Do you think Brennan could help us out? Could he collect you from the house once they leave?'

'I'll call and ask,' said Elena.

'Are you going to be OK with everything else? I know this isn't exactly what we planned, but we can still make it work.'

'I'll be fine. But they'll grill me about where you are. What do I tell them?'

Elena spied Barry coming back from the field and slid back behind the curtain.

'Tell them… tell them you have no idea. That I'm not answering my phone. Wipe all our messages and calls in case they check your phone, Elena.'

She peered back out again. Barry spoke to Fraser, laughed at something the Scotsman said, then headed down the side of the house and out of sight. 'You think that's one of them?' she asked.

'I think it must be. I don't know how they found him.'

Elena noticed Fraser jump into the van, start the engine, and drive away. 'How did it go today?'

'Good. Fantastic, Elena. I'll tell you all about it when I see you tomorrow.'

'Make sure I *do* see you tomorrow.'

'Be careful… I love you, Elena O'Carroll.'

Elena beamed. 'I love you too... Antonino!' She cut the call and took a deep breath. It would be a long night.

Barry emerged and an icy chill ran down her spine. He held a long length of plastic covered chain, part of which he dragged behind him. And a canister of petrol. She bolted for the door and locked it. Yes, this would be a long, scary night. She'd sleep with one eye open and a knife tucked under her pillow.

41

Page 4

"I phoned up the Bartells' landline and spoke to a miserable sounding woman, who I guessed was his downtrodden wife. The mother of his other three sons. When she put Jack on the line, he sounded calm, considering. He said he'd be willing to speak to me and discuss the situation and called me back a few days later. He even sounded pleased to hear from me and I started, foolishly, to believe that after all these years of pining, I might finally be able to be reunited with you. He seemed so sincere. Jack said he'd been harsh with me in Malta and that he'd felt bad ever since, and had even considered contacting me to arrange some meet ups so I could spend a little time with you. But away from the family home, because Maria could never know I was back in your life. He said he'd always regretted what happened. He told me about a place that I should go to meet him – a cafe near a town called Ashford in Kent. I drove to that cafe, but it was closed, abandoned and far from anywhere. When I tried to leave, an old white van blocked my way out and three boys got out and dragged me from my car. One of them was only a kid. I screamed for help, but the youngest punched me hard in the stomach and they manhandled me into their van. They blindfolded me, drove to a field, and they ripped all my clothes off as they forced me into a deep pit they'd already dug out. The one called Barry did most of the talking. He said I had two options. Leave England now, return to Malta and never come back. The second option was to stay and be tortured. He said they'd make me suffer, and they'd do… sickening things to me. The older ones said they'd take turns to have me. Afterwards, they'd lock me up and return daily to rip chunks out of me. He laughed when he said that one day he'd bring a potato peeler and would use it to slice off the skin from my nose until it was down to the bone. The next day he'd bring a hammer and chisel to remove a few toes, then pliers to remove my eyelids – and he'd make sure I lived, just to suffer some more. He sneered as he said he'd keep it up for days, weeks, possibly months, until I begged to die. The prolonged torture would continue until there was nothing left to hack off. And then, when he was ready, he'd burn me alive. He then joked that he personally considered the first option to be more appealing and that he suggested I went for that. I believed everything he said, so I was forced to flee. I know I am a coward… But I'd never been so terrified in all my life. And knowing you were there, living with those vile people… well, that awful thought stayed in my mind every waking minute. I didn't want to leave you. But I was powerless to save you."

42

Duncan became aware of voices and, for a moment, he didn't know where he was, but the night's events flooded back in rapid succession.

'He blacked out a minute ago, Barry,' said a voice.

'Wake him up,' snapped the other voice. This guy… this Barry, spoke harsher and sounded more intimidating than the first. He'd been the one doing all the talking since they'd grabbed him.

Duncan kept his eyes closed. Until the liquid splashed over his face and he smelt the unmistakable, pungent odour of petrol. Then he opened them and sobbed. 'Please let me speak… let me tell you what happened!'

More petrol flowed over his body, and he screeched and begged for them to stop as the liquid flowed over his raw, broken skin and stung like hell.

The men pulled him to his feet, removed his jacket, and shoved him forward a few steps.

The taller man shone his torch into a hole, and Duncan peered in. It looked deep and there were puddles of water down there, plus loads of crushed beer cans, bits of wood and various pieces of debris. The wood was black and charred, and he grasped that he stood on the edge of some sort of large fire pit.

'No... no, no, no, no... please don't... please, God no,' pleaded Duncan.

Barry was putting something around his ankle... some sort of metal bow-shaped shackle. Similar to a device that would be used to tow a car. Duncan felt a tight pressure around his ankle and pulled away. He realised that they'd also attached a thick chain to the shackle, but he couldn't see where the rest of the chain went or what they'd attached it to.

Barry tugged at the shackle and stood up. 'OK, Duncan, my name is Barry and this is my brother Johnny... and you are going to have a nice, long chat with us. Got that?' He then poured more petrol over Duncan's head and he gasped as it burnt his eczema.

Amy checked in on Francesca and stared at the baby in wonder. She was the most gorgeous little girl, and Amy felt so blessed. For reasons she could not fathom, she had the sudden urge to send Duncan a photo of Francesca, with a message that she was happy for him to forward it on to Karl. She wanted him to see her... to see what they'd created... the amazing child whose life he *should* be part of. But the urge passed. If Karl wanted to be involved, she would wait for him to do the chasing.

'Why didn't you call the police? You claim it was an accident, so why flee?' asked Barry.

'I... I just...'

'Did you know Craig?' asked Barry.

Duncan shook his head.

'So, why?' asked Barry.

'I... I'd heard... stuff,' said Duncan.

Barry grunted. 'So, you fled out of fear? Thinking that the last thing you wanted was to end up in the middle of nowhere, chained to a concrete block and swimming in petrol.'

'Something like that,' sniffed Duncan.

'And are you associated with the Chillcotts?' asked Barry.

'Never heard of them,' croaked Duncan.

Johnny sighed and shook his head as if this affair was nothing but a massive waste of time and a huge inconvenience.

'So, Duncan, we need to know where your mate Karl is,' said Barry.

'I don't have a clue. I swear I don't. He's travelling around Europe... but I can't—'

'Duncan! Don't, OK. Just don't. I'm going to need you to stop talking bollocks and unlock your phone. If I have to ask twice, then I will pull out my lighter and cook you like a stuck pig.' Barry held out the phone and Duncan took it and unlocked the screen. Barry snatched it back and opened up the contacts. He found Karl's listing and clicked on the circle icon containing a photo, then he enlarged the photo and held out the phone for Duncan to see. 'This him?' he asked.

Duncan didn't respond for a good fifteen seconds before giving a reluctant nod of his head.

Barry showed Johnny the photo. 'Who does he remind you of?'

Johnny shrugged. 'He looks familiar, I guess.'

Barry clicked his fingers. 'That nutty mush from the Jackass show. Dead ringer.'

Johnny nodded, appearing bored as he took a swig from a bottle of whiskey.

Barry turned his attention back to Duncan. 'Now, big lad. I need you to calm down and focus. Think carefully about what you say and how you say it. OK?'

Duncan said nothing.

'You need to call Karl and convince him to come back home. Tomorrow. So concentrate on every single word that comes out of your mouth.'

'But... I won't be able—'

Barry cut him off with a sharp slap to the side of his head that made Duncan's ears ring.

'No buts here, Duncan. I'm telling you how it's going to be. You fuck this up and I will boot your fat arse down there and light you up. You'll burn to death in that filthy pit. There is no third option here. Do you understand what I am saying to you?' asked Barry. 'Can you imagine dying like that? It won't be quick.'

Duncan tried to speak but words wouldn't come and his jaw chattered and he just made a pitiful whining noise.

Barry's eyes narrowed. 'We have your address. We will find your family. Everyone you care about will be drawn into this. Now make that call and get creative. Or we'll be the ones getting creative. You don't want that. I promise you now, you do *not* want that.'

'Please don't make me do this,' said Duncan, repeating the sentence over and over until Barry slapped him about the head again.

'Enough with this bleating. Use this phone,' said Barry. He typed Karl's number into a different phone and handed it to Duncan. He accepted it with a trembling hand. 'I'm not sure what to—'

Barry slapped him again. Hard. Duncan sobbed and moaned.

Barry spoke through gritted teeth. 'I'm getting bored with your shit. Think, boy. Make a choice on what's more important to you.'

Duncan's ears rang and his face throbbed from the strike. He gazed up at Johnny with a pleading look, but the man just returned with a cold, unforgiving stare.

Barry shook his head, exasperated. 'Look, it's him, or it's you and your family. Is this fella worth that much to you?' Barry pulled a chrome zippo lighter from his jacket pocket. 'It's the most important phone call you'll ever make, big lad. Don't you screw this up. Now get on with it. On loud speaker.'

Duncan pressed the call button, and the phone made the unusual call tone, confirming that Karl was still overseas. He willed the phone to go straight to voicemail, because if Karl didn't answer, then he'd have more time to think of a way to wriggle out of this situation. Think of a way he could somehow warn Karl this was a setup without these lunatics suspecting a double cross. There had to be a way. Surely there had to be.

'Hello?' came Karl's voice.

'It's me,' said Duncan.

'Hey, hey, Dunk. What's up, man? Is this a different number?' Karl's voice sounded cheery. He sounded drunk.

A few seconds passed before Duncan could force out any words. 'New phone. Where are you?'

'In the square. Eindhoven. Chilling outside under a lovely warm heater. Oh, hold up, it's turned off.' There was a scraping noise before Karl came back on the line. 'Sorry, switching the heater back on. Bit fresh now. Is it cold in the UK yet?'

Duncan, doing his best to stop his teeth chattering, said, 'It is super cold. Freezing.' That was an understatement, he considered as he looked at each brother in turn, receiving stony stares in return.

'You OK, Dunk? You sound distant.'

'I'm fine. I have a terrible cold,' said Duncan. His hands hurt, they were so frozen. His body kept shuddering involuntarily. 'Might be the flu.'

Duncan got a tiny nod of approval from Barry in response to his fib.

'You sure everything is OK, mate? You sound strange. Anything else I should be worried about, other than you having a snivel?' asked Karl.

Duncan looked past the two foreboding shapes and focussed on the bright moon that fought its way through the gloom. 'Karl, I… there is something I need to tell you.' Still focussing on the moon, Duncan tried hard to conjure up a scheme to save them both. But nothing came to mind. He closed his eyes tightly. He didn't know what to say. Shout a warning to Karl and suffer the consequences – or trick his best friend into coming home to face these men and whatever brutality they had in store for him. He thought about his parents and their part in all this mess. Would these men really go after them? Would they hurt them? He opened his eyes and focussed on Barry. Yes, he was certain they would. They'd be prepared to do anything.

'Well?' asked Karl.

Barry's expression couldn't be clearer. The expression said – *You dare and I'll kill you!*

Duncan closed his eyes. 'I spoke to Amy. There's something important I need to tell you.'

'Well, don't keep me in suspense, Dunk. What?'

Duncan could feel hot tears rolling down his cheeks and snot bubbled up in his nostrils. 'She had your baby. A little girl. Francesca.'

It was a good twenty seconds before Karl responded. 'You've seen her?'

'Yes. I've seen her,' said Duncan.

'What's she like?'

'She's got your hair, Karl.'

Duncan opened his eyes. The moon was now gone, hidden under a covering of mist and cloud. The brothers both fixed him with sinister stares. Duncan could hear Karl's heavy breathing. He closed his eyes again and detested himself for being so weak... for being so helpless... for being Duncan Parvin the gutless pushover. He wanted to spit in their faces and roar at them in defiance. Scream at them as he savagely steamed into them. But like the weakling he'd always been, he sobbed. Silent, pathetic, and feeble as usual.

'And what did Amy say? About me? About us... going away?' asked Karl.

Duncan took a deep breath. 'She... was angry, but she is desperate to see you.'

'Dunk, I... I want to come back. I do, but things are tight. The blog is still in the planning stages, and I'm only working two days a week with Joost now.'

'I'll buy your ticket. Just send me a screenshot of your passport,' said Duncan, hating himself.

'You'd seriously do that for me? I didn't even square you up for the Eurostar,' said Karl.

'I'll book on my phone tonight and send you everything you need.'

'Thanks, Dunk. I mean that. Christ, I have a kid. I can't get my head around that!'

'I gotta go, Karl. Take care, OK.' He ended the call and the racking sobbing flooded out.

'You did well,' said Barry, taking the phone from his shaking hand. 'Where's your bank card? You have a flight to book.'

'Do you want kids, Joost?' asked Karl.

Joost considered the question, then said, 'No... no. I mean, I dunno.'

Karl switched the overhead heater back on. 'I'd never thought about it myself.'

'I got really upset when I lost my dog,' said Joost, looking into space, wistful and wasted.

'And?' asked Karl.

'If you have a child, then you carry the responsibility for that person... for the rest of your life. I mean, some parents don't see it that way. But I'm sure if I had a child and something happened to them… I'd not cope so well. Sounds crazy, right?'

'Nah, it doesn't sound crazy. Worrying about kids you don't even have yet,' said Karl, considering that he sounded far more sarcastic than intended.

'Exactly. I'm worrying now. So imagine if I really had a child. I'd never sleep again. I like my sleep. So, no responsibilities, equals no worries.'

Karl laughed. 'Perhaps you smoke too many drugs, you mad Dutch tit.'

'I see, that's funny to you? Thanks. But I get enough lectures from Faas and Noah.'

Karl had been drinking some strange ruby lager which had screwballed him. He couldn't stop laughing. Joost's offended face was cracking him up now.

'I'm just being honest with you. But screw you, man… How is your big friend, anyway? He suffers from anxiety, right? I feel you were oblivious to that. The boy was in a dark place.'

'Yeah, right, cos you liked Duncan so much. You all ripped the piss out of him. Especially that muppet,' Karl jabbed a thumb towards Faas, who stood with another group of friends. Who did Joost think he was? Of course, he wasn't oblivious to Duncan's issues.

'Mmm yes, but Faas is just Faas. He is an arse, but he is an arse to everyone. I liked the big guy.'

'Faas is a bellend!'

Joost laughed. 'Man, you're being such a moody idiot tonight. Lighten up. Here, try some of my beer. It is amazing. Or as we say – *Alsof er een engeltje op je tong piest.*'

Karl took a gulp of the muddy-looking beer. 'Which means?'

'As though an angel is pissing on your tongue!'

Karl nodded, deciding that the beer, though alright, wasn't quite that fantastic. If angel piss could even be considered fantastic.

Joost patted him on the shoulder. 'Look, I understand—'

'You wasted all my money, Joost! You blew the bloody lot.' He'd wanted to have a go at Joost for ages about this, and tonight he would.

Joost sipped the beer as though he wasn't even listening, waved to get Faas's attention and pointed to his empty beer glass. Faas stuck up his middle finger.

Joost muttered, '*Gierigaard!*'

'I always thought you Dutch lot were meant to be frugal, Joost.'

Joost chuckled. 'Yep, but not with other people's money.'

Karl couldn't help laugh at this. He *had* always assumed that all Dutch people were tight, but apart from that tosser Faas who was a right stingy shit, his time spent in the Netherlands had contradicted that view completely and he'd found the people to be generous.

A rhythmic dance number started pumping through the outside speakers. The vocals sounded like they were being sung by a tribal Indian. 'Ahhhh hoo ahhhh hey ya whoo, hey.' This triggered another flashing memory of Amsterdam. He was heading down steep steps as the sounds of thudding music intensified.

'Joost, did you drug me with something... weird? I recall you giving me something... at a rave. But it's all vague.'

'No! I gave you chewing gum. You drugged yourself. Karl, you can't handle your weed. That's all. My tolerance is higher than most people. I've smoked every day for the last fifteen years.'

'Joost... how old are you?'

'Thirty-eight.'

Karl laughed. 'You told me twenty-eight. So you are clocking on forty!'

Joost shrugged and gave him a *does it matter* look.

Karl shook his head. 'Ah, God, I'm losing the plot. What am I doing here? My girlfriend had a baby and I'm just—'

Joost shoved him. 'You're having a blast, man. And we can make your blog work. Don't worry so much. These things... they take time, Karl. You shouldn't be quite so impatient.'

'The blog... what blog? It's just a load of nonsense.'

'No, don't think that way.'

'Joost, it's a blur. The last part of that trip is missing from my mind. And now I have to go back home with my tail between my legs.'

'I am still coming with you, yes? You promised.'

'But *did* I though?'

'You said you'd take me to London! Come on, all those nights you crashed at my house and now—'

'Alright. You can come. But Duncan is sorting my flight, so...'

Joost waved his hands around. 'I have some money. Plus, Noah will hit me up with the plane fare. Just tell me which flight you're on.'

Karl sighed. 'As soon as Duncan sends me the booking info, I'll let you know.'

Joost beamed. 'And we can go to Wembley? It's been so long since my last trip to London, Karl. Ah, I am so excited for this. And what's Canterbury like? It is a very historic, medieval city, yes?'

'Yeah, lots of cobbled streets and old timber-framed houses. I guess the city centre is pretty cool if you've never visited. Some amazing architecture.'

Karl wondered what he'd say when he got home. He didn't even know if *he'd* be welcome, let alone Joost. He could just imagine the conversation.

'Hiya, Dad, it's been a while. Oh, by the way, I've brought home a crazy Dutch dude. The one that helped spend all that money Beverly lent me.'

His dad would fix him with a harsh, disapproving glare. 'What?'

'Yup, wasted every penny. Yes, that money I begged my little sister to send me and she stupidly agreed, which we went on to spunk on a mental bender. There are at least forty-eight hours missing from my brain. Me and my new friend spent the lot on what I can only describe as total carnage. Including, but not limited to, the consumption of Northern Lights ganja, strong beer, fruity cocktails, coke – the drug, not the drink – space cakes and magic truffles. And apparently, I don't know if this is true because I can't remember, I tried to engage in sexual relations with a shop manikin. A sexy one with tights and a red wig, but yes you heard me, Dad, a shitten manikin.'

His dad's face would go red with rage at this point. 'Where the hell did I go wrong with you? I mean really, what did I do in a previous life to be saddled with such a dysfunctional, pointless, good-for-nothing son like you?'

'Must have been something bad, Dad. Something... truly awful.'

The pretend conversation made Karl chuckle and think of Duncan. As kids, they'd create fake scenarios all the time. Karl would start by being rude and Duncan would pretend to be Donald Rogers, putting on his best parade ground voice and they'd have a serious talk, well they'd act serious, but talk nonsense and make up silly situations. It always ended up with them in stitches. These acts weren't just used solely for Karl's dad. They did others too. Karl would say something like, 'Hey, imagine you asked the science teacher if we could try to light our farts with a Bunsen burner.' Then they'd act out the characters. It always sounded lame when he tried to explain it to others. Well, of course it was rather lame, but it entertained them though, so that's all that mattered. As they got older, they'd rarely do it, though on the odd occasion, when drunk, they would.

Karl hoped that one day, when they were older, settled down with massive mortgages, their own demanding teenagers and content with life (if anyone ever was) in the back of a cosy country pub, or on a quiet camping trip settled around a roaring campfire, Duncan would say, 'You know acting like a dick won't make yours any bigger.'

Then Karl would take up the role of Craig Bartell and they'd re-enact the exchange.

Afterwards, they'd both share a secret, sly chuckle and that would be it. They'd never speak about it again. They'd never speak about it at all… just a little re-enactment every decade, in order to remind themselves how lucky they'd been to have eluded justice. And more importantly the repercussions from Craig's mental family.

The music continued, 'Ahhhh ho, ho, ho ahhhh, hey ya whoo, hey.'

Karl saw Noah talking to a couple of women and he started playing an air guitar. Faas started dancing, and some others joined in. Karl smiled. The Dutchies loved a good dance. And they loved to party. Then a sudden flashback hit and he could picture himself dancing in some dark, smoke filled basement. The music, deep, twisted and industrial. The dancers all moved like tribal clones, and he'd been holding up that bloody Elvis duck… he'd been waving the damn thing around and pumping his fist. There had been two girls dancing by him. Both were tall, hot and dressed in Native American tribal costumes. He recalled one of them taking the duck and dancing with it wedged between her bulging breasts. It had then been tossed about the place a few times, and now he even visualised the duck peeking out of an older guy's crazy-high, spiky blond hair as he twirled around like some sort of bizarre techno ballerina. But somehow Karl left the place holding the stupid thing.

Joost was giggling now. 'I feel so high it's like my eyebrows are levitating from my face. What strain did I smoke?'

Karl stared at Joost, and the situation became clear. Duncan kept the balance in his life. Without him, he'd lost his way. He shouldn't have abandoned his best mate. Now they were both adrift. He could see that now and he'd been kidding himself. He'd been selfish.

Karl recalled the time when he'd became friends with Duncan. He'd always considered the lad to be a total geek, but he'd not been able to stand idly by and watch him descend to such a low place. Aged thirteen, Duncan's eczema flared-up terribly and he'd been unable to conceal it because it had covered his face, neck and back of his hands. Some of the other kids told Duncan to stay away because he was contagious. They'd call him sun-dried raisin boy, and shout stuff at the back of the class, like, *'Who dug up the rotting corpse?'* And, *'Hey, Parvin, have you been washing yourself with battery acid again?'*

Karl found Duncan sobbing in a toilet cubicle one afternoon. Some clown had pissed in his locker and stuck a yellow *caution radioactive* sticker on the door. That was his life at school. He had low self-esteem, zero confidence and, despite his size, no backbone whatsoever. Karl remembered hugging the big lad and promising him he'd always have his back. The skin on Duncan's neck had been cracked, sore and weeping and it seeped onto the shoulder of Karl's white shirt. The problem was that the more he stressed about the situation, the worse Duncan's condition got. It was a terrible affliction and Karl thanked his lucky stars he didn't have anything like that to deal with during his school years. Duncan ended up having what could only be described as a mental breakdown.

Karl tried to teach Duncan how to stick up for himself and how to use witty comebacks against the piss-takers, but that took time and lots of encouragement.

Aged fourteen, Duncan told Karl he wanted to kill himself. He'd meant it too. He was so depressed. That's the reason why Karl had got into the gaming with Duncan. It hadn't really been his thing, but he always made the effort to spice up the games and did his best to keep Duncan happy. Sometimes, after days of gaming, he'd desperately needed a break and so he'd be rude to his dad on purpose, or avoid doing his chores, knowing full well he'd get grounded. Seeing

Duncan's disappointed expression always made him feel guilty as he stood on his doorstep with a despondent expression plastered on his face, but there were only so many space battles Karl could handle in one lifetime. But it was the one thing that Duncan loved. It took his mind away from all the vile bullshit in his life. The ultimate escapism for him. During those moments of play, being transported to another place gave him some much needed respite from his shitty time in school. So Karl would masquerade as a geeky gamer, faking his excitement during those long and tedious gaming sessions, purely because Duncan was his best friend, and he wanted to keep him cheerful. He'd never, ever tell him that. It would break his heart. Even now.

Karl took a deep breath and realised Faas and Noah now stood at the table and Faas had brought them all a round of drinks. Karl almost fainted.

Faas flashed his shark-like grin. 'A drink, to congratulate you.'

'Hey?' said Karl.

'The baby! Fuck, man, this guy. He's forgotten already,' said Faas.

They all bellowed with laughter. Karl gazed around the outside seating area. It was packed, as usual. The entire square bustled with drinkers. He would miss this place so much, but it was time to return home and face the music.

Karl picked up his beer and took a sip, thinking he may as well make the most of his last night here.

43

Elena had just started dozing when the banging at the door woke her and sent her scrabbling for the knife. She slipped on her bathrobe, held the knife behind her back, and opened the door a crack. Barry glared at her. Dense mist surrounded him.

'It's gone midnight!' said Elena.

Barry sneered at her. 'He contact you yet?'

'No. And he hasn't replied to my messages. I'm worried, Barry. What if he's come off his bike, and he's injured out in the woods? We should look for him.'

Barry swigged from a bottle of whiskey. He could barely stand. 'Where did he go?'

'He never told me, Barry.'

Barry growled at her. 'Liar!'

She shook her head. 'I'm not.'

'He's staying away cos he knows he's in the shit.'

Under normal circumstance she'd have called Barry a fat twat and told him to sod off. But that wouldn't be wise tonight. 'What's he supposed to have done? And who's that guy in Hetty's paddock?' she asked.

Barry moved closer to her. 'Don't be a nosy little mouse. Or I'll...'

Elena gripped the knife tightly, ready to slash out at him. She heard a vehicle pull up but couldn't see who'd arrived because of the dense mist. 'I didn't do anything, Barry!'

'You've been whispering into Nino's ear and putting silly ideas into his head… How does he even fancy you? Hey? You buck-tooth… fucking, rat-faced little skank!'

'You're drunk and talking shite,' said Elena. Barry's words hurt, but she'd be damned if she'd let him know that.

Barry gritted his teeth and upturned the bottle.

Elena readied herself for his attack. 'I'm shutting the door now!' she shouted.

'Bitch,' he hissed.

A deep voice cut through the night. 'Barry!'

Jack emerged from the mist.

Barry staggered towards him. 'Dad? You're back?'

'You leave that girl be and sod off to bed. Now, Barry!'

Barry belched, retched, and wobbled off, almost tripping over Moose and Cracker as he went.

'We are going to have a long chat in the morning, son,' said Jack.

Barry dropped the bottle as he disappeared into the night. The bottle rolled off across the courtyard and the dogs chased after it, sniffed it, and raced off.

Jack gazed at Elena, gave her a thin smile, and left. She shut the door and slid down it, her heart racing. She decided to get dressed and check on Hetty. Elena didn't think sleep would come tonight.

Duncan hugged himself and shivered uncontrollably. He'd been too terrified to move from the spot, fearing the brothers would see him, assume he was trying to escape and reappear. Duncan wondered if they'd left him out here to die of hypothermia. He'd told them everything, so what use would he be now? The only explanation was that they'd keep him alive until they'd nabbed Karl, and the pair would be dealt with together. Every time this idea floated around in his head, he sobbed.

His mind continued to drift to grim places. He closed his eyes and wondered if he'd see the night through. He became drowsy, and his mind seemed in a fuzzy mess. Like he couldn't hold a single thought without confusion setting in.

Elena walked into Hetty's shed and rubbed the horse's snout. It was so bitterly cold tonight. The coldest night since mid-February. She threw a horse jacket over Hetty's back and secured the clips in place under her stomach. She couldn't see much, but she'd not brought a torch in case they'd see the light from the house. Elena hugged the beast and said her goodbyes. And afterwards, she'd locate the spare jacket.

Duncan's skin almost seemed to burn from the intense cold and when he felt a weight of material laying over his shoulders, he flinched and stared at the figure standing over him. He blinked his eyes. It looked like a young girl, but he knew he must be dreaming.

But she spoke and said, 'Wrap yourself right up underneath. Curl up into a ball. And stay inside.'

Duncan pulled the giant cloak around him. It smelt like damp horse and strong wax. 'Please help me escape. I'm begging you, help me!' he gasped.

She shook her head. 'I can't let you go. If you are not here in the morning... I'd be in real trouble.'

'It was an accident... I swear it.'

'Are you the one that... did *it*?'

Duncan shook his head. 'He attacked us... me and my friend... but it was an accident. We were only defending ourselves.'

The girl turned and started to walk away.

'Please don't leave me,' he said. 'I don't want to die. I want to go home. I want to see my mum.'

The girl stopped, tilted her head and removed a baggy hoody that she'd been wearing over a long dressing gown. She offered it to him. 'Put this on. It might be a tad small.' Then she left, racing away into the dense mist. Duncan yanked off his petrol-soaked top, tossed it away and tugged on the hoody. It was too small, but warm and smelt nice.

Like a girl's perfume and weirdly, this seemed to comfort him. He laid out the blanket, rolled on top of it, and pulled it around him until he'd cocooned himself. *A tiny glimmer of hope,* he thought.

44

2 December 2018 [05.00]

Duncan poked his head out from under the blanket to get some much needed air. Although morning seemed to draw close, a thick cover of dense mist still shrouded the area and a layer of wet dew clung to the outside of the blanket. It seemed like he'd woken up on a mysterious planet. And he still didn't have a clue where they'd taken him. Suddenly, a big shape made its way through the mist and Duncan shuddered, fearing the brothers were returning. Then he saw a white horse with chestnut coloured legs. No doubt the beast wanted to investigate the presence in its paddock. Duncan tried to guess the time and estimated about five am. He'd stayed relatively dry under the big horse blanket. He'd still been cold, but the sharp, numbing chill eased once he'd stay covered for some time. The girl had perhaps saved his life last night. Duncan slipped back under and closed his eyes. He pictured his mum in the kitchen, singing 'Silent Night' and baking cakes, and wondered if she'd been calling him… no, he *knew* she'd have been calling. She'd be going out of her mind with worry. 'I'm so sorry, Mum,' he whispered.

. . .

Elena sipped her coffee and checked the time. Not quite six. Brennan would soon be setting off from East Kilbride. He'd said he'd try to arrive around four this afternoon. That seemed so far off. She needed to keep a clear head, because freaking out and doing something rash would be stupid. Jack coming back complicated matters, but she couldn't do much about that now. One more day and she'd be rid of this damn place for good. She just prayed Nino knew what he was doing. She went to grab their passports that they'd secretly obtained.

Duncan peeked out from under the heavy blanket and took in the crisp morning. The mist had eased and now hovered in low, shallow patches, but he was able to inspect his surroundings for the first time. His breath plumed in front of him and a thin layer of frost had covered the grass. Everything was so peaceful, it seemed surreal. A line of wispy smoke flowed from a red bricked house situated some sixty metres away. A plane flew high overhead, and a cockerel called out from somewhere nearby. The field in which he lay was a good two acres, with a low, badly maintained stone wall around it, and a battered wooden gate at the entrance. Behind Duncan, beyond the paddock wall, lay dense woodland. There'd be little point in screaming for help. They would never have dumped him here if they'd had doubts. If he yelled out, they'd be the only ones to hear his calls. Duncan checked the chunky shackle again – as if by some miracle it had vanished during the night; obviously, it was still there and so tight it wouldn't budge. It must have been an inch thick.

In the far corner of the paddock sat a ramshackle, open-fronted shed made from corrugated sheeting. Inside, he could see hay and assumed that the horse slept there. Next to the shed sat a massive pile of dead leaves, some buckets, and a rusted wheelbarrow full of wood. Two sparrows splashed away in a semi-frozen muddy puddle that was filled with golden leaves. The birds seemed content with life and were unbothered by his presence in the field. The horse lazily grazed around and a crow cawed in the distance. These sights and sounds made him sob, because he started to think… really think. There were so many things in life he'd always taken for granted. All the little things that, once his time was up, he'd never get to experience again. And he was certain his time was running out. Once Karl arrived and the Bartells no longer needed him, they intended to take his life and the best he could hope for was a quick, painless end. He'd noticed the coldness in their eyes. Especially the shorter of the brothers, Barry. And he'd seen eyes like that before… they were identical to Craig's. This brought back the rasping sobs and before he knew it, he was crying and saying, 'Please save me. Please! God. Please. Don't let me die out here.'

A squirrel bolted across the gate and he spotted his peacoat strewn across the top. He took some calming breaths and tried to keep it together.

Duncan followed the chain attached to his ankle. The chain, coated in red plastic, must have been twenty feet in length and the end was attached to a ring set inside a square concrete block. They'd attached that end with another thick bow shackle, that even the Hulk would struggle to break free from. He scurried back to the pit's edge and dived back inside the blanket. Somehow, it seemed a bit safer under there.

Barry looked like utter crap. He stirred his coffee with bleary eyes and a distant look. Johnny's head was a tad muzzy, but otherwise he'd woken up feeling quite chipper, considering the amount of Jack Daniels they'd tucked away.

'Did you go back out and give that lad a horse's coat, Jon?'

Johnny sipped his tea and shook his head.

'Bloody Elena,' said Barry.

'Does it matter? It got mega cold.'

'Aw, poor chap. I dunno why you just didn't stick him in your room last night. He could've had a warm, cosy sleeping bag on the floor, or better still, you could have done top and tail like a couple of schoolgirls having a sleepover.'

'Keep talking, Barry, and you'll be having a sleepover in A and E!'

Barry flashed a teasing grin. 'Ooh, alright, Jon. Take it easy.'

'We may need him again to arrange everything with this Karl bloke,' said Johnny.

'Now isn't the time to get compassionate, Jon.'

Johnny grunted and picked up an old newspaper, snapping it open.

Barry, elbows on the table, leant towards him. 'I'm deadly serious, bro. We need to consider our options here. They are limited.'

Johnny pretended to read the paper.

'Two counts of kidnapping for a start. That's even before we consider the worst part. We can't get soft. I'm not spending the rest of my days locked up.'

'Yeah, you don't need to tell me,' said Johnny.

'They are not pets, Jon. We can't keep them. And we can't realistically set either of them free. You do understand that, right? I know you've been budding up with Nathaniel. But I don't believe we can let him go.'

'And what about Nino? We going to shoot him too? This is getting out of hand, Barry. We're losing control of the situation.'

'He lied to us and I want to know why! Fuck, Jon, why would he feed us such a big load of bullshit?'

Johnny sighed and run a hand through his hair. 'Look, I have been mulling this over... what if Nino didn't lie? Think about it for a sec... what if Stefan did say that stuff?'

'Why would he do that?'

'He was a loudmouth twat for a start. I bet he wanted to give it the big-un. It's possible, right?'

Barry nodded thoughtfully. 'So, if that were the case, why has Nino gone AWOL?'

Johnny shrugged. 'I dunno. We should go easy with him until we know for certain, hey? He might just be scared; you know what he's like.'

'And tell me this, Jon... why did Duncan say he'd seen someone else in Craig's motor?'

Johnny deliberated over what Nino had told them about the night Craig died. He'd said Craig made him take his BMW to stake out Trev Smith's flat on Stour Road in case the lowlife returned. Whilst Nino stayed there, Craig ventured around all Trev's local haunts searching for him. At around eight pm, Nino got a text from Craig confirming he'd located Trev and that Nino should meet him in a carpark on the outskirts of Canterbury. Nino drove there, walked around the place but couldn't find his brother and so phoned Craig's mobile. Nino heard the phone ringing, followed its sound, and made the shocking discovery.

But Duncan said Craig's car was at the scene and he was certain that someone else had watched the altercation from the driver's side.

'Nino saw the fight,' said Johnny. 'Didn't he?'

Barry nodded. 'He was there. There is no question about it. But why lie about it?'

'Either he felt bad for not coming to his aid and guessed we'd all be furious with him... or...'

'Nino was happy to sit back and watch,' Barry finished for him.

'We have to consider that... those boys had a rocky relationship, Barry.'

'We need to sort this out.' Barry let out a huge yawn. 'What are we meant to tell the folks about all this?'

'The truth,' said Johnny.

Barry grinned. 'Dad will march out there and put a bullet in the big lad's head.'

Johnny finished his tea and sighed. 'So will Mum given half the chance! In fact, she'd use her fists.'

'Are they still here, Jon?' whispered Barry.

'No, they both headed out first thing.'

'I bet Mum forgot her false teeth or something and made Jack drive back to Whitstable.'

'And is everything sorted with this flight, Barry?'

Barry flashed a wolfish grin. 'Yep, all arranged. I... sorry, Duncan sent Karl all the travel arrangements. And he's been texting his mum. She's worried sick, but Duncan's a good lad. He informed her he stayed at his friend's gaff.'

'Shit, Barry, you switched the location services off, right?'

Barry frowned and looked worried. Then he laughed. 'Yeah, I'm not a total muppet! The phone's off now. It's almost out of juice and I couldn't get a charge in the bastard thing last night.'

Johnny wondered if Barry would have been able to locate his own shrivelled cock for a piss, the state he'd been in last night. 'And the airport pickup?'

'All organised, Jon. When we get him here, I want to do that bastard myself. Understand? You can do that fat, blubbering lump... if you're up to it.'

Johnny shrugged. 'Fine by me.' Barry had a special bond with Craig and he'd see it as his duty to carry out the revenge killing.

Elena read the message from Nino and a flutter of excitement hit her stomach. She needed to be ready to move at three this afternoon. He'd assured her he would have lured his brothers away by then, and she'd have full access to the house. That only left Jack and Maria. They'd left early this morning, but she had a bad feeling they'd be coming back here and that might lead to complications. One option would be to nip inside under the pretence of having a bath and sneak into Barry's room. But the risks would be much higher if Jack and his shrewd bitch of a wife were lurking about the house. She'd cross that bridge later. Bloody bad timing or what? Why did the old bastards decide to come back today, of all days? So typical of her luck. She'd not bothered telling Nino about their return. She figured he already had quite enough on his plate and any additional worries would not help his situation.

Duncan peered up at the figure standing over him and blinked away his tears.

Johnny knelt and handed him a crusty roll laid on a piece of kitchen foil. 'Here. It's cold. Hope you're not a vegetarian.'

Duncan accepted the roll and inspected it. He wasn't in the least bit hungry, but didn't dare offend the man by not accepting the offering. 'Thank you.'

'Nice hoody,' said Johnny. 'Not sure about the size and colour. Go on, eat up, mate.'

Duncan forced a polite grin and nibbled on the bacon roll. It tasted good and after a few bites, he decided he was hungry and gobbled the food down.

Johnny placed a small flask onto the grass. 'Hot tea with sugar.'

Duncan smiled sadly, his eyes filled with tears, and he sniffed. 'When will you let me go home?'

'Drink some tea,' said Johnny, holding him with a stony stare.

'What will you do with me?' asked Duncan, feeling the tears rolling down his face.

Johnny let out a long sigh. 'You said last night you thought they'd been someone else in Craig's BMW... you certain of that?'

'Yes... I only caught a quick glimpse,' said Duncan. Over the months he'd thought a lot about the shape moving about in the car, and as time passed, the more he'd questioned what he'd seen. *If anything*. But now wouldn't be a sensible time to mention his doubts.

Johnny nudged the flask with his boot. 'Get that down you.' Then he turned on his heels and strolled away.

'Mr Bartell... I'm so sorry about your brother... I understand you must hate me, but not a day has gone by when I haven't thought about what happened and wished it hadn't... I need you to understand that... I just...' Duncan sobbed. 'I just really, really needed you to hear that.'

Johnny stopped walking, but didn't turn back to him. He bowed his head, shoved his hands into his pockets and continued his stroll back towards the house.

'I see his face when I close my eyes. I always... see his face,' said Duncan.

Johnny stopped.

'I promise... no, I swear on my family... on everything I love. If you don't kill me, I'll say nothing.'

Johnny didn't turn to face him but said, 'Yeah, well, I don't know you. So, your promises mean little to me.'

'I won't talk to the police. I give you *my* word.'

Johnny let out a long sigh. 'I tell you what... if you survive your stay here, I give you *my* word that we'll leave you be.' And with that, he marched off.

Duncan pondered on Johnny's words and what he'd meant by *if you survive here*... was this a glimmer of hope that they would let him go? He'd need to hold on to that hope, otherwise he might go insane.

Johnny pulled back the tarpaulin, sending wet leaves flying everywhere. 'Might need a jump start, but this motor should pass as a taxi.'

Davey scrunched up his face. 'That's Craig's… isn't it?'

'We have some false plates in the shed,' said Johnny.

Davey rubbed the bonnet and sighed. 'I'm not sure about this, guys.'

Barry's eyes narrowed. 'We don't give a fuck if you're sure! It's pretty damn simple, collect the bloke in the picture—'

'The one that looks like the Jackass geezer?' interrupted Davey

'Yes. Collect him and deliver him to the agreed spot. We'll take him from there.'

Davey lit up a cigarette and blew a plume of smoke out of his nostrils. 'And then what?'

'We'll take him out and treat him to a slap-up dinner! What the hell does that matter, Davey?' snapped Barry.

'I thought we were square… I sorted out that cash pick up, Barry.'

Barry's nostrils flared. 'It's an airport taxi run. It's hardly difficult.'

'OK, boss. No worries,' said Davey.

'Plus, I haven't forgotten those dents!' said Barry.

Davey pulled a face. 'Dents?'

'Look, just use that burner phone to text him your registration and meeting spot. He'll jump in, you'll drive back. We collect. Job done. Easy fucking peasy,' said Barry. 'Sign off the text, *Last Stop Taxis*. Make it appear professional, yeah.'

Davey took a long drag of his smoke and gazed around the courtyard. 'So, what happened to Nathaniel? Is he still—' Davey's gaze shifted to the paddock, and he did a double take. 'Funny looking horse that… Who *is* he?'

Barry grinned. 'Him? That's our last taxi driver. The wanker spoke way too much.'

Davey's jaw dropped open. He stared at Duncan and flicked his smoke across the courtyard. 'Righto.'

Johnny's eyes darted back to Duncan and then back to Davey. He couldn't help feel sorry for the big lad. He had been in the wrong place at the wrong time, but that didn't matter. Even if he decided to let him go free, Barry would never agree to let the matter drop. It was a shame, because the boy seemed sincerely regretful. He also seemed so guileless, and he'd clearly never been a part of the world they inhabited. Then it struck him. This was a kind of weird, poetic justice – his hot-headed brother had met his end at the hands of a couple of average Joes, when he'd faced off with some real crazy wide-boys and walked away unscathed. The world could be a strange, unpredictable place alright.

Davey got into the BMW and sat behind the wheel. 'Honk, honk… Taxi for Steve-O.'

That bloody car. He'd recognised it straight away and shuddered. Somehow, Duncan knew what they were planning. They were going to collect Karl in Craig's car and drive him back here to face the music. Would Karl notice it was the same car? He very much doubted that. He angrily tugged at the chain and a wave of panic, rage and terror washed over him. If he didn't do something quickly, his best friend's fate would be sealed. Then a cold sickness hit him, and he puked his breakfast into the pit.

45

2 December 2018 [15.30]

Nino parked his bike in a small wooded area opposite The Swan and took out the bottle of Jack Daniels from his rucksack. He never touched the stuff, but knew from experience that the whiskey carried a potent stink. He opened the lid and poured a good measure into his hands and splashed it over his cheeks as though he were applying aftershave. Nino swilled a big mouthful and spat it out. Then, to be doubly sure the smell wouldn't be missed, he tipped some over his riding jacket, which he'd already caked in plenty of mud. Now it was time to head inside.

Nino placed both hands around his beer and fixed his face into a gloomy expression. He spotted Veronica whispering to Reilly, and she nodded in his direction. As he'd hoped, Reilly strolled over to him. 'Everything alright, Nino?'

Nino sniffed and shrugged. 'Yeah.'

'You reek of booze. Bit early for a sess, no? I'm guessing by the state you're in, you rode here?'

'I came flying off and cracked my shoulder. In the woods near here.'

'You hurt?'

Nino shook his head. 'Just a bruise.'

'Anything I can do?'

Nino forced himself to appear tearful, wiped his eyes and spoke slightly slurred as he said, 'I need to see Barry and Johnny. Can you tell them to get me? With a ramp for my bike.'

Reilly nodded. 'Yeah, course I will. You sure you're alright though? Is there anything I can get you?'

Nino wiped the tears rolling down his cheeks, thinking, yeah and an Oscar for my epic acting performance would be fantastic. 'No. I just need to speak with my brothers.'

Reilly gave him the thumbs up.

Nino scanned the pub. Now he needed to get the hell out of here fast, but as he stood up to leave, Veronica arrived at his table and handed him a coffee. She gave him a warm smile. 'Drink that up, luv.'

'Thank you.'

Veronica sat down next to him. 'It's hard. I understand. Losing a brother. I mean, Stefan could be a total pain, but God, I miss that little sod like crazy. I bet you miss Craig terribly?'

Nino sipped the coffee. 'Mmm, yes.' *Oh, boy,* he'd not expected this.

'Seems so odd... the way they both went... I keep telling Reilly I'm sure the two deaths are connected somehow.'

Nino's mouth became dry. 'You do? But how?'

'Can't you think of anything that might connect them?' she asked, her voice soft, but her expression resolute.

Nino shook his head, avoiding looking into her hard, grey eyes, convinced that if their eyes met, she would somehow see right through his lies and learn the truth.

'Reilly swears he'll get to the bottom of this... but these things take time,' said Veronica.

Time, thought Nino... time was running out.

'Reilly, how's things?' asked Barry.

Johnny watched Barry, seeing the worry lines stretch across his face as he listened on the phone.

'OK, mate. I appreciate you calling. We'll be there soon. Cheers.' He ended the call and rubbed a hand over his head.

'What?' asked Johnny.

'Nino's at The Swan. He came off his bike and made his way there. Pissed up by the sounds of things. He's asked for both of us to go collect him. He's in a right state.'

'Barry, why would he go there? I mean, of all places.'

'I think the little shit stain is trying to send us a message. Trying to tell us he's not afraid to spill the beans. That must be his game.'

'He can't be that stupid!'

'I'll go, Jon. You stay here and hold the fort. We need Nino back home so we can get to the bottom of all this bullshit.'

'You sure?'

Barry nodded, though he looked peaky and apprehensive. 'Where's Fraser with my van?'

'He had a date with some local skirt. Must have got lucky.'

'Would you tell him to pick me up? He can come with me.'

Johnny nodded and picked up his phone. 'Sure.' As he dialled Fraser's number, he couldn't shake the worrying thoughts chasing around his head that there was major trouble heading in their direction.

Nino had run this conversation over in his head many times. His tone needed to sound right. Sincere and believable above all else, because messing this up wouldn't end well.

He prepared his best cracked, shaken voice and said, 'Reilly... Reilly, it's me.'

'Where'd you go? My sister's been searching the entire pub for you,' said Reilly.

'Look, I need to talk to you... to tell you... I *have* to tell you...'

'Spit it out, fella.'

'My brothers... that night... they...'

Nino pictured Stefan's over the top walk as he sauntered toward Barry's van, pissed up and full of bravado.

'You still there, Nino?' said Reilly.

Nino continued the pause, giving time for Reilly's rage level to crank up.

Nino remembered everything about that night with crystal clear clarity.

'Oi, oi, it's only the big man himself,' Barry had called to Stefan as he hung from the Renault's window.

Whilst Stefan was full of arrogance, Nathaniel looked like a nervy child as they approached the vehicle.

'You lads fancy going to a banging beach rave?' Barry had asked.

Stefan, steaming drunk, appeared well up for this. Nathaniel didn't want to go.

Barry had laughed. 'Come on, show the crumpet those big guns of yours, Stefan.'

The other end of the phone was silent. Reilly hadn't left the call, though.

'They waited for Stefan to leave the pub. Barry told him about some party and Stefan jumped in the back of the van,' said Nino.

'Which pub?' asked Reilly evenly. 'You were there?'

These questions not only threw Nino, but Reilly's calm tone also did. He didn't sound mad enough yet. He didn't sound mad, period.

'A place in Rosemary Lane in Canterbury. I didn't have a clue what they'd planned to do. Honest I didn't, Reilly… they didn't tell me. I don't think they'd thought it through themselves. They were blind drunk and not thinking straight. You have to believe that, Reilly. They never set out to—'

'Who told them where to find Stefan?'

Nino didn't answer. Another question he'd not even considered. He decided he'd been way too confident going into this.

'Who?'

'Reilly, I—'

'Was it Nathaniel?'

'Look, Reilly, I don't think he knew what would happen.' Nino felt guilty for stitching up Nathaniel, but at the end of the day he'd come too far to worry about the shit storm winging its way to all the other parties. It did kinda make sense to blame him. He didn't even know who had given his brothers the tip-off. This outcome just made sense as it gave more authenticity to his story. And would add more fuel to the fire. Nathaniel wouldn't likely get a chance to have his say and put the story straight.

'So what happened, Nino?'

Nino could visualise everything in that van.

Johnny up front necking neat Jack Daniels whilst at the wheel.

Barry and Stefan's raucous laughter.

Dance music thudding so loud the wooden panels vibrated.

Drinks flowing.

Drugs been consumed. Cocaine and pills.

Barry and Stefan were even dancing at one point.

Johnny's erratic driving.

The fear radiating from Nathaniel.

Nino's own fear. His anticipation of what would happen next. Of *how* far his brothers would take this.

'Everything was chilled out. Barry and Stefan were having a laugh. We all were, Reilly. I didn't have a clue things would play out like they did.'

Nathaniel kept catching his eye. Nino knew all too well the terror pulsating through the other lad. He'd stepped into something bad. Very bad. He could sense it. Perhaps Nino's body language gave the game away that night. Or perhaps some kind of sixth sense told Nathaniel that things would take a sinister turn. He'd drunk very little, refused the drugs and no doubt wished he'd not let Stefan convince him to head to some random party.

'Barry produced a joint and lit it up. Stefan smoked quite a lot but kept saying, "That weed smells dodgy, Barry. What *is* that stuff? That's a weird-arse smell, mate".' Nino had watched as Barry pretended to inhale a few times, before handing the smoke back to Stefan and said, 'Black Maaaambaaaa.'

'Isn't that Spice?' Stefan had asked, his eyes wide and animated.

'What did they do to my brother?' asked Reilly, his voice sounding odd and quiet.

'The music stopped, and we travelled a while in silence. The atmosphere changed and Barry's mood darkened. Then he said, "I bet you still wear that fucking chain when you're doing a bird! I bet you do, don't you?"'

Nino spotted headlights, snapping his mind back to the present. He froze. Barry's van came into view. He stepped further back into the shadows as it rolled past his position. If his brothers spotted him, the plan would be ruined.

'Stefan started freaking out. Saying he wanted to go home and that he couldn't face a party. He didn't like the buzz.'

Barry's van pulled into the pub carpark. He'd got there way faster than Nino had expected. Nino hadn't got out of the pub fast enough. After Veronica's heartfelt chat, he'd pretended to nip to the toilet and slipped out the back, only to forget his phone and have to rush back in. He'd have to hurry things along now after that gigantic cock up.

'So, Barry goes, "Let's get some fresh sea air and walk it off." But Stefan pleaded with him to stay inside, saying he couldn't face going outside. Then Johnny opened the side door.'

Nino pictured Barry's enraged features as he yanked Stefan's chain, breaking it free from his neck as he'd yelled, 'Out! Come on, I thought you were a tough nut! What are you afraid of, big man?'

Duncan peered up to the sky and could see the low winter sun peeking through jagged clouds. *Now or never*, he considered. After scanning the house and courtyard for a few minutes, Duncan seemed convinced that nobody could see him. At least one brother, Barry, had left in that van a short while ago and he decided this would be his only chance. Duncan felt around the edge of the pit and dug his fingers through the mud until he touched on some rock. He clawed frantically until it came loose and repeated the process until he'd removed two solid hand sized chunks of rock. He viewed the house again and placed the chain over one rock; selecting the piece as near to his ankle as possible. He prepared to slam down the second rock, but again, his eyes flicked back to the house. Now, sure he wasn't being watched, he brought down the rock onto the chain with such force it delivered a sharp pain up his wrist. He repeated the process several times and again checked the house. Still clear. He ignored the stabbing pain, clenched his teeth, and hammered away at the chain like a mad person.

. . .

Nino watched Barry head towards the pub's entrance. A surge of excitement washed over him, making him clench his jaw. But no Johnny. He'd brought that bloody knife-merchant Fraser Moore with him instead. Shit, shit, shit… *Why was everything going wrong?* This not only meant Elena would be stuck at the house alone with Johnny, it also meant the Chillcotts would head there next to find him.

'And what, you and Nathaniel just sat there and did nothing?' asked Reilly.

Yes, that's pretty much what happened, thought Nino. Although Nathaniel had quietly said, 'I swear I won't say a word, Nino. I'm done with that idiot, anyway.'

Nino couldn't be certain if Nathaniel said that as a way of saving his own skin or if there'd been any truth to the words. Maybe a bit of both.

'We did not know what they were intending to do. Honestly, Reilly. They came back from that coastal path ten minutes later without Stefan.'

Reilly began breathing heavily now. He'd stayed so composed thus far, and Nino would be lying if he didn't admit to being impressed by Reilly's placidity. It was unnerving.

Nino continued. 'They were laughing and joking and started drinking again. They drove back in a right state. It was a miracle Johnny didn't lose control and kill us all. They forgot all about Nathaniel. Until the morning.'

Nino recalled his brothers waking up with the most hideous hangovers as they began remembering the night's events in a panicked mess. The repercussions of what would happen next dawning on them in their now bleary, sober states. They'd messed up in spectacular fashion.

'Why didn't we *do* Nathaniel as well?' Barry had asked.

Johnny had slapped his own forehead. 'I don't even remember driving home, Barry.'

'Why? Why would they do this?' asked Reilly.

'Barry overheard Stefan telling some lad in the pub toilets that he'd done Craig over,' said Nino.

'No way. If Stefan killed your brother, he would have come to me.'

'It was a fallout over this association they'd set up… did you know about that?'

'The association was a load of bollocks. Why are you telling me all this?'

'My dad didn't have any involvement in any of this.'

'That's not a reason, Nino.'

Nino wasn't sure why he'd even said that. He didn't feel that he owed Jack Bartell anything, not after the lies he'd fed him for all these years. 'I… I don't think it's fair. Any of this. And I can't be a part of it. The truth will eventually get out, so I'm doing what needs to be done. I don't want to be blamed, Reilly,' he said in the most pathetic tone he could muster.

Silence on the phone now.

'Reilly?'

'Barry's at the bar,' whispered Reilly.

'What are you going to do now?' asked Nino, trying to sound freaked out. That wasn't hard under the circumstances.

'Are your brothers hiding Nathaniel?' asked Reilly.

Not expecting the question, Nino faltered and blurted, 'No… I mean, he was there, but he's long gone.' Even to his own ears, this did not sound convincing. He could have slapped himself. 'Reilly? Am I safe? I don't know what to do.'

'No Bartell will ever be safe again. So… leave.'

The call was cut.

Nino needed to warn Elena, and fast. The trouble he'd intended to bring to the pub would soon wing its way directly to the house. He phoned Elena, and she answered on the first ring. 'Elena, only Barry came!'

'Yeah, I saw him go. Did you poke the angry bull?' she asked.

'Yes, it's done. You need to leave the house, Elena. It's gonna all kick off.'

'Chill out. Bren will be ready to pick me up soon. I'm heading over to the house now.'

'How are you so calm? Wait, Brennan won't drive up to the property, will he? The last thing we need is him starting any shit.'

'No, I'll head up to the main road on foot. Once he's collected me, I'll call you and we'll meet at the agreed place.'

'Please be careful, Elena!'
'You too. And calm down.'

Duncan's fingers were numb, his palms hurt and blood seeped through his cracked finger tips, but he continued to hammer down the rock, alternating his hands and whacking it hard and constantly until the rock fragmented. As soon as that happened, he hunted around in the earth for more pieces to use. He'd managed to split through the plastic covering and laid bare the chain links. Now he'd really have to smash it.

Elena took her towel and washbag into the house. As she moved through the hallway and headed for the stairs, she glimpsed Johnny in the lounge, sitting on the sofa with a troubled expression slapped on his face.

'Hey, Johnny... I'm heading up for a bath. Any word on Nino?'

Johnny nodded. 'Yeah, Barry's gone to get him. Didn't he call you then?'

Elena dropped her lip and shook her head.

'No? That's weird. Normally, we can't get him to stop phoning you, Elena.'

Elena pursed her lips. 'Well, OK, if you must know, we had a big ding-dong. He's pissed me right off.'

Johnny stood up and headed over to her. 'Ooh, now that's a first.'

'Mm. Let's just say that I will not crack until he apologises for being a massive dick.'

'What'd you fallout over?' asked Johnny.

'It's personal,' she said in a haughty tone.

'You told Barry you were worried about Nino last night.'

'I was... I was worried he'd had an accident. But I'm still mega pissed at him.'

Johnny stared at her impassively, then said, 'OK. Enjoy your hot bath.' With that, he strolled back into the lounge and peered out of the window.

'Who's there?' asked Elena.

'My folks are home. This should be interesting.' Johnny's phone pinged, and she watched him carefully as he read a message and did not appear to look impressed at what it said.

'Good luck,' said Elena. She bolted upstairs, headed into the bathroom and whacked on the taps. She needed Jack and Maria coming home like she needed a bullet up her backside.

Duncan screamed inside as he bashed the rock against the chain with everything he could muster. His hands, now blistering, hurt like hell and after a surge of rage like nothing else he'd ever experienced washed over him, he began to shake, sob and curse the chain. It didn't seem to have hardly bent out of shape, let alone come close to breaking. All he'd managed were a few marks and scratches. As the hopelessness of the situation hit him, he cried out, and though he continued to bring down the rock, the energy and determination left him. He pictured the Bartells watching him and finding his actions hilarious. He closed his eyes and took a breather. If he didn't break free, then Karl would die, and he'd be to blame.

Nathaniel took a bite from the thin pizza. 'So, I was wondering if we're all done now, Johnny?' he asked.

'Warren texted me. What's all this about you taking his phone earlier?' asked Johnny.

Warren popped a straw into a can of Stella and sucked hard on it. Johnny noticed there were many empty cans scattered around the table and floor.

'He fell asleep and dropped it. I was only picking it up,' said Nathaniel. 'I don't get why he's babysitting me, anyway.'

Johnny crossed his arms. 'Warren said you were trying to make a call.'

'He's been drinking beer after beer and necking his painkillers like sweets,' said Nathaniel indignantly. 'He's not with it.'

Warren grunted and mumbled, 'Silly cunt.' Or at least that's what it sounded like.

Nathaniel stood up straight and jutted his chin. 'The toilet in here smells like a homeless man's pants… And… and the toothbrush Barry provided me with looks like someone unclogged a scabby sink with it.'

Warren sniggered, cracked open another can, and transferred the straw.

'You got the ransom cash, so why can't I disappear liked we'd all agreed?' asked Nathaniel.

Warren took two pills from a white tub and swallowed them down with the rest of the Stella, sucking vigorously on the straw.

'Yeah, you definitely shouldn't drink heavily on those, Warren,' said Johnny. Then to Nathaniel he said, 'Look, keep your head down for a while longer, until the heat dies off.'

Nathaniel tossed the pizza crust into the box and rubbed a hand over his head. 'I have a place to go. A friend in Ibiza. I need my cut… then I'm gone. If you don't want to cut me in the full amount, I'll settle for a few grand. I just need to go. I'm going nuts in here.'

Johnny guessed Nathaniel's sudden bold behaviour meant he was getting worried about what they intended to do with him. He'd do something rash soon if they didn't take action.

Warren sucked hard on the straw and drained the can. Johnny eyed the strange man. With those big, dark eyes, round like giant marbles and his slit-like mouth that seemed to spread right back to his ears. He sure was a freaky fella. He had the appearance of a supernatural being. Johnny thought the guy was a total creep, but Barry trusted the weirdo implicitly, so what could he do?

'I'll sort you out a new toothbrush. And you can pop up to the house for a shower, or bath later… Just a few more days. OK?'

Nathaniel didn't seem convinced by this, but nodded and said, 'OK. A few more days. But I don't need *him* watching over me.'

Elena listened at the stairs and could make out muffled voices. She gazed down the hallway at Barry's door and prayed the arsehole hadn't locked it. He often did, the paranoid twat. Happy nobody wasn't heading her way, she walked towards his room, her towel and washbag in hand. Then she stopped, peered over her shoulder, and eyed the stairs leading to the loft room. An icy shiver ran over her and she felt a strange sensation – almost like she was being watched. She imagined seeing Craig standing up the top of those stairs, watching her with a mistrustful glare. God, this house creeped her out more than ever.

Mills looked up from his paper and bag of pork scratchings. 'What?'

'I need you to call Silas and tell him we need him and as many bodies as he can muster. Tonight. They need to meet within an hour.'

Mills sighed and folded his paper. 'Where are we going?'

Reilly stared across the bar where Barry and his Scottish mate were busy ordering drinks. The arseholes were laughing and chatting with Veronica. 'We're going to the Bartells. I think Nathaniel is there. But there's more. I'll explain everything soon. Don't let Barry leave. You keep that fat prick here, Mills. Whatever you have to do, he does *not* leave.'

His brother gave him a hard nod. Reilly knew if he told Mills about Stefan, there'd be immediate bloodshed. Once again, Kreshnik's words echoed in his mind – *Your revenge will taste so much sweeter if you wait for the perfect moment.*

'Hey, Mum... Dad. Where have you been hiding?' asked Johnny.

Jack rolled his eyes. 'Problems with the damn electric down there. We came back last night because we lost all the power and then had to race back down to meet the electrician this morning.'

'All sorted now then?' asked Johnny.

Maria picked up the kettle and grunted, 'Bloody better be.'

Jack sat at the table and crossed his arms. 'So, you gonna tell me what the hell has been going on?'

Johnny bent down and patted Moose and Cracker. 'Got any decent whiskey?'

Elena placed her hand on the door handle and smiled when it turned and the door creaked open. She slunk inside and closed the door behind her, careful not to make a single sound. She took in the immaculate, open room. The double bed was made, the sheets crisp and prim. A tall oak wardrobe and matching chest of drawers were the only other items of furniture. A mobile phone and one candle sat atop the chest and nothing else looked out of place. The floor space was empty of items. It reminded Elena of a soldier's billet.

Reilly sucked down his rage and phoned his brother-in-law. He answered on the third ring. 'Kresh, I need some heavy tools.'

'Of course. I can get whatever you want. Same as always, what you don't use, you can return.'

'They will be used.'

Kreshnik laughed. 'OK. Can we meet tomorrow first thing?'

'I need them now.'

'No. I need more time to arrange with my people.'

Reilly took a few calming breaths. 'Look, just get anything you can. But I need them tonight, because tomorrow might be too late.'

'Fine. I'll rustle up what I can,' said Kreshnik abruptly and cut the call.

Reilly put down the phone and placed his hands on the bar. The old Reilly would have steamed over to Barry and smashed him to pieces without a moment's hesitation, but he held onto his temper. He needed to do this right. His dad had a few shooters stashed up somewhere, but last time they'd spoken about them, his dad couldn't remember where the guns were hidden.

Elena opened the wardrobe and found an array of shoes and boots that appeared to have been placed in a precise row. She moved them aside, pulled her penknife out of her wash kit and used the blade to pull up the base of the wardrobe. Then she angled the base, tugged it out through the doors and placed it down. Using the torch on her phone to light up the area, she delved inside and prised up the loose floorboards. And just as Nino said, she located the bag down there. Elena snatched it out and peered inside, and a grin spread across her face. As she fingered the rolls of cash, Elena squealed in delight. She dashed to the window, checked all was clear, and tossed it outside. She then dived back to the wardrobe, but a banging sound caused her to freeze.

Her eyes flicked to the door, and she listened. After convincing herself she'd been hearing things, she stepped back to the hole inside the wardrobe and explored it thoroughly. Elena removed a heavy, silver revolver, a box of ammunition and an ancient looking double-barrelled sawn-off shotgun. The weapon's stock had been roughly cut down, and the barrel appeared to be held together by a load of shabby gaffer tape. She slid the revolver and slugs into the washbag, placed the shotgun back in the hole and left the room. Her heart raced and she couldn't stop smiling. They were close. So close to a better life. The life they deserved.

Reilly saw Barry walk to the toilets, so decided to do a bit of fishing. He went over to the Scotsman and grinned. 'Hey, Fraser isn't it? How you doing?'

'Not so bad, pal. Yourself?'

'Yeah, sure, I'm great. Listen, someone mentioned that Nathaniel is staying up at the Bartells' place? Have you seen him?'

Fraser sipped his beer. 'I wouldn'y know anything about that. I don't know who that is. Sorry, pal.'

'No? Coz I'd like a word with him. He could answer a few very important questions I have.'

Fraser shrugged. 'Like I said, I dinnae know anything about this. Best talk to Barry when he's finished his jobby. He had a cheeky pick-me-up on the way here. It gave the fella a wee red alert on, if youse ken what I'm saying? Banging bit of ching that, mind.'

'Come on, Fraser, you must have heard something about Nathaniel?'

Fraser's eyes narrowed. 'I said I dinnae ken the boy. Which part of that are you noo getting?'

Reilly chewed the inside of his cheek. He knew of this Fraser's reputation. The bloke didn't piss about and if the stories were true, he made most of the so called hard-nuts around here look like fluffy, fairy princesses.

Fraser slid his hand inside his jacket and kept it there, eyeing Reilly with disdain. Was he about to pull a knife on him? That would be a big mistake.

'Where's Nino? We're here to pick the lad up? But I cannae see the boy here?' asked Fraser.

Reilly shrugged. 'He was here.'

Fraser made a big show of scanning the pub. 'So where did the wee fella go?' He peered over the bar. 'Nino, you down there, pal? Nope.'

'You wouldn't have been silly enough to bring a blade into my pub... would you?' asked Reilly.

Fraser flashed him a scathing look. 'Oft, I'm getting the impression I'm not wanted in your boozer, pal. I'm sensing some very iffy aura. I might head off before everyone gets too excited.'

Fraser tried to get up from the bar stool, but Reilly put a firm hand on his shoulder and stopped him. 'You should wait for Barry.'

Fraser glared at him. 'Now, I am gonna suggest you take your hand away. Or I will cut the thing off and use it to slap you about the puss!' He spoke with the air of confidence that suggested the guy carried zero fear.

'Oo, easy, mate. No need to throw threats around,' said Reilly in an appeasing tone. 'Let me get you another pint.'

A sly grin worked its way onto the Scotsman's face. Reilly, certain he'd spotted the flash of a blade, stepped away from the man. He'd already glimpsed the beer bottle nearby that he'd intended to snatch and whack the bloke with. But Reilly didn't have time to make a grab for it, because Mills intervened, grabbed Fraser by the back of the neck and slammed the guy's face against the bar. Once... twice... three... four times. Possibly even five or six. Reilly couldn't be certain because of the sheer speed of the attack. Mills shoved the injured bloke down to the ground like he was no more than a toddler and then stamped on his legs with such brute force, Reilly heard bones breaking. If it hadn't had been for Veronica's ear-piercing screams for him to stop, Mills most likely wouldn't have ended the attack until Fraser lay dead in a mashed-up heap. He'd not intended to stop his brother. Screw that.

Reilly scanned the pub. Seven patrons were in. All blokes. Most gazed in shock and others looked away, pretending that they'd not just laid witness to a man losing his front teeth and having both legs mangled. Reilly caught Sean Teller's eye. He could see the Liverpudlian texting, so he marched over to his table. 'You texting someone, Teller?'

Sean shook his head, turned his phone around to reveal a game screen. 'My clan was under attack. I had to act super fast.'

Reilly sniggered, shook his head and left him be.

A young man put his puffa jacket on and made to leave, but Veronica stood by the door and shook her head. 'It's an early lock-in, lovey. Sit down, yeah. Next few rounds are on us.'

The young man swallowed, gave a sheepish nod and sloped back to his seat, pulling his Nike baseball cap lower onto his head as if somehow this would shroud his identity.

Another man rose from his seat. This guy was older, perhaps sixty, with thick, lamb-chop sideburns and hefty shoulders. A scaffolder that drunk here on a regular basis; normally with a gang of mates, but today in for a quiet pint on his Jack Jones.

'Sit down, Keith!' hissed Mills.

Keith walked over towards the crumpled body on the floor and Reilly heard Fraser moan, gurgle and tilt his bashed up head to the side.

Mills squared up to Keith. 'I said, sit down!'

Keith stared Mills straight in the eye. Few people carried the size to do this. Reilly walked over to the pair, expecting more trouble to erupt.

'That chap is choking,' said Keith in a soft tone. With that, he bent down, tipped Fraser onto his side and fished around in his mouth, knocking out two loose teeth in the process.

As all this took place, Mills's outraged and disgruntled face was a real picture. Reilly would have loved to have snapped a shot, because the image would have looked wonderful as a huge canvas print.

Reilly watched in awe as Keith pulled out a chunk of mutilated tongue from the semi-unconscious Fraser, stood up, and placed it on the beer drip runner. Then he stayed put, elbows rested on the bar as if waiting to be served. 'That's not a blade,' said Keith, his voice void of emotion.

Reilly could now see that Fraser had been reaching for a shiny, silver vaping device, and not a knife. But this didn't make him feel too bad for the guy. You give yourself a reputation for being a blade wielding whack-job, then these kinds of misjudgements were bound to come about. You can't be too careful these days. There are all sorts of nutters about. He snatched up the vape and slid it into his back pocket.

Reilly would like to get to know this Keith better. What a legend. He turned to Mills. 'Go pull Barry off the shitter and take the prick down to the cellar.'

Mills nodded, then he turned and muttered, 'Barry's standing right there.'

Reilly followed Mills's gaze to the other side of the bar, where Barry stood. The expression fixed on his face suggested he'd awoken from a bizarre yet terrifying nightmare. Then he bolted.

'Cunt!' spat Mills, charging after him.

Reilly addressed the room. 'We don't tolerate blades in our boozer. So please remember that. We'd appreciate your patience whilst we clear up this little mess and get this bloke some medical care. As my sister said, free bar, so don't be shy, go get stuck in, guys.'

There were murmurs and mutters as the patrons drifted over to get their free drinks, whilst trying to avoid peering down at the beaten man.

Reilly smiled and patted Keith on the back. 'Do us a favour, Keith… give us a hand to get this mush into my car.'

Keith glared at him incredulously, let out a deep sigh, and nodded.

Elena could hear raised voices from the kitchen as she headed outside the house and strolled around to the back to collect the bag. She skipped back to her place, where she grabbed her backpack and transferred the money rolls into it. She took one last gaze around the place and breathed out a relieved sigh. Just two more quick jobs to do and she'd find her brother. She went outside, lit up a cigarette and scanned the courtyard. Not yet four o'clock, and darkness was already creeping in and a bitter cold now accompanied the sun's descent.

It was finally time to say goodbye to this place. She headed to the store shed to get the shotgun cartridges.

46

Page 5

"Help me take revenge. Help me destroy this evil family that stole our lives from us. We can do it together. You're a grown man now. I'm certain you have a fire in your heart and deep down, you carry a bitter hatred for these people. Think about all this. Really think! Write back to me at the address below. It's Evelyn's and she'll make sure I get any letters. I'm living and working in Naples, but I'm coming back to London soon. Evelyn will get a contact number for you, so we can talk. I'd so love to speak with you. To see you! The Bartells took our lives from us, Nino. They took you away from me and stole everything we should've shared together. They stole those precious moments. You can't forgive them for these things. I understand we can never get that time back, but we have the rest of our lives to make up for this injustice. And I'm sure when this all sinks in, you'll be outraged and may even want to lash out. Please don't! You mustn't. Stay calm and keep it together. We can take revenge, but it should be slow and well planned. We need to wait for the right opportunity to present itself. A time where you can take them for every penny and hit them where it hurts. I'm sure you'd love to return to Valletta. To once again see those honey-stone-coloured buildings and exquisite beaches. You'll fall in love. You'll feel like you've come home. You will have come home.

You are Antonino Borg Pullicino. You are a strong, passionate man and I know you'll do the right thing. My mother was a strong Maltese lady, Nino, but my father... your grandfather... was a fine, bold man, Nino. A proud Neapolitan whose blood runs strong in your veins. You're not a Bartell. You don't belong there, and I'm sure you've always known in your heart that you are a different breed to those ungodly animals.

My wonderful son, I love you so much. I always have. And I always will. You are my world. All I live for is the amazing moment when I can hug you again."

Selene Pullicino (Mum) xxx

47

2 December 2018 [16.30]

Ravi sat down at his desk and opened up his work emails. He'd promised his wife he would give the business his full attention in the coming weeks. No more working from home. It would be business as usual and back to full time in his London based office. He needed that; needed the grind of work and the distractions that accompanied it. After his ordeal with the ransom drop off, he'd been both relived and infuriated to learn Nathaniel had made that call to Chandra. That hurt. Because his wife had all but given up on Nathaniel, and despite the fact Ravi had been through hell and back to locate him, Nathaniel still broke his silence by calling his mother. After everything Ravi had done, Nathaniel still didn't have the respect to call and attempt to put things right. His son even phoned her from a withheld number, so ringing him back wouldn't be a possibility. Ravi did, for a brief moment, consider that the kidnapping wasn't real and somehow his son orchestrated the ransoming for his own game, though the very idea seemed preposterous, and he'd been annoyed at even letting that horrendous thought enter his head.

Ravi read a client's email, though its content did not sink into his muddled brain and this riled him further. His clients once felt they had implicit trust in him. He'd always seen it as his goal to not only assist them in their endeavours, but to educate them. Whether it be to understand the complexity of their investment, or administering their budgets sufficiently, Ravi would assist every client with the same degree of support and diligence, regardless of their standing or affluency. But he'd been so fixated by his son's disappearance, he'd let down so many clients who'd come to rely on him completely. There were bridges to mend, though Ravi suspected some would be way beyond repair now. He'd even lost two invaluable employees during his absent months spent searching.

A text came through on Ravi's mobile and his eyes flicked to the screen. A message from Arnie Baxter. He flicked open the text – *your boy's @ the Bartells. Go now, he's in real…* these words were followed by three poo emojis.

Ravi frowned and read the message again. Then he turned off his computer and went to grab his things. He knew what to do.

Nino gaped in total surprise as Barry came running out of The Swan. This made zero sense. Why would Reilly just let him go? He crouched low as he observed Barry fumble with his keys and jump inside his van. Had he fought his way out? As Barry's engine started, Nino spotted Mills come charging out of the pub and race to the rear.

Barry's van sped out of the carpark and almost run the huge man over as he sped down the lane. Mills roared as he launched a bottle at the fleeing van and it smashed in the middle of the road.

Nino didn't even dare breathe, let alone move, as Mills stood in the lane and screamed obscenities at the fleeing van. After shouting his barrage of colourful abuse, Mills stood silently in the middle of the road, eyes fixed forward as though in some sort of freaky trance. The van could no longer be seen, yet still he glared up the lane. Then, out of nowhere, Mills let loose a bellow that would have terrified a horde of bloodthirsty barbarians as he charged to the nearest car, a sporty VW Golf, and hammered the absolute crap out of the motor with his bare hands.

. . .

The dark-haired girl came through the field. She carried a satchel in one hand, had a rucksack slung on her shoulders and something Duncan couldn't make out gripped in her other hand. She walked over to him and crouched down. 'Here, I found these. They're pretty rusty and not super sharp, but they should work.' She handed him a set of bolt cutters.

Duncan took hold of the cutters and studied them. 'Thank you so much.'

The girl reached inside the satchel and pulled out a handful of what looked like shotgun cartridges. She tossed them into the fire pit. Duncan decided she was an odd-looking girl, with close-set eyes, a tiny chin and a small, skinny nose. And Duncan hadn't noticed those buckteeth on their previous encounter. Now he could focus on nothing else. Though he still thought she was cute, in a strange way.

'I need to get my phone back,' said Duncan.

The girl tipped up the satchel, emptying the contents. More cartridges tumbled out and disappeared into the pit. 'You need to start cutting that chain. Do you want to die here?'

'I have to get my phone back!' said Duncan.

The girl kicked at a few stray shells that missed the hole. 'People are coming here tonight. Dangerous people. There will be major trouble. You do not want to hang around. Trust me.'

Duncan sniffed, trying not to cry. He was done with tears. 'It's important. I need to warn my friend. Barry took it from me.'

The girl pulled out a gun from her rucksack and transferred it into the satchel. 'Fine. Upstairs bedroom. Back left. He has a phone up there. Could be yours, I guess.'

'Thank you... I mean it, thank you so much,' said Duncan. He wanted to know the reason this strange girl was helping him. Why she had a gun stashed in that bag and where she was heading. But there was no time for that. He needed to go inside that house and retrieve his phone.

'You'd be insane not to run now. If I were you, I'd leap that fence and bolt. Get as far away from here as possible,' said the girl. 'You'd be safer in the pits of hell!'

'I... I just can't.'

The girl sighed and nodded. 'Alright. Up to you. But I warned you.

Good luck.' She then jogged across the paddock, climbed a fence and scurried off into the dark trees beyond.

Jack poured a large measure of whiskey and slugged it. 'I see.'

Johnny watched his dad closely, but couldn't get a read on him. He'd brought him up to speed on everything.

'Who did the deed?' asked Jack.

Johnny frowned. 'I'm not following?'

Jack scratched his stubbled chin. 'Who shoved Stefan over the edge?'

'Well... if I recall things right, I did,' said Johnny. 'We were steaming, though.'

'I figured as much. Barry is full of hot air, but often when it comes down to it, he leaves others to get their hands dirty. He only has his reputation because he's been riding your coattails since he was a kid,' said Jack.

'It's all a total mess, Dad. I'm sorry.'

Jack shrugged and finished the dregs of his drink. He immediately poured himself another and topped up Johnny's. 'Yeah, well, it is what it is. I'll contact Delano.'

'That odd bloke from Sheerness who looks like a skeleton?'

'That's the one. Nice chap. Mad as a wet hen, but he can help us remove all traces of them.'

Johnny laughed. 'Will he do a deal? Three crispies for the price of two?'

Jack grinned. 'Technically, once the furnace is up and cooking, I guess it doesn't matter how many stiffs he slips in, hey?'

Johnny sipped his drink. He'd already known that his dad would suggest a full clean-up job. But the thought of actually carrying out the grim executions didn't fill him with joy.

'I know you reckon you can trust this Nathaniel lad, but you don't want him out there knowing what he knows and always worrying about it. Loose lips sink ships and all that bollocks.'

Johnny didn't believe that for a minute Nathaniel would talk about what happened, but he never went against his dad's commands.

'That boy's father was snooping around our pad a while back,' said

Jack.

'So what?'

'So… it means the bloke has linked us to his son. He might come back sniffing around again. And as for your big soft mate out there… well, he's still responsible for Craig's death, Jon. We can't let that go.'

'No, he was just a witness. It's his mate. Oh shit, what time is it? We're meant to be meeting Davey around seven.'

'You have plenty of time. I tell you what, son, we'll have a few more stiff drinks to prepare for what we need to do, then we'll round up the three amigos and… put this thing to bed tonight. Agreed?'

Johnny nodded and pulled his phone from the pocket of his jeans. He frowned. 'Damn, Barry's called me five times. My bloody phone was on silent.'

Ravi had been along the route in the daytime several times, and he felt confident he'd be able to retrace the route in the dark, especially with the new head-torch he'd recently purchased from the Cotswolds store. Ravi pulled on his thick beanie hat and placed the torch straps about his head and tightened them in place, before clipping the connecters under his chin. Ravi slid the stun gun into a holster on his belt and fastened it with the Velcro cover. He checked his boot laces were nice and tight and tucked away. He'd purchased cargo combat trousers and a padded military jacket for his excursions to the Bartells. He'd selected every item in black, because he'd always intended to undertake some night time investigations out here. He guessed he looked like a special forces soldier about to start a covert mission. He locked the Jag and placed the keys into one of the zip pockets in his trousers, then made for the overgrown trail that led deep into Craven's Cross Forest. It took twenty minutes to reach the house on his last visit, but he intended to get there faster tonight. He pressed the button to light up the torch unit and pressed it again to dim the settings. The knowledgeable guy in the store assured him that this costly model would be perfect for night hikes. He advised Ravi that the battery life worked best on the middle setting, and would still be bright enough for walking and was a popular piece of kit with night runners and mountain bikers.

As he entered the dark, twisting byway all fear left him. Tonight, this madness would all be over, he told himself.

They made it look so easy in the films and comics, but in reality, breaking through a solid steel chain was ridiculously hard work. Duncan tried snapping away in short bursts, and then tried clamping down and using prolonged pressure, but so far, he'd only managed to chew through a couple of millimetres of metal. He didn't have time for this. *Karl* didn't have time.

'So you left him there?' asked Johnny.

'I had no choice, Jon. Like I said, I strolled out of the khazi and Fraser was all smashed up,' said Barry.

'And you don't know why they decked him?' asked Johnny.

'No! Nino wasn't even there… the little bastard must have totally stitched us up. Led us into a trap.'

Johnny and Jack shared a look and Jack poured more whiskey. Johnny's phone lay on the table so both of them could hear the conversation.

'Maybe Fraser said something to piss them off,' said Johnny.

'Mills came charging after me like a wild beast. Nah, they wanted my blood. They'll be heading up to the house next, sure as shit they will. I think… *Nino* must have told them about… well, about…'

'He's told me,' said Jack.

'Oh,' said Barry. Then, after a brief silence, asked, 'What the hell is happening? Why would Nino fuck us over like this?'

'Barry, what about Davey?' asked Johnny.

'Oh, shit. Um, hold up, I'll call him. He'll be making the pickup any time now!'

'I'll call him. Just hurry back here, Barry,' said Johnny, then cut the call.

Jack finished his drink and slammed down his glass. 'I think once you've called your guy, we need to have a little chat with Elena and find out what Nino's playing at. Don't you? You can bet your hairy gonads that little madam knows what's going on.'

48

2 December 2018 [17.30]

Johnny stepped out into the courtyard and phoned Davey. He answered on the first ring.

'Yes, I'm here before you ask,' said Davey in a snarky tone.

'You see him yet?' asked Johnny.

'No, but he has already texted back after I confirmed my location and registration… wait, there is a guy pointing at my car. He's a ginger lad, but he has a beard. Could be him.'

'Listen, Davey—'

'This guy is definitely scanning the row of taxis, but he's walked away and started talking to a tall blond guy wearing a chequered shirt.'

'I don't need a description of everyone leaving the airport, mate.'

'I think it's him. But I can't work out if he's with that guy or just chatting with him. The blond guy has lit up a smoke and sniggered at something the ginger guy said. They could be together. Awesome.'

'Davey, there is a change of plan. We have complications, so we can't meet as arranged.'

'Hey? Where do I take him then?'

'I need you to *deal* with this, Davey.'

'Johnny, mate… that's not what I agreed. Fuck, he's coming over! It is him.'

'Just get it done. We'll wipe the slate clean and bung you a tidy wedge for the job.'

Davey sighed. 'I'm not a bloody hit man! What the hell am I supposed to do with him?'

'I dunno. Use your imagination. Craig kept stuff in the car. Might be a blade in the glovebox. There should also be a Tomahawk wedged under the driver's seat. Barry gave it to him on his nineteenth birthday. Craig kept it hidden for emergencies.'

'Sorry… a what? What do you think I am, a bloody Apache Indian? Shit, Johnny, you've stitched me up.'

'I'm sure you can handle it. Quickly message your guys to meet you somewhere.'

'I… Johnny, mate, come on. This is heavy stuff… can't I hold him somewhere instead?… Ah, shit… the other guy is heading over with him.'

'You're collecting the guy that killed my brother. Do you understand the importance of this? There maybe no second chance! Don't let me down, Davey. Don't you dare let me down!'

'Hey, man,' said a man's voice.

Johnny heard Davey suck in some air and say, 'No luggage for the boot, guys?'

'Nope,' said the man.

'Cool,' said Davey.

Johnny took a deep breath. The bastard that killed Craig was right there with Davey. He shook his head, furious that he'd not be able to deal with the matter himself. He'd been watching the darkened mobile home during his call, and suspected Elena had buggered off somewhere, or was hiding. He stomped back inside the house. 'Dad! Come on.'

Duncan gritted his teeth so hard he thought they might shatter as he gripped the tool and squeezed and squeezed until his cheeks almost exploded. Then the pressure let up, and he realised the screw holding the cutting blades in place had broken, rendering the tool useless. Now he wanted to scream blue murder and as the anger surged through him, he kicked out with his leg and saw that the chain link was now cut and his leg pulled free of it. So shocked by this unbelievable discovery, Duncan shot up, looked around in a blind panic, and raced off towards the house.

Nino came to a halt at the agreed meeting spot, jumped off the bike and raced over to a parked Transit van. A stocky, unshaven man sat at the wheel. He wasn't certain it was Brennan, as he'd not seen the man in years, but he banged on the window. The man wound it down and regarded him with suspicion.

'Bren?' asked Nino.

'Been a while, hasn't it, Nino?' said Brennan. He spoke in a slow, deep, Northern accent.

'Is Elena not here? Where is she?' Nino asked, panic washing over him.

'She is late. I was wondering if I should drive down to the house. But Elena was adamant I wait here. I just tried her phone… she didn't pick up.'

'You should have gone to find her, Bren!… I'll track her down. Stay here in case she turns up.'

'Nino… if you've dragged my sister into something that gets her hurt… there'll be murders. You hear me?'

The pair locked eyes for a moment.

'I know how much you love my sister, but she's a fool where you are concerned. She abandoned her own family to be with you,' said Brennan.

Nino considered that after his first savage encounter with Elena's brother many years back, he'd never want to experience his wrath ever again. 'I'll find her. I promise, Bren.'

'See that you do. You have fifteen minutes, then I'm coming down there myself! And I'll batter any Bartell or anyone else that gets in my path.'

. . .

Elena took the track that Nino often used as a shortcut that led from the house, through the woods and along the fields. The first part of the track ran parallel to Dead Lane, and she went with caution, concentrating on every tiny sound. She thought she heard a vehicle approaching. Then a sudden noise, like a huge thudding impact, made her stop dead, and fearing it might be Nino or Brennan, she made her way further down the track, snuck through the bushes and took a quick peek. What she found was Barry's van, on its side in the bush, wheels spinning and smoke spilling from the bonnet. It was clear he'd taken the bend too fast and lost control.

Elena froze, wanting to go back, but her intrigue compelled her to investigate further. An overwhelming sensation came over her to check the front and see if Barry lay trapped and injured in the wreck. How she'd have enjoyed waving at him. She'd even blow the fat twat a little parting goodbye kiss and perhaps wave the stolen cash in his stupid face. Elena knew she couldn't, of course, because she needed to get out of there. Then she glimpsed a figure move at her left, so spun, and found Barry standing in the road. He held a crowbar.

'And what's this nosy little mouse up to?'

Elena tried to move back, but ensnared herself in the coarse bushes.

Barry snarled. 'Where the fuck is Nino, you goofy slag?'

As Duncan raced across the courtyard, a severe pain jolted up his ankle and leg. The pressure of the tight shackle made running near impossible because it was so painful. The front door to the house flung open. Duncan plunged down behind the Land Rover. He waited several moments before stealing a glance. Two figures stomped straight past the vehicle. They headed in the direction he'd just fled, and they walked with real urgency. One he considered could be Johnny. Were they heading to the field to collect him? Duncan took a deep breath and exhaled. Then, crawling on his hands and knees, he slunk around to the other side of the vehicle, jumped to his feet, and raced for the front door.

. . .

Whilst Jack searched inside the darkened mobile home, Johnny gazed out into the paddock and squinted in the darkness. He jogged over to the pit and his fears were confirmed. He kicked over the horse blanket, revealing an old set of broken bolt cutters and a mangled chain. Johnny scanned the blackness surrounding the property and figured the chubby bastard would be long gone by now. A shame, he considered, because with the strong alcohol flowing through his veins and the anger now boiling inside of him, he'd have enjoyed beating the big pathetic lump with a shovel. He no longer cared. He no longer held any pity for him. Johnny clenched both fists and spat in the pit. He told Barry they should have stashed the lad in Craig's old room. As usual his brother did it *his* way. But right now, there were more pressing matters to consider than hunting down that useless pussy.

Duncan opened the door and walked straight inside. A light at the end of the hallway revealed a large, open kitchen area, and there were clanking noises that sounded like pots and pans being knocked about from within. He peered up the darkened stairs and made for them. Duncan heard his own heartbeat in his ears as he went up. The pain in his ankle felt worse on the stairs than from running. He tried to recall what the dark-haired girl had told him... *back left... or was it front?*

Elena tugged the revolver out of the satchel, aimed it at Barry, and stepped out from the undergrowth. 'Try it, you dumb shit!'

'You best be careful with... wait a minute, that's mine! Fuck! You sneaky little bitch. You've been in my room.' Then his face dropped as the reality of the situation struck him.

'Start walking... go on, piss off home. You come near me and I swear to God I will stick one straight in your kneecap.'

Barry coughed out a nervous chuckle. 'Yeah, course you will. You probably can't even fire it.'

'I'm an O'Carroll, Barry. You think my dad never stuck a shooter in my hands?'

'You're not keeping the money, Elena! I won't bloody let you!'

Elena grinned. 'Oo, Elena, now is it? That's a first, Barry.'

. . .

Duncan crept into the dark room and scanned the place. With slow, careful steps, he crept over to the bedside cabinet and there it was. He'd done it. He'd only found his phone. Duncan scooped up the phone and held it to his chest. He wanted to contact Karl immediately, but he feared making a call here, so as nimbly as possible, he slinked back out into the hallway and made for the stairs. The terror racked his body and his jelly-like legs almost gave way on the descent. But he needed to save his friend. There was no more time. He forced himself on.

49

2 December 2018 [18.00]

Johnny found Jack sitting in Elena's smoking swing-chair, reading a letter. His lips were pressed tight together, and he breathed heavily. Jack spotted him and handed him the crumpled letter. Johnny sat down next to him, causing the seat to creak in protest under their combined weight. He read the letter.

Elena heard the growl of the bike, then moments later the dazzling glare from the machine lit the lane.

Barry's eyes blazed as Nino stopped the bike, kicked down the stand, and dismounted.

'Get away from her, Barry,' said Nino.

Barry stepped towards Nino. 'Is this your subtle way of telling us you don't want to step up and help the family business? You should've just said, Nino. We all guessed you'd be no replacement for Craig. It wouldn't have been a big surprise to anyone.'

'I know, Barry! I know my mum's alive,' said Nino.

'Nino, please, please, please don't tell me this is all about *her* and you've actually been drawn in by her bullshit,' said Barry.

'I know what you did to her, Barry. You, Craig and Johnny,' growled Nino.

'We don't have time for this, Nino,' said Elena, backing away from Barry, but keeping her aim fixed on him.

'What did you do, you stupid boy?' said Barry, his voice barely audible.

Kreshnik slung open the old Volvo's boot and pulled back a threadbare blanket.

'These will do fine,' said Reilly, as he viewed the two pump-action shotguns and single handgun.

'There aren't a huge amount of rounds. Ah, and my cousin said, "don't get caught with the Glock. Get rid of that, even if you don't end up using it." Are you sure this can't wait? I can get you much better gear. Even a couple of Skorpion machine pistols. Those are crazy good.'

Reilly shook his head. He'd only use the guns to force himself inside the house, because he'd decided that he'd be taking a claw hammer to thrash their fat heads. He wasn't even keen on using guns anyway, and he was a terrible shot. 'You not coming, Kresh?'

'No. I'm very busy tonight. This is foolish. No?'

'Tell your cousin thanks for the tools.'

Kreshnik gave him a toothy grin. 'He said he owes you big for dealing with that competitor of his.'

'No sweat,' said Reilly, thinking it really wasn't... one quick phone call, in fact.

'Reilly, please do take care. Whatever you are up to. Don't screw up and leave me alone with that miserable, moody meathead, Mills.'

'He'll be heartbroken that you said that, Kresh.'

Kreshnik laughed. 'Mills doesn't have a heart... oooh, hey, Mills, how are you doing, my friend?' he said animatedly, as Mills suddenly loomed over them.

'What are you two jabbering about?' asked Mills gruffly.

'Skorpion pistols,' said Reilly, sharing a secret grin with Kreshnik.

'You got one?' asked Mills, a hint of a smile creeping on his lips.

'No, we don't,' said Reilly.

. . .

Nino had expected anger and aggression from Barry. He'd played out this confrontation in his mind, and this hadn't been how he'd envisioned it going down. Not even close. Barry appeared utterly defeated, hurt, and betrayed. There were even tears welling up in his bloodshot eyes.

'Have you even seen her?' asked Barry.

'We met yesterday. And I've been speaking to her on the phone for months. She hates this family with a passion!' said Nino.

'You're one of us. Why would you do this?' asked Barry.

Nino stepped forward. 'She tried to contact me years ago, and you threatened to murder her! All this time and I thought she'd killed herself. How could you all let me think that my own mother committed suicide? That's sick!'

Elena waved the gun. 'Nino, get away from him! You step back, Barry. I mean it.'

Barry, ignoring the warning, stepped closer to Nino. 'She was warned off. That's true enough, I won't deny that, but with good reason—'

'Nino, we're running out of time,' blurted Elena. 'I said get back, Barry!'

'You threatened to rape her!' said Nino.

Barry pulled a disgusted face. 'Hey, leave it out! Did I fuck?'

'So that's a lie?' hissed Nino.

'That never happened. I promise you, there is *so* much more to this, Nino. I swear it.'

'You're lying! You've all lied to me. I should never have been here. I should've had a different life. You didn't have the right. None of you did.' Nino felt the tears coming and fought them back down. All these years… all the lies. The betrayal. It was too much now. He'd held onto all of this pain and despair for a long time. Kept his rage caged up. But no longer.

Barry's shoulders slumped, and he shook his head. 'He saved you, Nino. Dad took you away because he had no choice. Selene no doubt claimed that Dad stole you from her, but that's not what happened.

Whatever bullshit she has spun, she's nothing but a lying, twisted witch!'

Elena's eyes flicked between the brothers. 'Nino, he's just trying to get in your head. You can't believe his nonsense. Shut up, Barry.'

Barry ignored Elena and continued. 'Dad told us everything one night when he was drunk out of his nut. The entire story, and he's kept the truth from you all this time, so you didn't have to suffer the real truth. That's why he said your real mother died. That was better than the reality.'

Nino shook his head. 'Don't spin a load of bullshit, Barry!'

'Don't tell me, she painted a wonderful picture of you two living a glorious life by the sea. All unicorns and rainbows. Am I right? When Dad finally took you away from her, you were living in a squalid flat in South London. You were living like a dirty savage!'

Nino's mouth was so dry he couldn't even swallow. He watched Barry closely as he stood in the lights of the toppled van, scrutinising his face for even a hint he was weaving an elaborate lie. But he wasn't. Nino was sure of that.

Johnny handed the letter back to his dad. He couldn't think of anything appropriate to say, so said nothing. The letter was dated last year, which meant Nino had been sitting on this dire information since then, biding his time and plotting his move. That was cold. He'd done well to hide it, he'd give him that. Things were starting to make sense. He had some idea as to why Nino was going feral.

Jack stood up. 'I'll get my shooter.'

Johnny watched his dad go. There were only a few times he could ever recall his dad showing his fear. He knew Jack was far more afraid of facing death by some debilitating illness than at the prospect of dying in a vicious fight to the death. He'd see the latter as a proper way to check out. He'd welcome that over Marcus Chillcott's fate of gradually fading away into oblivion and relying on others to nurse you. His worst nightmare. Just as it was Marcus's, who'd once told Jack that if he ever became so sick he was a burden to his family, then to slam a pillow over his mug and blow his brains out. The pair had a complicated relationship. Partners. Friends. Sometimes even bitter enemies. And they'd once fought a brutal battle in this very courtyard that ended in gruesome injuries to both parties. But they always held a deep respect for one another throughout the years. Marcus even helped his dad acquire this land; by deceit and treachery, of course, but all the same, the Bartells were all indebted to Marcus Chillcott. Johnny considered what Marcus would make of all this mess. He warned Jack about taking on the boy and said it would be a huge mistake. He ridiculed Jack and said he was soft and sentimental, where that bloody kid was concerned. Johnny remembered thinking it all rather strange, because Jack never once treated any of them like he did Nino. *They* all needed to be tough and unforgiving, like Jack. He'd not been jealous, unlike his brothers, just rather confused about why his dad treated the younger boy so differently. Johnny never told a soul he'd been listening at the lounge doorway that day – when Jack lied to Nino and explained to the youngster that his mum had died.

'Why did God let this happen?' Nino had asked, snivelling and gripping his frayed ape toy that Barry had given him.

Jack had replied in a soft voice, 'The angels need her, son... the angels *really* need her to dance for them in heaven. She had no choice but to leave. But she will miss you. She'll always miss you.' Then he hugged the boy. As Nino cried in his dad's arms, Jack told the boy everything would be OK.

Seeing this small display of affection from his dad always stayed with Johnny, because he, like his brothers, not once experienced anything like it from the man. Yes, he drank with them, cracked jokes and always let them do as they pleased. But he never dished out one hug or showed them any sign he actually cared for them. Not one show of genuine emotion like he'd witnessed that day, and years later, when Johnny learnt the truth about Selene's awful treatment of Nino, he came to understand that perhaps, at that time, Nino needed to see that side of Jack. It finally made sense. But that lie, albeit one told out of compassion, had returned to haunt not just Jack, but the entire family.

They'd all wanted Nino to have his name changed. He remembered Craig and Barry refusing to use Nino or Antonino and they'd only call him Ferret and Grunt. When Jack found out, he went ballistic. 'His name is Antonino! That's the name he was born with. That's the name he is keeping!' Jack had bellowed. They'd all tried to connect with Nino, even Craig in his own strange way – but Nino wasn't like them. He could be such an uppity, entitled little shit. He never wanted to be a Bartell from day one, and it always seemed like he was too good for them. So, as time passed, they all stopped bothering. It had been many years later that Craig added another layer to the tale and told Nino that his birth mother had topped herself because she'd resented Nino. Jack hit the roof upon learning that, and Craig received the bollocking of his life.

Johnny sighed. It would be a long night. And he'd need more strong booze to get through it.

Duncan raced along the side of the house, but the pain soared up his ankle, and this forced him to slow to a swift walk. He switched on his phone, scurried along past a chicken coop, and stopped as he noticed a bright light moving around in the darkness ahead. It seemed some way off, but it appeared to be heading in his direction. He decided not to chance meeting the torch bearer, fearing it might be another Bartell member, so he went into a wooden store shed, hid himself in the back and checked his phone.

His heart sank when he saw the battery display at only one per cent.

'She didn't just give you up, she used you as a bargaining tool. To drain as much money as she could from Dad,' said Barry.

Nino's heart began racing so fast he felt giddy. Because somehow, by the expression on Barry's face, he knew his words were sincere.

'She burnt your backside with cigarette butts when you were a toddler. I bet she didn't tell you that bit of info, did she?'

Nino opened his mouth to speak but clamped it shut.

'Did she tell you about the time she called Dad, threatening to drown you in the bath if he didn't come and take you away? No?

Didn't think so. Or what about the time she blackmailed Dad, saying she'd tell Mum about their sordid affair if he didn't pay her a hefty wedge?'

'We need to go!' shouted Elena.

'Dad screwed up. He met your mu—' Barry twisted his head as though in pain and corrected himself. 'He met Selene on one of his holiday jaunts and got swept away by a stunning bird who duped the silly fool into thinking she loved him. But she was scum. A slag. A stripper with drug issues. She took him for a ride and tried to ruin him. I refuse to use the word *mum* because she was never that.'

Nino glanced at Elena and it was clear enough by her disgruntled expression she believed it too.

'She hated you because you destroyed her dream of becoming a professional dancer. Which would never have happened, anyway. So she vented her anger on you, because she was a twisted, bitter, selfish whore. She even slapped Dad on the birth certificate, because she'd always planned for him to take you away,' said Barry.

Keeping her aim and eyes on Barry, Elena spoke softly to Nino. 'We have to go. Before it's too late.'

Barry jabbed a finger at Nino. 'We didn't want you here at first, because you almost ripped our family apart. Ever consider the impact on us? That's why Craig resented you. He found it hard to accept. Ever since you came on the scene, all our lives changed. You almost tore our parents apart. Don't you get that?' asked Barry.

Nino shook his head, wanting this to all be a pack of lies, but knowing it wasn't.

Barry's face darkened. 'Dad risked losing everything to bring you back here. He risked losing his wife, his sons and his home. But he still did it, because he said he'd never be able to live with himself if he'd left you alone with her. Because you were one of his own. That's how much he cared about you. And you repay him by destroying everything. So go! Piss off with your little mouse and go be with that hussy who tossed you aside and used you to line her own pockets. You deserve each other, you traitor!'

Nino felt Elena's arm across his chest. She pushed him back towards his bike.

'If you reckon your life would have been so wonderful... warm beaches and fond memories, then you are deluded. The woman has poisoned you,' said Barry. Then he glared at Elena. 'And she's no better. A scheming thief like the rest of the O'Carroll scum. Geez, Nino... how did you let these women mug you off like this? You're meant to be the smart one, bro.'

Nino couldn't hold it in any longer. He sobbed and Elena pulled him to her and held him, whispering words he was unable to hear through his rasping sobs.

As Ravi approached the property's perimeter, he switched off the head-torch and adjusted his eyes to the darkness. He saw a couple of lights on downstairs, but most of the main house was unlit. He clambered over the fence and, taking caution with every step, headed onto the Bartells' land.

'Remember when those men came here? When Dad got hurt?' asked Barry.

Nino remembered. He'd remember that day for the rest of his life.

'At a funeral Jack attended, he received a lot of stick about you. Some nasty stuff was said. One of Marcus's nephews got drunk and took things too far. He ripped the total piss out of our family and ridiculed us for taking you in. I don't know the full story, but Dad refused to take it and he belted the prat so hard he ended up in intensive care. That same night, Marcus and his family came searching for retribution...' Barry ran a finger down his own cheek. 'So, every time Dad has stared at himself in the mirror, he's always been reminded of what he went through... defending you. Can you imagine how he'll feel now? Because everything he's ever done for you... it was all for nothing. I guess he can mull over that when it all kicks off here tonight.'

Nino's face must have dropped, because Barry's eyes narrowed and he said, 'Oooh, you don't know? The folks came back. And I'll doubt we can get them to leave.'

Nino looked at Elena, but she didn't return the look. She kept her eyes focussed on Barry.

Barry spat in Nino's direction. 'We didn't ask for this. No more than you did. Mum made herself ill. She turned bitter and miserable. She's barely cracked a smile since the day Dad brought you home. It mentally ruined her. Seeing you every day. A living reminder of our father's betrayal.'

Nino realised he hadn't considered this. Yes, he knew that he'd come on the scene because of a sordid affair... but he'd not once contemplated the full impact of his presence.

Barry spun on his heels, walked away, and disappeared down the dark lane.

Nino put his face in his hands. What the hell had he done?

The battery was so low. Duncan knew he'd only get one call, and that was if he was lucky and the battery held. He'd have liked to have phoned for help too, but right now, saving Karl was his prime concern. He'd considered a text, but if the phone died before he replied, or he didn't receive the text... Duncan would never know. No, a call was needed. Duncan's hand trembled as he selected Karl's number. Not only would one per cent not last long, if Karl blurted out his name, and the driver got wind of the situation, he may not get a chance to escape. And suddenly the words came to him, or more to the point, how he should deliver them. As soon as Karl answered, Duncan didn't give Karl a chance to utter a word.

'Karl Rogers, you are a disgrace!' said Duncan, using his best parade-ground voice.

'Um, I—'

'Don't you utter a word, your father is speaking. Do *you* understand me? DO you?' Then, using his own voice, he whispered, '*Do* you understand?'

'Ah, yeah, Dad,' said Karl.

'That's not a real taxi. It's *not* taking you home. You need to get out!'

'OK... Dad. Yep, I'll definitely do that.'

'I'm sorry... I messed up. Big time.'

'Yeah, don't worry about that. Where are you now, Dad? Are *you* doing alright yourself? Are you at home now?'

Duncan went to speak, but the battery gave up and the line cut. He sighed in relief. He'd warned Karl and given him a chance, at least. Now, somehow, he'd need to get away from this awful place.

Then Duncan heard the dogs barking and slapped a hand over his mouth.

50

2 December 2018 [18.30]

'Wow, man. I mean, shit. I heard your dad shouting for real,' said Joost.

Karl's jaw tightened and his eyes flicked to the driver. 'Could we do a pit stop at the services, please? Busting here.'

'Um, yeah, OK,' said the driver, though he sounded unconvincing.

Joost grimaced. 'Is he angry that you've brought a friend to stay?'

'Nah, it's… something else… hey, mate, the service's turn off is right here… ah, you passed it now.'

'You know, it is against company policy to make unauthorised stops. Best keep your legs crossed,' said the driver, trying to make a joke about it. 'Too many cheeky beers on the plane, I bet.'

'What taxi firm do you work for again?' asked Karl in a surly tone. Then he sent Duncan a text – *Where are you??? All OK?!!*

The driver coughed and fiddled with his baseball cap. 'Um, The… *Last Stop Taxi Company*… don't leave a negative review, mate. I am new to the firm. I'll speed up!'

Joost caught the song playing on the radio. 'Hey, turn this up! What a tune.'

The driver cranked up the volume and Joost started singing along.

'My mum loves Erasure,' said the driver, nodding away to the tune. ''*Sometimes*' is her favourite track.'

Karl gazed around the taxi and as Joost started bellowing out the lyrics, he wondered if he was dreaming.

'Here he comes, the hero of the hour,' said Jack. He followed this comment with a swig of his drink and a smirk.

Johnny observed his brother as he took in the scene before him, his expression a mixture of outrage, confusion, and even a little embarrassment. Barry viewed the bottles of whiskey, one of which lay empty, and he focussed on the weapons and cartridges. He scooped up the neglected sawn-off, cracked open the barrel and slid two twelve-gauge rounds inside. 'We should take them by surprise. We'll ambush them on the lane as they drive in.'

Jack took another sip of whiskey and let out a harsh laugh. ''Ark at Mr Tactical Warfare over there. You were running away earlier, and now you're Rambo with a huge hard-on.'

Barry pursed his lips and snapped the barrel shut. 'OK, let's just sit here and get blitzed instead. And wait until they're kicking the door down.'

'I'm doing sausage sandwiches. You want one, Barry?' asked Maria in a chirpy tone as she stood at the kitchen counter cutting open a packet of sausages.

Barry stared at her in disbelief. 'You should go, Mum. Now, whilst you can. You too, Dad. This is our doing! You've no reason to get caught up in this.'

Jack let out a hoarse cackle.

'Crispy onions for everybody?' asked Maria.

'Mmm, ta,' said Johnny.

'Nah,' muttered Jack.

Barry gawked at them. 'Onions? Fucking onions! Nino's stitched us up. Elena's taken our cash stash, and the Chillcotts are coming. As in, they'll probably be rolling up any moment.'

Jack and Johnny shared a look, then they turned back to Barry. His contorted, wide-eyed expression sent them both into a fit of hysterics.

'I'm dreaming here. Mum, sort these two muppets out for Christ's sake,' said Barry.

'Sort these two muppets out, Mum,' mimicked Jack.

Maria huffed. 'Stop teasing Barry, Jack. And ease off that swill!'

'Elena nicked your Colt Python, Barry,' said Johnny.

'I know, I've just had it aimed at my bloody head!' grumbled Barry.

Jack sniggered. 'It's a big enough target, I suppose. She could hardly miss that massive bonce.'

'Ah, but I bet you didn't know she also set Duncan loose?' said Johnny.

'And I bet he didn't know that she's been at my ammo stash,' said Jack, amusement showing in his glazed eyes.

Barry gave them both a dirty glare. 'Right under your noses? What the actual fuck? And have you checked on Nathaniel? Or have you been too busy getting rat-arsed to bother?'

Jack sneered and sniffed. 'Says this idiot, who's happy to have cider on his Frosties for breakfast.'

'Only when there's no milk,' said Barry tartly.

Johnny knocked back his drink. 'Yeah, I checked on Nathaniel. He wants to come up for a soak in the tub.'

'Wants you to scrub his back,' said Jack with a big grin.

Barry put down the weapon and scanned the table again. He began counting the cartridges. 'Twelve.' His jaw dropped. He picked one up and rolled it around in his fingers. 'Twelve!'

Jack turned to Johnny and winked at him. 'Wow, and he even did that without using a calculator.'

Barry growled, went to speak, but instead scrunched up his lips. He noticed the letter under Jack's Browning shotgun. He snatched it up and read it. Barry shook his head and glared at Jack. Nobody said a word about its contents. Nobody would dare with Maria present, Johnny surmised. They'd been lucky she'd not seen it, and his dad surely hadn't meant to leave it out in the open. As if this dawned on Jack, he snatched the letter from Barry and stuck it in the pocket of his long wax jacket.

'Sausages won't be long. Someone grab the HP sauce,' called Maria.

Barry sat down and put his head in his hands. Jack poured him a large measure of whiskey and slid it across to him. 'Here.' Jack turned to Johnny. 'Message that creepy berk and tell him to bring this Nathaniel kid up here. The way I see it, they'll be after him too, so he doesn't have much choice but to stand with us.'

Johnny nodded in agreement and texted the instructions to Warren.

Barry hit back the drink, picked up the sawn-off and stood up. As an afterthought, he snatched up two more shells and slid them into the pocket of his jeans.

Jack laughed. 'Oooh, watch out. Our saviour is on the move.' He whistled the theme tune to *The A-Team*.

Barry jutted out his jaw. 'I'll head back to the gates. I've already put the chain on.'

'Well done, Barry. That should stop them,' said Jack.

'The dogs keep barking out the back,' said Maria.

Johnny picked up his dad's Browning and the rest of the rounds. 'I'll take a butcher's out back. I'll meet you out front in five, Barry.'

Barry nodded. 'Sure. But I'm going to change my pants. Because I think I shat myself a bit.'

Johnny patted him on the back. 'Thanks for sharing that.'

'You dirty bastard,' said Jack.

Ravi scanned the courtyard. No sign of the van, but the Range Rover, Land Rover Defender, and Ford Ranger were all parked up. The place looked even larger than he remembered it, especially the huge open courtyard. He peered down at the entrance where he'd spoken to Jack. The converted barn was his first point of investigation. He'd noted that before, as it seemed like the ideal place to hold someone. The windows were thin and high, and he could see dim lights flashing from what looked like a TV screen. Something in his gut told him he'd find Nathaniel there. So he jogged towards it.

After seeing a distant beam of light, Nino took the first opportunity to leave Dead Lane. He zipped the bike through a skinny gap in the trees and switched her off. The pair climbed off, stashed the bike behind the thicket and ducked into the undergrowth. And not a moment too soon, because as they huddled together, they heard the deep rumble of vehicles approaching. But now they were trapped in an enclosed pocket, and Nino cursed himself for not taking a different route. If he'd double-backed, he could have nipped onto the route across the fields. But his encounter with Barry had muddled his mind, and he'd hurtled off in an aimless daze. Then headlights streaked through the trees. Nino felt Elena tense as the lights danced amongst the tangle of bushes and he was certain they'd be discovered in the dead-end hole they'd ended up stuck in.

Elena squeezed his shoulder. 'I'm sorry I didn't tell you Jack came—'

'Ssh. Keep low, Elena!'

The vehicles appeared. They began to pass by the gap. They moved slow and ominous. If Reilly collared them holed up here, Nino didn't know what he'd do. He didn't care to find out. Three cars and a van crawled past. The noise from the shrill van reverberated in the hole. They came so close Nino could smell faint cigarette smoke and see shadowy shapes sitting inside the vehicles. Nino held Elena tight as Nino closed his eyes and willed them to keep going and pass them by. That chilling moment lasted an eternity. As the grumble of engines finally faded, it felt like he'd signed a death warrant for the entire family and the severity of what he'd done hit him like a bolt of lightning. He'd treated this like a game. But this game had severe consequences.

Ravi crept up to the barn's entrance. He tried the door. Locked. As he considered his next move, he heard a key turning in the lock. He made a clumsy grab for the stun gun, and almost dropped it as he un-clipped the unit. The door opened a few inches.

'Wait. I need a quick wazz,' said a voice from inside. Nathaniel's voice. Ravi was certain of it.

Ravi scanned all around him, and good thing he did, because a stout figure was marching across the courtyard. They were heading in his direction.

'I need to go now,' said Nathaniel.

Ravi barged into the building and closed the door behind him. He took in the scene.

Nathaniel stood staring at him, aghast. Although he'd seen him in that jittery footage, Ravi nearly didn't recognise his son in the flesh, with the goatee beard and shiny, bald head that almost matched his own. But he looked like a common criminal now. The man with him, a skinny, ghastly fella with beady eyes, shot him a confused glare. The man appeared to be on drugs, because his eyeballs were glazed and bloodshot.

Then followed a brief pause before Ravi said, 'Now listen here. I'm taking my son. If you try to stop me—'

Before Ravi could finish the sentence, the man's face screwed up in anger and he yanked out his phone. He started fast texting.

'Dad, stop him!'

Ravi thumbed the charge button on the stun gun and once the unit crackled, stuck the device against the man's neck. The man yelled out, stumbled backwards and lost his feet. He crashed down on his back and jolted about like a giant worm break dancing.

Nathaniel bounded over and tried to grab the man's phone. The man snatched it back. They wrestled for the device, with Nathaniel falling on top of the man. Ravi, amazed the nutcase was still functioning after the zapping, could only gawp at the scene.

'Dad... blast him again! Blast him!'

The man punched Nathaniel hard in the temple. Then he rained down thump after thump, and one shot made a loud clomp as his fist connected with his son's face.

Nathaniel toppled sideways, clutching the man's phone in both hands and groaning in pain.

The man hissed as he tried to find his feet. They'd provoked the maniac now.

Ravi, stunned by the violence, fumbled to charge the unit. This time, remembering Arnie's words, he jammed it against the man's groin.

The man let out a long, painful, 'Oooooff!' He rolled around, kicking his legs and clutching himself in agony.

Nathaniel dragged himself to his feet. 'What are you doing here?' he asked, chest heaving and his nose streaming blood. 'You shouldn't be here, Dad!'

Ravi, shocked by what he'd just done to the complete stranger, struggled to find any words.

'We need to leave, Dad. Now! I'm meant to be going to the house. They'll come looking.'

'There's another one... walking this way,' spluttered Ravi.

Nathaniel chucked the man's phone on the floor, then stamped it to bits.

Duncan skulked further back into the darkness. The dogs were yapping right outside the store shed and he shuddered with every bark. He desperately wanted to leave this place, but fear gripped him now, and he became convinced the dogs would bring unwanted attention, so froze. He prayed they'd go away. Then he heard a gruff voice calling to the animals. And the door creaked open. A bright torch beam streamed inside, and in a wild panic, Duncan scrambled around the messy shed, fumbling for an object to use as a weapon. Noticing what he thought looked like a police battering ram, he heaved up the heavy tool. He felt a sudden fury bubbling up inside of him, the like of which he'd never known. His mind flooded with all the injustices he'd suffered. All the torment and hate. All that was wrong in the world. It almost overcame him. It almost made him pass out, the sensation was so intense... so powerful and oppressive. But he fought off his woozy head and strode forward like a crazed, marauding creature. It was like he was steaming drunk and he'd now become fuelled by hysteria, fear and bitterness.

'I can see you in there, Duncan,' said the voice. He thought it sounded like Johnny, though couldn't be certain.

Like a trapped beast about to be unjustly slain, that fury subsequently exploded in Duncan and he charged at the torchlight. He caught the glimpse of a shadowy shape – and a gun.

Duncan slung the ram forward as hard as he could, putting all his weight behind the thrust. It crashed into the figure's chest and they let out a grunt of pain as the pair of them pitched forward and landed in a heap outside of the shed.

The dogs barked like crazy as Duncan scrambled to his feet and ran.

. . .

Johnny pulled himself up and searched the ground for the shotgun. His ribs hurt like hell where the big lump had bundled the ram into him, knocking the air right out of his lungs. He snatched up the gun, and went after Duncan. He spotted the lad some twenty-feet away, clambering over the fence by the chicken coop. He took aim with the gun. With his finger stroking the trigger, he hesitated for maybe five seconds and considered letting him go. Then decided against that idea. He fired and Duncan toppled from the fence and fell out of view.

Johnny started heading towards the boy, thinking that he couldn't afford to waste any more rounds on Duncan, so hoped the single shot would have been enough. Otherwise, he'd finish the job another way. Then Johnny's phone rang, and he stopped walking and answered it.

'What's going on?' asked Barry.

'I found Duncan. He's down.'

'Never mind him… There are headlights coming, Jon. This must be them.'

Johnny turned on his heels and started jogging back to the courtyard. 'Make every shot count, Barry.' He didn't even look back in Duncan's direction. The boy wouldn't make it far.

Nathaniel locked the barn door and tossed the keys away.

'That was a gunshot,' said Ravi.

'Where's your car, Dad?'

'Look!'

Ravi pointed to headlights that were streaming along the lane and heading up to the gate. He identified the shape of a man, crouching, as if lying in wait.

Ravi and Nathaniel kept low, and they moved across to take cover behind a couple of oil drums filled with broken-up wood.

'What shall we do?' asked Nathaniel.

The man left the shadows and started running away from the gate. His run appeared ungainly as he tried to duck down. He dived to the ground and scrambled down the side of the skip, just as the lights dazzled straight through the gates and illuminated the track leading into the courtyard. At least three vehicles had pulled up. A few moments passed, and Ravi caught sight of people at the gate. They were shaking it, as if trying to open it. Two figures climbed over and tried to break the chain that held it. The car engines were cut, and the lights went out.

Ravi studied the figures standing at the gate. They were scanning the property with a silent coolness that made Ravi want to turn and flee immediately. But more dark shapes materialised at the gate. And they all surged over it to join the first pair.

The group swarmed into the grounds, silent and bold, as they marched up the long driveway. Ravi felt like he'd been glued to the spot as he watched the mob with a mixture of utter dread and intense fascination.

'Who the hell are all these people?' whispered Ravi.

'I can't see who they are.'

Then a sudden banging from behind them made them both jump. It sounded like fists pounding against the door of the barn. Nathaniel had locked the man inside, and he was livid.

Elena climbed off the bike. Brennen leapt out of the van to greet her.

She beamed at him. 'Hey you.'

Brennen pulled her into a tight embrace. 'Come here! I was getting worried, girl. Another minute and I was heading down.'

'Elena, stay with Bren. I'll catch up with you both in an hour,' said Nino.

Elena broke free of the hug and looked mortified. 'Nino, no. Don't you dare!'

'I need to fix this,' said Nino.

Elena shook her head. 'You don't owe them anything... you don't need to do this.'

'What's happening down there? Is it kicking off?' asked Brennen.

'I'm going back to the house,' said Nino.

Elena grabbed Nino's arm. 'I know I should have told you, but I thought you wouldn't care about Jack. After the lies—' She stopped herself from finishing the sentence.

Nino pulled his arm free. 'I need to fix this,' Nino repeated. 'I messed up, Elena, and I'm going to put it right.'

'Fine, I'll come too,' she pulled out the revolver. 'I'm not afraid.'

Brennan and Nino shared a look. Words were unnecessary. They both acknowledged what the other was thinking. Brennan took hold of Elena and held her tight, and as Nino tore off, he heard her wild shouts of protest.

51

2 December 2018 [18.50]

Karl eyed the driver. The guy glanced back at him, and Karl got the sense that he somehow knew all was not well... perhaps he'd been giving off nervous vibes since taking Duncan's call. Now the atmosphere in that car was tense and his heart was drumming in his chest.

'Where are we?' asked Karl.

They'd driven off the motorway and were heading down a dark A road.

'Satnav took me this way. I'll pull over down here. I need to check the tyre pressure. You can take a quick leak too,' said the driver. 'Screw that policy, hey?'

A sudden feeling of deep dread came over Karl and he guessed something terrible awaited them.

The car slowed and moved into a long, gloomy lay-by set back from the main road. It was overshadowed by tall trees and thick, coarse bushes that were dotted with roadside litter, ran alongside it. The place looked gloomy and unwelcoming.

'Watch yourself, I heard this is a local dogging spot,' said the driver, laughing nervously.

'You have a flat tyre?' asked Joost, letting out a gaping yawn.

The driver was gazing out of his windows, as if trying to spot something. Or someone. 'Um, yeah,' said the driver, sounding distracted.

The car came to a sudden stop.

'I'll have that pee now,' said Karl, nudging Joost to get his attention. He said, 'Joost… loop, loop… ah, shit, um… gevaar!'

The driver vaulted out of the car and was tapping on his phone. He looked flustered and twitchy. He made a brief show of booting the front tyre.

'What is going on?' whispered Joost.

'Go!'

Ravi dare not even breathe. The group was a real ragtag group of bruisers and ruffians. They strode along the track towards the courtyard in total silence. They proceeded straight past the figure, hiding behind the skip without discovering him. The banging on the door had ceased, and Ravi wondered if the weird man trapped inside had seen the approaching thugs and had decided to lie low and keep quiet.

As the mob passed the skip, one of the group, a hooded, yobbish looking lad, broke away and dashed back. At first, Ravi assumed he'd noticed the other man hiding, but then he tossed away a beer can and started urinating.

The rest of the group were passing their way now. Ravi smelt them; rank tobacco, reeking booze, and pungent petrol.

Nathaniel slumped further down behind the oil drums. His eyes were shut tight and his hands were over his mouth and nose.

The intruders were armed with bats, bars, and machetes. Two carried shotguns. Ravi recognised two of them. Mills and Reilly Chillcott.

The hooded lad finished up his wee, and as he turned, the man hiding shuffled out from behind the skip, snuck up behind the lad, and raised a stumpy shotgun.

Ravi gasped, expecting to see the lad get blown away right in front of them, but the gunman didn't fire, he just stayed frozen in the aiming position.

Ravi jolted as if anticipating a loud gunshot. Time seemed to freeze in those few moments – but the hooded lad trotted after the gang, zipping up his flies as he went, and the gunman stayed fixed to the spot. The hooded lad was oblivious to the danger right behind him.

'That was Barry Bartell,' whispered Nathaniel.

Barry slunk away into the darkness.

'Move,' said Ravi. Even though his own legs were like rubber and didn't want to work.

'Now. Leg it, Joost!' shouted Karl, as he dashed along the lay-by. Total darkness surrounded the area, and he wondered where exactly they could run to. He glanced back to make sure Joost was behind him, but to his complete surprise, Joost strolled along like he didn't have a single care in the world. Then he noticed the axe-type weapon in the driver's hand.

'Joost! What are you doing?' yelled Karl.

'You need to get back here, mate. Now!' shouted the driver.

Karl half expected the driver to tell him it was company policy for passengers not to flee.

Johnny stood in the shadows and aimed the shotgun at the approaching mob. He'd counted sixteen men. He wanted to fire at the crowd whilst they were bunched, and would have done if he'd been holding more ammo. But he knew every shot must count, so he'd wait for the opportune moment before striking. They needed to be closer.

The gang entered the courtyard, and some started fanning out. He saw Mills was armed with a shotgun, Reilly a hammer. Those sly bastards Silas and Grey were here too, with the former holding another shotgun. Two younger lads, with jug-ears and wearing matching grey tracksuits, carried petrol cans.

Johnny inhaled and exhaled several times. The booze flowing through him helped steady his nerves. He was ready for this. Or as ready as he ever would be.

. . .

The driver pointed the axe at Joost. 'Just tell your mate to jump back in the car. Or else.'

Joost held up his hands. 'OK, man, chill out... please, there is no need for this aggression. Be reasonable, my friend.'

Karl approached. 'He has nothing to do with this matter. Please, let him go.'

The driver stared at his phone. His eyes flicked to Karl, then to Joost, and settled back on his phone. 'In the car. I won't ask nicely again. Understand?'

Joost smiled. 'Hey, you know, I'm good friends with a guy in Rotterdam that can get *the* best coke in Europe. As much as you like.'

'What?' said the driver incredulously, as if this was the last thing he expected to hear from the Dutchman.

Joost flashed a genial grin and shrugged. 'Is that something that would interest you? We could make a deal. And avoid all this craziness. What do you say?'

'Yeah, stop talking shit, mate,' said the driver. 'Best coke in Europe my ball-sack... You... bloody clog wearing spunk bubble!'

Joost shrugged again. 'No, I am serious, man. Deadly serious.'

The driver lowered the weapon, only a touch, and went to speak again, but out of nowhere, Joost let loose an epic round-house kick that floored the guy. It caught him square on the face and sent him, and the weapon, bouncing and skidding across the ground. Joost, in a relaxed manner, knelt down and struck two super fast jabs straight into the side of the guy's head.

'Is this one of the drug dealers you've been hiding from, Karl? Seriously, man. What a total penis,' said Joost. He glared down at the driver. 'How about I beat your ugly face with my clogs? Yeah? Sound good? Stupid arsehole.' Joost pinched the driver's bashed nose, and he let out a pathetic yelp.

Karl, awestruck by the insane move the Dutchman had so effortlessly pulled off, said, 'How do you know about that?'

Joost walked over to the weapon, scooped it up, and examined it. 'You told me when you were twisted. You don't remember?' He spoke in such a breezy tone it was as though they were chatting over a couple of nice, chilled pints and not standing over a decked man, that only a few moments ago, was threatening them with a weapon that resembled something straight out of the film *Last of the Mohicans*. Holy crap, thought Karl... had the universe somehow been trying to warn him about this threat?

Karl gazed down at the crumpled figure on the floor. The man, dazed and moaning, held both hands to his battered nose. The speed with which the magnificent kick had been delivered was so swift, it had taken the guy by total surprise. Karl felt confident the extra punches were overkill.

'Where did that move come from?' asked Karl.

'Dutch kickboxing. I once run a class,' said Joost.

'That's a thing?'

'Of course. I'm sure I told you. Your memory is terrible, Karl.'

Johnny tensed as he readied the shotgun. He didn't have a clue where Barry had disappeared to, and only hoped that once the trouble kicked off, his brother would charge in from the rear and take the intruders by surprise. Then something took *him* by surprise. An engine roared to life. At first, he'd not been sure from where, until he perceived it was Jack's Land Rover racing across the courtyard. The lights, spotlights included, burst on, flooding the approaching mob in harsh, blinding beams.

Then total mayhem erupted.

The vehicle steamed forward like a lethal dreadnought.

The shocked men were firing wild shots off in every direction.

Some of the gang were frantic and screaming curses.

The vehicle's back window shattered from one of the stray shots.

Then, the moment the Land Rover struck into the line of unlucky trespassers, Johnny witnessed one guy get tossed up in the air and thud down in a twisted heap.

Another tried to leap out of the vehicle's path, but got whacked on the hip and thrown to one side. The guy did a dramatic roll as he howled in pain.

Two fortunate lads did dive from its path, but the unluckiest of the mob got slammed hard against the front. And with the lower half of his body dragged underneath the motor, he got scraped along the ground a few feet before the vehicle collided with the paddock wall and crushed him between the chunky grill and the lumpy stone wall. Johnny didn't think for a second that the guy had any chance of surviving the brutal battering. He was unable to see clearly, but reckoned his head must have been caved in on impact. He witnessed a limp arm hanging out from the steaming carnage.

As thick plumes of steam poured from the wreckage, the mob started recovering from the assault and made for the ruined vehicle.

Silas yelled in rage as he fired off round after round, which pulverised the windows. This mob was baying for blood now.

Ravi watched in utter horror as the man was crushed under the vehicle and total anarchy ensued in the courtyard. He witnessed a horse, spooked by the ruckus, rear up and gallop about the paddock near where the collision had taken place. Nathaniel grabbed him by the arm. He started dragging him, as booming gunshots rang out and gruff shouting filled the uninviting night. The next thing Ravi knew, he was running behind his son... fleeing the deadly tumult and murderous screams.

'Joost, that was just... incredible... like some mental Van Damme shit,' said Karl.

Joost threw the axe into the darkened bushes. 'Pfffttt. He's a Belgian.'

The driver rolled onto his back and Karl could see his nose looked bent and swollen.

'They say we are tooo loud. We talk tooo much and our sense of humour is offensive. And don't even get me started on their fries.'

Karl didn't want to ask about their fries. Now didn't really seem like the ideal time to debate *fries*. He wanted to go. Now.

'They think their damn fries are so much superior. No. They often fry them in pig fat, don't you know?' said Joost.

Joost walked over to the BMW and slipped into the driver's seat.

The driver dragged himself up. 'Get out of there... get out, you crazy bastard,' he moaned.

Karl got in the passenger seat and slammed the door. 'We can't steal his car, Joost!'

Joost locked the doors. He revved the engine, and the car kangarooed forward a few metres.

'Out of the car!' yelled the driver, now up and bashing his hands on the driver's window, as blood streamed from his nose and spatters of it sprayed over the glass.

Karl heard the screeching noise of bikes coming. Mopeds by the sound of it. The pair shared a worried glance.

The lights of the bikes flooded the dark lay-by in zigzagging streaks. There were at least six of them.

'Drive!' shouted Karl. 'Go, go, go!'

Then the driver started punching at the window and screaming, 'You're screwed now!'

The mopeds started circling. Several stopped, jumped off, and raced over to join the driver to attack the car. They looked very young, but they were enraged and at least one carried a blade. They were yelling and cursing, and Karl thought they were going to be killed.

One youngster booted a wing mirror clean off.

Another young lad used something to crack the passenger side window.

Karl slid down in his seat, petrified.

Joost finally got the car moving and drove away. Karl tensed as the Dutchman powered forward and crashed straight into a bike, sending it spinning out of their path, with the rider diving out of the way without a moment to spare.

Joost chuckled. 'Wow. Weird driving this side!'

As the car bolted onto the road, Karl turned to check behind him. 'Some of them are chasing us! Oh, God!'

Joost laughed and floored the accelerator. 'Fuck those little bitches. No chance!'

As the passenger door of the Land Rover flung open, Johnny saw Jack trying to clamber out of the wreck. The rest of the mob were heading his way and circling him. They wanted to rip him limb from limb now.

Jack dropped from the vehicle, crawled a few paces before leaping to his feet and making a dash for the house.

As Jack made for the door, limping as he ran, a young lad with a baseball bat tried to block his path, but Jack barrelled into him, and using his forearm, Jack slammed him out of his way, sent him sprawling onto his back and stamped the youngster on his way to get to the front door.

Another lad prepared to swing an iron bar at Jack from behind, and Johnny fired a shot, caught the attacker in the back of the knee and he buckled over and hit the deck, bellowing in agony as he rolled about the ground clutching the wound. Johnny fired another shot at the mob, and now major panic erupted amongst the gang as they dived for cover and searched for the new threat.

Silas spotted Johnny and fired off several badly aimed rounds his way that hit the wall of the house.

Johnny ducked down and slid down the wall of the building.

Then Jack bellowed, 'Giddy uuup, mother-fuuuckkkers! Come inside and party. I'm just getting started.'

Christ, thought Johnny, the old man was even more pissed than he'd realised. He'd made it look like he was on a drunken jolly boys' outing which would have messed with the trespassers' heads no end.

Johnny peered around the wall. He was relieved to see Jack rush inside the house. So Johnny raced to the rear, charged in through the back door, and locked it shut. He couldn't be certain, but he seemed sure he'd heard what sounded like Nino's bike somewhere out there as he started using the table and chairs to block the door and windows.

The chaos outside had all taken place within the space of about sixty seconds, yet in that short time, they'd caused absolute bedlam out there. At least Jack had, anyway. Craig's death and the situation with Nino had finally sent his father over the edge.

Duncan staggered in blind panic, but he could no longer keep to his feet and so collapsed to his knees. The pain was overwhelming and total hysteria began to set in. He'd never make it out of here alive now, that seemed clear enough to him. He had no way of knowing how badly the shot had damaged him, but without receiving medical care, he'd bleed to death. Would that take a few more minutes, or many pain ridden hours? Duncan tried to force himself to stand, but that seemed impossible. He let out a feeble cry for help and closed his eyes. He'd heard the thunderous gunshots and terrifying yelling, so guessed the dangerous people the girl had warned him about were here. Now his only hope of survival lay in the hands of some random stranger hearing distant gunshots and notifying the police. But this place seemed so cut off from the rest of the world. He doubted that any help would come. He collapsed and grunted in pain.

Then a voice said, 'Dad, help me get him up.'

'Who the hell is this?' said another shaky voice. 'Oh my goodness. He's been shot.'

'He's not with the others. Grab his arm, we can't leave him here.'

And Duncan found himself being dragged to his feet.

These strangers were helping him walk. They were saving him.

52

Johnny charged into the lounge, flinching from the sound of windows smashing. The room lay in darkness, but he could see the windows were already barricaded, with two upturned sofas and a large oak display cabinet. Maria sat in the corner with Moose and Cracker on either side of her, both dogs anxious and growling. A meat cleaver lay between her feet. She wore a pair of tatty white slippers and a faded robe over her clothes. She stroked the dogs, seemingly unbothered by the frightful uproar in the courtyard. Behind her hung the large black and white canvas print displaying Jack's previous dogs. Charles and Reg both lived long, content lives, but Rita died of a heart defect at a young age. Nino held such a strong bond with the bitch and had been inconsolable when she'd passed away. He didn't speak one word for about ten days straight. When he did finally speak, he blamed Craig for deliberately over exercising Rita to make her condition worse. But Johnny refused to believe that.

Johnny reloaded the gun, annoyed he'd already wasted some rounds. 'They won't dare touch you, Mum.'

'I knew that boy would one day ruin us,' she said. It almost sounded like she was gloating.

Jack stood in the shadows, drinking whiskey neat from the bottle.

He gripped Craig's zombie crossbow in the other hand. Johnny had seen his brother penetrate full paint cans with that dangerous thing. But Jack would only have time to take down one assailant should the mob flood into the house in a wave of angry madness.

'Where's Barry?' asked Jack, slurring now.

'Maybe he's holed up in The Den with the other two,' said Johnny.

More windows smashed and the dogs cowered.

The shouts outside intensified – vile threats, curses, and taunts. Jack's actions had caused panic and chaos out there, but the gang were also fuming and they'd likely tear them all to pieces given half the chance.

Jack gritted his teeth. 'Let's chase back outside and face them!'

'No! They don't know we're low on rounds, Dad. Plus, they have no clue how many of us are holed up in here.'

'Son, they'll burn us out... that's what I'd do.'

Johnny grimaced, recalling seeing the petrol cans. He raced to the window and peered through a small gap between the curtain and the wall unit. Men were milling about the Land Rover. Then he could see they were trying to shift it back to free the limp and crumpled body under it. Jack joined him and gazed out.

'Let me go out and fight that big, ugly shithead!' slurred Jack.

'Leave off, Dad, he'll batter you senseless!'

Jack let out a hoarse laugh. 'You go out and take him on then, son.'

'No one is going outside,' said Johnny, thinking he'd rather face a pissed off grizzly bear, then go up against that giant crackpot.

Jack sneered. 'Look at that... a bloody hammer. Has that arrogant piss-flap come for a good tear up, or to erect a bookshelf? Marcus always used to complain Reilly was a jumped-up little psycho. He needs a good kick up the arse, that one.'

Johnny spotted shadowy figures run across the courtyard. They hurled threats and bellowed in outrage, though none made to head directly out the front of the house, no doubt fearing they'd get shot. In a sudden flash, his Ford Ranger burst alight, and several gunshots rang out, causing him to move instinctively to the side. Jack fell backwards.

Then crashing and loud thudding sounds came from the kitchen.

'Dad! Watch the front window,' he shouted, as he raced to the back door, gun aiming forward. 'Come through! Go on. I DARE you!' To emphasise his point, he let loose one round into the door, the piercing sound making his ears ring and fizz. The thudding stopped, but the kitchen window smashed in, causing a chair to come flying down. He caught a sudden sight of shapes moving outside.

'Come ON then!' he snarled, so loudly his throat felt as though it was on fire.

The mob were hurling projectiles and taking pot shots at the house, but Reilly's focus lay on his cousin, Silas, as he dragged his brother and best friend, Grey, from the wreckage. When he bore witness to the extent of the damage, Silas cried out. Grey's misshapen head flopped forward and for a moment Reilly expected to see it fall away from the body. He looked utterly mashed up and he couldn't help remembering that lowlife scum-bag Tristan Vickers and what he'd done to him back in his younger days.

'I'm not leaving him here,' cried Silas.

Reilly puffed out his cheeks, thinking that he'd underestimated the Bartells. He'd get some major grief from Silas's family for dragging them into this shit-storm. Another lad, Tyler Lovell, had been shot in the back of his knee, and one of Lovell's mates had been inches away from getting his head blown straight off attempting to boot down the back door. Not to mention the two youngsters who'd been bashed up by Jack's motor. He'd not completely thought all this through, Reilly concluded. Kreshnik would rib him for this cock up.

Silas started screaming blue murder and ran to the darkened house, firing wildly, but some return fire from the downstairs window sent him running for cover behind the wreckage of Jack's motor.

Now things were turning into a siege situation, and he visualised scores of armed police and helicopters descending on the gaff. The Bartells wouldn't call the police. Not in a million years, but even this far off the beaten track, gunshots and fire could still draw unwanted attention eventually.

Jack... *that mad, batty old lemon.* Not so mellow then, he decided. What a total legend. Reilly knew his dad would have relished in all this madness. He considered shouting out an offer to Johnny or Barry to step outside and have a square go, but thought better of that idea.

They'd not leave the building now, and he knew they'd have the front and back under watch and would murder any of them that were foolish enough to attempt to force entry.

Mills came and stood next to him, chest heaving. 'Right, we rush the place. Half of us will steam around to the back and storm in. Afterwards, we douse the entire house. Ready?'

Reilly, about to point out that half of them were not in a position to stroll back to the cars, let alone storm a well defended house like a bunch of battle-hardened marines, when the roar of a motorbike stopped him. The bike halted some thirty feet across the courtyard and the helmet-less rider gazed at the carnage and revved the engine.

Mills growled and went to move forward, as did Silas, shotgun at the ready.

'Wait! Hold up. I'm sure that's Nino. Leave him be. Let me speak to him a second,' said Reilly, marching towards the bike. He wondered if the boy had some information that could assist the situation.

As Reilly approached, Nino didn't dare cut the engine. When he got within ten paces, Nino said, 'Don't come any closer, or I'm straight outta here!' Nino revved the bike and Reilly stopped, hammer hanging at his side.

'No closer, Reilly!'

Reilly flashed him a cold grin.

'I told my brothers Stefan killed Craig. But I lied about that,' said Nino.

Reilly's eyes hardened and his face twitched.

'But even after I told them, they refused to go after Stefan, because they were too afraid of the consequences. So… I went and did it myself. *I* got Stefan blitzed on drugs, took him for a seaside stroll and I shoved him… Though thinking back, it was only a tiny nudge to be fair… I wanted to get you guys at each other's throats. I'm getting the sense it worked quite well.'

Reilly's eyes blazed with ferocity. With the flames raging behind him, he looked like a cruel, terrible demon, and Nino felt his entire body trembling. It seemed pointless to explain the hows and whys of the situation. How he'd been duped by his own mother into doing her bidding and ripping his own family to pieces. He doubted Reilly would care about all that stuff, anyway. It wouldn't change the fact that, given the chance, Reilly would bash in his skull with that claw hammer.

Reilly's nostrils flared. 'Come closer, Nino. Jump off your bike for a moment. Speak to me like a real man. Show me you're not a complete, sly coward.' He spat these words with venom.

Mills, Silas and the rest of the mob gathered around Reilly. Surrounded by the light of the burning vehicle, the gang looked like something from a horrifying nightmare. Pure malice radiated from them as they snarled like hideous fiends that wanted to hack him into tiny pieces. Nino felt so isolated and small, like he was trapped in a dark cave full of approaching, savage beasts intent on murder. Somehow, he stayed himself. 'Go ahead... kill each other... But I can assure you my family has been set up. Same as you have. I'm surprised you fell for all that bull-shit, Reilly. You made it way too easy, mate.'

Reilly laughed. A psychotic, sinister laugh that sent a chill through Nino's entire body.

'Elena is waiting down the lane with Brennan and the O'Carroll clan. If I don't return in ten minutes... then they'll be coming with enough firepower to take you all down. So... I better get back.'

This lie did nothing to deter Reilly, because he let forth an incoherent scream and bolted forward. The man's wrath was petrifying as he thundered towards him. Nino was aware of the other figures charging for him, too. Then it all became a blur of fast running shapes and baleful faces as he revved the bike and searched urgently for the safest route from the fast approaching dangers.

Several shots rang out as he crouched low in the seat and sped off across the courtyard. He took a sharp right and doubled back. The rear wheel wobbled as he made the critical turn and he nearly lost all control of the machine. Then he rocketed away from the gang.

Nino dared a glance back. He saw Reilly sprinting after him and preparing to throw the hammer.

Four, or maybe five more shots rang out, quicker lower pitched sounding. He ducked down low and zigzagged his way along the side of the house. He saw Mills aiming a handgun, and something heavy thudded against his back, causing him to gasp. Then, gripping the handlebars with every ounce of strength he could muster, Nino swerved from side to side as the pain racked his lower back. By some miracle, he stopped the bike from toppling sideways and he fought fiercely to keep his balance. A pinging noise rang out and sparks spurted from his front wheel. Nino whizzed around the far side of the house and was forced to swerve when he glimpsed a shape pouncing from the shadows. He just about dodged a crazed, hooded figure swinging a lump of wood and bellowing like a frenzied animal.

He careened along and circled the house, zipped through coiling black smoke in the yard and made a dash for the track behind the paddock. His bike shot through the gap in the fence and powered off into the gloom as another gunshot echoed into the night.

His heart was thrashing wildly against his chest as he fled into the darkness.

The flight from the Bartells seemed like a vivid dream. Duncan had followed the bright torchlight through the creepy, old woods, across broken ground, wading through thick, sludgy puddles and high, ropy reeds. All the time the two strangers guiding him, dragging him in places and heaving him up when he'd fallen to the ground. It took the strangers a long time, but they'd managed to transport him to a car, bundle him in the vehicle and place him across the backseats.

And now they were moving fast. The pain was agonising and his mind swam. He thought he heard his name spoken, but surely he couldn't have.

'Hold on, Duncan,' said one of them. 'Stay with us! You stay with us!'

Yes, they'd said his name. But there seemed no time to consider who these people were, because Duncan's mind went black.

Hospital staff and paramedics rushed to the car to assist Ravi and Nathaniel with Duncan's unconscious body.

'We found him on a roadside,' said Ravi, though no one seemed to pay him any attention as they were far too busy tending to Duncan.

'He said his name is Duncan,' added Nathaniel.

Within moments, Duncan was being placed on a stretcher and wheeled quickly into the emergency area. Ravi heard one of the staff asking him to move the car from the ambulance drop off zone, but not to leave the hospital. But the pair were racing out of Medway Maritime Hospital without a moment's hesitation.

The car pulled up in a Tesco carpark. With the adrenaline now subsiding, Karl couldn't stop shaking as he used his mobile to call Duncan for the fifth time.

'No luck?' asked Joost.

'Straight to voicemail. God, I hope he's alright.' Karl turned to Joost and gave him a questioning look.

'What?' asked Joost.

'Why didn't you mention it?'

Joost shrugged. 'You were so trashed. I guessed you couldn't remember what you'd told me.'

'Aww, I am a total bloody liability.'

'You're a good friend. To take the blame like that.'

Wow, thought Karl, he had told him the entire story. 'If he knew... *if* Duncan... remembered... he wouldn't be able to cope.'

'But what I don't understand is how he can forget like that,' said Joost.

Karl sighed. 'I've been dealing with Duncan's issues the entire time we've been friends. I love the guy to bits... honest I do... but it's hard to always be responsible for him. I worry if he will do it again.' Karl rubbed his beard and stared out of the window. 'The doctors called it a type of psychogenic blackout. They say it's hard to diagnose completely. Another doctor described it as a stress induced seizure.'

Joost pulled a confused face. 'A seizure?'

'The first time I witnessed one of his... episodes, if you like, was at school. We were only fifteen. It terrified the life out of me, Joost. He'd been getting real shit from some gobby twats all day at school. And bang... his anger sparked out of nowhere and he smashed up the boys' loos. He almost pulled a door off its hinges. Then, like a switch, he flaked out and collapsed onto the floor!' Karl shook his head from the memory. 'He stayed out for maybe ten seconds. And afterwards he had no recollection of those moments before he crashed out.'

'So, is it the anger that causes him to switch off?'

'Yeah, it can be the anger. But not every blackout... sometimes they'd happen when he was under pressure, or feeling low. But you have to understand, he's not had an episode for about a year... before... well, until the Craig Bartell incident happened.'

'The mind can do crazy things, Karl,' said Joost.

'I panicked... I tried to run for help, but as I did, that nutter stopped hitting Dunk and came after me. And Duncan jumped to his feet, yells like a madman and grabs the fella. Then he... he bloody hurled him! Straight after, Dunk dropped to his knees and was out like a light. It was surreal, I can tell you.'

'And Duncan threw that guy over a wall?' asked Joost.

Karl nodded. 'Yes. Craig flew backwards over it, crashed down, and his head got impaled on a bit of metal. Sorry, I don't know what I already told you.'

Joost smiled. 'I got the general idea before, but you explained it a bit more clearly this time.'

'I was prepared to take the rap. But... Duncan suggested we run.' Karl grinned. 'Even though he thought I'd shoved him. Which does kinda show he was looking out for me. And oddly enough, he stayed calm and took control of the situation. Normally he gets in a mad flap about everything.'

'And you have no doubt he can't remember? He's not using this as... a pretence to shift the blame on you?'

'Trust me, Joost... Dunk didn't remember that part. He'd have been fretting about like an idiot if he'd known he was solely responsible. That was my way of keeping the situation under control. It made sense at the time.'

The pair sat in silence for a while and, for some reason Karl couldn't fathom, he realised *this* was the BMW. At that very moment, Karl noticed a pair of blue, mini boxing gloves hanging from the interior mirror. He studied them. The name Craig was imprinted on them in black, italic lettering. Here he sat in the dead guy's car and now he needed to get out. 'Come on. It's time to abort the stolen motor... Hey,

Joost, why did you tell that guy about the dealer in Rotterdam? Was that true?'

Joost grinned. 'Sure, yeah. Best stuff ever. No lies. I wanted to throw his concentration… to give me the edge.'

'Edge? I don't think you needed it,' said Karl. He considered there was far more to this intriguing Dutchman than he could have ever imagined. He'd certainly view him in a different light from now on.

The pair snatched up their rucksacks and got out. As they headed away from the car, Karl stopped. 'Wait up a sec.' He trotted back to the car, tugged the Elvis duck from his pack, and placed it on the dashboard. Then, as an afterthought, unhooked the boxing gloves and hung them over the duck. He didn't know what drove him to carry out the action, only that it was a massive relief to be rid of the damn duck. Although he'd not be at all surprised if he found the bastard thing hiding at the bottom of his backpack, grinning up at him, when he unpacked.

As the pair walked away, Joost locked the car and tossed the keys into a bin.

'What a night,' said Nathaniel. He gestured to the blood smeared all over the leather interior. 'I remember getting a scolding for spilling a dab of ketchup.'

'I flushed all that powder away. The… stuff you hid in your room… in my house!' said Ravi.

'So, you went to all this trouble to find me… *Why*? To give me a stern telling off? Gee thanks, Dad.'

'Now is not the time for your smart-arse comments. I should have gone to the police, yet I've risked everything to drag you out of this mess. So you can salvage your life that you seem dead set on destroying.'

'Yeah, well, I didn't ask you to play the brave hero,' said Nathaniel testily.

Ravi gripped the steering wheel and went to speak, when Nathaniel spoke in a softer voice and said, 'But I'm glad you came.'

'How do you know that boy?' asked Ravi.

'I don't exactly know him. I've never even spoken to him before.

He used to game with the Howard brothers. Those boys I used to play the war games with. Callum Anderson's best mates. I'd often see Duncan at the local Games Workshop. Everyone used to rave on about how crazy-good his model painting skills were.'

'So… what was *he* doing in that place?'

'I have zero idea on that. He's a quiet, geeky type.'

Ravi considered that he'd have put his own son in that category until recent years. There was, however, no time to wonder about the hows and whys of another lost youngster. That would be another parent's concern.

Ravi sat for a while and said nothing, then reached over to his phone, and clicked the play button on the file he'd prepared.

Nathaniel gazed at him questioningly.

The audio on the clip started playing.

'Yeah, but how does that work, Stef?' The voice was low and muffled, but unmistakably Nathaniel's.

'They tell him stuff, and he gives them a few cheeky tit bits here and there,' replied another voice, who Ravi presumed belonged to Stefan Chillcott.

'What, like an informer?' came Nathaniel's reply.

'Nah, not exactly like that… not big stuff. Just bits and pieces.' There were clear traces of nervousness in Stefan's voice. As though he realised he'd said too much. 'But… but it's just bullshit stuff. Just to keep them sweet and off his back.'

Nathaniel let out an uneasy laugh. 'Yeah, I get you. Makes sense. Your brother has got his head screwed on.'

Ravi reached over and paused the clip. 'Just how much trouble are you in?'

'You must have pulled my room to bits to locate that, Dad.'

Ravi slapped the steering wheel. 'Were you blackmailing him? Or are you working with the police? Have you put us all in danger? Well? Answer me!'

'No, Dad!'

Ravi stabbed a finger at his phone. 'Is *this* what got the boy killed?'

'No… no way. The recordings were, I dunno, my insurance policy, I guess. I started to feel like I was… in too deep with his family.'

Ravi shook his head and grunted. 'Which brother are you discussing?'

'Reilly... And Stefan was my partner, Dad. Do you understand?'

'Why would you go into business with—'

'No! My partner... as in we were together. A couple.'

'He... but... you... I... you never...' said Ravi, stammering the words.

'I didn't understand what I'd got myself into. I really liked him, but he was dragging me into a world which scared me. I became torn between my feelings for him... and my fear of a life that I didn't belong to.'

'Are you trying to tell me he *made* you deal drugs? Is that what you're saying?' asked Ravi. 'Were you stuck in an abusive relationship with him?'

'I dunno, not quite... though, I guess... kind of. It's complicated.'

'Nathaniel... were you involved in what happened to that boy?'

Nathaniel closed his eyes and a pained expression darkened his features. 'I was there, yes. It wasn't me... But I did nothing to stop it.'

'Oh... my...' said Ravi, feeling sick to his stomach now. How much more could he take?

'I wish I'd helped. But they'd have killed me too. So, I opted to keep my mouth shut and forget the heroics. I'm lucky they didn't do me in.' Then he added, 'It was those Bartell brothers.'

They stayed silent for a long time, and Ravi couldn't look at Nathaniel. It may as well have been a stranger sitting next to him. The dark road ahead blurred and Ravi rubbed his eyes, as punishing tiredness, the like of which he could never recall ever experiencing before, hit him hard.

Nathaniel sighed. 'I take it we're not going home. Are we going to stay in London?'

'No. To a friend's place. Where we will be safe.' Ravi didn't see Arnie Baxter as a friend, but he'd been the only one to achieve any real results during this entire search, albeit to line his own pockets. He'd texted Ravi an address near Rochester and told him to come there straight away and lie low. Though no doubt he'd want paying for his information too.

· · ·

Nino brought the bike to a halt under the heavy branches of an overhanging tree. It now sank in how close he'd come to being killed tonight. He'd stared death right in the eyes. He cut the bike's engine and checked himself over to make sure it was just the hammer that struck and not a stray bullet. Then he pictured Selene's face. Her staring at him in wonder. 'Please forgive me, Nino. Please!' she'd repeated over and over as she held him in her arms and sobbed at his shoulder. 'We can help each other, son. We can finally be there for each other. You have the chance to get away from these monsters.'

Nino pictured her pretty face... her genuine, sad smile. Then he closed his eyes and gritted his teeth. Since receiving that letter a year ago, he'd betrayed his family, stolen from them, told foul lies that had led to people being killed, and ripped two families apart in the process. He knew he'd never be safe again. Nor would he be able to stare at himself in the mirror again without regarding himself with utter loathing. And it had all been for nothing. Elena would get her wish of being free of his family. But that wasn't enough. Not to warrant all the chaos he'd caused. There were other ways they could have gone about things, but he'd not been thinking clearly with all the emotions spiralling around his mind. He should have guessed Selene's twisted angle. She'd bleated on about ripping the Bartells off... about stealing enough from them so he could set up an entirely new life elsewhere... but now he guessed she'd been conning him from day one, for her own gain.

Reilly had enough egg on his face to make a bloody giant omelette. And they'd possibly be enough left to bake a Victoria sponge for afters. The tale of Jack Bartell's epic and brutal defence of his land would soon ripple through the criminal community and make Reilly sound like a total plum. Still, what could he do now? Maybe listen to Kreshnik's advice in the future might be a wise idea. This was the sort of thing he'd warned him of many a time, yet he'd let blind rage cloud rational judgment. He'd tried to convince himself he'd needed to act fast, but he could have bided his time. Nino had played him. And he'd known exactly what strings to pull to unlock his anger. He'd used his younger sibling.

Everyone thought Stefan was a twat… Reilly supposed, to some degree, that was true. He was well aware people in their inner circle ridiculed Stefan and thought the lad a total joke, though never in his presence. But most people only saw one side of Stefan. They hadn't watched him on his fourth birthday, jumping for joy as he unwrapped his presents. Or seen him return home despondent and rejected after his first day at school because he didn't fit in with the other kids. They'd never found the boy sobbing quietly under his bed, too scared to admit to his father that he'd pissed the sheets again and was loath to receive another bashing as punishment.

Stefan could be a boisterous lad, but in reality, he was nothing like the character he passed himself off as. And nobody in the family, save himself and his sister Veronica, had any idea regarding Stefan's sexuality. This had been because their father had always been so openly homophobic. He'd say that if he ever learned that one of his sons turned out gay, he'd beat the fucking queer right out of them. And failing that, they would be disowned and banished from the family. His dad could be a real bloody dinosaur. So, Reilly and Veronica held that secret and Stefan tried to surround himself with young, ditzy girls as a smokescreen. Reilly just wished Stefan would have listened to him. He'd told his brother to settle down with a reliable bloke, get a sensible job and stay out of their shit, troubled life. He might have been happy, especially now with their father no longer in the picture, to screw matters up. But his last boyfriend, the Sookdeo guy, Reilly had just known that the bloke was unsuitable. He was confident from day one he'd been the one who betrayed Stefan. Reilly wanted to find him. He wanted to stare him straight in the eye and ask him. Then, if not satisfied with his response, beat him until his brains popped out of his ears.

Stefan's personality… his *gangster* persona, had been nothing more than an act. He wanted to be like Reilly and Mills, but he wasn't. He came from a different generation. Just another kid forced into an environment that wasn't suited to them; shadowed by notorious figures that everyone respected or feared. Nino had reminded him of Stefan. Although their situations were slightly different, neither boy belonged to the habitat they were born in to.

How he'd misjudged *that* one. The cunning little traitor. Now he didn't have a clue what to bloody believe after today's events. So Reilly would take his time. And even if it took a decade, he would chip away until he learnt what happened to Stefan, and then he'd methodically deal with anyone that played a hand in the matter. They would receive no mercy.

'Arrgghh,' came the whimper from behind Reilly that dragged him back into the moment. Reilly glanced around to the young kid, moaning and wailing in the back. He was only sixteen. Another of Silas's clan. He'd been tossed right over Jack's motor and Mills reckoned he'd most likely fractured his skull, broken his arm, and his left leg. Reilly agreed with the leg, because he'd seen a few inches of snapped bone protruding through his jeans that were soaking wet with blood when they'd shoved him in the back.

Mills glanced at Reilly from the driver's side, sucked in some air, then focussed back on the road. His brother had taken some serious convincing to abort the attack. He would have the major hump with Reilly for ages. But he didn't have an endless stream of cannon fodder to toss at the Bartells. These were Silas's family members, and some of them were pissed up and only joined the expedition, expecting a drunken dust-up. They'd not expected murders. Silas and Grey knew the score, but Reilly guessed some of the other guys didn't quite grasp how dangerous the opposition would be.

They left Dead Lane and the convoy of cars followed behind as they sped out of the area to go and lick their wounds and wallow in their swift, miserable defeat.

Johnny shone the torch down the track and scanned the gate, aiming the shotgun low as he walked. The lock hung down, broken, and the gate lay open. He stepped out onto the lane to check all was clear. Once content the mob had fled, he jogged back to the courtyard.

Jack was busy using a high-powered jet wash to try and stem the flames engulfing Johnny's Ranger, though he still held the whiskey bottle in the other hand and took the odd swig as he doused the fire. He could have been washing a patio on a warm Sunday afternoon he appeared so calm.

Johnny walked towards the back of the house. He clambered over the fence, and expecting to see Duncan either dead or dying, he was very surprised to find him gone. Johnny scanned the chicken coop and surrounding area. He found plenty of blood, and after a further search, the boy's phone, but no body.

When Johnny returned to Jack, he found Barry scanning the damage. Warren stood there too, shoulders slumped and looking very sheepish.

Johnny eyed Barry, but he didn't return his stare.

'I got cut off by the mob. Had to lie low,' said Barry, as if he sensed Johnny required an immediate explanation for his absence.

Johnny wanted to ask his brother at what point he intended to join in the defence, but made do with a spiteful sneer.

Jack continued to fight the fire and seemed to be winning the battle. The Ranger looked a real mess. Thick, black smoke continued to swirl around it, though most of the flames were waning. The smell was choking.

Huge fires, gunshots, and noise in general weren't unusual around here, so Johnny doubted anyone in earshot would have paid much attention and notified the authorities. But the Duncan situation would be a serious issue now, and he cursed himself for not shooting him in the head.

'We need to do a full search of the area. I can't find this Duncan kid, so he must be out there somewhere. We need to locate him, or his body. He can't have wandered too far,' said Johnny.

'Um, we have another problem,' said Barry, catching Warren's eye. 'Nathaniel... he's gone, too. Someone came and took him. His dad. Or I think that's what Warren said.'

Warren said something to Barry, but it sounded like mumbled gibberish.

Johnny eyeballed Warren, who also didn't return his gaze. Johnny could have easily shot him in the chest. For a second, he even pictured himself doing it. Pictured seeing his scrawny body go flying across the courtyard. The stupid, ugly dickhead.

It all seemed clear enough now – Nathaniel and his dad had helped Duncan scarper. That seemed like the only plausible scenario, because he could never have just picked himself up and trotted away with a slug in his back. He reckoned they had until dawn, before the police swamped the place. They'd need to act fast.

'We need to clean up. Now,' ordered Johnny. 'There can be no trace that those lads were here. Barry, your van needs dragging out the ditch and cleaning. And get those false plates removed.'

Barry huffed and grumbled. 'In the morning.'

Johnny stepped towards Barry and leant in close to him. 'Tonight!'

Barry, his face muscles tightening, nodded.

'We also need to sweep away the glass. And collect all the spent shells,' said Johnny. Then he looked at Warren. 'Use Barry's Range Rover to pull out the van. Then tow Jack's motor away from here! I'll send you the address to take it to.'

They all gazed at the vehicle. It was peppered with bullet damage, many dents, and every window was cracked or smashed.

Warren flashed him a doubtful look.

'Just get it done, Warren. It's not far,' said Johnny, thinking that a driving ban was the least of Warren's concerns if he got tugged.

Jack fired off the jet wash next to Barry's shoes. 'Go on, you little goose's cock. Get to it. You've been sod all use to us for most of the night.'

Barry snorted. 'I'll grab some bleach.' He stormed off towards the house, then stopped and said, 'My bird in Bridport… she's having my kids. Twins.'

Jack and Johnny gazed at each other in astonishment.

'Right,' said Johnny.

'Jesus wept,' said Jack.

'Thought you should know,' said Barry. Then he marched off into the house.

Jack laughed. 'Twins. That fella can't even take a whizz without spraying piss up the wall. How will the dope cope with two brats?'

'He can cook at least,' said Johnny, thinking he had no desire to bring any kids into this world of theirs. Not now, not ever. His eyes went to the blackened mess that was his Ranger. He loved that motor. That's screwed my five years with no claims, he thought.

· · ·

Ravi pulled into the wide driveway and viewed the house, a large semi-detached Victorian property under renovation. The unattractive building stood in darkness, was covered in scaffolding and white tarpaulin clung to the sides, which flapped in the breeze. He'd not been expecting such a big house, so checked the address again.

'Whose gaff is this?' asked Nathaniel, shifting around uneasily as he viewed the place.

'His name's Arnie. This is his ex-girlfriend's place. She's away, and he said we can hide up here for a few days.'

The pair got out. Both were slick with blood and their trousers sodden with mud.

'Let's go to a hotel. I don't want to stay here,' said Nathaniel as he scanned the house, wary and tired.

Ravi locked the car and ignored his son. He walked down the side alley, and went inside using the side door, as per Arnie's instructions. Nathaniel followed, his eyes flicking about as he took hesitant steps.

The strip lights flashed twice before coming on, the brightness revealing a garage room, its floor painted dark red and the walls a brilliant, stark white. There were two huge, gleaming motorbikes parked up, a tall metal rack laden with tools, and some exercise equipment placed on a gym mat in the corner. Ravi also noted a metal disabled ramp that led into the room via a newly painted white door.

'Dad, you sure about this?'

'This life you've been leading makes you paranoid! Relax,' said Ravi, although he had to admit to himself that something didn't sit right with him either. This place *didn't* seem right.

The door slammed shut behind them, and Ravi heard a lock clunk into place. His mouth went bone dry.

The white door opened and Arnie rolled down the ramp and stopped in front of them.

Ravi couldn't help noticing how different the man looked. Clean shaven and his attire appeared neater. Not only that, he appeared much fresher and dignified.

Then Ravi saw the look of shock on his son's face.

'Glad you made it out in one piece,' said Arnie, speaking in a clear, well-spoken voice that Ravi had not heard him use during any of their previous encounters. Then Ravi felt more than a nagging sense that all was not right. Something was very off indeed.

'Just about,' said Ravi, watching Arnie with suspicion now.

'Dad! He's not who you think he is,' said Nathaniel.

Arnie snorted and shot Nathaniel a venomous glare.

'What is going on here?' asked Ravi.

'That's Sean Teller,' said Nathaniel. 'With no accent,' he continued, though he almost said this to himself.

'What? Nathaniel, what's going on?' asked Ravi.

The man, Arnie, or Sean, or whoever he was, spat in Nathaniel's direction. 'Go on, tell him what you did.'

Nathaniel backed away, his eyes darting left and right as though he were planning to make a rapid dash for it.

'You can't get out,' said Sean, his tone dripping with scorn. Then he locked eyes with Ravi. 'I am sorry that I used you like this. That's no lie.'

Nathaniel slapped his own head. 'I didn't even know! I swear. I didn't know.'

Sean kept his focus on Ravi. 'You asked me in the cafe who did this to me. Well...' he jabbed a finger at Nathaniel. 'He did!'

Ravi, altogether stunned, could not speak. Or breathe.

'I got slapped about a bit by Mills and Stefan, but I'd have lived... I'd have definitely walked away.' Sean took a deep breath and moved his harsh gaze back to Nathaniel. 'But *he* took it upon himself to assault me with... with... I don't even know what... a sharp object the surgeon said. And he damaged my lumbar spine beyond repair! Hit me from behind, the vile little shit.'

Ravi's focus moved between the pair, but he still found himself utterly speechless.

Sean punched the sides of his wheelchair with both fists. 'And this is the result. This is my life now!'

Nathaniel's jaw dropped and his eyes were wet with tears. 'I was drunk. I swear I didn't mean to take it that far!'

Sean snarled. 'Trying to impress those thugs! You make me sick. You have a family that loves you. Yet you hang around with those scumbags pretending to be a criminal. That makes you worse than them.'

Ravi put up his hands. 'Right… right. OK, this has got out of hand. Nathaniel, it's time we speak to the police. I'm done with sweeping all your mess under the carpet. I'm done with that!' shouted Ravi. His heart now raced so quickly he became faint and hot. His wife had been right all along. Nathaniel was beyond redemption. He'd been too pig-headed to listen.

A figure came charging through the door. They were clad in black military wear and sporting a black baseball cap with a camo bandanna covering their face.

Ravi considered making a grab for the stun gun, but before he acted on that idea, he'd been set upon, knocked over and pushed face down on the floor.

'Don't you move!' shouted a female voice. 'Keep still.'

Ravi's wrists were handcuffed behind his back. He wriggled sideways and found Nathaniel was receiving the same treatment, and although he was trying to fight back, he got overpowered with ease as his cuffs were violently applied, making him squeal in agony.

It was obvious that this woman was a trained individual. Police or military, without a doubt. Ravi couldn't work out if this was an official arrest. He prayed it was. The alternative meaning… he didn't care to summarise what the alternative might mean.

The woman applied duct tape to their mouths, doing Ravi's first. She stood up and studied her hands. 'Shit. The pair of them are covered in claret!' She took a deep intake of breath and vigorously searched Ravi, as though inspecting him for injuries. She repeated the process on Nathaniel. 'It's not their blood,' she exclaimed.

There was a long silence. Then the woman said, 'I should get this checked out.' She bolted through the white door.

Sean glowered at Nathaniel. Then wheeled himself out.

And they were left alone to wonder about their fate in a cold, despairing silence.

'How is he?' asked Brennan.

Elena shrugged. 'He's not said much since he came back.'

'Where will you go? I mean, what's your plan? Do you even have one?'

Elena shrugged again. 'I guess we won't be flying off to Malta with his mummy now.'

'Elena… you can't seek help from our family. Dad won't protect you against them. He'll be mega pissed if he finds out I came down to help you.'

'I made my choice, Bren. And I stand by that.'

Brennan kissed her on the forehead and spoke in his slow, steady voice. 'I'm two doors down if you need anything. You'll be safe tonight. There is no Bartell or Chillcott alive that will get past me.'

Elena hugged him. 'They wouldn't dare try.'

'And tomorrow… I'll help you both disappear. I know a place.'

Elena found Nino on the bed, curled in a ball, wearing only his boxers. An angry, purple bruise had spread across his lower back and hips, though she did not know how he'd received the wound, as he'd not yet spoken of the night's events.

Elena kicked off her heavy boots, joined him on the bed, and stroked his wound. She could see his reflection in the mirror, and he just gazed into space, sad eyed and lifeless.

Elena understood his angst. He'd done some awful things, but only to escape a life he felt he did not belong. A life he'd been led to believe had been unfairly thrust upon him. The Bartells were bad people, but Selene was no better. She'd turned out to be worse. She'd manipulated a confused, lost soul and left him broken and even more lost than ever. That was unforgivable.

'Did you ever consider she was playing me, Elena?' he whispered. 'Did you just go along with everything because you were desperate to get away from my family?'

'No… No, Nino. Never think that!'

He didn't answer for at least five minutes, then softy said, 'OK. I believe you. But we should return the money we took.'

'Without that cash, we have nothing! We can't make a fresh start without it. Besides, they extorted that money.'

'I meant return it to Nathaniel's father. Not my brothers.'

'Right, I see,' she said, thinking hell would freeze over before she'd let that cash go. They'd taken a massive risk stealing it. Nino would see sense after he'd evaluated the situation properly and stopped with the self-loathing.

Elena hugged him. At least she'd never let him down. Not ever. She glimpsed the bag containing the ransom cash. And she'd die before letting that twisted bitch get her lying mitts on a single penny. Selene's betrayal would not go unpunished. Not whilst she drew a breath.

The woman drove like a maniac. Ravi and Nathaniel knocked shoulders as they bounced about in the back. Blackness flitted by, and Ravi had no inkling where they were heading.

The woman yanked the steering wheel. The car swerved off the road and Nathaniel fell sideways, cracking the top of his head against Ravi's temple.

Ravi tried to shout slow down, although what came out was a muffled, 'Mmm ahh.'

The car skidded to an abrupt stop, and the woman leapt from the seat. 'Out. Both of you! NOW!'

They both obeyed, clambering out in a clumsy muddle.

'To the front!' the woman yelled. She wielded an extendable baton and looked intent on using it. 'On your knees!'

Ravi and Nathaniel shuffled to the front of the Jag, and in the harsh glare of the headlights, dropped to their knees. No sooner had they knelt down, the woman slammed Nathaniel onto his back with a thump and he grunted as he connected with the ground. Ravi planted himself down before she got the chance to force him.

The woman stepped out of view. Ravi couldn't see what was taking place, but listened as she clunked about and guessed she was retrieving Sean's wheelchair from the boot.

The woman returned, rolling Sean over to them and struggling to move the wheelchair across the sodden mud. Sean now wore an identical black cap to the woman. Ravi quivered when he saw the handgun in Sean's hand. It looked like the silver Beretta he'd seen when he'd been searching the Dark-web.

Sean cocked the weapon and Ravi rolled over, placing himself between Sean and Nathaniel. Ravi scrambled backwards until he was right on top of his son. Silent, blue flashing lights appeared behind his

Jaguar, illuminating Sean and the woman. For a few seconds, he considered they'd been saved, but their captors didn't bat an eyelid at this new arrival.

Sean shook the gun at Ravi. 'You can't protect him any longer. I accept this will be hard.'

Ravi tried to speak. He tried to force some words, but they would not leave his mouth through the tight binding.

A shadowy figure approached. Not close enough for Ravi to see their face, but close enough to notice the unmistakable uniform of a police officer. So this substantiated the fact they *were* dealing with the police. Yet this wasn't an arrest.

The officer summoned the woman over. As she approached him, he spoke to her in a deep, clear voice. 'There's an APB out on this Jag. This pair dropped off a victim with a gunshot wound and fled the scene. ARV teams have been scrambled and it's all hands on deck. The last sighting was two miles away. A traffic camera picked them up heading out of Medway.'

The woman threw back her head. 'Shit!'

'They're not convinced the victim will pull through. This is likely to be a murder case,' said the officer.

Ravi eyed Sean, who was listening to the exchange too.

'They are tracking these two individuals as a priority,' said the officer. 'This motor is hotter than Satan's gonads in a boiler suit.'

The woman patted the officer's shoulder and nodded her thanks. He stepped back into the darkness and folded his arms. He didn't look as though he intended to leave.

Ravi continued to eye Sean defiantly, and again he tried to speak through the binding.

The woman crouched and whispered in Sean's ear. Then he nodded and whispered something back to her. She grumbled, stepped over to Ravi, and yanked the tape from his mouth.

Ravi gasped and said, 'Just arrest him. Why can't you arrest him? Stop this insanity. Please stop. I beg you. Don't kill my son!'

Sean shook his head. 'He doesn't deserve you, Ravi.'

'No… No… I've always been a terrible father,' sobbed Ravi. 'I've bullied and intimidated that boy endlessly. I have made him feel insignificant his entire life. His choices of late are on me… I've never wanted to admit it, but it is my actions that pushed him into this life... He deserves a second chance. He really does!' he cried. The desperation in his voice was pitiful to his own ears. Never had Ravi grovelled or begged for a single thing. At this moment, he didn't care.

Sean shook his head and offered a grim smile. 'Your failings as a father won't hold as excuses for his behaviour, Ravi. I'm not buying any of that old shit. He will be judged on his own actions.'

'Then you'll have to shoot me first!' said Ravi.

The woman pulled Ravi away from Nathaniel and shoved him down. He landed with a thud in the mud and let out a low wail. Then she dragged Nathaniel over to Sean. Nathaniel struggled insanely, squirmed, and his eyes widened. But she held him in position – down on his knees, facing Sean, who wedged the gun under Nathaniel's chin. There was no mercy in Sean's harsh eyes. Ravi could see that clear enough.

Ravi struggled onto his knees. 'NO... Stop. There is no going back after this. You do this and you'll be sorry. This won't change anything. You must know that. You MUST!'

Sean ignored Ravi and focussed on Nathaniel. He shoved the barrel of the gun upwards, forcing Nathaniel's head right back so he was gazing into the sky. 'I don't hear you laughing now.'

Nathaniel's eyes bulged.

'Yeah, I heard you,' said Sean, pushing the barrel harder. 'You sick little bastard! I heard your deranged laughter. What was it you said? "I'll teach that mouthy Scouse prick to keep his big trap shut!" Remember saying that?'

Nathaniel closed his eyes and mewled.

Time seemed to stand still. Ravi could only watch, silent and helpless.

Nathaniel let out a long, distressing moan and wept. Sean sniggered at this.

'Just know...' Sean whispered in a nasty tone. 'This crazy situation has got far, far too messy. That is the only reason you get to live tonight. Understand?'

Sean relaxed the gun and Nathaniel's head slumped forward.

'Look at me!' bellowed Sean. 'Do you understand?'

Nathaniel, eyes glazed with terror, nodded.

'When we meet again, and we will, I won't hesitate to pull the trigger!' said Sean.

The woman roughly un-cuffed Nathaniel's wrists and clipped the cuffs onto her belt. 'Get down. Hands on your head! Do it now,' she yelled in his ear.

Nathaniel obeyed.

Then the woman un-cuffed Ravi, but used far less force with him.

And Ravi lay there, whimpering in the mud. He didn't move for a long time.

When he finally sat up, Sean and his companions were no longer present, and Nathaniel lay rooted to the spot they'd left him.

Ravi dragged himself up. They were in a field in the middle of nowhere. Some sort of boggy marshland. He shook his aching wrists, then tensed as he took in large lungfuls of air.

Nathaniel, stunned, stood up and gingerly removed the tape from his mouth, then waggled his lower jaw. As Ravi watched his son shaking his wrists, a strange, intense sensation flowed through him. He trembled all over. His only son had crippled a man. That fact now echoed in his mind and appalled him. Nathaniel had been happy to launch a vile, cowardly attack on an outnumbered man from behind during a drunken fight, but yet he'd left Stefan, his own boyfriend, to his doom when the guy was desperate for his help. What sort of son had Ravi raised? He'd utterly failed at being a father. That was now strikingly apparent. He did not want to be here. He wished to be far away from the son he'd spent months searching for. He suddenly longed to be back in Trinidad. Alone with the love of his life, Chandra. He imagined warming his toes in the glorious white sand. He missed his wife... now he pined for her in this desperate moment. He imagined them both as teenagers again, laughing, carefree and jubilant. He closed his eyes and was sure he heard his favourite Ennio Morricone score playing. But then Ravi felt very peculiar and his vision swam frantically. A pain thudded into his chest like a lightning bolt striking the ground and exploding.

'I can't believe it... I swear I didn't realise I'd injured him that severely. I was trying to prove myself to Stefan's family... I only wanted them to accept me... Dad? Dad?'

Ravi could barely hear his son's voice now, as severe, stabbing pains shot up both of his arms. Fire seemed to spread across his chest as he fell to his knees, clutching his heart.

Ravi thought he heard his son sobbing and saying he was sorry, but he tried to block that out and take in the music, but absolute darkness swept in and bore him away.

53

5 December 2018

Matthew sat drinking a cold can of Coke, wishing it was alcohol. As he deliberated on the last eighteen months of his life, he perused the scores of photos on the lounge wall and a heavy melancholy weight hung over him. The sadness could often be overwhelming and unbearable, but this morning, it seemed to suffocate him entirely. Those many shots of him riding his Road King Harley-Davidson around southern Spain no longer filled his heart with excitement. Only a bleak feeling of anguish that they were days he'd never be able to experience again. His eyes fixed on one of the collages – the shots of his time spent with his cruising buddies in the States, when they'd set off from Long Beach to Fort Lauderdale and enjoyed the adventure of a lifetime. He'd lived for those trips. His passion to ride was an extensive part of his life. It's what he worked every day for, but now all he had was this piece of junk which he'd be spending the rest of his dismal days stuck in.

He viewed the photo taken on the day of his passing out parade. So fresh-faced and full of hope. He no longer resembled that young man. The job had chewed him up and spat him back out. If only he'd refused. If only he'd not stepped through *that* door.

There'd been a lot of speculation about the mysterious goings on behind that solid grey door. The door lay far down the long, cold corridor, way past the cafeteria's entrance. Lots of gossip about secret meetings and undercover operations. There seemed no other way to access that private part of the station, and no staff ever seemed to go in or come out. Matthew had been both surprised and intrigued to get the email requesting that he attend a conference in that remote part of the building.

If he'd had any insight into what would follow, he'd have outright refused to even discuss the possibility of working as a UC officer. At the time he'd felt privileged to have been offered a place on the special operations taskforce assigned to tackle the influx of cocaine, amongst other drugs, flooding the East Kent area. A chance to make a real difference.

That office – drab, damp and windowless, was where Matthew met with Chief Inspector James Henfield and Detective Constable Ray Simmonds. Being unknown to the area and carrying a look they said would be a great fit for UC work, they confirmed Matthew would be perfect for their unit. So, he went ahead and filled out the application form. He took a training course, which included some role play, lectures and firearms practice. And he was made to watch a string of disturbing videos about jobs gone wrong, including some real footage of operations where officers became compromised and attacked. *He should have bailed out then.* Simmonds later approached him about accepting a long-term operation, and Matthew returned to the office for a full briefing. Matthew's task would be to go deep undercover and become a recognised face in the Chillcotts' family pub. To become a person who the punters expected to see. His assignment, once an established local, would be to needle his way into the Chillcotts' business, at which point he would invite them to meet with an old friend from his days spent working with an organised crime firm in Liverpool. Another legend was already set up in the guise of Clive Tremblay, a level-headed dealer who would be drafted in as a buyer once Matthew's bosses deemed it was the correct time. He'd not been introduced to the officer who would be taking on this legend, but Matthew had already named-dropped Clive into several casual conversations in order to add more layers to the narrative. He'd spun several wild anecdotes about his escapades with his fantastic mate, Clive. But he'd been told he was playing the long game and that he needed to prepare for spending countless hours in the company of the Chillcott family and the reprobates that frequented the unsavoury establishment. Simmonds made it clear that continual surveillance would not be an option, and for much of the time, he'd be working alone.

It soon become clear to Matthew that he should've considered a career as an actor. He could switch into character with ease. Not even other Liverpudlians would've spotted his fake accent. He'd lived in the city for two years, which had helped craft the tone and lingo. But even still, he was good. Bloody faultless.

It was not the glamorous undercover work he'd aspired to. He'd spent so many hours talking complete shite with such an abhorrent and unsophisticated bunch of arseholes, it had become mind numbingly dispiriting. He'd started drinking. At first to blend in with the drunken gobshites, and after a time, to help pass the miserable days away. This led him to rely on the strong booze in order to cope with his existence in that depressing place. Weeks blended into months, and soon he lost all purpose. You could say that inadvertently, he became the type of total drunken scumbag he despised. When he'd report back to his handler, Simmonds, his only contact in the force, he kept protesting that it would be fruitless to keep him fixed in this position, that none of the Chillcotts would ever accept him into the fold, and he'd never infiltrate the family this way. But his superiors insisted he kept his cover intact and that all the work he was doing wouldn't be in vain. They had a plan.

And Matthew got left there. Stuck in an inebriated limbo.

Then there'd been that foolish, drunken barney with Stefan that escalated so fast.

And the gutless attack by the Sookdeo boy that changed everything.

On his third day in the hospital, Matthew opened his eyes, feeling zoned out on morphine when he'd spotted Henfield sitting in the room.

Henfield asked how he was and wished him a speedy recovery, but he'd not come to dispense pleasantries. 'PC Yates, you've done fantastic work. Exemplary. It is tragic that it should end this way.'

'Have they made any arrests, sir?'

'It is unfortunate, but arrests won't be possible.'

'Sir, did you not speak with DC Simmonds? I know who did this to me! I have a recording of the entire event.'

'PC Yates, there have been... changes.'

Matthew had winced.

Henfield then smiled tightly. 'We now have an informant within the family. They are to be an integral part of a bigger, ongoing operation to snare a significant Eastern European crime network. This one is out of my hands.'

'But... what about my work... sir?'

'Your reports will be a tremendous help, I'm sure.'

'No... no, they won't, sir. I told DC Simmonds my efforts were going to be fruitless.'

'I'm sure it just seems that way.'

'So... I don't matter? None of this matters, sir?'

'PC Yates, if arrests are made at this crucial point, your previous position would be divulged. We can't risk tossing a spanner into the works. They can't know. It's for the greater good.'

'My spine is snapped, but it's for the greater good,' he'd muttered.

'I am so sorry. You'll be well compensated for what's happened. We'll ignore the reports about your underhand tactics, loutish behaviour and your gratuitous indulgence with alcohol and drugs... For now,' Henfield had said in a curt tone.

In that moment, Matthew had considered *what Sean Teller's response would be.* And so he'd offered Henfield a stiff smile, and whispered, 'You can go and fuck your wife's tight arse with my compensation. It's only justice I want... sir.'

That response hadn't gone down too well at all. But seeing the hilarious expression of utter shock and outrage on the arsehole's face was priceless.

Matthew was told that under no circumstances should he contact any persons associated with the case, but Matthew made a beeline for The Swan the moment they discharged him from the hospital. He'd never forget the sea of aghast and nonplussed faces when he'd rolled himself into that bar, and just like nothing had changed, waved at Veronica and said, 'Usual, cheers, Veronica. Ta love.' He'd forced a brazen smirk and gazed about the room. 'What are these wet-lettuces all gawping at?'

At first you could've cut the atmosphere with a chainsaw, but Reilly took him aside and spoke with him. The guy was livid to learn what happened and that he'd received such a horrific injury over a trivial argument. Matthew, or should he say Sean, started gaining respect and got treated differently from that moment. At this point, he could've infiltrated the family with ease. But he no longer cared about any of that. He'd not ignored his superiors and returned to continue carrying out the original operation. This was his own quest. For revenge. But now Stefan was dead, and Sookdeo was in hiding. Matthew was a tad disappointed he'd not even been under suspicion. He would have booted the mouthy shit over the side of a cliff given half the chance. Stefan was partly to blame, after all. But Matthew supposed he, or Sean, was an unlikely suspect because of his predicament. As the time slipped by, he'd all but given up hope of finding Sookdeo, or learning any fresh news. His colleagues in the force were also hitting brick walls. The last sighting of the elusive lad had been at an ATM in Broadstairs, but they'd not tracked any fixed address. He'd fallen off the map and Matthew considered that he may never locate him.

Then luck struck. The boy's father showed up, so Matthew ditched the Sean Teller guise, and took on the role of Arnie Baxter, offering up his help to the man. Though not too willing, as he'd not wanted to arouse suspicion. He'd made Ravi wait over two weeks before he contacted him. He'd hoped that during that time, Ravi would have found the boy himself. Matthew could see how determined he was. He knew this man would be his best chance of finding that bastard. Gail was with him one hundred per cent and vowed to help him; she'd even shadowed them during the ransom drop off and taxied him around like his personal chauffeur. Like Ravi, Matthew was obsessed with finding the boy, though for very different reasons.

Matthew heard a door slam shut, breaking him out of his moment of reflection. Gail came in. She was wearing her police uniform, including her yellow Hi-Vis bomber jacket. She gestured at the soft drink. 'Fancy something stronger?'

'Only if you do.'

Gail took off her jacket. 'I do.' She tossed her jacket on the sofa and left the room. She returned with two cans of lager and slumped onto the sofa.

'Have you been digging?' he asked, accepting a can.

'The victim is called Duncan Parvin. Some lad in his mid-twenties with no links to organised crime. It may be a case of mistaken identity. Oh, yeah... I found out about your Scotsman from the pub too. A cyclist found him in a roadside ditch. He's on life support. Not looking too good for him.'

Matthew wasn't surprised. After the harsh bashing Mills dished out, he was quite shocked the man still drew a breath.

'Nothing called in on Dead Lane?' he asked.

'Nope. Whatever kicked off went unreported.' Gail put her feet up on the sofa. They drank in silence for a while.

'I still think you should've pulled the trigger,' she said. 'We could have somehow dealt with the situation.'

Matthew smiled. 'It was too risky, Gail.' Besides, he'd decided long before Ravi and his son walked into the garage of the rental property that he'd not be able to go through with actually shooting anybody. He wasn't a murderer. He'd done what he set out to do. Which was to stare that scumbag straight in the eye and let him know the true consequences of his disgusting actions. To put the absolute fear of God into him. To let him go with the dark knowledge that one dreaded day he'd have the barrel of a gun shoved back in his face. So he could spend every single day wondering if *today* was the day his enemy would return to commit the deed. If he'd wanted him dead, Matthew would've just let the Chillcotts have him. That wasn't how he wanted it to go down.

'Besides, you can't shoot someone with a replica, Gail,' he said with a wry grin.

Gail raised one eyebrow. 'Well, you had me there, too. Would never have guessed. Anyway, I think you made your point.'

'My pal acquired it,' said Matthew, draining his can. 'It was confiscated off some ten-year-old pikey kid.' Matthew fancied a decent pint now. Perhaps it wouldn't hurt to pop down The Swan for a few swift ones. Just to get the full lowdown on what happened the other night. So Sean could hear the juicy gossip. He wouldn't tell Gail. She'd not understand his desire to return to that loathsome place now he'd completed his objective. In truth, even he didn't quite understand why he was so inclined to return. But he felt compelled to go.

Karl got into the back of Ryan's Polo. Ryan started the engine, but didn't say a word. Clara turned and smiled at him, though he could see anger in her eyes.

They travelled for a few minutes before Karl broke the awkward silence. 'Are the police still guarding him?'

'Why? Worried you'll have to face the music?' asked Ryan.

Karl tutted. 'I don't even know what happened.'

'Yes you do. Somebody shot him. In the back. And the police believe he was held captive somewhere. The nurses had to cut a shackle from his broken ankle.'

Karl said nothing. He gazed out of the window, his heart racing as he digested the news.

'He almost died in surgery,' said Clara, her voice monotone and cold. 'He needed an emergency blood transfusion.'

'What's he say happened?' asked Karl.

Ryan took a deep breath. 'He said he can't remember. That he was about to buy fish and chips when several masked men bundled him into a vehicle and sped away. That he thinks it was a case of mistaken identity.'

They all drove in silence for a moment. Then Ryan said, 'This is on you, Karl. You need to talk to Dunk and make him come to his bloody senses!'

'I will,' agreed Karl.

'I mean it! You tell him to stop protecting you. You need to come clean and admit *you* killed that guy! Then this will all be dealt with and those sickos can be arrested,' said Ryan.

Karl nodded. 'OK.'

'This isn't fair! None of it is. You get him to talk… or… or I'll do it myself. I mean it, I will,' said Ryan, his face reddening. 'You can go in alone and speak with him first.'

Clara reached across and rubbed Ryan's leg. 'Karl will do the right thing.' She turned to Karl and fixed him with a stern stare. 'Won't you?'

. . .

Johnny sipped his tea and answered the phone. 'Davey.'

'Have you seen the news reports?' asked Davey.

Which one, thought Johnny, the mysterious shooting of local lad Duncan Parvin, or the horrendous attack in Margate. Johnny sipped his tea again. 'Yeah, I saw it.'

'I should have been there, Johnny! Not pissing about running errands for you!' said Davey.

'If you'd have been there... we wouldn't be having this conversation.'

Davey snorted. 'We'll never know now.'

Johnny rubbed his forehead and tried to block the image he kept seeing of Davey's little brother sitting in the lounge wearing ear defenders, whilst playing on his games console. Tried to erase the image of those big, brown, sad eyes watching him mistrustfully.

'I tried to fix that entrance door, but it was beyond repair. And they waltzed straight in unhindered,' said Davey.

Johnny guessed retaliation from the County Lines crew would be merciless... but they'd gone way further than he'd imagined. Attacking Davey's gang was one thing, but going after his family was an evil move. Especially the boy. This lot didn't mess around. They were in a different league. They'd beaten his mother to death and left his kid brother on a life-support machine.

'This is not over,' said Davey.

'You're talking nonsense,' said Johnny, and was almost tempted to add that Davey couldn't even deal with Karl Rogers and his kick-happy Dutch buddy, let alone face off against a bunch of hardened London criminals that were prepared to go to any lengths to take revenge.

'I need your help, Johnny.'

'This is not my fight. You started this off when you bombed out that house.'

Johnny heard Davey swallow hard. 'My brother's head has swollen to the size of a fucking giant watermelon. That's how hard they booted him! If you turn your back on me... I'll make you regret it. I swear on my mother's soul, Johnny.'

Those words sent a tiny chill down Johnny's spine, but that changed nothing. 'I'll speak to Barry. But regardless of what happened, you let the guy responsible for Craig's death get away. So I'm not sure he'll be feeling particularly charitable, Davey.'

'Like Barry's even calling the shots these days. You can make up your own mind, I'm sure.'

'What do you know about this posse?'

'That they're all dead men walking,' said Davey matter-of-factly.

'Anything else?'

'Not yet.'

'Call me when you've got some information,' said Johnny, then he cut the call. He walked to the kitchen counter and made himself a fresh brew. As he stirred his tea, he thought about Duncan. The lad, it seemed, hadn't blabbed about his ordeal and that amazed Johnny no end, considering what a snivelling drip he'd come across as. He'd given Johnny his word and kept it. Along with a monster of a bruise and a terrible pain in his ribs. Johnny had yet to decide if he'd keep *his* word. Then, feeling pain in his hands, he looked down at his knuckles. They were broken and cut. And a sudden flashback hit him. He took his tea into the lounge.

Johnny heard a muffled moan and glanced down at the figure slumped on the sofa, his back to him.

After Jack and Maria headed back to Whitstable, he'd had a blazing, drunken row with Barry over all the recent events, which then erupted into a ferocious fight. After overpowering his brother, he'd decided to teach the man a real lesson in family loyalty and thumped him senseless. He left Barry in a crumpled heap against the washing machine and took himself off to bed. It seemed Barry did not make it in upstairs.

'Rise and shine,' said Johnny in a buoyant tone.

'Go fuck yourself,' mumbled Barry.

'Come and get some breakfast,' said Johnny.

Barry turned over and Johnny took in a deep intake of breath. The damage was much worse than he'd expected.

'What did you do to me?' groaned Barry.

Barry's entire face was an absolute, pulverised mess. His lips were cracked and demolished, his eyes swollen and purple. His right ear lacerated and enlarged.

Barry gazed at him with pure, murderous hatred in his eyes, though he looked fit to pass out at any given moment.

'Not hungry then?' asked Johnny.

'Piss off!'

Johnny, already over the shock of seeing the aftermath of his handy work, decided he quite fancied an omelette, so headed out to get some fresh eggs.

Amy stuffed her clothes into a suitcase. Francesca screamed, desperate for her afternoon feed, but Amy couldn't spend one second longer under the same roof as Oscar.

Then he came rushing into the bedroom, flinging his arms around as if fighting off an invisible foe. 'We need to discuss this, Amy! We need—'

Amy cut him off. 'We have nothing to discuss. Except the fact you'll soon be dealing with a charge for conspiracy to commit a kidnapping. And possibly attempted murder. I'm going to make a full statement. I'm going to speak to the police detectives this afternoon.'

Oscar pursed his lips and took a step back. Francesca's screams intensified.

'Whatever you've been told, I can assure you—'

'Ahh, just leave off, Oscar. I know what you did.'

Oscar cast her an insulted glance. '*Did*? What are you talking about?'

Two days earlier she'd seen the shocking news about Duncan Parvin narrowly surviving a shooting, and she'd visited him in the hospital this morning. After speaking to the police officer guarding Duncan's room, Amy was granted access to see him, but received a very frosty reception indeed. When she'd managed to wangle some words from Duncan, he'd spoken in a meek voice and said, 'Why did you set me up like that, Amy? I don't understand why you'd do that to me.'

Then, between them, they soon established what happened that night. She'd felt so sickened by the turn of events, she'd raced home and started packing.

Amy picked up the wailing baby, grabbed her suitcase with her free hand and barged Oscar from her path.

'Will you not let me speak? Amy? Please?'

'We're done. I'm going to my mum's.'

Oscar stormed down the stairs and raced into the kitchen behind Amy. He couldn't believe any of this was happening. His world was caving in and he took in a sharp intake of breath. 'Please don't go. I'm begging you! I need you, Amy.'

Amy, now strapping Francesca into her car seat that was perched on the kitchen worktop, shot him a nasty glare, but said nothing.

'It's *him*, isn't it? You're going back to him?' yelled Oscar.

'It was a huge mistake thinking this would work,' she said, more to herself than to him.

Without even thinking, Oscar grabbed a carving knife from the wooden block by the microwave, and shoved the blade against his own throat. 'I can't carry on without you. That's the truth.'

Amy's eyes widened in shock, but she appeared to remain calm and reached for the car seat handle.

'I will!' cried Oscar. 'Please, just stay and let me explain.'

Amy curled her fingers around the handle. 'Stop being so melodramatic. This is insane!'

Oscar pushed the blade harder and felt the edge slice through his skin. 'You've never said *I'm your world*. Not even once. But I heard you, Amy... what you said about Karl.'

'You're acting crazy. Put that down!' she shouted.

Francesca continued screaming, her face going purple now. Amy tried to quieten the baby by shushing her, but the crying did not abate. Then Amy tried to leave... and before Oscar even knew what was happening, he'd removed the knife from his neck, bolted forward and slashed the blade in a wide arc. It tore across Amy's throat.

Amy let go of the car seat. It hit the floor and rocked backwards, toppling over, causing more harrowing screams from the baby.

Oscar dropped the knife.

Amy's hands grasped the mortal wound, and the blood showered the kitchen.

Oscar grabbed the car seat and fled into the living room, crying and howling as he went.

He put down the car seat and wedged the palms of his hands in his ears to block the noises. But this didn't work.

Unable to listen to the ghastly sounds of his girlfriend dying in the next room, he switched on the TV and increased the volume to its maximum capacity. That helped drown it out. Then he unclipped the baby and held her in his arms as she wailed ceaselessly. He stayed put for a long time. All he could see in his mind was the sheer panic and terror in Amy's eyes as he'd ripped that blade into her flesh. And the blood. All that blood.

He'd ruined everything now. How could he escape from this mess? There was only one person he could think of that might possibly help him out of this shambles.

Duncan peered over his iPad to find Karl standing at the end of the bed.

Karl shuffled closer. 'Still in bed at this hour. Anyone would think you'd lost four pints of blood the other day.' He gave Duncan a goofy grin, though Duncan saw his friend's eyes were red rimmed and wet with tears.

'I'm so glad you're safe,' said Duncan. 'I'll never forgive myself for setting you up like that. Karl, I'm so sorry. What else can I say?'

'Christ, stop being a silly tit. I'm fine… you're the one all messed up. What did those bastards do to you?'

'Doesn't matter.'

Karl shook his head. 'When I couldn't get hold of you, I started imagining the worst. I called all the hospitals, but they hadn't identified you… because you didn't carry ID… then I…'

'I'll be OK.'

'Dunk… we can't hide from this any longer. I'm gonna come clean… they'll understand why we didn't talk. And after what went down, it's obvious enough we were right to flee. I'll take the rap and say I forced you to stay quiet.'

'No.'

'It will all come out anyway, Duncan.'

'Not from me.'

'Dunk, you can't continue to lie about this!'

'That family knows everything about me.'

'That's even more reason to tell the truth! These maniacs need locking up. They'll keep hunting us. This won't be the end. I'll tell them myself.'

'No, you won't. And keep your voice down,' said Duncan, wincing in pain. 'We chose to hide this secret. And we faced the consequences. Besides, it would turn our lives upside down. Court hearings, death threats, and no doubt a media frenzy that all our family would be dragged in to.'

'As opposed to what? A constant fear of being burnt alive in our houses. Or beaten or shot to death whilst putting the bins out,' whispered Karl.

Duncan closed his eyes, recalling the gunshots ringing out that night. Those angry men screaming and baying for blood. There'd been some sort of major feud going down, and with any luck, the Bartells were the losing party. Whatever the scenario, it sounded heavy stuff, and he only hoped that the Bartell family would now have far more pressing concerns. And, if Johnny Bartell's word could be trusted, perhaps *Duncan's* part in all this chaos was now finished. Weirdly enough, Duncan believed him, which seemed absurd considering the man had shot him and meant to kill him.

'Karl, you should go back to Eindhoven. You'll be safe there. Your dad's sold his place, and he'll be in Cambridge and away from here. You have no reason to stay.'

'And what about you?'

'I reckon they are done with me.'

Karl's eyes bulged in shock. 'You can't bank on that. This is idiotic, Dunk! Please consider what you're saying. The police won't just drop this case... it's serious stuff. You had a bloody armed officer outside your ward! You're not thinking clearly. Neither of us will ever be safe again!'

'Either way, we'd never be safe. This way I have a small chance.'

'You're making a mistake, Dunk.'

'Maybe. But I've made up my mind.'

Karl bowed his head. 'Ryan said he's going to blab.'

'I'll speak with my brother.'

Tears rolled down Karl's cheeks. 'Will you at least come with me?'

Duncan shook his head. 'We should, perhaps... stay away from each other. I know what happened was an accident, Karl... but you started all this. Your actions sparked this chain of events. I... think it's best we go our own separate ways now. Don't you?'

'*My* actions,' said Karl. He puffed out his cheeks. 'My actions,' he repeated. He curled his lips into a snarl and went to speak, but stopped himself, yanked at his beard, and let out a long sigh.

'Go start your blog. If you put in the effort, I bet it will be a success,' said Duncan.

'I need to see my daughter before I go anywhere,' said Karl. 'She is a reason to stay.'

'You should leave them to get on with their life. You'll only rock the boat and upset everybody.'

Karl narrowed his eyes. 'Are you serious?'

It didn't fill Duncan with joy to crush his best friend this way, but it needed to be done. A necessity in order to keep Karl safe. The further away Karl was from here, the better. 'I'm being honest. I lied about Amy wanting to see you. It's the last thing she wants. Sorry. That was such an awful thing to do. I'll never forgive myself.'

Karl sniffed, wiped a few tears that trickled down his face, and said, 'OK. I should go now.'

'Take care, Karl. I mean it. Stay out of trouble. And ease off those chocolate sprinkles over there.'

'If you ever need to talk or...'

'I know.'

Duncan felt awful for not showing Karl the photos of Francesca that Amy had airdropped to his iPad during her visit. But would that have helped the situation? Would that only make it harder to leave? After Karl's sour departure, Duncan fought down the urge to cry and won. He'd decided on some things in the days after his ordeal. The first was that he'd always underestimated himself, and he would never again consider himself as such a weak-minded coward. He'd put Johnny Bartell *on* his arse, and he'd wager few people could lay claim to such an undertaking. He'd survived the Bartells. And everything he'd endured would make him stronger than ever before. Going forward, he intended to make himself physically stronger, too. He'd turn every inch of useless fat on his body into pure muscle and bulk himself into an unstoppable force that would make the Hulk look like Shaun the Sheep. Duncan wouldn't be the scared sheep in the headlights any longer… he'd be the terror that stopped the car in its tracks. He'd learn kung-fu, Thai-boxing and advanced self-defence and morph himself into a cruel, supreme killing machine… a deadly force that would rival even the most aggressive of opponents. He'd unleash a rage so fierce upon his adversaries that they'd rue the day they screwed with Duncan Parvin. And if the Bartells dared to come for him, or harm his family, he'd rip them apart with his own bare hands and grin conceitedly whilst doing it. If that meant taking medication to help with the sweating and the constant fear of the outside world, then so be it. The old Duncan could piss off to the darkest depths of hell and burn to a tiny cinder. He didn't want to be *him* any longer. He'd toss that useless turd aside and brush him away.

'Has Karl gone already, luv? I made him a cheeky egg sarnie.'

Duncan snapped out of his crazy, dark thoughts and gazed at his mum. She stood at his bed with a two Tupperware boxes and several neatly wrapped packages.

'Homemade mushroom soup and nice crusty bread with inch-thick butter. And your dad got some comics from the newsagents. He decided you might want something to read instead of watching TV on your ePad thingy.'

Duncan considered that after he'd eaten, perhaps he would send Karl a photo of Francesca. It seemed mean and compassionless not to share it with him.

Duncan smiled his thanks and accepted the food. He felt safe right now, and that's all that mattered at this very moment. Everything else could wait. For now.

THANKS FOR READING!

Did you enjoy reading *The Feud on Dead Lane*? Please consider leaving a review on Amazon. Your review will help overs discover the novel.

THE WRONG GIRL

How well do you know your husband?

Alex and Natalie seem to have the perfect life.

But Alex is haunted by terrible events from his childhood. He thought he'd escaped his past, but lately it's been surfacing in the terrifying nightmares that plague his sleep.

As Alex's behaviour becomes increasingly strange, Natalie fears the worst. Has he been keeping things from her? And who is the mysterious Sheryl he calls out to in his dreams? She is determined to save their marriage by digging up the truth no matter what it costs.

Natalie follows Alex when he returns to his hometown to face the demons he thought he left deep in the forest. But the trip takes a deadly turn when shocking secrets from the past are revealed.

Can Natalie face the terrifying truth as she unravels the mystery that could shatter her world?

The Wrong Girl – *the gripping psychological thriller perfect for fans of K L Slater, Daniel Hurst and Mark Edwards.*

Originally published as *The Tests*.

COMING SOON

Shattered

One mistake can ruin everything – one mistake can come back and smash your life to pieces…

Vanessa has been married to Curtis for eighteen years and life couldn't be better. But when Vanessa's ex-boyfriend, Hayden, shows up out of the blue, cracks start to appear in her world.

Hayden is brash, unpredictable and has a warped sense of humour. And he seems intent on making life very difficult for his first love.

Curtis starts to suspect that Hayden might have a bizarre hold on his wife, and when Vanessa comes up with a plan to remove Hayden from their lives, he becomes convinced she's lying to him.

But has Vanessa underestimated just how unpredictable and dangerous Hayden is? How far will he go to get what he wants?

And how far will she *go to stop her ex from destroying her idyllic life?*

ABOUT THE AUTHOR

I was born in 1979 and live in Kent, England, with my family and bonkers Dalmatian, Dexter. I ran a private investigation agency for over fifteen years and dealt in cases that involved breach of contract claims, commercial debt recovery, and process serving. My agency also specialised in people tracing, so much of my work revolved around tracking down debtors, dealing in adoption matters and locating missing persons. Since 2014, I have worked self-employed in the pet care industry, and I am a keen trail runner, mountain biker and kayaker. I've had a passion for screenwriting for many years and started writing novels during the pandemic. My first novel, *The Tests*, published on Amazon in June 2021, was based on a spec screenplay that I originally wrote back in 2009. This has now been republished with Inkubator Books under the new title, *The Wrong Girl*.

My next novel, *Shattered*, is a phycological thriller based in the Kentish seaside town of Whitstable. If you would like to be informed about my new book releases, you can subscribe to my newsletter at www.robertkirbybooks.com/subscribe

Printed in Poland
by Amazon Fulfillment
Poland Sp. z o.o., Wrocław
27 October 2022

19053141-2baa-4f72-a61a-456343617a70R01